DEATH RANCH

A Novel
By

Arley Owens, Jr.

SHORTY MAE PRODUCTIONS

DEATH RANCH
Copyright © 2013 Arley Owens, Jr.

Bible quotations from the
Authorized King James Version

Red River Valley
(Public Domain)

La Grange
(Billy Gibbons, Dusty Hill, Frank Beard)

Cover Art: CL Owens
Editor: Pitman Sanders

First Printing January 2014
Printed in the U.S.A.

Soft Cover Edition
ISBN: 978-0-9848195-8-4

SHORTY MAE PRODUCTIONS
P.O. BOX 81102
MIDLAND, TEXAS 79708

To

Juanita & Christine

the late wives of my drummer, Joe Prater,
& lead player, Dan Kinser

ONE

Two thousand acres lying east of Texas' Big Bend were alleged to be haunted by the ghost of a confederate colonel named Klell Ridgewall. Still known as the Ridgewall Ranch, its narrow southern section bordered the Rio Grande while the east and west boundaries fanned out northward, forming a rough triangle that terminated in Tomahawk County.

Ridgewall's struggle to turn the fledgling spread into a paying proposition came to an abrupt end when a band of Chizos Indians slaughtered his entire family. After driving a small herd of longhorns to Fort Davis, Klell got back to his cabin shortly before midnight to find his wife and their four teenage daughters lying naked on the floor in a bloody heap. His feisty spouse had managed to empty a pistol before succumbing to her attackers, a fact he'd learned by forcing a dying brave who spoke English to tell him what happened. They'd been beaten and savagely raped before being scalped alive, suffering unimaginable agony until their hairless heads were separated from their brutalized bodies by tomahawk. Determined to avenge their deaths, he'd ridden away on a white steed with his officer's saber held high in the air. That was the last time anyone saw Klell Ridgewall alive.

Carlson Loggins had been informed of the legend two days after being forced to buy the entire Ridgewall Ranch because the owner refused to sell his magnificent three storey mansion by itself. Located a quarter mile behind the midway point of the northern edge of the spread, the massive colonial structure fit his and his girls' needs perfectly. None of them had wanted to leave Houston but when a careless celebrity almost got them exposed, Carlson realized a change of location was in order—some place far away from the sophisticated law enforcement of a metropolis. Other than having a landing strip built to service the private jets of his elite clientele, the ranch remained unaltered.

Constructed by a rich eccentric in nineteen-eighteen, the mansion's entryway led to a deep foyer which emptied into a wide interior hallway separating the four sides of a magnificent ballroom from the other rooms on the first floor. It boasted a nine-foot Steinway grand piano perched on the bottom section of a three-tiered bandstand. An old fashioned liquor bar with saloon mirrors in back faced twenty-five hundred square feet of hardwood dance floor, encircled by antique table-and-chair sets resting on marble tiles twenty feet below an array of chandeliers imported from France.

The outer edges of the hall gave access to an enormous living room with a beautiful stairway gracefully rising to the second floor. Clockwise from there the hall continued past a library, capacious bathroom, study, billiard room with three pool tables, conservatory the last owner converted into a home theatre, a formal dining room, recently remodeled kitchen accessing an immense patio, and a four-shower exercise room with electric-eye sliding doors for swimmers to come and go from an outdoor Olympic-size pool, twelve person hot tub, and two Jacuzzis lying south of the patio.

Immediately after obtaining ownership Carlson had hired a construction crew to expand the carport, get rid of a slew of strategically placed security cameras, mount his wall safe, and install a deadbolt lock on ten of the fourteen bedroom doors for his clients' peace of mind. They were all located in the upper stories. He slept in the master suite on the second floor, his girls occupied the bedrooms with deadbolt locks, and the remaining three were used by his butler, cook, and maid.

They'd gotten settled in seven months ago.

Six cowboys who'd been working there when he bought the ranch had agreed to stay on and continue tending the livestock. They lived in a bunkhouse situated five hundred yards south of the mansion. None of them knew he was a drug-dealing blackmailing pimp. Like Uncle Sam, they believed him to be a successful entrepreneur with legitimate business interests who employed ten personal assistants that by chance happened to be amazingly beautiful women.

Blessed with good looks, charisma, and charm, Carlson learned as a teen that women wanted to be mesmerized, and he'd mastered the art before his eighteenth birthday. By the time he turned twenty he'd cultivated his first stable and blackmailed several important people by secretly filming their indiscretions. He'd let them off the hook only after forcing them to introduce him to their socially-potent friends, and using the same technique, had maneuvered his way up the ladder, rung by rung, into the upper echelon of powerful people with secret lives—politicians, renowned businessmen, sports figures, Hollywood celebrities, and even a few members of the clergy. Now in his late forties, he could retire to a life of ease and luxury if he wanted to, but his millions didn't satisfy him. Power was his opiate, and he proportionately relished bringing prominent citizens under his control to how deviously he achieved the conquest.

Carlson combed his thick, fine hair—still naturally black despite his age—plucked three gray whiskers from his pencil moustache, and left the bathroom. He smiled while approaching his customized brass bed, upon which he'd laid out a white shirt, blue suit, and red tie before showering. He'd pleasured his newest whore on it last night. Sonya had chosen to sleep in her own room afterwards, claiming her face was a hideous sight to behold when she first woke up. Unable to imagine her looking anything but ravishing, he suspected she snored and didn't want him to know it.

The memory of her thrashing orgasm started playing in his mind as he got dressed. He forced the scene from his thoughts and concentrated on knotting his tie. His stomach needed satisfying at the moment, not his penis. Allowing himself to relive Sonya's violent climax would turn it to steel. His sexual potency hadn't waned at all and he attributed it to two things: constantly being around beautiful women eager to please him, and his insatiable lust for power.

He wriggled his feet into a pair of black wingtips, put on his jacket, and made for the door.

Montella stepped out of her bedroom as he passed, and followed him down the hall to the stairs. The voluptuous blonde had been with him twenty years now and served as madam/mother-figure to the other girls, none of whom had yet reached thirty. She'd been instrumental in helping him ensnare a senator when she was twenty-five, and he still held the politico in the palm of his hand.

They descended to the living room. Selena, his Mexican maid who he bopped at least once a month to keep her happy, switched off a vacuum cleaner long enough to bid them good morning. They did likewise and the Hoover once again started sucking away whatever might have settled on the carpet overnight.

He entered the dining room in time to see his gargantuan black butler and henchman, Lambert, place the last of eleven sterling silver place settings on the table. A china coffee cup accompanied all but one.

"Good morning, Mister Carlson, your steak's almost done."

Only he and one of his girls never altered their breakfast choices. He sat down at one end while Montella took the other. The sixteen chairs between them, eight on each side, were empty at the moment.

"What would you like this morning, Miss Montella?"

She puckered her full glossy lips while thinking on it, and smiled at the ex heavy weight boxer upon reaching a decision. "Think I'll have a Denver omelet and a glass of milk."

Lambert poured their coffee and went to inform the cook, Rico, a big Italian that also doubled as bodyguard and bouncer. The pleasant aroma of breakfast meats frying and biscuits baking escaped into the room when he went through the swinging door.

Montella sweetened her coffee, took a sip, and acquired the challenging look she always wore when about to say something she anticipated he'd disagree with. "I think we should let Sonya go."

Carlson spooned sugar into his cup and stirred it. "And you think this because?"

"I don't trust her."

He shook his head no. The tall brunette had been with him less than a year and the new had yet to wear off. Just the sight of Sonya's naked body still gave him an immediate hard on. Though she'd never said it, he knew Montella feared she would be replaced as his favorite by the failed actress. She'd most likely spotted her leaving his room last night and had been stewing over it since.

"She'll wind up hurting us, Carl."

"How?"

"How?" she cynically laughed out. "By exposing us. You know her brother's with the FBI. I can't believe you kept her on after I found out about it."

"They're estranged, have been for years." He savored a gulp of premium Peruvian blend. "Even if they weren't, she knows better than to betray me."

Her sensuous mouth firmed with irritation. "Just don't say I didn't warn you."

Angela walked in and pecked him on the cheek. "Good morning, Boss." The oriental beauty flipped a lock of black hair over her shoulder while seating herself on the first chair to his left.

He'd recruited the slim twenty-two-year-old at a Las Vegas bus depot at the tender age of sixteen. He hadn't planned on replacing Nadia so quickly that day he'd bought her a one-way bus ticket back to Texas, telling her she wasn't worthy of plane fare and that he'd have Lambert break every bone in her body if he ever saw her face again. The bitch had decided to give it away to a rock star she'd met in the casino instead of servicing the headliner like she was supposed to so Montella could film them on the sly. That had been the sole purpose of the Las Vegas trip but Angela kept it from being a total waste of his money and time.

Seeing the pretty girl sitting by herself, nervously clutching her suitcase, he'd sat down beside her and asked where she was heading.

"I'm going to Los Angeles," she'd answered.

Sensing she might be running away from home, he'd posed the question.

"In a way, I guess I am."

"Mind telling me why?"

Eyes bubbling with tears she'd said, "Because my uncle is working me to death."

"Doing what?"

"Sewing. He runs a sweat shop and works everybody sixteen hours a day, seven days a week to make his quota."

"Don't you go to school?" he'd asked.

She'd shaken her head. "I'm from China and graduated at fifteen because I started school earlier than most. That was a year ago. My mother died so I came here because my uncle promised I'd make a lot of money doing easy labor. What a fucking liar. I'm going to L.A. and I don't care if I have to wash cars to make ends meet, I never want to touch a sewing machine again as long as I live."

He'd pulled out a wad of cash and waved it around. "I'm holding five hundred dollars in my hand. Come to work for me and I'll pay you this much every week and you won't have to spend a penny of it on food, clothing, or shelter if you're as good as I think you'll be. And if you're not, I'll teach you."

"What would I have to do?" she'd asked, greedily eyeing the greenbacks.

"Look, let me be brutally honest. The easiest way for a

pretty girl like you to make a lot of money is to come to work for me. I'm a man with a lot of wealthy friends who count on me to provide them with an intimate partner for an evening without any emotional complications. You'll never have to worry about being physically abused or catching a disease."

She'd gasped and brought a hand to her throat. "My god, you're a pimp!"

"The best in the business," he'd responded with a prideful grin. "If you want to scratch out a living working a third of your life away, fine. But picture yourself living in a mansion rent-free, wearing beautiful clothes, eating nothing but the finest food, drinking expensive champagne, and working only a few hours a week pleasuring my clients. Some weeks you won't even have to work at all, and yet your salary will remain the same. I'll even furnish you with a car."

Knowing she found him attractive because of the look in her beautiful slanted eyes, he'd gone for the kill shot. "Of course I'll expect us to sleep together once in awhile, but you'll enjoy it, I promise. Ever been with a man before?"

She'd given him a shy nod.

"No you haven't. Come with me and let me show you what a real man can do."

After a little more coaxing he'd talked her into accompanying him to his hotel room and soon had her begging to become one of his girls.

Lambert returned with a plate containing a four ounce steak, two poached eggs, and a generous helping of fried potatoes, which he set before him. The beef came from the tenderloin section of a flame-broiled porterhouse, the remainder of which Rico would consume with his breakfast after cooking everyone else's.

"What'll you have for breakfast this morning?" the big guy asked Angela with a smile while filling her coffee cup, his repeatedly broken nose causing his upper lip to curl outward.

"Waffles and sausage, please. Two links."

Carlson sat with his back to the kitchen. When he heard Lambert walk through the swinging door to pass on Angela's order, he turned to her and said, "Montella thinks Sonya's untrustworthy. What do you think?"

Angela cut her eyes to Montella and grinned. "I think she's just jealous and insecure because she's about to turn forty."

"For your information, bitch, I won't turn forty for another two years!"

Angela's opinion didn't mean shit to him. He'd asked the question to provoke Montella. Her regal features were so damn sexy when she got pissed. "You'll always be young to me, darlin'."

"I like Sonya," said Angela, aiming a harsh glare at Montella.

"So do I, but keep an eye on her for me. Montella's instincts are usually right." He sliced up his eggs and started dissecting his steak into bite-size pieces. "Reverend Snow will be flying in this evening and he's requested you."

Angela winced. "I was hoping that old geezer would never pick me. Wonder why he decided to this time?"

"He's been asking for you since you first started working for me, but didn't want to pay double."

Her pretty Asian face blossomed with a flattered smile. "You charge double for me, Boss?"

"No, but the preacher doesn't know that. I could tell by the gleam in his eye when he first asked for you the sky would wind up being the limit. I did the same thing with an actor who had an incurable case of the hots for Montella."

"Oh really, who is he?"

"It was before your time with us. He's dead now, but you'd know his name if we were to tell you." He forked a chunk of juicy beef into his mouth.

"But you won't?"

He shook his head.

"Why not?"

Her response prompted the cold stare—the meaning of which none of his girls ever misunderstood. Montella called it his *Dracula look.* He chewed the meat harshly, to intensify Angela's dread. When her trepidation reached its zenith, he swallowed and downed a sip of coffee—never taking his eyes off her. "What did I tell you about questioning me when I say no?"

She shrank in the chair and lowered her head. "Sorry, won't happen again."

"Reverend Snow uses his own medication for erectile dysfunction," instructed Montella, "so don't offer him any Viagra. He likes his women to think he can get it up naturally. And he doesn't do coke."

His apex regulars were provided complimentary cocaine but the preacher deemed it and all other drugs as Satanic. The parson did, however, enjoy the free champagne. Snow's electronic flock, which numbered in the millions, would freak if they knew about their pastor's insatiable sexual appetite and how he illicitly satisfied it on a weekly basis. If the good reverend ever decided to stop using his services, he'd enlighten him to his method of achieving a huge amount of severance pay—films and photographs of the famous cleric being screwed, blued, and tattooed by pretty whores. Under threat of them being sold to the media, the Man of God would most certainly cough up the cash.

Lambert came back with a tray holding Montella's and Angela's breakfasts. After serving them, he refilled everyone's cup.

Angela brightened up as she swabbed her waffles with a light coat of butter and drowned them with maple syrup. "By the way, Boss, the legend about this place is true. I saw the ghost last night. I woke up needing to pee and when I stepped into the hall I saw a man on a horse riding away from me. I was too sleepy to be scared so I just stood there and watched them go all the way down the corridor and disappear into the wall without making a sound."

He almost spit out a mouthful of potatoes but managed to hold the laugh until he worked them down his throat prematurely. "You only dreamed it, silly."

"Mm mm, I really saw it . . ." she stabbed a sausage link and bit off a small piece.

"Saw what?" queried Rosemary, entering the dining room. The gorgeous redhead was the shortest whore in the stable, standing five-three. She'd been with him four years now and had celebrated her twenty-third birthday a few days ago.

"Angela thinks she saw the ghost last night," answered Montella.

Rosemary giggled and lowered her sexy butt onto the chair to his right.

Lambert filled her cup and asked for her order.

"One egg scrambled, two bacon, and hash browns."

"No toast?"

"Mm mm." She tossed Angela a facetious smirk. "So did you see him at midnight like the cowpokes?"

"I didn't notice the time but it could have been."

"They claim the ghost *disappears* at midnight," said Montella, raising her glass.

Each of the cowboys claimed to have seen the same apparition at one time or another—a ghostly sword-waving confederate officer atop a pale horse, galloping down the prairie, disappearing at the stroke of midnight after a few seconds' ride.

Watching Montella's luscious lips part for a swig of milk, he recalled coming in her mouth the first time. She'd never swallowed before and had decided to find out what it was like. None of his clients would ever know the thrill of watching her burst into spontaneous orgasm the instant semen hit the back of her throat because only his seed could trigger it. She lived to have sex with him and detested having to pleasure a john. None of them ever suspected it though, he'd turned her into a consummate pro.

His muse flittered away as Angela started to recount seeing the ghost. "Look, it was just a dream. I don't need you putting bubbles in everybody's blood about a ghost. If the cowhands weren't just pulling our legs I'm sure they were liquored up every time each of them thought they saw it. The power of suggestion is an amazing thing, especially under the influence."

"I didn't dream it, Boss. I saw a man ride a horse down the hall and that's all there is to it. I won't bring it up again, but I know I wasn't dreaming."

"What did he look like?" asked Rosemary, no longer teasing.

"He was practically translucent but his coat and hat were gray and the horse was white."

Tweezed red brows arching higher than normal, Rosemary glanced his way, an awestruck gleam twinkling in her cobalt eyes. "Sounds like a confederate soldier to me, Carlson."

"Oh hell, she dreamed it! I ought to fire every one of those fucking cowhands for planting it in her mind."

Montella bellowed a dry laugh. "Like you'd know what to do with five hundred head of cattle. Besides, you know as well as I do all six of them are as convinced as Angela they saw Klell Ridgewall's ghost."

He wiped his mouth and dropped the napkin. "All right, so we might have a ghost. At least he's harmless."

"I'd love to see it," said Rosemary excitedly.

Nicole appeared and made her way to the table. "See what?"

"Don't ask," Angela warned the shapely caramel-skinned girl he'd seduced seven years ago when the then seventeen-year-old was working as a waitress in a truck stop near Texas City.

"Judging by the look on the boss's face, don't think I will." The tall Jamaican sat down next to Rosemary and ordered biscuits and gravy when Lambert came to take her order. Five-ten, the same height as Sonya, Nicole was a preferred choice for many of his black clients, especially basketball players. She believed in voodoo and claimed her grandmother had the ability to remove tumors without performing surgery. Her ailing mother and disabled father thought she worked for him as his personal masseuse and were very grateful for the money she sent them every week.

Rosemary gave him a defiant grin and turned to Nicole. "Angela saw the ghost last night."

"No shit?! Eew, tell me about it!"

Cheeks puffing out from trying not to laugh, Angela zipped her lips.

He groaned and threw his hands up. "All right, go ahead. I can see I'm fighting a losing battle over this."

Nicole squinted at him. "You don't believe her, Boss?"

"He thinks I only dreamed it but I didn't."

"You know what's weird, Angela . . .?" Nicole clasped her hands together beneath her chin. "I dreamed last night that you and Sonya were horseback riding and Sonya's horse reared up to make her fall off, then trampled her to death."

Noticing the corners of Montella's glistening lips turn up slightly, he chuckled inside. Jealousy *so* became her. It made him miss Nadia—no one could incite Montella's envy like that hot half-Gypsy bitch.

"Anyway," said Nicole, "tell me about the ghost."

"I saw a man ride a horse down the hall and vanish through the wall."

"She said he looked like a confederate soldier," added Rosemary, "so it has to be the ghost of Klell Ridgewall the cowboys told us about."

"Oh how exciting!" Nicole folded her long fingers together and flexed them. "I wonder why he appeared last night."

Angela shrugged and took a bite of dripping waffle.

"I hope I get to see him."

As usual, instead of dressing before breakfast like everyone else, Dorian ambled in wearing a bathrobe and scooted up to the spot at the table missing a china cup. He'd reeled in the black-haired blue-eyed beauty ten years ago after meeting her in a Little Rock barber shop where she'd been working shining shoes, having migrated from Louisiana with her hair-stylist cousin a few months before. A blackmail caper had brought him and two of his girls there—Montella and Nadia, who would betray him in Vegas four years later. The buxom hayseed still often slipped back into hick-speak despite the time and effort he'd invested refining her diction—calling a window 'wender', a corner 'coner', a fork 'fark', exercise 'exreesize' and the like. She'd turn twenty-nine on her next birthday but still couldn't buy liquor without getting carded because she didn't look any older than the day she'd buffed her last pair of shoes—his.

Dorian didn't drink coffee and was the only one besides him that never deviated in her breakfast preference. Soon after she sat down Lambert placed before her an oblong platter containing three fried eggs, a thick slice of ham, two large sausage patties, four strips of bacon, and a big square of hash browns. He then unloaded the rest of the tray: a bowl of grits, biscuits smothered with sausage gravy covering an entire plate, a tall glass of buttermilk, and eight ounces of orange juice.

She attacked the food like a starving dog. Before long the platter, bowl, plate, and glasses were completely voided. Dorian leaned back with a loud burp. Her voracious appetite also included consuming prodigious amounts of alcohol on a daily basis, yet her weight somehow stayed at one-ten, which kept her five-five frame perfectly proportionate.

"Gonna step outside for a smoke, be back directly."

He watched Dorian's marvelous ass waggle as she walked away, relieved no one had brought up Angela's ghost in her presence because she'd have retaliated with some tall swamp tale to top it.

Nicole shook her head with wonderment. "Man I wish I could eat like that and not gain weight."

"No you don't," he reprimanded, grimacing at her. "It's very un-ladylike. I've tried and tried to get her to consistently use the manners I taught her, but she usually only abides by them when on the job."

Montella laughed. "Tell us something we don't know, Carl."

Dorian appeared outside one of the dining room windows and lit up a filterless Camel. He hated she wouldn't give up smoking but at least she'd quit dipping snuff. When he met her she often did both at the same time. If the girl hadn't been so resplendently pretty and exceptionally built he wouldn't have wasted a moment trying to recruit her. As it stood, she was currently his most sought after whore, and loved sex even more than she did food and drink.

"Good morning, darlings . . ." Tillie waltzed in, platinum hair still wet from showering. A blue t-shirt clung to her braless breasts and her nipples angled upwards provocatively. An ex-smoker, she gazed covetously at Dorian outside the window.

Her twelve-year tenure trailed only Montella's. She had big dark eyes that compelled a man to look into them, especially when she bleached her naturally brown hair. He'd discovered her one summer while she was working as a lifeguard. Noticing her examining his physique as he lay sun tanning, he'd decided to strike up a conversation. Having just graduated high school, she'd been undecided about attending college or joining the army like her boyfriend.

"Oh, so you have a boyfriend," he'd said. "What a shame."

"Why's that?" she'd asked with a flirtatious smile.

"Because I was about to ask you out to dinner."

"So who's stopping you?"

"Your boyfriend, of course."

"How can he stop you when he's overseas?"

"I meant the fact that you have a boyfriend."

Her smile had then turned seductive. "What he doesn't know won't hurt him."

After wining and dining her, he'd gotten her coked up before giving her a throttling, the likes of which she'd never known. Turned on by the prospect of easy money, residing in a mansion, driving a brand new car, and knowing he'd be her part time lover, she'd quickly agreed to give up college, the army, and her boyfriend.

Finally taking her eyes off Dorian's cigarette, Tillie sat down and glanced around the table. "Where's Cynthia?"

"Guess she decided to sleep in," said Montella while daubing her gleaming lips.

"Her bedroom door was open when I walked by and I noticed her bed was made."

Angela donned a puzzled frown. "Carolyn's door was open too, and her bed was empty. She must have been in the bathroom since she didn't beat me down here. I hope there's not a flu bug going around."

Sonya burst into the dining room crying, flailing her arms like a maniac. "Carlson, come quick—something horrible has happened!"

He leapt from his chair and followed her through the living room, up the stairs to the second floor and the flight leading to the third, demanding to know what was going on. But she merely kept running and didn't stop until she got near Babette's room. She pointed towards the open door and covered her face with trembling hands.

What he discovered made him stagger to catch his balance as he almost vomited.

TWO

Babette, Carolyn, and Cynthia stared at him through lifeless eyes from heads carefully arranged on the top of the shelved headboard of Babette's bed. Their naked bodies lay atop the covers, intertwined as if they'd been in the process of grinding crotches when the triple decapitation occurred. Little blood had dripped from the stubs of neck remaining beneath each chin. Most of it had flooded onto satin sheets from the severed arteries. Each girl had been beheaded with such precision it looked as though a guillotine had been employed.

Stomach still threatening to empty itself, Carlson stepped back into the hall where Sonya had remained. "Why were you on the third floor?"

"I came up to the storeroom for toilet paper."

He'd asked because she slept on the second floor in one of the bedrooms with a bathroom. Some of the girls shared one between two rooms, the rest had to use one of the hall facilities. "Did you open the door?"

"No, it was already open. That's what made me glance inside and I wish to God I hadn't."

"They surely must have screamed. Did you hear anything?"

She shook her head.

His spine tingled with the rare sensation of fear. Whoever did this might not be finished and could be lying in wait somewhere in the mansion. Seldom failing to formulate an immediate contingency plan when things went awry, he couldn't see any way to avoid calling the police.

Hearing footsteps he quickly closed the door and turned to see Montella being trailed by the rest of the girls except Dorian.

"What's the matter?" gasped the bosomy blonde in a labored voice.

He fished out his master key, secured the deadbolt, and shoved it back in his pocket while heading for the stairs. "None of you need to see this. We're going to have to call the police."

* * * *

Gary Stoner had resided in Tomahawk going on four years but still sometimes felt like a newcomer. His older brother, born almost a decade before him, was a high-salaried petroleum engineer, and his younger brother had taken the same career path. They'd lived in Fort Worth all their working lives while he'd moved several times, earning a modest living. It was almost like destiny had decreed he should be different from his only siblings. He'd inherited his mother's dark complexion, dirty blonde hair, and gray eyes while they took after his fair-skinned father, whose irises were brown and hair originally black before age turned it silver. Their height differed as well. They were a couple of inches shy of six feet and he stood three-quarters of an inch past that mark. His older brother wore a full beard and his younger a goatee— he'd never even grown a moustache or let his sideburns lengthen. The three of them were similarly built with V-shaped upper bodies but his brothers had developed paunches and love handles as a result of living the high life. He rarely drank and didn't carry any excess weight.

As kids, he and his younger brother had been consumed by the same ambition but practicality kept them from pursuing it after high school, so Gary chose his secondary passion, despite knowing he'd never make anywhere near six figures a year like is older sibling.

He'd beaten incumbent Dody Massey for county sheriff in the last election, and his first three-year term would expire in fourteen months. Everyone in Tomahawk County knew Massey was as corrupt as they came, but because of his enormous reach and willingness to retain his office through any means, no one had ran against him since a popular army vet suffered a mysterious fatal accident while leading the polls. Gary had come aboard as deputy and Massey made the mistake of thinking he suffered the same lack of character as the crooked sheriff. Appalled to learn Tomahawk County's Finest received large monthly payments from a Mexican drug cartel in order to provide a pipeline for massive shipments of heroin to cross the border, Gary had resigned and ran against him the following election. Though only twenty-eight at the time, some rugged life experiences had made him far wiser than his years, and integrity meant a whole lot more to him than money, a character trait he felt every lawman should possess.

When the argument that he was too young to have acquired enough experience to be a competent sheriff didn't cause Gary to slip in the polls, the ruthless gangster tried a different tactic. Three of Massey's deputies, little more than hired guns, took turns punching him out while the other two held his arms behind his back—warning him to drop out of the race if he valued his life. Anticipating such action, he'd hidden a web cam inside a potted plant situated with a view of his entire living room, and had his friend, Tank Green, recording everything from his bedroom. A six-four ex-linebacker who'd kept himself in shape, Tank had been heavily armed in case the goons had something more than a beating in mind.

He'd distributed copies of the video to the district attorney, state police, and all the newspapers and television stations in West Texas. Massey tried to save face by firing the three badge-wearing thugs, claiming they'd acted without his knowledge, but one of them turned state's evidence and though the corrupt sheriff managed to stay out of jail through a series of legal loopholes, Gary had won the election by a landslide. Dody Massey left town in disgrace—to where, he had no idea.

His first act as sheriff was firing Massey's entire staff, including the dispatcher. After cleaning house he'd hired Tank as his main deputy, and being they weren't running a covert drug line, needed only one more to keep the peace in Tomahawk County, whose entire population barely cleared fifteen thousand, less than half of which lived in the county's only town, Tomahawk. Alfredo Parra—a young and eager-to-please Mexican, born and raised in the area like Tank—fit the bill aptly, and Alfredo's girlfriend Ilian Herrera took over dispatching duties. Although also deputized as alternate to Tank or Alfredo, neither had ever called in sick so she hadn't gotten to act in that capacity yet.

He was finishing a hearty breakfast at Carla's Café when his cell phone started ringing. Noting the call came from his office it figured to be Ilian.

"Yeah?"

"Gary, a Carlson Loggins just called and said three people have been killed at his place."

A cold twist of nerves unsettled his stomach. Not only had the hope of never having to deal with one been dashed, his first murder case turned out to be a triple homicide. He ran a hand over his face and took a deep breath. "Isn't he the guy that bought the Ridgewall Ranch here while back?"

"Yeah. He said three of his employees have been beheaded and requested someone get out there immediately because he's afraid the killer may still be on the premises."

"Holler at Tank and Alfredo, tell them to head for the office, and I'll pick them up."

* * * *

The three of them drove out to the Ridgewall Ranch in his

cruiser, Tank riding shotgun, Alfredo sitting in back. Though as nervous as his deputies, Gary tried not to show it. He glanced at Tank, fidgeting with the cowboy hat on his lap. The big redhead was too tall to cover his flattop with it in a car. "Isn't the Ridgewall Ranch where so many people claim to have seen a ghost?"

"Yeah," said Tank, "but it's a bunch of hooey. Me and some buddies used to party on Pussy Mountain all the way through high school—it's what folks around here call that big sand dune south of town. It got the nickname back in the fifties because it was the favorite place for teenagers to go parking in those days. You can see a ridge on the Ridgewall Ranch from there where a lot of people claim to have seen Klell Ridgewall but none of us ever did."

"*No es verdad,* Tank! I've never seen the ghost either, but my uncle has four times—he used to work on that ranch years ago. He never saw him on that ridge near Pussy Mountain but at different locations on the ranch."

Gary eyed the rearview mirror. "What was that Spanish you just rattled off, Alfredo?"

"Not true."

"Oh. Well I grew up in several different towns scattered across Texas and just about all of them have some kind of urban legend. One in particular I remember is a gal named Bloody Mary. Seems she drowned in a lake and her ghost comes out on occasion and walks across the water to kill whatever livestock might be nearby at the time, ripping them apart with her bare hands. And if a human should venture near while she's manifesting, the poor soul gets eaten by her."

"My uncle ain't a liar," Alfredo firmly declared, "the Ridgewall Ghost is real. That Bloody Mary chick sounds spooky as hell."

Tank chuckled. "Well nobody's ever accused Klell Ridgewall of doing anything except riding his horse for a short spell then vanishing into thin air at midnight."

"He's right about that, Gary, that ghost didn't kill those people. That's gruesome they got their heads cut off."

He grimly nodded in agreement.

The ranch came into view and a few minutes later they drove through a set of opened gates, crossing a cattle guard in the process. Gary had seen the mansion from a distance but had never driven onto the ranch. As it loomed near, he marveled at its size and grandeur. "Now that's what I call a *nice* abode. Wonder how many square feet that thing is?"

Tank squinted at the mammoth colonial structure. "I'd say it has to be at least two hundred feet wide, and about as deep. And with three stories, I'd guess it would have be well over a hundred thousand."

A huge carport on the left side of the mansion housed over a dozen vehicles, some of which Gary couldn't afford even at twice his salary. He parked near a porch spanning the front of the house. The place looked so much like an old-time southern plantation he imagined being greeted by a black slave groomed to work indoors rather than the cotton fields.

Ironically a black man did appear when they rang the doorbell—a muscular giant that had to be near seven feet tall. A smashed nose made him look angry and intimidating despite the formally polite smile he wore.

Gary touched the rim of his brown Stetson in greeting. "I'm Sheriff Stoner, believe we're expected."

The colossus led them through a long foyer and down a wide hall where they crossed a humongous living room to an elegant stairway. After climbing a second flight of stairs they encountered a man standing in a much narrower hallway who introduced himself as Carlson Loggins.

"The bodies are in here." Loggins opened a door and stood to the side, entering the room after them.

Alfredo slapped a hand over his mouth, looking like he might puke. Tank didn't bother covering his, but it'd also fallen open with shock. Gary couldn't help grimacing at the sight of three beautiful faces pressed together, peering at him through death-glazed eyes set in heads bereft of torsos. Heavy bookends on either side kept them from falling forward or rolling sideways. The women's nude bodies were on a big bed, shoved together at the groin, making it appear their last moments were spent having lesbian sex.

A search of the room following a brief conversation with Loggins turned up nothing—no axe, hatchet, knife, or any sharp implement capable of slicing through flesh and bone. Gary instructed Tank to search the rest of the house, told Alfredo to get the victims' names and personal information, then made his first official call to Bob South, the coroner.

While his deputy jotted down Loggins' words, Gary perused a large closet filled with feminine evening wear, daring lingerie, jeans, and t-shirts. A shoe rack contained rows of stiletto heels, other sexy footwear, and several pairs of sneakers. Not a single item remotely resembled anything a secretary would wear to work, everything belonged to one extreme or the other—totally erotic or blatantly casual—yet Carlson Loggins claimed all three dead women were his personal assistants.

"Whose room is this?" Gary asked.

Loggins pointed towards the head on the left. Curly brown hair cascaded downward over the varnished wood where the neck ended beneath a face that was so lovely even death couldn't nullify its beauty. "This was Babette's room. I have no idea why she, Carolyn, and Cynthia were singled out or why no one heard anything. We were all eating breakfast when another of my employees happened by and saw them here."

Gary pursed his lips, hating he had no choice but to pry into the victims' personal lives. "Were these women lesbians?"

Loggins shook his head. "Whoever did this had to have arranged their bodies like that, or forced them to before—"

"I see," he interrupted, trying to spare the man any added grief. "You say they worked for you as personal assistants.

What is it you do?"

"I'm an entrepreneur. Being that most of my business can be conducted over the phone or internet, I no longer use a conventional office structure. All my employees are encouraged to consider my house their home and dress as they see fit. I learned some time ago that such an informal atmosphere really increases productivity. We all consider each other family, even though I'm their boss. I have no idea who did this, Sheriff, but please search the place thoroughly because they may still be here."

"My deputy's doing that as we speak. I'd like to talk to your other employees. Are they all here?"

Loggins nodded and motioned for him to follow. "I told them all to wait in the dining room so my cook and butler could protect them if the killer tried to get to any of them. They're both ex heavyweight boxers."

When he walked into Loggins' extraordinarily ornate dining room Gary couldn't believe his eyes. With the exception of the black butler and a punchy-faced white cook, all his employees were not only female but astoundingly beautiful like the three dead women. One looked a few years older than the rest, otherwise they all appeared to be in their early or mid twenties. A pretty Mexican, dressed like a French maid, lacked the glamour of the other women—like a supporting actress whose facial features weren't as eye-catching as those of the leading lady—but she, too, had an exceptional figure. She asked if they wanted anything to drink.

He declined as did Alfredo.

A dazzling black-haired girl with sparkling blue eyes spoke up. "I seen you through the wender at Carla's Cafe the other day. Thought you wuz kinda cute but I didn't have no time to chaw the fat. What's yer name, lawman?"

Hoping he wasn't blushing over the compliment, Gary tried to answer nonchalantly.

She tossed him a flirty smile. "You any kin to them Stoners what lives 'round Morgan City down in the bayou country by chance? That's where my mama shit me out and raised me."

"Um no, don't have any relatives in Louisiana."

"Boss won't let me smoke in the house, and won't let me go outside on account of that killer and all." She turned towards Loggins with a sly grin. "Reckon it'd be okay if I promise to stand right outside one of them wenders where the high sheriff can see me?"

"That's up to Sheriff Stoner," said Loggins, clearly irritated with her.

She refocused on him. "Well, Sheriff, how 'bout it?"

Her intense gaze was hypnotizing. The other women were casually attired but she wore a white bath robe forced slightly apart at mid-chest by her large breasts despite a tightly cinched sash that revealed a narrow waist and very shapely hips. She looked so refined her redneck accent had startled him, sounding radically out of place with the surroundings. "Uh, yeah, I suppose that would be okay."

He couldn't help eyeing her butt as she headed towards a swinging door that apparently led to a kitchen. She suddenly stopped and whirled around with a teasing grin. "Sure you wouldn't like to 'company me, cutie?"

Loggins scowled at her. "Dorian, the man's here on serious business, quit clowning around."

She flicked her fingers at him and left the room. A few moments later she appeared outside one of the windows and lit a cigarette.

Gary shifted his attention to Loggins. "You say you were in this room when your employee told you about the victims. Were all of these people here at the time?"

"Yeah, except Sonya who first saw the bodies. Sonya, stand up so the sheriff can identify you."

A tall brunette rose tentatively to her feet, a slack expression indicating she still hadn't gotten over the shock of seeing the slaughtered corpses of her three coworkers.

He stepped towards her. "Okay, Sonya, tell me how you discovered the bodies."

"I was out of toilet paper so I went up to the third floor to the storeroom to get some. It's across the hall from Babette's room. I saw the awful scene because her door was open. I totally freaked and ran down here to get Carlson."

"By here, you mean the dining room?"

"Mm hmm."

"How did you know he'd be here?"

"Because it was breakfast time."

"You all usually gather here for breakfast every morning?"

"Well, eventually we all get down here," she replied. "Some of us sleep longer than others. Carlson gets up the same time every morning, that's why I knew he'd be here."

"You getting all this, Alfredo?"

The young deputy nodded while scribbling on his notebook.

"What are your duties for Mister Loggins, Sonya?"

A nervous glint flickered across her dark eyes.

"Like I told you, Sheriff, she's one of my personal assistants," Loggins answered for her. "Sonya's duties vary from day to day—from hour to hour actually. I might have her call my broker, or my lawyer, or one of my many business contacts for this that or the other. I might need her to compose a letter for me, witness the signing of a contract, things of that nature. Montella, my executive assistant, sometimes requires her help as well."

Gary scanned the women. "Which one of you is Montella?"

The oldest of the lovelies—a stunning blonde with amazingly pretty lips—raised her hand. "That would be me."

"And what are your duties?"

Montella rapidly fired off a long list of chores she routinely performed for Loggins. "And sometimes he might only need me to scratch his back. He pays us all very well and we're happy to work for him."

Loggins cleared his throat. "Am I under suspicion, Sheriff? You seem awfully curious about my occupation is why I ask."

He shook his head. "I'm merely trying to find a possible motive. The three women worked for you and lived in your house, so I'm starting with what they all had in common. How long have the victims been in your employ?"

"About three years."

"Each of them?"

Loggins nodded.

"Where are they from and what was their backgrounds before coming to work for you?"

"I'm not sure. Montella?"

The blonde crossed one arm beneath a pair of very generous breasts and raised the other, thoughtfully touching a high cheekbone with the long polished nail of her index finger. "Babette grew up in Houston, Carolyn was from Utah originally—Salt Lake City, I believe—Cynthia moved to Texas from Nebraska. Each of them came to work for us when we were located in Houston. Babette was fresh out of high school, Carolyn sold cosmetics door-to-door, and Cynthia was an intern at NASA."

"So Carolyn and Cynthia didn't leave their respective states just to come to work for Mister Loggins?"

"No, they'd lived in Houston for awhile before joining us, and as I said, Babette's from there."

Gary's cell rang. He pulled it out of the holder on his belt and brought it to his ear. "Yeah?"

"Tank here. This place has more rooms than a Hilton Hotel. I searched the second and third floors and didn't find anybody or any weapons. I'm heading downstairs to have a look around. Where are you?"

"On the ground floor in the dining room. Keep looking towards the outside of the house while you circle the hall and you'll spot it." He killed the connection and stashed the phone.

"We'll need a statement from each of you. Is there anybody else in the house?"

"Not in the house," said Loggins, "but there's six cowboys on the ranch."

"I'll need to talk to them. Can you call them in?"

Loggins produced a cell. "I'll call the bunkhouse, the cook should be there. For some reason cell phones can't pick up signals beyond a short distance south of the mansion so none of the cowboys have one."

While waiting, Gary gazed through the window and watched Dorian smoke. She reminded him of a raven-haired woman he'd seen several times at Carla's Café that appeared to be single. He planned to introduce himself if he could ever catch her alone—ask her out if their personalities meshed and she wasn't already seeing someone. She'd been sitting with the same two women every time. Tank and Alfredo didn't know anything about any of them and he'd refrained from querying the waitresses, not wanting to start rumors. Dorian's flirtation had been purely facetious or he'd have considered getting to know her if she cleared as a suspect. Both brunettes had something very special in common—they were physically cut from the same cloth as his late wife.

"No one's answering . . ." Loggins lowered his phone. "I leave the ranching operation totally up to them, so they could be anywhere over a span of two thousand acres."

He wondered why a businessman would want to live on a ranch he appeared to have no interest in running. Loggins struck him as the sort that belonged in a fancy office suite in a big city, and all his female employees would look right at home working as bunnies at a Playboy Club. He found the arrangement very odd. "How do I get to the bunkhouse?"

THREE

Gary waited for Bob South to arrive before going to the bunkhouse. The coroner had a young assistant with him who'd been trained to lift fingerprints.

"I'd hoped we'd never be working together, Gary."

"That makes two of us," he sadly assured. "If you don't need me for anything I'll leave you to your business and continue on with mine."

"No, you go right ahead."

He went to the bunkhouse alone. Alfredo remained at the mansion to record everyone's statement while Tank continued searching the area. The front door was unlocked so he let himself in.

Though roomy and sturdy, the building obviously hadn't been constructed with the idea of impressing anyone like the mansion did. Six plain bedrooms, a storeroom, and a large bathroom equipped to handle all the cowhands at once were positioned on either side of a hall running from a spacious living room to a big kitchen.

It concerned him to find the place empty, the cook should have been preparing lunch. His watch read eleven-twenty yet the stove was cold, the double ovens empty, the pantry void of anything to make sandwiches with, the industrial refrigerator didn't contain any leftovers to be warmed up, and there were no frozen dinners in the freezer waiting to be microwaved.

* * * *

Hank Best had spent the first ten of his thirty years on the Ridgewall Ranch working as a grunt before making it to ramrod and finally foreman. When Carlson Loggins bought the place he feared his job had come to an end and hadn't relished the idea of having to look for work at sixty. Thankfully the city slicker had been as worried about having to find someone competent enough to run the spread as he'd been of being fired. He'd donned his best poker face when Loggins asked what it would take to keep him on and not only managed to retain his position with a hefty increase in pay, he'd gotten the other hands a decent raise as well.

He dropped off three hay rolls on a barren forty and headed for the barn, tooling along in third gear so the John Deere could travel at top end—thirty miles an hour. An empty flatbed trailer banged along behind him as he whistled *The Red River Valley,* hoping Munchie was making tacos like he'd requested. Lunchtime would be arriving about the time he got the tractor stowed.

Othello Vance had hired on the same day he did and they hadn't been on the Ridgewall a month before the greenhorn got fired for sassing the boss. The cook had quit a few days prior and Othello begged for a chance to show he knew his way around a cook stove, promising to keep his sharp tongue in check. Impressed by his knack for preparing large quantities of tasty grub, the boss had started calling him Munchie and it stuck.

Nearing the barn, Hank backed off the gas but something caught his eye and he abruptly stopped whistling. The bunkhouse stood less than two hundred feet away and he'd spotted the sheriff's car parked in front. Not bothering to unhitch the trailer, he pulled the accelerator stick to full throttle and motored towards the adobe structure he'd called home for half his life.

* * * *

Gary was heading for the front door on his way back to the

mansion when it swung open. A tall cowboy wearing a dusty gray hat and a scowl on his face walked in.

"What's the problem, Sheriff?"

"Who are you?"

"Hank Best, the foreman of this ranch. Where's Munchie?"

Before he could say anything the man hurried past him and went down the hall. "Munchie, what the hell's going on?"

"There's nobody here," Gary hollered after him.

The foreman returned to the living room with an anxious frown tattooed on his lean mug. "What's happened to Munchie?"

"I don't know, you're the first person I've seen since I came inside. Three of Carlson Loggins' personal assistants were murdered in the mansion. I need you to round up your hands and bring them here so I can talk to them."

"Good god-ah-mighty . . ." wrinkles deepened at the corners of the puncher's stern blue eyes as his craggy sun-beaten features turned pallid. "Well I can tell you right now none of them did it, anymore than I did, Sheriff."

"I didn't say they did, but I need a statement from everybody, yourself included."

Hank ran the back of a weathered hand across his thin chapped lips and billowed a heavy sigh. "Something ain't right here either—Munchie's gone. He's regular as clockwork and should be in the kitchen getting chow ready for me and the boys."

That's what I was afraid of, he thought glumly. "Reckon he had to go to town for some reason?"

The apprehensive cattle boss took off his hat and edgily scratched at a patch of thinning gray hair. "Wish I could tell you that might be likely, Sheriff, but it ain't. Munchie's been working on this ranch for thirty years same as me, and he's never once been late getting a meal ready. Something's happened to him, I feel it in here—" he tapped his chest with his free hand.

"Well I looked all over and no one's here."

"Did you check the basement?"

He shrugged. "Didn't know it had one. I've opened every door in this place. How do you get to it?"

Hank put his hat back on and started walking. "From outside. It serves as a storm cellar. The man who built the place was scared a twister might collapse the house on an interior door and make it a tomb."

Gary followed him to the side of the bunkhouse and the lanky cowboy pulled open a wide steel door, slanting at a forty-five degree angle a few feet above the ground. When they descended the stairs and entered the basement, Munchie's whereabouts were a mystery no longer.

The poor cook lay naked, spread eagle on a cement floor— one hand gripping a penis which had been amputated with the scrotum intact, the other grasping the back of his severed head. For some reason the genitals had turned black. His lifeless eyes were open and aimed at the ceiling. The bloody cavity at his crotch appeared to be the wound he'd suffered first, judging by the lack of blood around the headless neck.

* * * *

"Man, I wanna fuck that bitch so bad."

Dooly snickered at Bobby Joe's remark but kept his eyes glued to the binoculars as he also ogled Dorian from atop his horse. It had become a pre-lunch ritual ever since they'd discovered the amazing beauty always stepped outside for a smoke around this time of day.

When Carlson Loggins bought the ranch he'd thrown a big barbecue so everyone could get acquainted. Hank had warned the crew to be on their best behavior, especially Bobby Joe and him since they were the youngest. He'd managed to get everyone a raise and had feared Loggins might renege on it if they chapped his hide in any way. They'd heeded their foreman's advice and had been invited to several other functions since. Loggins' personal assistants appeared to be beautiful snobs at first sight but had turned out to be friendly women. Every one of them looked like they'd stepped out of the center of some classy men's magazine but Dorian was the prettiest. Bobby Joe agreed with him while Geraldo insisted Sonya edged out the others as the cream of the crop. Jeremy thought Nicole Anderson topped the list and Munchie argued Montella Pace did. Hank claimed that honor belonged to the platinum blonde Tillie with Montella and Dorian running a close second, and the luscious brown-haired Babette and steamy redhead Rosemary tied for third place.

"Enough pussy dreaming, Bobby Joe. Let's get on to the bunkhouse and see what Munchie's got on the menu. Ten to one it's tacos." He lowered the field glasses and eased his gelding into motion.

Bobby Joe reluctantly did the same, his homely face drenched with more horniness than a rapist's in a topless bar. "If I was a lady's man like you, Dew, I'd ask her to marry me."

He laughed and shook his head. "Hell she wouldn't marry me unless I won the lottery. I'd like to bone her as much as you, but the sad truth is we're just a couple of cow punchers and she's a high class filly. That's just the way things are."

"She don't talk so high class."

"Aw that's just a game she likes to play. I've seen her speak and act real prim and proper, like a real lady. Let her go, hoss. There's a lot more fish in the sea. What the fuck?" Dooly reined to a stop and squinted ahead. "That's the sheriff's car. What the hell is he doing at the bunkhouse . . .?"

* * * *

Geraldo Toya had worked under Hank Best for the last seven years and planned to replace him when the venerable foreman retired at sixty-five. Being three rungs from the top wasn't how he'd envisioned himself upon reaching thirty, but Jeremy Hicks didn't have the brains to advance beyond ramrod so that didn't worry him none. Dooly and Bobby Joe certainly weren't a threat, being only twenty-one and twenty-two respectively. That Dew was a sharp customer and would probably acquire the savvy needed to run a ranch this size by the time Hank stepped down, but he had four years seniority over him and Bobby Joe. Bobby Joe didn't have any leadership qualities, and a man either possessed such attributes or he didn't, they couldn't be learned.

He fished a brown paper bag from his saddle bag and sat down on a smooth bolder by the riverside to eat lunch. Munchie had rustled him up some burritos upon hearing he'd have to eat on the range today. Geraldo really liked the old geezer—he watched over them all like a mother hen. No doubt he'd be serving up tacos about now since that's what Hank had asked for when everyone received their workday instructions during breakfast.

Gazing at the Rio Grande's glistening surface, he savored a bite of beef, beans, and cheese wrapped inside a tortilla as his thoughts whirled around Sonya. The first time they'd laid eyes on one another he'd felt the chemistry and knew she had too. Carlson Loggins might have everybody else fooled but not him. He couldn't tell the other hands or anyone else because Sonya had sworn him to secrecy when she'd confided in him. The dude was running an elite brothel and she wanted to bring him down. Once she had enough evidence gathered to bury Loggins, she'd present it to her brother who worked for the FBI as an analyst.

The first time they'd made love had been on a Saturday night when Loggins and all his girls had come to town for the rodeo. He and the other hands had been invited to sit with them, and when Sonya said she wasn't feeling well after winking at him, he'd volunteered to drive her home. They'd consummated their love in the bunkhouse and had only managed to get off to themselves long enough to be intimate twice since—once in the back seat of her Nissan Maxima, the other in the barn. But after she exposed Loggins they'd have all the time in the world.

* * * *

"Jeremy Hicks," said the grief-stricken foreman when asked for the name. "He was my ramrod."

Gary stood with hands on hips, viewing the second body to be found in the bunkhouse basement. Like the cook, the poor devil had suffered total castration and the killer had once again arranged it so the victim appeared to be jacking off. The cook's genitalia hadn't turned black after all. He'd been holding this black man's pecker and Jeremy Hicks held his. Placed in a sitting position in a dark corner totally nude, back leaning against the wall, a pool of blood covered the ground between his spread out legs while hardly any exuded from the head resting on the ramrod's other hand.

They left the basement and Hank Best ordered two long-haired cowboys, who'd shown up for lunch only to learn their cook and ramrod had been murdered, to round up the other hand and bring him back to the bunkhouse.

Gary hoped they'd find him with his head attached and still breathing.

Shortly after three o'clock the two cowpunchers rode up with their crony—a Mexican who also wore his hair shoulder length. By that time Bob South had examined the two bodies in the basement and his preliminary findings were that both had indeed died from exsanguination.

They'd been castrated while still alive.

FOUR

Carlson had never been through such a harrowing experience before—three of his girls decapitated, two of the ranch hands having their genitals ripped off as well as their heads. The moment they were out of the deputies' sight he'd told Montella to contact Reverend Snow and tell him to cancel his trip. Since no other clients were due on the ranch the next seventy-two hours—a rare event—he decided to hold off on further cancellations unless conditions warranted it.

He'd rented eight rooms at the best motel in town after Sheriff Stoner advised him it wouldn't be safe for anyone to stay on the ranch for the time being—one for himself, four for his girls and Selena to roommate in, one for Rico and Lambert, and two for the remaining cowhands, who'd be heading back to the ranch for work in the morning. Once again the sheriff had offered advice, saying it wouldn't be wise for any of them to be isolated and that the best thing would be for the four cowboys to stay together throughout the day.

Stoner had also stated that until the coroner verified the time of death no one living on the Ridgewall Ranch was above suspicion, including its owner.

The smell of fajitas and refried beans permeated the atmosphere of the Mexican restaurant. Carlson drank his supper, having no appetite for solid food. None of the girls ate much either, except Dorian, who'd put away more tamales and enchiladas than any of the cowboys.

"This was the most dreadful day of my life," said Montella, sitting across from him, morosely eyeing a platter of nachos.

He nodded while lifting a pitcher of Sangria. "May there never, *ever* be another like it."

"Who would do such a thing, Carl?"

"Don't know, but what worries me is how they were able to do it without anybody hearing them." He filled his glass and downed a mouthful. "Lambert locked us in tight last night like always, so the killer is someone who can pick theft-proof locks and carve people up like a surgeon."

Montella grimaced. "I can't see any connection between those poor cowboys and Babette, Carolyn, and Cynthia."

"Neither can I . . ." he took another long pull and swallowed hard. "To definitely change the subject, why do you think Sonya might hurt us, and don't say it's because her brother's with the FBI."

She picked up a nacho, studied it a few seconds, and dropped it back on the platter.

"Well?"

"She's sneaky, Carl."

"Hell, all women are sneaky," he snickered.

"Did you know she has a thing for Geraldo?"

"Oh does she now."

"Mm hmm."

He shifted towards the cowboys' table and examined the Mexican. "Well why not? He's a good looking guy."

"I'm serious, Carl."

"I know you are."

Sonya sat with the other girls around a large round table near the cowboys. Dorian was swilling beer like a sailor on the first day of shore leave and smoking one cancer stick after another. Sure enough he caught Sonya exchanging glances with the Latino, but that didn't mean she planned to betray him. After all, his whores were free to do as they pleased so long as they used protection and were able to perform their erotic duties at the high level expected of them.

The young bucks, Dooly and Bobby Joe, were watching Dorian's every move. Poor Hank obviously hadn't gotten over the shock of losing his long time friend Munchie along with his ramrod. An unlit cigar hung from his mouth and a mug of beer sat before him untouched like his taco platter. Carlson felt sorry for the foreman and could certainly relate—Babette, Carolyn, and Cynthia would be hard to replace.

Nicole came over, swiped one of Montella's nachos, and washed it down with a sip from his glass. She set it on the table and folded her long arms beneath her firm Jamaican breasts, one of the finest set of tits he'd ever had the pleasure of sucking and squeezing. "Boss, I've been thinking. I believe the ghost committed those murders. I sense a voodoo priestess may be involved, causing Klell Ridgewall to become malevolent."

Aware she was serious he forced himself not to laugh. Montella donned a sad smile and merely shook her head.

"And if I'm right, none of us dare go back to the ranch. According to all I've heard no one has ever seen him anywhere else, so I'll bet his spirit is confined to its boundaries. If that's true, we're all safe so long as we keep away. Angela saw him last night, so you can't say my suspicions aren't warranted."

He glanced at the girls' table and saw Angela's chair empty. She'd been sitting beside Dorian, who was lighting yet another Camel. "Where is she anyway?"

"Went to the ladies room. I need to pay it a visit myself. Be back in a minute."

When she got out of earshot he grinned at Montella. "That girl has some imagination, doesn't she?"

"Mm hmm . . ." she lifted a nacho and once again the cheese laden corn chip embedded with a slice of jalapeño found its way back to the pile a few moments later, completely intact.

A blood curdling scream split the air, followed by a continuous stream of them, all coming from Nicole. He made a mad dash for the ladies room, beating the cowhands and some of the other male patrons, and found her running in place, arms pumping, still hysterically bellowing.

"Somebody call the sheriff!" he yelled while shoving Nicole outside. Then he slammed the door and locked it to keep the crowd back.

Angela's head lay sideways on the toilet's tank while her body was doubled over on the bowl with her panties pulled down to her ankles. Her right arm was thrust up her skirt, sandwiched between her thighs as if she'd been masturbating when her throat got severed.

FIVE

Gary had asked for help but the FBI didn't investigate murder, even multiple ones except in special cases because homicides weren't a federal offense. Since none of the victims were employed by any government agency, this case didn't fit the criteria of being special.

It couldn't have been a single person acting alone but he had no clues to the killers' identity. However, Angela Yang being decapitated at a busy restaurant last night had eliminated everyone presently residing on the Ridgewall Ranch. Though any of them might be accomplices, they were all in each others' presence from the time she went to the ladies room until Nicole Anderson saw her.

Carlson Loggins had said they might as well all return to the ranch for what good it had done seeking safety in town. Unable to convince him or the ladies otherwise, Gary had implored them to at least share rooms rather than sleep alone. Loggins had eased his mind a little by requesting the ranch hands—who all claimed to be proficient with firearms—spend their nights in the mansion until the killers were apprehended. Meanwhile Gary had assigned his deputies to take turns staying on the ranch at twenty-four hour intervals. Loggins had eagerly agreed to supply a bedroom for them to sleep in.

Angela Yang's time of death was a no-brainer, and Bob South concluded the other three female victims had been slaughtered at least six hours before the cook and ramrod. Othello Vance, who the hands called Munchie, and Jeremy Hicks were last seen alive when Hank and the surviving cow punchers left the bunkhouse after breakfast. Hicks was supposed to make a run to a feed store for anthelmintics to worm a batch of three-month-old calves but his pickup never left the ranch.

Gary replenished his coffee cup and got comfortable at his desk, preparing to go through everyone's statements and bios. He started with Carlson Loggins.

Born and raised in Beaumont, Texas he'd been self-employed all his working life. He allegedly had no prior history with any of the female victims before becoming their boss, and they'd all been in his employ when he purchased the Ridgewall Ranch. After being called to the restaurant over Angela Yang's murder, he'd pressed Loggins and his personal assistants for more details about how they earned their living. All the information he'd been given had been either too generic or just plain vague. He'd then privately interviewed the butler, cook, and maid.

Lambert Jackson, the butler, and Rico Mircanti, the cook, had been hired by Loggins to double as bodyguards and servants. Both claimed that injuries had ended promising boxing careers and Loggins had been a loyal fan of each. When their sports tenures prematurely ended Jackson had gone to work for Loggins while Mircanti spent two years training as a master chef before being hired by the entrepreneur. High school dropout Selena Lopez, the maid, started working for Loggins five years ago at seventeen.

He'd then talked to Hank and the other three ranch hands, asking if they'd noticed any unusual activity since Loggins acquired the ranch. Other than being bothered by the noise of private aircraft landing and taking off after Loggins had a landing strip constructed, none of them had noted anything out of the ordinary. However, they weren't allowed in the mansion without being invited so they had no idea what went on inside when Loggins received visitors. Hank had been given strict instructions to call Loggins' cell phone rather than approach him in person if he needed anything.

"He let us know real clear that it'd be our jobs if any of us ever went inside his house without his permission," the old cowboy had said.

Gary had a feeling Carlson Loggins was nothing but a high-priced pimp and his so called personal assistants hooked for him. That scenario could mean the killers were out to end his operation because of anger or to eliminate competition. He hadn't voiced his suspicion to anyone, and planned to keep it to himself for the time being.

His opinion of Dorian had changed dramatically. Even if she wasn't a whore, he felt in his gut she and the other girls were assisting Loggins in some form of illegal activity. The beauty had been as difficult to pin down as the others when he'd tried to get precise information about her boss's business activities. Her hick accent had disappeared the moment he'd started questioning her, and each reply seemed carefully rehearsed, as if she'd been rigorously schooled in dodging queries concerning Loggins' affairs.

The cell phone startled him. He retrieved it from the holder and saw Tank's name on the screen. He'd taken the first shift on the Ridgewall Ranch. Hoping he wasn't about to hear bad news, he brought it to his ear. "What's up, Tank?"

"Just checking in. Nothing new to report."

"Good."

"I do have something interesting to tell you though."

"What's that?"

"I think one of the girls has a crush on you. She's been quizzing me about you all morning."

Despite his hunch over her being some form of bottom-feeder, he couldn't help hoping it was Dorian. "Which one?"

"Sonya Bain."

"Oh? What's she been asking about?" He tried not to sound disappointed.

"Are you single, where did you grow up, how long have you been in law enforcement, are you as honest as you look?

Stuff like that."

"Hmm. Maybe she knows something and is trying to find out if it's safe to tell me."

"Could be, but I don't think so. Well I'll let you go, we're about to have lunch."

* * * *

It had been over a month since Geraldo had been in the mansion. As he lunched on spaghetti and meatballs he fantasized about living in the splendid structure with Sonya after Loggins got sent to prison. In reality he had no idea what would become of it when the pimp finally got what he deserved, but felt confident he'd be able to convince whomever took over the ranch afterwards to keep him on.

The big deputy Tank Green sat across from him between Sonya and Rosemary, so enjoying the lovely sight of Rosemary's cleavage that he'd missed his mouth on two occasions, sending a trail of noodles and tomato sauce racing down the front of his khaki shirt. The dark red smear almost matched the color of Tank's and Rosemary's hair. Sonya had doused her napkin in a glass of water and tried to clean it for him after he'd wiped the bulk of it off with his own for the second time, but it would take something much stronger to remove that stubborn stain.

How can such a beautiful woman eat like such a pig? he thought while glancing at Dorian. Totally unconcerned about others witnessing her gluttony, she sat on the other side of Sonya, slurping up pasta and Italian bread as greedily as a pregnant sow trying to fill her belly before getting pushed away from the trough by other ravenous swine. His fellow cowhands could learn a thing or two about etiquette as well. Hank at least showed a modicum of table courtesy by occasionally wiping the corners of his mouth between bites, but Dooly and Bobby Joe were almost as bad as Dorian.

He noticed Loggins frowning at her and realized he and the pimp actually had something in common—disdain for ill manners. Montella, occupying the end of the table opposite her boss, swirled spaghetti around a fork in petite portions, bringing it to her lovely lips gracefully, chewing with her mouth closed the way a lady should. Sonya, being a vegan and refusing to eat any carbos other than beans from which she procured the bulk of her protein, pecked daintily at a garden salad.

Lowering his right hand, he secured the pistol strapped to his side while shifting in the chair. Nestled within a leather holster, the three-fifty-seven magnum had a cartridge in each of its six chambers and he had twenty-four more bullets inserted in the slots of his gun belt. Hank preferred a forty-five while lightweights Dooly and Bobby Joe wore twenty-two long barrels. A twenty-gauge pump-action leaned against the table to his right. His cohorts each had one too. The sight of the shotguns marred the genteel atmosphere of the magnificent dining room, but their presence was vital. Deputy Tank had doled them out and kept one for himself.

He'd been carefully analyzing the murders but couldn't see any correlation between the girls and poor Munchie and Jeremy. One thing was certain though, whoever did the bloody deeds had to be a sexual pervert. Nicole had been talking about Klell Ridgewall's ghost being behind the murders, saying she'd been certain before Angela's death that he couldn't venture off the ranch. Now she feared he could go anywhere and insisted they needed to find the voodoo priestess who'd somehow managed to turn a harmless phantom into a merciless killer.

Despite having seen the ghost one rainy night along with Dooly and Bobby Joe, he found her theory absurd. Hank, Munchie, and Jeremy had seen Ridgewall on several occasions, and the confederate spirit always disappeared a few seconds after manifesting atop his stallion, harmlessly waving his sword in the air. The night Dooly, Booby Joe, and he saw it, Ridgewall's ride hadn't lasted much longer than a shooting star. Besides that, Angela had been killed around eight-thirty, and no one had ever seen the apparition except shortly before the stroke of midnight.

* * * *

Nadia Mars had licked her wounds in Houston for a few weeks after being shipped back there from Las Vegas by Greyhound. Though afraid to work without a pimp's protection, she'd had no choice but to go independent when her bankroll thinned out. Having been coaxed into hooking as a teenager by the smoothest talking man on the planet, she had no marketable skills and was too accustomed to a life of luxury to work for minimum wage or wait tables for a living. One night a rodeo star picked her up and convinced her to accompany him across the state to watch him compete in a high stakes bull riding event at the Tomahawk County Arena. That's where she'd met and soon started working for Sheriff Dody Massey six years ago. He'd left her in charge of The Hog Farm when he fled to Mexico.

She couldn't believe Dody had lost the last election which negated his ability to fully protect his underground activities, but what she really had a tough time swallowing after finally getting used to the necessary adjustments was Carlson Loggins buying the Ridgewall Ranch. The selfish bastard didn't know she also resided in Tomahawk County, and she planned to keep it that way as long as possible.

Sitting naked in front of her vanity, brushing her thick black mane, her tits caught her eye and she panicked— according to the mirror they were sagging ever so slightly. She leaned forward to study her face, searching for any signs of aging. *Thank God, skin's as taut and creamy as ever.*

Age had only recently started showing on her mother, and

at thirty-five, Nadia hoped she wouldn't have to worry about losing her looks for at least two more decades. She sat the brush down and did her chest exercises, promising herself never to slack off again, having neglected her exceptional bosom for several months.

She'd often wondered if any of the members of ZZ Top had ever visited the brothel before she wound up there. *La Grange* described the place perfectly, for it *was* that type of home on the range. Located eleven miles from town, along the northeastern border of the Ridgewall Ranch, The Hog Farm had housed various whores from nineteen-eighty-nine until Dody got defeated by Gary Stoner. Since then she'd retained only two girls and had curtailed all prostitution business except for a handful of clients whose discretion could unquestionably be trusted. Jared Soul and his two helpers took care of the livestock—mostly hogs—on the thirty acre spread. They earned meager wages and resided in a converted barn, but free home-cooked meals and an occasional piece of pussy on the house kept them from seeking employment elsewhere. She only permitted the handsome Jared to touch her, leaving Erma and Sally to handle the other two losers.

A mass murderer was on the loose in Tomahawk County, killing four of Carlson's whores and two of his cowboys yesterday. She'd laughed out loud when the newscaster called the female victims, whose names were being withheld pending notification of their families, *personal assistants of Carlson Loggins*. As much as she hated the bastard, she'd give anything to feel his dick inside her again. No one knew how to pleasure a woman like Carlson, and she certainly never would have failed him intentionally.

She'd been crazy about The Francesco Brothers ever since the rock group broke into the limelight, and couldn't believe her idol, Antonio Francesco, had actually hit on her in the casino that night. How could she refuse him? Stars in her eyes, giddy with joy, she'd gone with him to his room figuring she'd be able to keep her appointment with the famous middle-aged singer Carlson planned to blackmail. Losing track of the time, she'd gotten to the headliner's room too late and incurred her boss's wrath to the terminal degree. The last time she saw Carlson he was chatting up a pretty Asian girl in the terminal as she weepingly boarded the bus.

Midday sunbeams streamed through the large window of her bedroom, bathing her in light and warmth. Resisting the temptation to climb back under the silky covers, she slipped on a robe and made her way downstairs. A horrible nightmare had woke her in the middle of the night and she'd tossed and turned for at least two hours worrying about it before slumber finally returned. She'd slept so soundly afterwards she hadn't stirred until noon.

The bout of insomnia had been induced by fear the night terror wasn't a mere dream but a psychic vision, for it had been an exact repeat of the same nightmare she'd woken up from at four a.m. yesterday.

SIX

Dooly had meant it when he'd told Bobby Joe neither of them had a chance with Dorian, but danged if he hadn't caught her giving him the eye all the way through lunch. Sitting in his saddle, ambling southward alongside Bobby Joe as they tailed Hank and Geraldo, he tried to think of a way to lure the scrumptious hottie away from the mansion so he could talk to her privately. She'd never marry him of course—a woman like that was high maintenance, way beyond anything he'd ever be able to afford—but maybe, just maybe, she might want to fuck him. The look in her eyes as she'd inhaled her grub sure made him think she wanted to. If he did somehow manage to get into her pants he could never tell Bobby Joe, it would break the poor boy's heart.

The chore ahead only required two hands but since Munchie and Jeremy had been slaughtered in broad daylight, the four of them had committed to stay together during work hours until the mad butcher got caught as Sheriff Stoner advised.

Loggins had rented enough motel rooms yesterday that nobody had to have more than one roommate, but after Angela's murder they'd all gone back to the ranch. Dorian had bunked with Sonya, giving up her bedroom to Bobby Joe and him. Just the thought of sleeping in the same bed she usually occupied had been enough to give him a hard on. If Bobby Joe hadn't been laying on the other side he'd have jacked off so he could get some sleep. He'd lain awake for hours fantasizing about her.

The late October air was arid and still, but an occasional breeze carried the nostalgic fragrance of blooming sage past his nose. A windmill fan needed repairing and as they drew near he spotted a newborn Hereford bull abandoned near the water trough fed by a concrete tank. His mother lay on her side near a prickly pear cactus, a glob of afterbirth exuding from her bloody twat like a mass of deflated jelly fish. Swarming blowflies served notice she'd borne her last offspring.

"Got a dead one," said Hank. "Dooly, you and Bobby Joe take that calf to the barn and bottle feed it. Geraldo and me'll tend to the windmill. We'll let the buzzards have mama."

Bobby Joe frowned. "Thought we were gonna stick together, Hank."

"We are, but that calf needs to eat right now, and if we don't get the windmill pumping again we're liable to have more casualties. That's why I'm sending the two of you instead of just one, so none of us will be by himself."

Dooly dismounted, lassoed the wailing calf, and heaved him across his horse behind the saddle. Bobby Joe held the infant in place while he tied its front hooves together, ran the rope under his gelding's belly, looped it several times around the protesting baby's back legs, and pulled it taut. Winking at Bobby Joe, who had a worried mope on his homely face, he climbed back in the saddle, wrapped the horn once, and kept a firm grip on the uncoiled rope. "It'll be all right, hoss. Anybody tries to bother us we'll blow 'em away." He patted his pistol with his free hand.

* * * *

The deputy had shown them all how to fire the shotguns and use the pump action to reload. Carlson used to hunt rabbits with a twenty-two rifle during his teens but hadn't touched a firearm since. Lambert and Rico needed no instructions and could operate a machinegun had one been handy. A Glock dangled on Rico's hip and Lambert had his nine millimeter tucked away in a shoulder holster.

He'd been shocked to learn Dorian had never fired a weapon in her life. Being such a swamp rat, Carlson figured she'd not only killed every type of game animal inhabiting the south but knew precisely how to skin and butcher them as well.

They were lounging around the billiard room taking turns at the tables. Carlson eased back in an armchair, watching Tillie take Deputy Green apart in a game of nine ball, Dorian slaughtering Lambert in bank pool, Nicole and Rosemary evenly matched in a round of eight ball. He was bored out of his mind and halfway hoped the murderer would appear so this mess could be over with. A glance at Sonya's gorgeous butt sticking out provocatively as she leaned over the pinball machine made his balls tingle. Letting his eyes roam over the tall brunette's sexy body, he eventually found himself focusing on her pouting lips and got an idea. Rising from the chair, he told her to come with him and headed for the door.

"Where are you going?" asked the deputy.

"Need to discuss a business matter in private, we'll only be about twenty minutes."

"Where are you planning to discuss this matter?"

"In the foyer."

"Be back here in fifteen and take a shotgun with you."

Carrying one of the twenty-gauges, he guided the hot pretty-mouthed bitch out of the billiard room and made for the luxurious bathroom down the hall.

A blowjob would relieve the boredom.

* * * *

Watching Nicole rack the balls for another game, Rosemary tried to ignore the jealousy that had been tormenting her since Carlson left the billiard room with Sonya. She knew the only business on his mind was sex.

Deputy Green's constant staring had become annoying and she wished he'd start ogling one of the other girls. At first she'd been flattered he had eyes for her alone amongst such an attractive group of women, but the luster had dulled and no longer warmed her ego. The poor yokel had no chance but the lovesick look on his face assured it wouldn't be long before he'd try to hit on her. Situations like this made her all the more resentful of not being able to publicly show her feelings for Carlson. She loved him madly and wished she could let the whole world know. Of course all his women loved him, but she doubted their affections were anywhere near as strong as hers. Dorian's certainly weren't, but the gluttonous nymphomaniac probably didn't possess the capacity to truly love anything beyond having her bottomless stomach and insatiable vagina gratified.

Her would be paramour checked his watch and frowned.

"I'm going to check on Loggins, everybody stay put."

* * * *

Gary hadn't ran against Dody Massey because of ambition. The desire to oust the corrupt lawman had driven him. Now he almost wished he'd turned his back on the matter and moved far away from Tomahawk County. Sonya Bain had Loggins' dick in her mouth and one of her tits dangled sideways from her employer's clenched teeth. Both the penis and breast had been severed from their respective bodies, as had the heads. Loggins' had been placed inside the toilet bowl, face looking towards the ceiling. Sonya's lay in the sink, eyes also looking skyward. The beheaded bodies were atop one another in the bathtub—Loggins' above with Sonya's hands clutching his shoulders as if they were having intercourse. He inspected the shotgun Tank had insisted Loggins take with him. It hadn't been fired.

Bob South removed Loggins' death-shriveled penis and

examined Sonya's oral cavity. "She has semen in her mouth. If it's Loggins' they were taken by complete surprise since she didn't have time to swallow or spit it out. The weapon or weapons used are extremely sharp with smooth edges. Their throats, her breast, his penis were sliced with the same surgical precision as the other victims. And like them, each amputation appears to have been done with one fluid motion. We're dealing with an exceptionally skilled monster, Gary."

"I know," he numbly agreed, "and he has a helper or two."

"Yeah, bound to have."

He stepped into the hall where Tank waited with Montella Pace. "Loggins told you they were going to the foyer?"

Tank nodded. "He claimed they needed to discuss a business matter in private. I told him I'd give him fifteen minutes. When he didn't come back by then I waited another five and went to check on them."

Gary looked at Montella, her beautiful façade was a mishmash of fear and grief. "You were alone when you found them?"

She answered with a meek nod.

"Okay, enough bullshit about Loggins being an entrepreneur. He was a pimp wasn't he, and you and the others are prostitutes. You need to tell me the truth because I think someone's trying to kill off the competition."

The offended glare that sprang to her face didn't quite ring true. "How dare you infer that I'm a whore! I ought to sue you for slander, and I just might if you don't apologize immediately. I'm a highly skilled business woman with a college degree, not some uneducated tramp."

He grinned, patronizingly. "I'm sorry, how classless of me. A high dollar lady of the evening would be a more accurate expression. Now cut the bullshit and tell me the truth or you're about to have four call girls think you ratted out their boss voluntarily. Square with me right now and you've got my word none of them will ever know I found out the truth about

Loggins from you."

Montella tried to keep up the farce so he said, "Tank, don't let her leave this spot. I'm going to the billiard room and have a chat with the other ladies."

"Okay . . .!" she grabbed his arm as he started to leave. She released it when he stopped moving, and lowered her head. "You're right. Carl was a pimp and I'm . . . I *was* his number one consort. We all hustled for him. He paid us very well and treated us with dignity and respect. Please don't tell any of the others I told you."

The agony twisting her striking features revealed she hadn't merely betrayed a boss but the man she loved.

"Don't worry, I won't—a deal's a deal. Besides, I want them to think I'm still in the dark about Loggins' true profession. A guy like that is bound to have made some enemies along the way. Who hated him enough to want to kill him?"

She raised her chin and steadied her eyes on him. "Sheriff, Carl pissed off a lot of people—*a lot* of people because he was also into blackmail. Am I going to jail?"

"That'll be up to a judge, but if you'll help me—not lie to me or send me on any wild goose chases—I'll do everything I can to get you leniency, you've got my word. Has anyone else seen the bodies?"

"No. I followed Deputy Green out the door when he went to look for Carl and Sonya but none of the others did."

He cut his eyes to Tank. "Does that square with the facts?"

"Yeah. After Montella chased me down and told me what she found I went back to the billiard room and warned everybody not to leave, no matter what, until I got back. They know something's up but I didn't tell them anything."

"Good. If one or more of them are involved, they might overplay their hand." He'd arrived with Bob and his assistant, and they'd entered without ringing the bell because Tank had let them him, being directed to do so over the cell phone. Only Montella knew he was on the premises. "Tell me about the blackmail."

She drew a deep breath through her nose, gripped her waist with slender fingers terminating in long polished nails that appeared capable of slicing the fabric of her blouse, and exhaled a haggard sigh. "There's two large walk-in closets in my bedroom but appears to be only one. The door to the other was replaced by what appears to be a normal full length mirror attached to a wall. In reality it's a two-way mirror with highly sophisticated audio and video recording gear behind it. Every new client spends his first night in there. Everything he says and does is carefully captured. We did the same thing back in Houston."

"So all the rooms aren't monitored by video cameras?"

"No. The first thing Carl did after buying this place was have all the security equipment removed because such devices would have made his clients very uncomfortable. Plus Carl didn't want to take a chance on any of his activities winding up on tape. The only video recorder in this house is the one in my bedroom. Carl won't—" she closed her eyes and tears dribbled from each corner "—*wouldn't* even let us have cell phones with the capability of taking pictures."

Confident her grief was genuine, he knew she didn't have anything to do with Loggins' death. If Montella was an accomplice the killers had surprised her by taking him out. "Okay, here's what we're gonna do. Tank, go back to the billiard room and tell everyone about Loggins and Sonya but include Montella as a victim too. Don't let anyone out the door until I tell you, which will be right after Bob gets the bodies out of here. Montella, you're coming back to town with me, I want them to think you're dead for the time being. There seems to be some sort of plan being followed, and since you weren't really a victim, if any of the others are involved it'll cause confusion and they'll want to find out what's going on, so they'll have to contact the killers. Tank, watch and see if anyone uses their cell phones after you break the news. Don't try to stop them, just listen carefully."

Tank gave him a puzzled look. "Why do you think there's a plan? Seems to me whoever's isolated from the crowd is getting picked off."

"I don't think so, Tank. There's nowhere in this stretch of hall to hide, so Loggins would have seen them if they were lying in wait when he stepped out of the billiard room. He was totally caught off guard or he'd have fired the weapon. Bob found semen in Sonya's mouth and you can bet the bank it's Loggins'. She was going down on him in the bathroom when the killers burst in. Since he and Sonya obviously didn't see anyone in the hall, the killers couldn't have seen them leave the billiard room, which means someone had to have notified them Loggins and Sonya were vulnerable."

"Why do you say killers rather than killer?" asked Montella.

"There's no way one person is capable of this. There'd be signs of a struggle and blood everywhere instead of precisely where the killers want it to be if it was one person acting alone. There's at least two, maybe more. You say the door was open when you found them?"

She nodded.

"Loggins definitely would have locked it, yet the doorframe's intact, so someone either had a key or picked the lock—it wasn't kicked in. You said you followed Tank. How is it you spotted the bodies first and he didn't?"

"Deputy Green went the opposite direction."

"You told me you followed him."

"I did follow him out of the billiard room but I knew what Carl was up to—wanting a quickie with Sonya—so I went to warn him the deputy was looking for them so they wouldn't get caught in the act. This bathroom was the nearest place to do that. With the deputy around, Carl wouldn't have run the risk of trying it in any of the other rooms because on this floor only the bathroom doors have locks."

He glanced at Tank. "Is she telling the truth?"

"All I know is I was heading towards the foyer when she ran up from behind me crying, and told me what she'd found."

Gary stepped into the bathroom and told Bob to call him the moment they had the bodies in the hearse. Back in the hall, he turned to Montella. "Okay let's go. Tank, you know what to do."

"I'll need to pack a few things first, Sheriff."

He put a hand on her back and prodded her forward. "A dead woman doesn't pack. If anyone noticed something of yours missing it might give us away . . . ."

SEVEN

Geraldo couldn't believe his beloved Sonya had been taken from him. If only he hadn't pleaded with the deputy to tell him everything he would have been spared that part of the torment. Tank's description of the crime scene had so defiled his mind he feared the mental image would torture him forever. Actually seeing Sonya in that condition most certainly would have driven him insane, so he thanked God he hadn't. He'd immediately excused himself after hearing the gory details and had cried his eyes out in the foyer. There were no more tears to shed at the moment. Many more would surely follow, but for now his grief had retreated into the empty void he felt inside.

The deputy had staunchly refused to discuss Montella's slaughter, saying only that she'd been a victim too. Her body must have been so violated Tank just didn't have the heart to put it into words. He grieved for her also. Though a whore, the woman had been a rare beauty and possessed such a refined air she came off like a privileged member of high society rather than an upscale madam.

Alfredo Parra and three highway patrolmen had been called in to help Tank ensure no one left the premises, even though none of them could have killed Sonya, Montella, or Loggins. Hank and he had rejoined Dooly and Bobby Joe after repairing the windmill, and everyone else had been in the billiard room when the murders occurred, so they all had unshakable alibis. Nonetheless, like the butler and cook, he and his fellow ranch hands had been required to surrender their pistols to the lawmen, who'd confiscated all the shotguns.

The empty chairs at either end of the dining table served as ominous reminders their usual occupants were dead. One patrolman had attempted to take Loggins' seat but the pimp's surviving whores—except Dorian, who'd seemed to find the outburst amusing—had chastised him, saying no one should ever sit there again. The pig was presently bent over an overloaded plate, stuffing her face with fried shrimp and ketchup-saturated French fries, not bothering to close her mouth while she chewed, or wipe the goop off her lips and chin.

He sat properly erect, supping on beans and cornbread, forgoing the shrimp and potatoes for this one meal in homage to Sonya, who would've shunned both due to her vegan anti-carbohydrate diet. Careful to keep his left arm off the table and mouth closed while chewing, he felt guilty over not refraining from the carbo-laden cornbread. But if he ate nothing but frijoles he'd be farting before he finished supper.

Nicole once again voiced her concern that the police had better start looking for the voodoo priestess manipulating Klell Ridgewall's ghost.

Deputy Parra, sitting next to her, winced. "What makes you think that?"

Nicole cut her arresting dark eyes to him and smiled, her brilliant white teeth contrasting sharply with the light chocolate of her face. "I know this sounds foolish to the uninitiated, Deputy, but I speak from experience. You can ask these cowboys here, every one of them have seen the ghost. Angela Yang saw it the night before her death. That same night Angela saw Klell Ridgewall ride down the hall I dreamed she and Sonya were horseback riding and Sonya's horse bucked her off and trampled her to death. And now she's been attacked too. I tell you, it's no coincidence."

Dorian popped a jumbo shrimp in her mouth, tail and all. "It's a known fact back'n Cajun country where I growed up, way deep in the Looz-ee-anna swamp, that voodoo's real.

What's yer name again, poncho?"

"Alfredo Parra."

She gave him a wide grin, crisp breading peppered sporadically between her teeth, lips coated with ketchup. "That's a right purty name. You hitched?"

The deputy nervously shook his head.

"Gotta girlfriend?"

He nodded.

The smile vanished and Dorian stuffed her mouth with fries. "Damn shame. I'd have let ya fuck me if'n you wuzn't spake fer."

Alfredo and every other male dropped their jaws, and the astonished deputy's grip failed as well—his fork bounced off the table and onto the floor. Geraldo wanted to throw his glass at the uncouth bitch as Dorian hee-hawed and resumed pigging out.

Dooly and Bobby Joe were pale-faced with shock. Or was it excitement?

* * * *

Gary couldn't afford to have anyone in town see Montella or he'd have taken her to Carla's Café for supper instead of having a pizza delivered to his house. When The Department of Public Safety granted his request for assistance, he'd called Tank and told him not to tell any of the patrolmen Montella was alive, and until he said otherwise, even Alfredo and Ilian weren't to know. Tank had informed him no one used their cell phones after he'd conveyed the gruesome news. Though the ploy hadn't worked so far, he wasn't ready to call it a bust just yet.

He'd finished eating by the time Montella finally took a second bite from the smallest slice in the box. She dropped it on her plate and started crying. "I just can't believe Carl's dead."

She'd asked if he had any wine and he'd apologized for not being able to offer her anything stronger than coffee or tea. He could only imagine how out of control her emotions would be if she'd tried to douse her sorrow with booze. Loggins' death had apparently really thrown her for a loop.

"I'm s-sorry," she sobbed, "I just can't help it."

"Don't apologize, I can handle it."

When she finally collected herself he guided her to the living room and insisted she take his comfortable recliner. He sat down on the couch a couple of feet to her left.

"What are you going to do, Sheriff, stay up all night to make sure I don't run away?"

"Nope, a couple of years ago I converted my spare bedroom into a makeshift cell."

"Why'd you do that?"

"My nephew took a turn for the wild and my older brother asked me to take him in for a spell, hoping I could straighten him out since the boy admires me because I'm a lawman. He'd fallen in with the wrong crowd at his high school in Fort Worth so I agreed with my brother that a change of scenery could only help. Well, he liked attending school here so I was able to get him to quit skipping classes but couldn't convince him to stop sneaking out at night. So I boarded up the window, installed a one-way deadbolt lock on the door, and bought a baby monitor so he could wake me up when he needed to use the bathroom. I'll dig it out of the closet and put it back on the nightstand. Just press the buzzer if nature calls."

A quizzical smile rose up. "So what happened to your nephew?"

"After a few months he finally saw the light—went back home, stayed away from bad company, and finished high school. Now he's a freshman at Baylor and wants to be a lawyer."

Her lips returned to their natural pout as a wistful gleam appeared in her eyes. "I wish somebody had done the same for me when I was a teenager."

"Is that when you went astray?"

"Mm hmm. I was sixteen and smarter than anybody on the planet, especially my parents. I ran away with a guy who swore I was the love of his life. Good thing he was underage too or my father would have seen to it he went to prison for taking a minor across state lines. We hid out with his cousin in Houston for a few weeks before a cop who'd seen my picture on the runaway hotline spotted me at a restaurant, and before I knew it I was back home in Minneapolis, Minnesota.

"I finished school and all, but that short stint in Houston had been such a liberating, fun time for me, I went back there right after graduation. I was only planning to spend the summer, using graduation money I'd gotten from friends and family to live on before going back to attend Minnesota State that fall. But before I'd been there a week I met Carlson Loggins and my life hasn't been the same since. Unfortunately I became addicted to the thrill of the hunt, not to mention Carl's unbelievable skills as a lover."

Loggins had to have been one lowdown hellatiously selfish bastard, corrupting this beautiful intelligent woman. "Maybe things will work out for you yet. You're still young and like I said, if you keep helping me I'll do all I can. Minnesota State's still there, you know."

She giggled. "I've got a degree in economics from Rice, silly. Carl made me do it so I could manage his affairs more efficiently. I don't regret not getting my education at Minnesota State, I regret letting the character my parents tried so hard to instill in me erode. They are so proud of me, thinking I'm the indispensable right-hand woman of a legitimate business tycoon. They love Carl to death—his ability to con people is . . . was amazing."

If it hadn't been for the astounding beauty of his so-called personal assistants and the imprecision of their duties for him, he'd have never made Loggins for a pimp. The dude had somewhat reminded him of Howard Hughes in his prime. That period of history fascinated him and he often found himself wishing he'd lived in that time. Things were so much simpler then. Men were men, women were women, and God had yet to be kicked out of the classroom. He wondered if the rest of Loggins' whores had also been addicted to his bedroom skills but didn't voice it. "You honestly have no idea who might be behind this?"

"Mm mm. Ironically I didn't trust Sonya. Her brother's with the FBI, a tidbit I found out while secretly going through her things when she first came aboard, which was part of my job description. I told Carl about it and I think he was a little suspicious also, but was still too enthralled with the new kid to be objective. It's hard enough to believe he's dead, but it blows my mind he was with Sonya when it happened."

That enlightenment made him feel pretty certain Sonya had never had a crush on him like Tank suspected. She'd most likely been feeling him out through his deputy, planning to rat out the pimp. Before long his thoughts turned to Dorian and how she'd wound up with Loggins. Montella seemed to be shooting straight, so he decided to satisfy his curiosity. "That one girl, Dorian, seems like she must have been recruited right off the farm."

A throaty laugh escaped Montella. "Oh believe me, Dorian is one serious piece of work. Carl picked her up in Little Rock, Arkansas after she shined his shoes in a barber shop. He and I spent a lot of time teaching her how to talk right, walk right, apply makeup correctly, proper dining etiquette—the whole nine yards—but for whatever reason, she prefers her old way of life. The girl has an IQ off the Richter scale, yet she dropped out of school in the ninth grade. Every meal she eats would satisfy the appetites of two male athletes if not three, and she drinks like a fish but never gains an ounce of weight. And she's not bulimic—I know because Carl had me spy on her when she was a rookie, expecting to confirm she was. She smokes several packs of cigarettes a day—filterless now—and has done so since she was seven, but doesn't have a smoker's hack. She used to dip snuff as well but Carl finally managed to break her of that. She's twenty-eight but as you can attest, she looks like a high school senior."

He raised his brows. "Man, some set of genes, huh?"

Montella nodded. "She's also a bona fide nymphomaniac."

A sour jolt of disappointment rippled through his gut at hearing that. "Okay, enough about her. Who's in line to take over the operation with Loggins and you removed from the scene?"

"Tillie, I suppose. I only say that because she's been there longer than any of the other girls. Although Lambert might have designs on taking the reins, as might Rico."

"Which one's Tillie?"

"The bleached blonde with inviting dark eyes."

"Oh . . ." he remembered her well.

She leaned towards him and cast a sultry smile. "You've heard my life story, Sheriff. Care to tell me yours?"

He grinned. "Don't try to hustle me."

"I'm not, I swear—I really wanna know. To be honest, I'm surprised you're not married, being such an attractive man with obvious integrity. Or are you?"

Her question prompted the saddest day of his life to spring to the front of his mind. Some painful memories fade with time but he knew this one never would. If he died a senile old man, that fateful episode would follow him to the grave. "I lost my wife in a camping accident. She was eight months pregnant with our only child."

Her eyes widened and immediately turned moist. "I'm so sorry . . . for your loss, and that I asked."

"No, don't be. It always haunts me and talking about it doesn't make it any more painful like it used to. It happened seven years ago. We decided to spend a weekend in Big Bend National Park to celebrate our first anniversary. That's where we met—she was a park ranger and I was working as a deputy in Alpine at the time. We'd hiked up on this ridge where the Rio Grande was so far below it looked like a narrow ribbon winding through the canyon. She leaned over to snap a picture, and that very moment a rattler snagged a cottontail nearby. The rabbit's shrieking startled her. She lost her footing and fell."

A tear traced its way down her cheek. "How horrible. You must have married really young. How old was she when it happened?"

"We were both twenty-three when she died."

"So you're thirty, huh?"

"Yeah, but not for long. My birthday's in January." He resisted an urge to inquire about her age.

His curiosity must have shown because her sleek lips spread with a knowing grin. "Go ahead. It's okay, you can ask."

"I thought it was forbidden to ask a lady such things."

Her smile turned bright. "Oh you called me a lady, how sweet. If only that were true. Anyway, I recently turned thirty-eight."

* * * *

Candles burning, fetishes properly hung, she began the chant. "Klell Ridgewall, I summon thee. The Indians have returned to take thy wife and children yet again. You must avenge them by the justice of thine powerful swift sword. I summon thee Klell Ridgewall to heed the call. Heed the call, Klell Ridgewall—yea verily yea—I summon thee to heed the call—"

Awaking in a cold sweat, she flung off the covers and rose to a sitting position. Unbearably hungry, she didn't bother with a robe. She stepped naked through the door and headed for the stairs, hoping a trip to the kitchen would ease her troubled mind over dreaming it again.

Despite her agitated state produced by the nightmare, she was horny as hell. The expensive vibrating dildo wouldn't suffice any more than her fingers. She desperately needed a flesh and blood dick—stiff, throbbing, satisfying. No, no, no, one cowboy wouldn't do. Two would be required. One to ream her pussy, the other to rape her ass. No, no, no, she also needed to suck cock while getting mauled. Three cowboys. Yes . . . three were needed.

Tres vaqueros.

She awoke with a start. *It happened again . . . dreaming I woke up in a dream. Am I dreaming now?*

EIGHT

He hung up with Ilian and phoned Tank.

"Yeah, Gary?"

"Get to my house soon as possible. Ilian just took a call from a Nadia Mars who lives at The Hog Farm. Three men were butchered there. I need you to watch Montella while I'm gone. She's asleep in my spare bedroom and I've locked her in. I'll leave the key on the coffee table . . . ."

Gary arrived at The Hog Farm at nine-oh-two a.m. Infamous for being Dody Massey's whorehouse during his corrupt tenure as county sheriff, no suspicious activity had been reported since he'd taken over the sleazeball's job. Not wanting to pull Alfredo off the Ridgewall Ranch, he'd again requested assistance from the DPS and they'd dispatched a patrolman to meet him at the crime scene.

He got out of the cruiser and shook hands with trooper Lawrence Kerns, a crusty incorruptible vet who'd soon be retiring from the highway patrol. They'd met during his short term as one of Massey's deputies.

"I sure don't envy you, Gary—talk about being baptized by fire. A dozen murders in three days in Tomahawk County? Who'd have ever thought such a thing was possible around these parts?"

A twinge of guilt stabbed his gut at hearing him say a dozen when in reality the number was eleven. "Not me, that's for sure. How are you doing these days, Lawrence?"

"I'd been getting by pretty good till this shit started. People are liable to start moving away if that bastard isn't caught soon."

"Bastards with an S. I know it's not just one sicko acting

alone." He headed down the walk towards the rambling two-storey house from which the first of Dody Massey's illicit revenue streams had started flowing years ago.

His stomach flip-flopped with jarring disappointment when the door opened. He'd expected a woman to answer the bell but not this one. She had lavish coal-black hair cut at the shoulders, its luster so brilliant the sunlight streaming through the door cast a band of shimmering blue highlights around her head as if she'd been crowned with a halo. Her beautiful dark eyes turned abruptly down at the corners as though unable to bear the weight of her long, thick lashes. Vibrantly sexy, yet girl-next-door sweet, the large glistening orbs compelled a man to get lost in them. Pouting beneath a pretty nose, her ruby lips—sensuously full but not fat—hinted at pleasures impossible to find in another's kiss. She stood about five-six and had a perfect hourglass figure with large, proudly protruding breasts. It devastated him to find her here because only a whore would reside at The Hog Farm. She was the brunette he'd been hoping to introduce himself to at Carla's Café.

She looked terrified.

"I'm Sheriff Stoner and this is Patrolman Kerns."

The heartbreaker stepped back and motioned them inside. She nervously volunteered her name as Nadia Mars while leading them down a short hall on the first floor, where she stopped, inhaled a deep breath, and pointed.

Gary entered the room and almost gagged from the smell of human feces that had oozed onto a bed from three naked Caucasian males lain side by side with their legs spread—each one headless, castrated, and missing an anus. "Where are the heads?"

When no one answered he turned to find she hadn't come into the room.

"Shit, what the hell's going down here?" whispered Lawrence, fear coating his shock-paled face as he gawked at the carnage.

Fighting a wave of nausea, Gary heaved a bitter sigh and wearily muttered, "I wish I knew."

They searched the room and finally located the heads in a chest of drawers. As Gary anticipated, the genitals and anuses were with them—penises and testicles covering the eyes, rectums stuffed inside open mouths. The killers had pulled each man's tongue through an anus. He decided to wait for Bob to get there and clear their faces before having Nadia Mars identify them, if she could.

* * * *

The lawmen would only permit mandatory chores and a patrolman had accompanied them through each. Hank hoped he and the boys still had jobs when the dust settled and the ownership of the ranch got transferred. They were heading to the mansion for lunch, and memories of Munchie depressed him as they'd done every meal he'd taken since his best friend died. He wondered if he'd ever get over losing him. His thoughts drifted back to that fateful day Othello wound up becoming a cook.

"When you boys get that hay truck unloaded, get to painting the barn," the boss had ordered Othello and him.

"I hired on as a puncher not a painter," Othello had protested.

"You hired on to do what you're told, mister."

"Well you'd best tell me to do something else then 'cause I ain't painting no fucking barn."

An impatient man with a quick temper, the boss fired him on the spot.

Othello apologized and tried to make out like he was only funning him but the boss didn't buy it. Always a sly dog, Othello came up with an idea. "Well can I at least have one decent meal before you kick me off the Ridgewall?"

The boss had coughed out a sour laugh and said, "You know there ain't been a decent meal served on this ranch since the cook quit. Head on to the bunkhouse and get packed. If you wanna torture yourself with another lousy supper, be my guest, but it'll be your last meal here."

"Um, mind if I do the cooking? I promise you'll like it, and if you don't, well hell it couldn't be any worse than what the other boys have done since filling in."

The boss had refused at first, fearful he'd slip something in the grub to get even. But Othello kept swearing with a solemn oath he wouldn't and was finally granted permission. He made chicken and dumplings. The boss loved it, as did the other hands, and turned the kitchen over to him when Othello begged for the job. Before long he seldom got called by his given name anymore.

Hank's memory zoomed past Munchie and landed on that cold rainy night he'd returned home after being honorably discharged from the army. The water tower had the school's mascot painted on it, as did most small Texas towns. His homesickness had gotten swallowed up with elation and hometown pride upon seeing the old familiar Tiger on the round tank looming high above Main Street. But those emotions were soon stricken down like the Tiger's paper image the football team ran through when taking the field for a Friday night battle. His sweetheart wasn't expecting him and he'd surprised her only to discover she'd taken up with another guy. That was the day he'd said "I do" to his right hand and they'd lived happily ever after since.

He'd never let a woman hurt him again.

* * * *

Watching the hearse drive away with the bodies, Gary told Lawrence he could get on with his regular duties. As the patrolman left he fetched a notebook from the cruiser and headed back towards the house to interview the three women who lived there.

The victims had been identified as ranch hands, and the ladies were left with no one to run the place but themselves. He found it difficult to picture the ultra feminine Nadia Mars slopping hogs, and had a feeling she'd be delegating the ranch chores to the other two girls since she claimed to be in charge of the place. None of them had heard anything so once again the killers had somehow managed to accomplish their gory task quietly, as they'd done when butchering Angela Lang at the Mexican restaurant.

When he got to the porch his cell rang. He checked the ID and raised it to his ear. "What's up, Alfredo?"

"We found Loggins' will."

A technician had been dispatched to drill open a wall safe in Loggins' bedroom on a judge's orders. "Has anyone read it yet?"

"Yeah, he left everything to Montella Pace."

He raised his brows. "Did he make provisions in case he survived her?"

"No."

"Good. Listen, Alfredo, I don't want this getting around but Montella's not dead, I've got Tank watching her at my house. I'm trying to flush out any conspirators among Loggins' employees. Tell the guy the judge sent that I'll handle notifying Loggins' relatives. Now not a word of this to anyone, you hear? Not even Ilian."

"You can count on me. Suspect anyone yet?"

"Everybody. I don't want any of Loggins' employees hearing about the will either. Gotta go."

He stowed the cell and pulled a pen from his shirt pocket while stepping through the door. Nadia had collected herself somewhat but still seemed on edge. The other two women—a cutesy blonde and a stacked brunette—were still obviously in shock. They were the ones he'd seen with Nadia Mars each time he'd spotted her at Carla's.

All three were standing, rigid and nervous. "You can sit down if you want."

None of them did.

"Who saw the bodies first?"

"I did," said the blonde, a glum pout tainting features overly accentuated with makeup. "Nobody uses that room except when we have an overnight guest. I noticed the door was open so I thought Nadia or Sally must have been in there looking for something. I went in to see if I could help and . . . saw the bodies."

"You're Erma, right?"

She nodded.

"And what time was this?"

"Somewhere between seven-thirty and eight."

He scribbled it down. "And what did you do when you found them?"

"I completely wigged out and couldn't stop screaming. Nadia and Sally came rushing in to see what was wrong."

"Is that the way you two remember it?"

Both women corroborated Erma's statement.

"When did each of you last see them alive?"

"Allen spent the night with me," said Erma. "Everything was fine when I went to sleep. I woke up alone and thought he'd left to do his morning chores."

"I told them all goodnight here in the living room and went upstairs," Sally reported.

Nadia gazed at him with a sickly expression. "They had dinner with us last night. I developed a severe headache and lost my appetite so I went to bed while they were still eating. That's the last time I saw them. This was done by the same person that killed those people on the Ridgewall Ranch, wasn't it, Sheriff."

"I'm afraid it sure looks that way." He found it sadly ironic he'd finally managed to meet her at The Hog Farm of all places. All the thoughts he'd had about approaching her when he finally caught her alone had flittered away the moment she'd opened the door. "I'll be checking on you from time to time. If any of you decide it's not safe to stay out here you need to let me know so I'll be able to find you."

"Well I can tell you right now I'm leaving," declared Erma. "I'm bailing for Dallas and moving back in with my parents just as soon as I get packed."

He shook his head. "Sorry, I can't allow that because none of you are above suspicion right now. You can't leave Tomahawk County until I find out who's behind these murders. If any of you attempt to I'll track you down and book you for suspicion of aiding and abetting a serial killer."

"Bullshit!" Nadia ejaculated. "We could be next on that son-of-a-bitch's list. You might be signing our death warrants if you don't let us leave."

The vexation clinging to her face accentuated the mesmeric sexuality it always exuded. "That's the situation. If you'd like I could put you in jail under protective custody, but you'll have to be locked up like regular inmates. County regulations won't permit the use of the facilities for mere lodging purposes."

They all took him up on it, which surprised him. "Who'll feed the hogs?"

Nadia belted out a sarcastic laugh. "To hell with those hogs, I'm not gonna hang around and get butchered like one. Every head of livestock on this ranch is up for sale as of right now. I'll call the paper and place an ad, then you can take us to jail."

An hour later the three women were sharing a cell furnished with two steel bunk beds. He'd instructed Ilian to provide sheets and pillows to make the thin mattresses a little more comfortable. Regular inmates had to sleep with nothing but a wool blanket.

* * * *

The ballroom didn't have any windows, being centered on the bottom floor and surrounded by the hall. Double doors in front and back were the only way in or out. Alfredo and a patrolman stood guard at the front while two other patrolmen manned the rear. The glamorous structure had been created for the purpose of entertaining a large number of guests and contained an elaborate ladies room and men's room. Supper was being served buffet style from the bar, to be eaten on one of the many saloon tables surrounding the dance floor.

Gary took a head count—the four ranch hands, surviving whores minus Montella, the maid, cook, and butler were all present and accounted for. They'd be sleeping on cots borrowed from the boy scouts. He picked up a cardboard box, exited at the front hall, and told Alfredo he'd have Tank relieve him as soon as he got home. The box contained a large plastic storage bowl filled with salad, bottle of wine, and a pan of lasagna confiscated from Rico Mircanti, who'd prepared several for the evening meal. He hadn't planned on taking the wine but Rico had tossed it in, saying his lasagna couldn't be savored to its fullest without the beverage. Thankfully the ex heavyweight had been flattered rather than curious that he'd wanted so much of his expertly prepared cuisine, and hadn't questioned him about it.

Montella wouldn't have to settle for pizza and iced tea tonight.

* * * *

Nadia stood at her cell door chatting with the lovely Mexican dispatcher Ilian Herrera, standing outside the bars. The young girl radiated a very endearing naïve sweetness and had just confided that she and her boyfriend, Deputy Alfredo Parra, planned to marry someday.

"We grew up together," she continued. "Been sweethearts since like forever. I call him *mi vaquero quapo.*"

"Which means?"

"My handsome cowboy."

"How romantic. Do you guys live together?"

Ilian's brown skin turned pinkish. "Oh heavens no, that would be immoral. Not that we don't . . . you know."

"Make love?"

A full scale blush appeared as she nodded.

"How long have you worked for Sheriff Stoner?"

"Since he started. As has Alfredo and Tank Green, the other deputy."

"Sheriff Stoner seems like a nice guy."

"Oh he is. I call him *senor honesto audaz y fuerte.*"

Nadia grinned. "And that means?"

"Mister honest, bold and strong."

"And what do you call Deputy Green?"

"Tank."

She had to laugh even though the girl hadn't meant to be humorous.

Ilian glanced at her watch. "It's almost suppertime. We feed inmates food from Carla's Café but since you're not exactly hardened criminals I can order from some other place, but you'll have to pay for it. Gary told me to let you guys have whatever you want within reason."

"Oh I often eat at Carla's. I'll have a cheeseburger and fries." She turned towards Emma and Sally, facing each other on a bottom bunk, engrossed in a game of spades. Ilian had provided the cards. "What's your dinner order, girls? The county's treating us to Carla's . . . ."

* * * *

Dooly couldn't believe Dorian had chosen to sit at the same table with Bobby Joe and him. The white tank top she wore really showed off her braless tits—nipples ripping at the fabric like two bullets, cleavage shaking as she attacked her lasagna. She'd shelved the hick vocal and allowed her lady's voice to come out.

"I caught you boys staring at me through binoculars while I was outside smoking day before yesterday. What do you say to a threesome?"

Bobby Joe started coughing, apparently choking on a hunk of garlic toast, while he could only gawk at her speechlessly.

The sexiest smile he'd ever seen in his life crawled across her killer face. "What's the matter, boys, cat got your tongues?"

"Come on, Dorian, quit teasing us."

The smile turned into a sheepish grin. "So who says I'm teasing, Dooly?"

Bobby Joe looked quickly left and right, blubbery lips flapping in the process. "There's no place to do it, girl."

"Oh yes there is. There's a cozy little closet behind the bandstand that's practically soundproof. Meet me there when everybody goes to sleep."

Dooly scanned the area she referred to and saw several closet doors. "Which one is it?"

"The one closest to the back wall." She slowly traced her upper lip with a delicate pink tongue. "It's just big enough for me to lay down and spread my legs."

Blood surged into his dick.

She rose from the table and leaned over to fetch her empty plate, making sure they could see all the way down to the upper ridges of both nipples. "If you two think you're man enough, I'll take you one at a time. Then after you both rest awhile, one of you can fuck me in the ass while the other's working my pussy. If you can still get it up after that, I'll suck both your peckers bone dry. Of course I'll expect some pussy and ass licking in return. You show up first, Dooly, by yourself. When I'm through with you I'll take care of Bobby

Joe here."

Bobby Joe scowled at her. "How come he gets to go first?"

"Because he's better looking than you, dumbass. You're as ugly as a sack full of armpits. Didn't anybody ever tell you that?"

Rubbery lips drooping on a face reminiscent of the scarecrow's from *The Wizard of Oz,* Bobby Joe meekly shook his head.

"Well you are, take my word."

"Why are you gonna let me fuck you then?" he mumbled, looking more intimidated than a cowed dog.

"Because that bulge in your pants hints at a big dick. Or do you just always walk around with a hard on?"

"No . . . least I don't think I do."

Dorian laughed and put her free hand on her hip. "Hell you're dumber than a box of rocks too, ain't ya? If I wasn't so fucking horny I'd withdraw my offer and just screw Dooly's eyeballs out. Consider yourself *luck-ee,* Bobby Joe. Gonna fetch me some more grub, be back quicker'n you'n cum from watching my ass."

Dooly hated himself for not being able to keep from ogling her amazing butt after the cruel way she'd humiliated Bobby Joe. From the corner of his eye he saw the tortured cowboy couldn't take his eyes off it either.

"We ain't really gonna punk her at the same time are we, Dew? We'll just take turns right?"

"Hell no, she's just having fun being a cock tease. Neither one of us are ever gonna get any of that pussy, I guarantee you."

Bobby Joe winced. "You mean you're not gonna meet her in the closet after everybody sacks out?"

"Nope, because she won't be there. She's just planning on making fools of us, that's all."

Dorian returned to the table carrying a plate with enough lasagna on it to choke a Suma Wrestler. She wolfed it down in silence and wiped the platter clean with a remnant of toast which she plopped into her mouth while standing up. "Gonna sneak a smoke in the little girl's room, then I'm gonna get me drunk at the bar. See you boys after everybody sacks out."

"She seems serious to me," said Bobby Joe after she walked off.

He cocked his head and grinned. "Hell, if you can't tell she's just funnin' us then you really are dumber than a box of rocks, Bobby Joe."

* * * *

Montella had been overjoyed to see the surprise he'd brought home from the Ridgewall Ranch. She'd tried to convince him to share the wine with her but he'd refused. He sat down at the table with a fresh cup of coffee as Montella filled her glass for the third time, the first reload after they'd finished eating several minutes ago.

"Do you know if Loggins left a will?"

She shook her head and readied her moist lips to receive a dose of fermented grape juice, imported from Italy according to Rico Mircanti. They puckered alluringly as the sophisticated prostitute swallowed.

"Seems to me he'd have told you about it since you were his second in command, so I suppose he probably didn't. And that means everything he owned now belongs to his nearest relative. Any idea who that could be?"

His bluff didn't elicit a reaction, which surprised him. Montella merely shook her head. "I know his parents are dead—at least that's what he told me—and he claimed he didn't have any siblings, so I have no idea. Carl never mentioned any other relatives."

If she really didn't know about the will then most likely nobody did except the lawyer Loggins had used. He'd looked the document over and its legal fluency clearly indicated the work of a professional. "You said he put you through Rice so you could better manage his finances. That sounds like a guy who thinks ahead. Why would he neglect to make out a will since he was obviously concerned about handling his money correctly?"

"I didn't say he didn't," she replied nonchalantly, "only that he never told me about it. Carl *was* a careful planner and he did tell me just about everything. If he made out a will the only reason he'd have for not informing me is because he bequeathed something substantial to yours truly."

Boy, honey, did he ever, he thought with a silent laugh. "Are you saying he might have been afraid you'd do him in to collect it?"

"That's what I'm saying, Sheriff. Carl didn't trust anybody."

"Not even you?"

"Mm mm, at least not totally, but he trusted me more than anyone." She sipped more wine, set the glass on the table, and brought her palms together beneath her chin, the tips of her pointed nails almost touching the taught creamy skin beneath it. "Tank told me three men got murdered on a ranch next to Carl's."

It dawned on him he'd made a mistake by not telling Tank to keep Montella in the dark about the murders at The Hog Farm. He'd lost an opportunity to catch her off guard and perhaps get her to slip up if she knew who was behind it. Now she'd had hours to figure out the best way to dodge any question he might ask. "Do you know Nadia Mars?"

Montella's features warped into a look of unsettling surprise that couldn't have been more extreme if he'd just climbed out of the casket at his own funeral. "My god I haven't heard that name in years. Did she show up at the ranch?"

"No."

"What is she doing in Tomahawk County?"

"She lives on a ranch next to Loggins'."

"You're kidding me!" The shock on her face was either genuine or she deserved an academy award for best actress ever.

If Montella didn't know a competitor lived next door then Loggins hadn't been aware of it either. "It's called The Hog Farm. The sheriff before me ran a whorehouse out there. I have a feeling she took over for him after he left the area. How do you know her?"

"She used to work for Carl. He fired her in Las Vegas several years ago. Angela Yang was her replacement as a matter of fact. I can't believe she moved here of all places. How long as she been on that hog farm?"

He ignored the question. "So she worked for Loggins in Las Vegas, huh? You told me you guys moved here from Houston. When did you live in Nevada?"

"We didn't. Carl had set up a sting to entrap a singer who was headlining one of the hotels. Nadia was supposed to screw him while I filmed them from a closet with slatted doors. When she didn't show at the set time the singer stormed off in anger and told Carl never to call him again—that he needed a reliable pimp. Carl, Nadia, and I had flown down there for the weekend solely for that purpose. He took Nadia to the bus station and came back with Angela, who he'd found there."

He'd asked Montella if she knew Nadia because they lived on neighboring ranches. Hearing the raven-haired beauty had once worked for Loggins had been an entirely unexpected piece of information which shed a new light on everything. Could Nadia have migrated to Tomahawk County to exact revenge for being canned by Loggins, wanting vengeance so badly she had her own ranch hands killed to divert suspicion away from her? As far as he knew Dody still owned The Hog Farm so he and Nadia had to know each other. If she moved out there before he lost the election she'd no doubt been working for him. Had she convinced the ex-sheriff to arrange the slayings in exchange for something Dody wanted and couldn't get his hands on otherwise?

The thought of Dody being involved unnerved him. He wouldn't give a damn about helping Nadia, his motivation would be to get even with him for winning the election. If that was the case the puzzle couldn't possibly be pieced together. Anyone could be the next victim because the murders were being committed for only one reason—to get him railroaded out of town for failing to stop the killings. He shook the disturbing notion from his mind. Evil though he was, Massey wouldn't go to those extremes.

Would he?

NINE

They'd been herded into the dining room for breakfast, Tank Green having accompanied Rico to the kitchen some forty minutes prior so he could prepare copious amounts of oatmeal, biscuits, and gravy. There wouldn't be any other breakfast options this morning because Rico hadn't been allowed to leave the ranch yesterday to do his weekly grocery shopping.

A surge of bitter grief engulfed Rosemary as she stared at Carlson's empty chair. She'd sat to his left at breakfast two days ago, fondling his dick beneath the table. He'd pulled it out of his trousers just for her before slyly whispering, "I think there's something on my lap, would you check it out for me?"

She'd stuck her head under the table and had immediately turned wet at the sight of his hard on. Being ambidextrous, she'd managed to eat her eggs while jacking him off at the same time, giggling inside at the thought of him purposely spilling water on his pants to disguise the semen stains as he'd done at a restaurant in Houston. Unfortunately, even though she'd kept her right wrist's action light so her upper arm movement wouldn't give them away, one of the cowboys had taken note of it and she'd had to stop before Carlson came. It would be her last experience with his magical cock, and the loss left an aching void inside she doubted would ever be filled.

Even though four years had passed—flown by actually— the memory of meeting him remained as vivid now as it had when it happened. Sitting with a boy who'd tried to impress her with dinner at a pricey restaurant—both of them freshmen at the University of Houston—she'd spotted a handsome man giving her the eye. Though she hadn't returned his flirty stare because he was not only a generation older than her but had a beautiful woman with him, he came over to her table when her date went to the men's room.

Sitting down in the vacated chair uninvited, he'd stuck out his hand. "Hi, I'm Carlson Loggins and I must know—is that your natural hair color?"

"Yes, if it's any of your business," she'd retorted, refusing to shake hands.

He'd leaned back with a sigh. "You've got to come to work for me, you've just got to. How much are you making at your present job? I'll top it, whatever the amount."

She'd leaned forward and leered at him. "Listen, mister, I don't know you and I want you to leave me alone."

Firing back a disarming smile he'd boldly insisted, "No you don't. I've got your curiosity up, I can tell. Listen, I need a redhead, and you're perfect."

"A redhead for what?"

Expecting him to make up a lame line about being a movie director or some similar bullshit, his reply had rattled her to the core. "I have a nose for women. You're a girl that really appreciates sex and you like to do it a lot. Give me one night and I'll show you what you've been missing all your life. I promise you'll forget every guy you've ever been with once I have you looking down from the upper regions of heaven. I'll pay you a generous salary to entertain rich men—many of them celebrities—while providing a steady dose of me on the side. What is it you do anyway?"

Feeling belligerently indignant she'd started to tell him to go straight to hell but wound up silently gawking at him with slack-jawed incredulity instead, because something in his eyes made her think he *would* have her looking down from the upper regions of heaven if she gave him the chance.

"Your boyfriend's heading this way so I'll be leaving now. Here's my card—give me a call, I promise you won't regret it."

As he'd returned to his table, the stunning blonde sitting there had given her a pleasant smile. The next day when an overwhelming compulsion to know if his bragging was fact or fiction had forced her to call him, she'd learned the woman's name was Montella Pace.

Never had a man touched her so expertly, kissed her with such passion, or driven her to such orgasmic heights. Far from lying, Carlson had actually understated his sexual prowess, prompting her to quit school, planning to remain with him for the rest of her life.

Feeling tears form she closed her eyes. *Oh, Carlson, I loved you so much. How could you leave me?*

She opened them when Tank set a bowl of oats and a cup of coffee before her. Lambert refused to serve anybody since he was being viewed as a possible suspect like everyone else. Rico, on the other hand, chose to continue his duties and had gotten miffed only when Alfredo refused to let him go to town to replenish the pantry yesterday.

The others had lined up at the kitchen, going through one at a time before returning to the dining room with one of the breakfast choices. Dorian sat two plates heaped with biscuits and gravy on the table, went back to the kitchen, and reappeared with a glass of buttermilk in one hand, orange juice in the other. She planted her somehow fat-free ass and started her feeding frenzy. Rosemary quickly looked away, repulsed by the freak-of-nature's disgusting eating habits.

Tank stood behind Carlson's chair, arms folded, hardly disguising his intentions since she was the only one he'd served. Wishing he'd stop ogling her she partook of the coffee but had no appetite for oatmeal. Biscuits and gravy didn't appeal to her either because she was deeply mourning Carlson's death.

Not knowing what else to do, she figured on returning to Houston once the sheriff allowed her to leave the ranch. Her parents thought she'd spent the last four years working for a legitimate enterprise. They'd be more than happy to resume paying for her college if she wanted to go that route, but the future held no interest to her at the moment.

Tillie and Nicole were worried Sheriff Stoner might discover they were all hookers and arrest them for prostitution, but even if they were incarcerated it would only be for a short while—nothing like the sentence a murder rap would entail. These horrendous crimes called for the death penalty, not time behind bars. Since Carlson alone did the blackmailing, all they had to do was keep their stories straight like he'd often dictated: "Just say you had no idea you were being filmed or that anyone was being blackmailed."

Tank walked over and put his hands on her shoulders. "Can I get you some more coffee?"

She almost pulled away, but not wanting to hurt the bumpkin's feelings, looked up with a smile instead. "I'm fine thanks."

He gave her a light squeeze with both, released his grip, and assumed his station at the hall entryway. A few minutes later Alfredo stepped into the dining room. Tank's shift had ended, thank God.

Having no doubt the psycho's killing spree would continue, she wondered who the next victim would be, but had no fear of being selected—she couldn't be lucky enough to be put out of her misery.

Nicole sat down beside her, having opted for biscuits and gravy. She knew that behind her brave front the girl had to be taking Carlson's passing really hard as well. Many a time he'd selected the two of them to spend the night with him, preferring them more often than any other pair of girls when he was in the mood for a ménage a trios. As a result they'd grown very close. Nicole had already been on board for three years when she'd arrived on the scene, and though they were only a year apart in age, the sweet Jamaican had mothered her from the start.

The last time she'd been in Carlson's bed, so had Nicole, and they'd finally learned the reason he'd so relished them for a threesome.

"You need to keep your strength up, eat your oats."

"I've got *no* appetite, Nikki."

Nicole gave her a love pat on the thigh. "I know it's hard, child, but life must go on."

She put her hand on Nicole's and gave it a light squeeze. "I miss him so much."

"Me too. I'm telling you, if they don't start looking for that priestess we're all done for."

Everyone except Dorian scoffed at Nicole's notions of a voodoo priestess manipulating the ghost of Klell Ridgewall, and she certainly didn't believe it either, but it troubled her that none of them had heard Angela cry out at the restaurant or any sounds coming from Carlson, Sonya, and Montella while they were being slaughtered. Carlson might not have screamed but surely the two women had, and it seemed to her their frightful wailing should have been loud enough to at least be partially discernable from the billiard room. The absence of any sound from people being hacked to death was extremely abnormal. Could it in fact be supernatural after all?

A morbid chill iced its way up her spine at the thought.

* * * *

Tongue as sore as his dick, Dooly couldn't enjoy his biscuits and gravy. He glanced over at Bobby Joe, noting him shifting uncomfortably in his chair as well. Dorian hadn't been a cock-tease after all. Having no intention of taking the bait last night, he'd drifted off, only to be awakened by someone shaking his shoulder.

"Psst, wake up, stud, you fell asleep."

Making out her beautiful face in the pale illumination of the ballroom emanating from the chandeliers, dimmed so everyone could sleep yet be able to find their way to the restrooms during the night, he'd been completely flabbergasted. A quick glance at Bobby Joe had revealed Dorian hadn't bothered with him. Not about to miss such a golden opportunity he'd quickly risen and followed her into the closet, hormones surging over knowing the gorgeous ass swaggering before him would soon no longer be hidden by a bathrobe. What followed started playing in his mind like a porn flick:

The smell of stale cigarette smoke filled his nostrils as they entered the closet. Dorian closed the door and flipped on the light. It took a moment for his eyes to adjust and when they did he saw the room was a lot bigger than she'd described. A thick blanket had been spread out on the hardwood floor, and in a corner sat a bottle of champagne, pack of camels with a butane lighter resting on top, a saucer with a cigarette butt on it, and a box of condoms.

She took a deep gulp of champagne, sat the bottle down without offering him any, and quickly shed the robe. He nearly came on the spot at the sight of her body. Dorian's big gorgeous tits were obviously natural, yet they appeared too heavy not to droop like an old woman's instead of sticking almost straight out the way they did. Her dark-pink nipples were so hard they looked as if they might split open any second, and a glance at her bikini-waxed pussy made his gonads pulsate. She had such a pronounced clit it bulged like a glistening wad of bubble gum between her beautiful legs.

"Like what you see, doncha, Dooly."

He'd gone to bed with his jeans on but had taken off his shirt. Before he could blink twice she had him butt naked.

"I'm clean, are you . . .?" she pointed at the condoms.

"Yeah." His throat was so dried out by lust the word came out hoarse.

"If there's any doubt, use one."

"No, no doubt, but guess I should in case I don't pull out in time."

"Nah, there's no chance of knocking me up. I was hoping you could ride me bareback." She hit her knees and inhaled his dick, turning it instantly hard. Then she pulled her way up his body and mounted him—clamping her arms around his neck as her tight, wet pussy slid up and down his shaft. It took all his willpower not to pop when she started undulating her hips like a maniac. A few seconds later she cried, "Oh, Dooly, this is what life's all about—feels so fuckin' good I can't stand it—I'm gonna cum, you handsome motherfucker! Oh-oh-oh-aaaaahhhhhh . . .!"

She pulled off him just as he exploded. His jism coated her upper thigh as they collapsed to the floor in each others' arms, tongues locked in deep wet kisses as he crushed her tits with his hands—their silky firm texture compelling him to squeeze as if his life depended on it.

"I love the way you kiss me," she tenderly declared. "Hungry yet romantic, that's a rarity. I feel something special for you, cowboy."

His waning adrenaline reversed directions as a rush of excitement flooded him. "You are so beautiful, Dorian."

"Yeah, yeah," she said sarcastically while reaching for her bathrobe, which she used to wipe his sperm off. "Figured you'd appreciate not getting cum on your face."

Before he could ask what she meant by that, Dorian forced his head to the floor and planted her cunt on his mouth. He stabbed his tongue inside it and she went wild—gyrating so aggressively he feared she'd break his nose.

Thankfully it didn't take long before she reached a second climax and rolled off him, panting like a winded dog. "Tell Bobby Joe to get his ass in here pronto so he can fuck me while you reload."

Not bothering with his underwear, he slipped on his jeans and crept into the ballroom. "Wake up, hoss," he whispered in his pal's ear, "this is the luckiest night of your life."

The instant Bobby Joe processed the information, he jumped off the cot like it was on fire and they snuck to the closet.

Bobby Joe's bottom lip nearly hit the floor when he saw Dorian's bare body.

"Get naked," she demanded while stubbing out a smoke.

The homely cowboy obeyed in a flash and already had a full hard.

Dorian grinned and tossed him a rubber. "Dayum, that dick looks like it belongs on a donkey. Get it covered and get to work."

While Bobby Joe sheathed his long, thick pecker she laid down on the blanket and spread her legs.

Dooly took off his jeans while watching them from a corner. His libido gained renewed life as Dorian moaned, grunted, and soon squealed with satisfaction

"All right, get off me." She pushed him away while saying it.

"But you didn't give me enough time to shoot my wad," Bobby Joe protested.

"Quit your bitching . . ." she rose from the floor and turned to him. "Get over here and stick your dick back in my snatch where it belongs, Dooly. We'll fuck with you standing up again. Bobby Joe, you can get off pumping my ass."

Once again she mounted him and wrapped her legs around his lower back. "Oh, Dooly, I love the way you feel inside me."

She grunted painfully when Bobby Joe shoved his jumbo rod into her rectum, but the guttural sound carried a hot note of pleasure. "Fuck fast and hard, Bobby Joe. Dooly, don't move a muscle."

Every piston stroke from Bobby Joe caused her pussy to squeeze his dick tighter, making it extremely tough for him to hold back. When she heaved a loud gasp and hissed, "Empty your balls in me, Dooly, let's cum together!" he let loose with a fury.

A lustful groan signaled the end of Bobby Joe's frustration.

After they pulled out of her, Dorian stood with eyes closed, rubbing her sweaty breasts, savoring her afterglow. Before long her lids parted and she said, "Dooly, get your mouth on my clit and fuckin' eat it. Bobby Joe, get to licking my ass. Make me cum hard, motherfuckers."

Dorian climaxed so intensely that time she let out a shrill scream that could wake the dead. Since it apparently hadn't done the same to everybody in the ballroom, she'd been right about the closet being practically soundproof.

She dropped to her knees. "Bobby Joe, shed that slimy rubber and I'll jack you off till you get hard again. Dooly, shove your dick in my mouth."

Once she had them both erect, she ordered Bobby Joe to put on a new condom and ride her butt again. "Dooly, do just like last time—I wanna feel you cum inside me once more with Bobby Joe's big dick up my ass."

Bobby Joe obediently worked her corn-hole and he pumped another load in her twat at her orgasmic command. She lit a cigarette and let them rest until she finished it. Then she got them stiff again using a hand on Bobby Joe, her mouth on him.

"Put on another rubber," she huskily commanded Bobby Joe. "You boys do exactly like before, but this time I'm gonna lay on my side on the blanket. Cum with me again, Dooly, and kiss me while you're doing it. Don't take your lips off mine until every last drop has squirted out of your dick."

After she came that go-round Dorian couldn't get Bobby Joe up again. She finally turned loose of his limp pecker and put her hands on her hips. "Shit, you're more size than substance ain't ya, Bobby Joe."

"Use your mouth," he pleaded. "I know it'll get hard again if you suck it."

"Are you kidding?" she chided disgustedly, face puckered like she'd just taken a full bite of lemon. "I'd never let an ugly man even kiss me, much less give him a blowjob."

"But you said you'd suck us both dry at supper."

"Yeah? Well you're stupider than I thought if you believed it. Now get on back to bed."

Head hanging low, Bobby Joe did as he was told.

Completely drained of energy, feeling green from breathing the smoke polluted air, sweating from lack of ventilation, he was more than ready to crash himself. He reached for his underwear but she grabbed his hand. "I'm not fucking through with you yet, Dooly. Bend over so I can eat your butt."

"Dorian, I've had it."

"Please . . .?" she ran her fingers through his hair and kissed him.

Instinct took over and he eagerly plunged his tongue between her thrilling lips, loving the feel of her big tits crushed against him as they held each other in a death grip.

"Okay," he breathlessly consented, coming up for air.

"Good, now get down on all fours and let me make you feel *real* good."

She started licking his ass and steadily fondled his dick until it barely got stiff enough to penetrate, then she made him lie down on his back and started riding it. He popped almost immediately due to the odd sensation of her canal squeezing his steadily shrinking shaft, but she kept gyrating on it—her throaty moans showing she liked the feeling of having his limp noodle inside her, and didn't stop rocking her hips until getting off once more.

So exhausted he couldn't see straight he said, "I've got to call it a night, Dorian."

"Make me cum with your mouth one last time, then you can go to bed. I love the way you eat me, Dooly. You might have the best set of lips that's ever kissed my pussy."

His ears burned from the friction of her thighs as she clamped them around his head during the throes of another orgasm. Before he could get off the floor she had his worn out dick in her mouth. Fatigue kept it from reaching even half mast but that didn't stop his sperm from gushing down her throat. She gave his balls a final lick, rolled towards her supplies, took a swig of champagne, fired up a Camel, and said while exhaling, "You're my kind of man, Dooly. Get some sleep. See ya in the morning."

Unable to quit yawning, he gazed across the table at the insatiable nympho, marveling at how unaffected she appeared—sitting comfortably at the table in her bathrobe, looking like she'd had a full rejuvenating night of undisturbed sleep. Shoving a spoonful of gravy-soaked biscuit between her pretty lips, Dorian winked at him and smiled as she chewed.

* * * *

Gary made coffee and phoned Tank, whose ranch shift had just ended.

"What's up?"

"Head to my house and stop by Carla's on the way, I called in an order of pancakes for Montella. You'll have to watch her while I'm gone. I found out last night Nadia Mars used to work for Loggins. I'll relieve you after I interrogate her, then you can go home and sack out . . . ."

Ilian smiled and bade him good morning when he walked in.

Gary grinned back. "What did our guests order for breakfast?"

"They all wanted glazed doughnuts so I picked up a dozen."

"Must be on a health kick," he kidded while grabbing the ring of cell keys. He entered lockup hoping they'd spared a few because he hadn't eaten.

There were seven left in the box. He wolfed one down and munched on another while escorting Nadia to his office, where a fresh pot of coffee waited, prepared by Ilian as she did every morning.

"Have a seat in that chair by my desk." He filled two cups and handed her one before sitting down. "How long have you lived at The Hog Farm?"

"Six years."

"How long have you worked for Dody Massey?"

"Who says I do . . .?" she took a light nip of coffee and gave him a timid smile.

"I know you used to hustle for Carlson Loggins and now you're living out at Dody's cathouse, so don't bother trying to bullshit me."

She tried to look insulted but couldn't hide the anxiousness that sprang to her face at hearing Loggins' name. "I have no idea what you're talking about, Sheriff."

"Look, busting you for solicitation is the farthest thing from my mind at the moment. I have something just a little more important to get to the bottom of. Several of Loggins' whores, two of his ranch hands, and Loggins himself are dead. Your three hog farmers are dead. All of them were perversely butchered so there has to be a connection. Now how long have you been working for Dody?"

Her breasts rose with a deep breath and sexily fell as a sigh of resignation breezed through her scarlet lips. "Since I moved to The Hog Farm."

"Where is he?"

"Somewhere in Mexico. I don't know what town, he wouldn't tell me."

"Does he know Carlson Loggins?"

"Not that I'm aware of. He left Tomahawk County long before Carlson bought the Ridgewall Ranch, so it's unlikely they ever met. How did you know I used to work for Carlson?"

"I'll ask the questions. When's the last time you talked to Dody?"

"A couple of months ago."

"Where do you send his money?"

"Excuse me?"

He raised his cup. The coffee's aroma temporarily diluted the enticing smell of her perfume, which had been taunting him since she'd walked through the cell door. Why did this beautiful woman have to be a whore? Eyeing her contrived frown of confusion, he took a sip, set the mug on his desk, and crossed his arms. "His piece of the action, where do you send it? Don't make me ask again, Nadia."

"Oh, that money." The phony smile of recognition she wore made her look plastic and cheap. "A highway patrolman picks it up every Monday morning. I don't know how he passes it on to Dody."

"What's the patrolman's name?"

"I can't tell you," she fearfully avowed, the tone of her voice matching an anxious glare that obliterated the bogus façade she'd been projecting.

"Can't or won't?"

"Take your pick."

"So that's how it's gonna be, huh . . .?" he rose from his desk. "Nadia Mars, I'm charging you as an accessory after the fact for the murders of Jared Soul, Allen Smith, and Carl Ray. You have the right to remain silent. Anything you say can and will be used against you in a court of law. You have the right to an attorney, if you can't afford—"

"Knock it off, Sheriff, you win. His name is David Nevers. Do you have any idea what Dody will do to me if he finds out I told you?"

He pointed at her cup. "You're in protective custody, remember? Enjoy your coffee."

Nadia took a quick gulp as if to settle her nerves. She had the look of a woman standing on the roof of a burning skyscraper with only two choices—stand there and burn to death, or jump.

"You're not worried about what Nevers might do?"

"Not as much as Dody. You ought to know, Sheriff. He had you beaten up as I recall."

"That he did."

She shot him a puzzled squint. "You don't seem surprised by the name."

"I'm not. Nevers used to be one of Dody's deputies before joining the highway patrol. Can I count on your full cooperation?"

"Since you're threatening to charge me otherwise, how can I refuse?"

"Smart girl. . ." he pulled out his pen. "Tell me everything you know about Carlson Loggins and Dody Massey."

TEN

Pete Lemmon, the district attorney, had relieved him of the burden of dealing with the victims' families. Each one's car had been impounded along with their personal effects to ensure no one claiming them had any reason to set foot on the Ridgewall Ranch or The Hog Farm.

When Gary spoke to reporters after Loggins' murder, he'd not only refused to release any of the victims' names but also held back the number of fatalities. If any member of the law enforcement in Tomahawk County leaked it to the press they'd be naming one number too many, a fact only he, his two deputies, and Pete knew. He'd instructed Tank to quiz everyone present in the billiard room when Loggins and Sonya were being murdered, and none of them had seen anyone walk out the door except him and Montella. Since the cowboys were outdoors working at the time, everyone on the Ridgewall Ranch thought she'd been murdered too. But the lie hadn't borne any fruit so he'd concluded that continuing to babysit her would only hamper the investigation. He phoned Alfredo and told him Tank was on his way to the ranch with her.

"That's right, Alfredo, I want you to tell them all Montella's alive. I don't want anyone keeling over with a heart attack thinking they're seeing a ghost when Tank walks in with her. And about that complaint from the cook, he can go to town for groceries as long as you, Tank, or one of the patrolmen accompanies him to make sure he winds up back on the ranch."

Montella didn't know it, but she was now footing the bill for everything Rico Mircanti charged.

* * * *

When he entered the dining room at suppertime Geraldo thought he had to be hallucinating. At the end of the opulent table, occupying her usual spot, sat Montella Pace, looking ravishing and very much alive. Dooly let out a crude "What the fuck?" upon seeing her, and Hank stumbled backwards a few steps, grabbing his chest. Bobby Joe looked like a pale-faced statue as he froze in his tracks. The patrolman who'd spent the day monitoring them while they'd performed their ranch duties looked very confused, and Geraldo could only imagine how silly his own stupefied expression must have appeared as some of the girls laughed at their reaction.

Montella quickly cleared things up. "It wasn't my idea, guys—the sheriff made me do it. As you can see, I wasn't murdered after all."

Pulsating surges of joy and relief overwhelmed him. "So my Sonya's still alive? Where is she?"

The sadness draping Montella's countenance sent a sharp burning pain through his heart like a flaming arrow.

"You mean she, she—"

"I'm sorry, Geraldo, but I'm afraid Sonya and Carlson really have been taken from us."

"But why—" his voice broke "—why the lie?"

"You'll have to ask Sheriff Stoner about that, though I doubt he'll tell you."

"That's enough discussion on the matter, Montella," said Tank, eyeing him suspiciously. "So you and Sonya were an item, Geraldo?"

He lowered his tearful gaze to the intricate patterns engraved in varnished hardwood tiles covering the dining room floor. "I guess it doesn't matter now. Yes, we were lovers. We kept our relationship hidden because Sonya didn't want Loggins to know."

Dorian issued a cruel laugh. "Hell, that's gotta be the worst kept secret on the Ridgewall Ranch, poncho."

"Geraldo!" He glared at the ill-mannered pig, for the first time in his life wishing he was a woman so he could punch that sneer off her face.

"Whatever. Shit, all of us knew you two were fucking."

"Enough! You're lucky I'm a gentleman, *perra sucia*, or I'd physically take you to task for using such vulgarity to describe our lovemaking."

Dorian shot him the finger with both hands, holding them high in the air. "Hey, Selena, what'd he just call me?"

"Take a seat, Geraldo, and cool off," Tank intervened before the maid could tell the pig that perra sucia translated to *you little bitch.*

Trembling with anger, he wanted to tell the deputy to fuck off, but knowing Tank was only doing his job, he chose to sit next to Tillie in the chair farthest from Dorian. The other hands seated themselves, and Selena—who, like Lambert, had refused to continue her duties—sat down next to him.

Rico stepped in from the kitchen. "Okay, folks, soup's on. Line up and help yourselves . . . ."

* * * *

Nadia placed her half eaten chili dog from Carla's on a sprinkle of fries and rose from the thin mattress to give her leftovers to Ilian.

The pretty Mexican accepted it through a horizontal slot in the bars used to pass food trays through. "You didn't eat much of your supper. Are you sure you don't want to finish this? It's a long time until breakfast."

She patted her stomach and smiled. "I ate most of the fries, I'll be fine."

"I'll save it for my dog then, he loves weenies."

"What's his name?"

"Maton. It's Mexican for Bruiser." Ilian stepped to a long

steel table and set the food in a cardboard box she'd brought their meals in. "He's a golden retriever."

A wistful sigh rose from her throat as she recalled a tragic childhood moment when a doctor determined what had caused her to break out in hives. "I love dogs but can't have any type of pet with hair because I'm highly allergic to animal dander."

"I'm sorry, how sad for you. I can't imagine not having pets. I've got a good-for-nothing fat lazy cat named Foo-Foo too. Would you believe she's scared of mice?"

"I can relate."

"Can I ask you a personal question?"

Certain of what Ilian wanted to know, her stomach twisted with a knot of shame as she geared up to explain why she'd chosen the world's oldest profession as a career. "Sure."

"Are you part Mexican?"

She grinned with relief. "No, my father was Romani and my mother's Welsh."

"Romani?"

"Gypsy."

"Oh. When I first saw you I thought, 'She looks Latino but her skin's too light.' I love your peaches and cream complexion, by the way."

"Why thank you. I admire yours as well."

Ilian giggled. "Yeah, year-round suntan. Can you tell fortunes?"

The query evoked a painful recollection of her recurring dream.

"Oh, please forgive me. I must have offended you by that look on your face. Sorry."

"No, it's quite all right, no offense taken . . ." she brought her hands to her temples and indented the skin with her fingernails. The mock acupuncture sometimes prevented a headache and she felt one coming on. "Your question just stirred some unpleasant memories, that's all. I can't tell fortunes per se, but unfortunately I did inherit a clairvoyant gift."

"She calls it a curse," Erma laughingly enlightened, still working on a chicken fried steak.

Ilian's brows rose. "A curse?"

Pressing her fingers a tad harder, she gently nodded. "I sometimes dream about things before they happen, and most of the time they're very negative. Rarely do I receive a predictive vision where something good is about to occur. Thankfully most of my dreams are no different than other people's."

Ilian fingered her badge, absent mindedly tracing its edges. "Speaking of dreams, I've been having some weird ones lately. Have you ever dreamed you woke up from a dream, only to discover you're still dreaming?"

* * * *

Dinner was being served in the ballroom again. Rosemary gazed at her plate without really seeing it. Her mind was locked on a memory—the last time she and Nicole had been in Carlson's bed. The three of them were naked and sated. Carlson had deposited his semen on her waiting tongue a few minutes prior and she'd given Nikki a wet kiss, sharing their man's jism. Neither of them were bi, they'd done it strictly for his sake because it *really* turned him on. As they'd lain on either said of him, he'd fondled their breasts while confiding something she would never forget.

"The first woman I ever slept with was a friend's mom. He and I were only fifteen at the time. His dad was going to take us on a weekend fishing trip but somebody gave him two Cowboys' tickets and he decided to take my buddy to the game instead. They were going to head out Saturday and come back after Sunday's game. About an hour after I got home from school that Friday my friend's mom called and invited me to have dinner with them and spend the night if I wanted. When I got there she answered the door and I knew right then something was up by the look in her eyes when she told me to come in. She locked the door—said her husband and son had already left for Dallas—then she kissed me. I'd always had a hard on for her but thought I'd done a good job of hiding it until then.

"She asked if I'd had sex with a girl yet. I was practically speechless but managed to tell her no. I'll never forget the sexy smile that came over her face as she said, 'Well you won't be able to say that after tonight.' Then she grabbed my hand and pulled me to her bedroom. Nervous as hell, I told her I didn't know anything about making love. 'That's all right,' she said, 'I'll teach you.'

"After we did it that first time she went on and on about what a natural lover I was. I thought she was just stroking my ego at first, but soon learned otherwise. I didn't leave her house until Sunday afternoon. We must have screwed a million times and enjoyed every conceivable form of sex two lovers could have by the time I graduated high school and moved away from Beaumont. We never got caught because she was slick and I kept my mouth shut, but a long distance affair carried too many risks of being discovered so she told me we had to call it quits. By then I'd bedded down more than my share of girls and had discovered what made them tick. But little did I know she had one more thing to teach me.

"Three months after we broke up I ran into her at a Rangers' game. She and some friends were having a girls only weekend. One of them was a gorgeous black chick who couldn't take her eyes off me. My buddy's mom whispered in my ear, 'Have you ever been with two women at the same time?' I shook my head no and she whispered, 'You won't be able to say that after tonight.' She slipped me a note with the name of her motel and room number. The black chick was rooming with her. Well, that was my first threesome and I'll treasure that memory forever." Carlson had then cut his eyes to her and smiled. "My buddy's mom was a redhead, Rosemary, and built just like you."

* * * *

"... heed the call, Klell Ridgewall—yea verily yea, heed the call—"

Gasping for air while waking, she was terrified, yet keenly aware of the wet stream, induced by an overwhelming erotic craving that demanded immediate satisfaction, oozing from her vagina. *Debe tener dos putas . . . Debe tener dos putas . . . Must have two whores. . . .*

* * * *

Nadia insisted she had no recollection of anyone unlocking the door and making her move to the next cell. "I don't know why Erma and Sally aren't here, Sheriff, or why I didn't wake up where I fell asleep."

Tank, Alfredo, and Ilian swore they didn't have a clue who'd done it either. Besides knowing none of them would do such a thing, Gary had proof they weren't lying. His deputies had spent the night on the Ridgewall Ranch, spelling each other as guards every four hours alongside the patrolmen who'd done likewise. Ilian had gotten an urgent phone call from her mother saying her sister had gone into labor. Gary had relieved her so she could go to the hospital where she'd remained with her family throughout the night, and Erma and Sally had been there when he'd locked up. Finding the two women gone and Nadia in the wrong location when he'd arrived this morning, he'd called Ilian first. Her mother had answered the cell phone and handed it to Ilian, standing in the viewing room admiring a new niece.

Whoever did it had returned the ring of cell keys to its

proper place after moving Nadia and freeing the others. If she hadn't been left behind he'd peg Dody Massey as the culprit, but having the most damning information on the corrupt ex-sheriff since he'd left her in charge of his whorehouse, she'd have been the first one taken.

As baffling as the whole thing was, it presented the possibility of a silver lining. If Erma and Sally were taken against their will then they'd been kidnapped—a federal offense—one the FBI would be forced to respond to. Unfortunately, at the moment he couldn't prove they hadn't left voluntarily with whomever unlocked their cell.

Nothing was missing and the intruder hadn't done any damage in gaining entry. He'd had the locks changed on all the exterior doors of the jailhouse after being elected, and there were only four sets of keys. Since neither he nor any member of his department had ever lost or temporarily misplaced one, providing an opportunity for a duplicate to be made, an expert lock-picker or an actual locksmith had to be involved.

Nadia sat next to his desk sipping coffee and eating one of a dozen doughnuts he'd picked up for the three voluntary inmates' breakfast. She wasn't groggy as if she'd been drugged during the night, yet didn't appear to be lying either.

"You say they must have moved you in your sleep. I just don't see how that could be accomplished without waking you up."

She shrugged and dunked the doughnut in her coffee. "Neither do I, but that has to be what happened. All I know is I went to sleep in the bunk beneath Erma's with Sally lying on the other bottom bunk, and had no idea I was in another cell and they were gone until you woke me up."

He'd sent Tank to The Hog Farm to see if Erma and Sally might be there, and had told him to take one of the patrolmen with him for backup. He expected a report any minute since they'd set out from the Ridgewall Ranch. While waiting he began picking Nadia's brain over her missing friends.

"How long have you known Erma and Sally?"

"I met them shortly after I started working for Dody."

"How long had they been with him before that?"

She seemed mildly offended by the statement. "I'm the one that hired them."

"Who came aboard first?"

"Erma. Sally started working with us a few weeks later as I recall."

"As whores for Massey."

She lowered her eyes and nodded.

His cell phone rang. It was Tank.

"Yeah, Tank. Find anything?"

"Um, Gary, you'd better get out here."

He frowned. "Are they there or not?"

"Well, there's two females here but I'm not sure it's them. Gary . . . their faces have been removed and—"

"You mean they're dead?"

"Y-Yeah . . . and they've been scalped."

* * * *

The two women were bound to be Erma and Sally but even their mothers couldn't verify it by sight. Like the first victims they'd been decapitated and their naked bodies had been arranged to make it look like they'd spent their last breath grinding vaginas. Two brass poles at the foot of the bed, impaling open throats, supported their hairless heads. Only the ears retained skin—the other epidermis, along with flesh and cartilage that once formed noses, had been so expertly removed the ghastly faces looked like medical dummies that could be taken apart layer by layer to study anatomy. Again the killers had left blood only where they'd wanted it but had added a new twist by making off with their scalps. The macabre cleanliness of exposed muscle, tendons, blood vessels, and bone revolted him almost as much as the gaping, lidless eyeballs perched above triangular nasal cavities grossly emphasized by permanently smiling teeth.

A scowl entrenched on his face, Gary turned to Tank, whose ashen expression revealed he felt the same dismay at being powerless to stop the insane butchers. "We need expert help on this and we're gonna get it if I have to go all the way up to the Governor."

ELEVEN

Though dressed as a civilian the tall sandy-haired man carried himself like a marine so he assumed him to be the Texas Ranger from Company E in El Paso he'd been promised. Rising from his desk with a big smile, Gary extended his hand. "I am *some* glad to see you, Ranger. Heath Crow, right? I'm Gary Stoner."

"Be glad to shake hands with you, Sheriff, but my name is Dunmark Finley."

Gary chuckled while pumping the reciprocating palm. "Sorry about that, must have been a change in plans. They told me to expect Ranger Crow." He pointed to the chair beside his desk and invited him to have a seat.

Finley cleared his throat as he sat down. "Before we go any further, Sheriff Stoner, I need to clear up your confusion. I'm an investigator, not a Texas Ranger."

"Oh? Who are you with?"

"I work independently, Sheriff. I investigate metaphysical activity, especially malevolent forms thereof."

Expecting Finley to be a last minute replacement for the ranger, he'd figured him to be an investigator with some branch of law enforcement. He pointed towards the door. "I don't believe in that bullshit. You know your way out."

Finley appeared unfazed by his reaction. He calmly rose to his feet, pulled a card from his shirt pocket, and tossed it on the desk. "I researched the Ridgewall Ranch phenomenon some time ago and have seen the ghost seven times. On each occasion the ectoplasm had only enough energy to briefly appear, and couldn't possibly have manipulated anything in the physical realm. But recently a dark power has somehow altered what heretofore has been a passive manifestation. Believe me, Sheriff, this will only get worse. Your skepticism will evaporate eventually because circumstances will dictate it. Call me when it does, and let's hope by then it's not too late."

A shudder reverberated through him as he watched Dunmark Finley walk away. Montella had laughingly told him Nicole Anderson believed a voodoo priestess had turned the ghost of Klell Ridgewall into a bloodthirsty killer. He'd snickered at the theory as well, but now it unnerved him how closely that allegation aligned with Finley's.

The man's words carried an eerie weight.

Thinking about yesterday's horrid sight at The Hog Farm, he leaned forward while crossing his arms atop his desk, dropped his forehead on them, and closed his weary eyes. Since they'd been in protective custody the women hadn't been required to exchange their clothing for county duds, and a thorough search of the house had turned up the items Erma and Sally wore when last seen alive. The DPS had been given two sets of fingerprints lifted from the corpses. Though he'd yet to receive confirmation, there wasn't a doubt in his mind they'd match those of the two women mysteriously taken from his jail.

"Sheriff Stoner?"

Gary sat up and turned to see a man about the same height as Dunmark Finley remove a white cowboy hat from a head of neatly groomed dark hair. He wore a pleasant smile on his face and a circular badge on his chest. Arcing across the top over a star that read SERGEANT were the words DEPT. OF PUBLIC SAFTEY with TEXAS RANGERS looping across the bottom.

"I'm Heath Crow."

* * * *

Nadia didn't want to stay in jail upon learning Erma and Sally had most likely been stolen away from there by the killers. Still not cleared as a possible accomplice, Sheriff Stoner had given her only one other option—take up temporary residence on the Ridgewall Ranch. Deputy Green had driven her to the mansion after taking her to The Hog Farm so she could pack some clothes. Trembling during the process, she hadn't been able to stuff a suitcase fast enough because Erma and Sally had been found in her bedroom.

Montella looked well, though faint lines at the corners of her blue eyes hinted at approaching middle age. Carlson's death must have exorcised the demon of jealousy because the blonde madam actually seemed glad to see her. Tillie had bleached her pretty brown hair but otherwise hadn't changed too much in the last six years.

Dorian ran up and gave her big hug. "You're a sight for sore eyes, Nadia! Shit it's good to see you!"

"You too, girl. I swear you haven't aged a day since I last saw you."

"Hi, Nadia, remember me?"

She'd forgotten about the Jamaican girl Carlson had recruited during her last year with him. Freeing herself from Dorian's embrace, she turned towards her. "Um, yeah but you'll have to forgive me, I don't recall your name."

"Nicole Anderson."

"Oh, that's right. So good to see you again."

Nicole introduced her to a beautiful redhead named Rosemary, who hadn't been around when she'd suffered Carlson's wrath. She shook the girl's hand and turned to Montella. "Those women that were killed here, how many of them did I know?"

"None of them."

Nadia took in the ritzy ballroom where the police were keeping everybody. "I don't see Debbie, Cheryl, or Twila. Are they still around?"

"Carl cut them loose three years ago."

"Why?"

Montella crossed her arms. "A football star paid an arm and a leg for the three of them at the same time. He talked them into sneaking out for a night on the town and a reporter snapped some pictures. When Carl saw them in the paper he canned them on the spot. It was their replacements who were first murdered as a matter of fact."

Carlson didn't tolerate insubordination on any level. Leaving the premises with a john was a big time no-no. Realizing she was thinking of him in the present tense, a melancholy lump formed in her throat as it cruelly hit home that she'd never see him again. "I can't believe he's dead."

"None of us can, Nadia."

"I've been angry with him ever since he fired me, but never got over him. I miss him so much."

Montella's glossy lips spread with a perceptive smile. "We all miss his dick, dear."

A crude way to put it, she thought sadly, *but oh so true.*

* * * *

Gary had given Heath Crow all the details of the murders and the mysterious abduction of Erma and Sally. The ranger was inspecting the cell they'd been taken from. "Nadia Mars knows more than she's saying."

"I thought so too at first but not anymore. I'm satisfied the whole maneuver is as big a mystery to her as it is to me."

Heath donned a half grin. "You taking the word of a prostitute?"

"No, gut instinct. She's not lying."

"I can appreciate that since I usually follow my hunches too. But you said there were no indications of her being drugged, so someone being able to move her without waking her up stretches the boundaries of logic."

He eyed the bunk Nadia claimed to have fallen asleep on the night of the abduction. "You're right, Heath, but everything about these murders is illogical. The way the killers can butcher people without anyone nearby hearing a sound, the strange compulsion to leave the severed heads blood-free as possible and the torsos a bloody mess doesn't lend itself to a logical explanation either. Anyway, she's at the Ridgewall Ranch if you want to interrogate her."

"Oh I want to talk to everybody out there."

"Just one thing. I gave my word to Montella Pace I wouldn't tell any of her cronies she ratted out Loggins. I'd appreciate it if you'd do likewise."

* * * *

They got to the ranch around suppertime and found everyone in the dining room. Most of them had finished eating, including Nadia. Gary instructed her to accompany the ranger and him.

He guided her down the hall far enough from the dining room entrance to not be overheard, and listened as she reiterated what she'd told him about her mysterious ignorance of the deadly jailbreak.

Heath gazed at her stoically until she finished, whereupon he conveyed his skepticism with a patronizing grin. "Who are you protecting, Miss Mars?"

"No one," she emphatically declared. "Erma and Sally were my friends. I wouldn't spit on the sick bastards that killed them if they were on fire, much less do anything to help them."

Seemingly unaffected by her answer, Heath cut his eyes to him. "When everyone's finished with dinner I'd like to commandeer the dining room for interrogation, one person at a time. I assume everybody that lives on this ranch is in there?"

Gary nodded.

* * * *

"Who told you I was a prostitute, Ranger Crow? This is crazy—I was Carlson's personal assistant."

Standing near the dining table, Gary stifled a yawn as the redhead sitting across from Heath spouted the same flim-flam he'd gotten from her after Angela Yang's murder. He'd given the ranger a list with the names of everyone residing on the ranch and Rosemary's had been called first.

A denigrating smirk spread across Heath's firm athletic face. "We know what you really did for Carlson Loggins but you can worry about the consequences of that later. What should presently concern you is leaving us unconvinced you're not in cahoots with the people that murdered him."

Realizing the jig was up, she demanded to know how he'd ascertained Loggins true vocation. Heath ignored her and glanced at the list. "Please have Montella Pace come in."

Gary escorted Rosemary to the billiard room where they'd stationed Tank, who'd been keeping an eye on Nadia. Then he went to the ballroom where the others were being guarded by patrolmen, and fetched Montella. When Heath finished with her she'd have to wait in the billiard room as well, so no one would know what to expect before being interrogated.

Heath beckoned Montella to take the chair directly across from him and she sat down. "First off I want to thank you for cooperating with Sheriff Stoner, Miss Pace."

A sigh streamed through her glistening lips. "I hope you won't tell any of the others I'm the stool pigeon."

"Your secret's safe for now . . . ."

* * * *

Dooly had never spoken with a Texas Ranger before and felt honored in spite of the situation. Ranger Crow sure fit the mold. Built like he could whip his weight in wildcats, he didn't mince words and had an air about him that said he couldn't be outwitted. When the lawman asked if he'd ever had sex with any of Loggins' female employees, he sensed a lie wouldn't stand long before the ranger unraveled it. "Yes, sir, I have."

"Which one?"

"Dorian." He noticed Sheriff Stoner seemed offended at hearing the name.

Ranger Crow started scribbling on a legal pad. "Did you pay for it?"

"Pay for what?"

"Sex with Dorian."

"Oh no," he laughed out, "she came on to me."

"How many times have you had sex with her?"

"Several times, but it all happened the same night."

"When and where did this take place?"

"Three nights ago in one of the ballroom closets while everyone was asleep."

The ranger stopped writing and eyeballed him. "Do you usually get it for free from prostitutes?"

"Say what?" He cut his eyes to Sheriff Stoner. "Dorian's a pro?"

"We'll ask the questions," said the sheriff.

At first he just sat there stunned with confusion, then the pieces came together and he laughed at himself over what a dumbass he'd been. "Hell I'm an idiot. No wonder all the women working for Loggins are so dang pretty—they're high class whores. Loggins didn't have that landing strip built so those rich dudes could fly out here on a regular basis to do business with him like he told us. They were paying him for pussy. Man oh man . . . wonder what that wild ride Dorian gave me would have cost. Bobby Joe got her for free too."

"When?" asked Ranger Crow.

"That same night. She took turns with us, wore us both smooth out. She'd planned on making it a regular thing but scrapped the idea later the next day when one of the women complained about hearing weird noises when she got up during the night to use the restroom."

"According to Bobby Joe he was never intimate with any of the women residing in the mansion."

"Yeah? Well he's lying out his ass, Ranger Crow. Get him in here and let him try to say that in front of me. You'll see right off who's telling the truth and who ain't."

"That won't be necessary." He scanned an open spiral notebook lying beside his legal pad and resettled his eyes on him. "According to the statement you gave Sheriff Stoner, you've worked on this ranch for three years. How well did you and the cook get along?"

"Me and Munchie? Heck I loved that old fart. He treated us all like he'd taken us in to raise, except Hank of course."

The ranger put his pen down and meshed his fingers together. "How about you and Jeremy Hicks?"

"We got along fine most of the time."

"I understand you two had a heated argument a few weeks ago. What was that about?"

He shifted in his chair, wondering who'd blabbed about that. "I told him I was tired of Bobby Joe and me getting all the shit work—that Geraldo needed to eat his share of it too. Jeremy said I didn't have any say in the matter, that he'd dole out the chores however he saw fit, to which I replied that he could suck my dick. We dang near went to fist city after I told him that and most likely would have if Hank hadn't shown up when he did. After we both cooled off we apologized to each other and went on back to work."

"Did you and Jeremy ever come to blows on other occasions?"

"No, that was the maddest we ever got with each other. I'd been stewing for a long time over him showing partiality to

Geraldo, and when he told me to clean out the horse stalls I blew—told him it was high time Geraldo got his turn at it because me and Bobby Joe had gotten stuck with it far too long."

Ranger Crow scooted his chair back and rose to his feet. "Okay, we're done."

Glad to hear that, he got up and stretched, looking forward to hitting the sack. He'd been the last one called into the dining room and it was almost midnight. "Who told you about my argument with Jeremy?"

"No one, it was in the sheriff's notes."

"Never mind who told me," said Sheriff Stoner before he could ask.

"If I find out it was Bobby Joe he's got an ass whooping coming."

The sheriff patted him on the back. "Let it go, Dooly. I'd hate to have to haul you in for assault."

When they stepped into the hall he saw the ass end of a white horse silently galloping away from him. The confederate officer riding it was waving his saber as if leading troops into battle. The Texas Ranger and Sheriff Stoner wore the same look of baffled amazement while watching Klell Ridgewall disappear through the far wall.

TWELVE

The chief of the DPS had said Heath Crow would be sent to assist him because during the ranger's marine days he'd been part of a task force that apprehended an elusive child killer. After being tortured and sodomized, the dismembered bodies of five boys had been deposited on the lawns of separate houses at a military base. Since none of the abducted children's parents served in the armed forces the investigators had been stymied as to why those residences were chosen as dump sites.

USMC Corporal Heath Crow brought a lengthy investigation to an end after deducing the killer appeared to be obsessed with the number five. Each boy—kidnapped separately five days in a row—had been a fifth grader. Their arms and legs had been amputated and arranged in a star-like pattern on five lawns, the torso and limbs equaling five body parts. And Camp Pendleton, chosen for the morbid display, housed the fifth regiment. Corporal Crow painstakingly searched the records for every marine receiving a dishonorable discharge from there and his diligence paid off. A captain had chosen to resign rather than face possible court martial after coming under suspicion of molesting a young boy. Acting on that information, the task force apprehended the man a short time later and collected enough evidence to convict the homicidal pervert not only of murder, but for impersonating an officer to gain access to the base.

Gary sat across from the ranger at Carla's Café. The two of them had been discussing what they'd seen last night.

"There has to be a rational explanation for it," insisted Heath, working on a bacon and egg breakfast.

Swallowing a bite taken from a triple stack of syrup-drenched pancakes, Gary chased it with coffee and set his cup down. "Dooly said he'd seen the exact same thing out on the range. Whether or not it was the spirit of Klell Ridgewall, that has to be what so many people have reported seeing on the Ridgewall Ranch. A short while before you showed up a man came in my office claiming to be a metaphysical investigator. He thinks Ridgewall's ghost is doing all the killing."

Heath chuckled.

He sliced off a piece of sausage from a large patty and forked it into his mouth. Mixed with diced jalapeños and green chilies, it burned his tongue but he willingly suffered the agony because of the extraordinary flavor. A Carla's specialty, he'd gotten addicted to it the first time he'd ordered breakfast there. Water only intensified the pain but any type of bread, including hotcakes, help neutralize the acid to a tolerable degree. "Does anyone rouse your suspicion?"

"Nadia Mars. I admit she doesn't appear to be lying but I just don't see how she could have been moved from one cell to another without remembering at least something about it."

Following the spicy sausage with a wedge of pancake, he chewed slowly so as to relieve his misery. When his tongue started feeling numb instead of on fire, he swallowed and took a very light nip from his water glass. "I think she's just a real sound sleeper. My nephew's like that. You could heave him over your shoulder and not wake him up."

Heath grinned. "At least you're not saying the ghost miraculously moved her."

"No, not at the moment anyway."

"The other thing that stands out about Nadia Mars is the fact she used to work for Loggins, which makes her the only connection between all the victims."

Preparing for another round of savory torture, he cut into the sausage patty again. "According to her statement the only Ridgewall fatality she knew personally was Loggins himself.

Montella and the other three prostitutes that were around when she was still whoring for Loggins verified it."

"Which makes her all the more suspicious, Gary. Why is it none of the women she knew before Loggins dumped her have been killed?"

He hadn't thought about it from that angle and had to admit Heath might be on to something. "So you think she hired some goons to butcher all those people just to hide the fact she wanted Loggins dead?"

"Possibly. I'm not ruling anything out at this point."

"Neither am I. I pondered that very thing when I found out Loggins fired her, but if she's behind it, having Erma and Sally abducted was a dumb move because her being left behind put her right in the spotlight."

Heath mopped up some egg yolk with a biscuit and bit into it. "Not necessarily. What better way to be cleared as a suspect than having it appear you're being framed?"

* * * *

The gentle motion of his horse threatening to rock him to sleep, Hank let out a long yawn and rubbed his eyes. After the Texas Ranger interrogated him last night Sheriff Stoner had kept him penned up in the billiard room until everybody got grilled. He hadn't been able to hit the sack until after midnight. It was hard enough trying to fall asleep with a crowd in the ballroom anyway, but when Dooly spouted off about seeing the ghost in the hall the place hadn't quieted down for at least an hour afterwards. When that fiasco finally ended, Dooly had started badgering Bobby Joe about telling Sheriff Stoner he'd had it out with Jeremy, somehow convinced he'd done so despite Bobby Joe claiming otherwise. Geraldo had settled that by confessing he'd been the culprit and was more than willing if Dew wanted to try a little of his honor on. Dooly had merely shot him the bird and climbed into his cot.

"Wonder why Ridgewall decided to show up indoors?" said Bobby Joe, hands resting on his saddle horn, reins draped through fingers sheathed with cowhide gloves.

Geraldo adjusted his blue Stetson. "It's not the first time he's done it. Angela saw him upstairs the night before she died."

"Hope that don't mean you're about to buy the farm, Dew."

Dooly grimaced from atop his mount. "You and me both, Bobby Joe."

The work day had ended and they were heading for the stalls to put up the horses before calling it a day. The lawman on horseback to his right would drive them to the mansion in his patrol car from there. Hank wished Rico Mircanti would rustle up some Mexican grub for supper like Munchie used to, but knew the odds were slim to none against his recurring hankering for tacos being satisfied tonight.

An ache stabbed his heart as he thought of his old friend. He'd love to get his hands on Othello's killer and rip the son-of-a-bitch's balls off like the bastard had done to the poor cook. Jeremy could be a real shitass at times but he wouldn't mind avenging his departed ramrod as well. He sniffed a dribble of snot back through his nose, hawked it into his mouth, and spit. "Something better give soon is all I can say. I'm tired of being rounded up every evening like a herd of cattle."

The rest of the boys echoed his sentiments.

A grin appeared on the patrolman's face, straddling the roan Jeremy used to ride, eyes hidden behind a pair of pilot's shades. "You think I like having to hang with you cowpokes all day? Believe me, none of us are enjoying this any more than you guys."

He fired a smile back at the lawman. "Thanks for helping us out. It was almost like having a full crew again. Much obliged."

"You're welcome, Hank. I'd have been bored out of my

mind otherwise."

"You must have done some ranch work before somewhere down the line, Mister . . . what'd you say your name was again?"

"Lawrence Kerns. Yes I have, and call me Lawrence."

Hank gave him an appreciative nod. "Where abouts did you cowpunch, Lawrence?"

"I grew up on a dairy farm outside Killeen."

"That explains it. Pretty country up there, doesn't have to be irrigated like this desert prairie."

"Yeah, it sure is."

"So how long have you been with the highway patrol?"

"Too damn long . . ." he pulled off his sunglasses, rubbed both eyes with the index knuckle of the hand holding them, and slipped the shades back on. "I'll be retiring soon."

"Hell, come to work for me. If I still have a job when this is all over that is."

Lawrence snorted a short laugh. "Got plans to open a little bait store near Amistad."

"Ah, Lake Amistad. Haven't been fishing there in years. Caught a thirty pound cat last time I was there. Maybe I oughta come to work for you."

That brought another chuckle from the patrolman.

"So what do you think's going on with these murders, Lawrence?"

The lawman blew out a mournful whistle and adjusted his hat. "Did you happen to see any of the casualties on this ranch?"

"Yeah, I'm afraid I did. Othello Vance and Jeremy Hicks . . . it was gruesome."

"Well I saw the three butchered hog farmers. When somebody comes up with a rational explanation as to how somebody can do that without being heard, and tell me why three strong cowboys let themselves get slaughtered like sheep without any evidence of putting up a fight, then I'll have a foundation to base a theory on. Until then, there's no way in hell I'd try to figure this shit out. When I heard about the first murders I thought Dody Massey might be behind it all until I found out nobody heard anything while that Chinese girl was getting cut up in the ladies room at that Mexican restaurant."

Hank jerked his head back with surprise. "For gosh sakes, why'd you think that?"

"Revenge. During the last election his big thing was claiming Gary Stoner didn't have enough experience to adequately serve as sheriff. I thought he was banking on Gary being forced to resign for not being able to solve those homicides. Massey's a cold-blooded snake with a handful of loyal punks that would hack up their own mothers if he told them to. But his goons don't have anywhere near the expertise needed to pull off these mysterious slayings."

* * * *

She placed the fetish carefully among the rest and began igniting candles. The dangling talismans felt cool against her naked breasts, sweating from the heat of a nearby boiling caldron. "Klell Ridgewall, I summon thee. The Indians have returned to rape and torture and butcher thy women yet again. You must avenge them, Klell Ridgewall. Rise from thy grave and draw thy sword. Rise, Klell Ridgewall, I summon thee—"

"What . . .?" she looked around frantically, head bobbing from side to side on a sweat-soaked pillow. "Where am I? Oh my god I'm still dreaming! Why can't I wake up?"

Craving a man's hard dick and a woman's soft tongue, she rose to her feet. The dripping juices of arousal snaked down her inner thighs. *Un hombre y una mujer . . . un hombre y una mujer . . . un hombre y una mujer . . .*

* * * *

"Yes, it's true, darling, you're the only one I really love. The others can't begin to compare but I have to pretend, to keep morale high. You understand, don't you?"

Heart fluttering with joy, she nodded and stroked his lovely hair. They were lying sidewise in each others' arms, having returned from heaven where they'd flown on the wings of orgasm.

"Good." He caressed her breast and rolled her onto her back, preparing to make love to her again.

A protesting bladder woke her.

She got out of bed and made her way to the ballroom ladies room, not at all disappointed at being pulled away from Carlson, for she'd join him again the moment she went back to sleep. Her every unconscious moment had been spent with him in dreams since he'd died.

When she flipped the light switch Rosemary no longer required a toilet. Hot piss squirted through her panties at the sight of Lambert and Tillie.

* * * *

Despite having seen the three headless corpses at The Hog Farm, Nadia had never witnessed anything so horrendous. The first to reach the ladies room to see what the screaming was all about, she'd seen Lambert's head lying sideways on the lavatory countertop with the end of his severed neck resting on the left edge of the sink. Tillie's had been placed on the right side of the porcelain depression. The killer evidently wanted to make sure what little bodily fluids remained would empty into the drain from the base of their throats. Only a scant amount had.

Lambert's naked body had been placed on the toilet as if taking a dump while Tillie, also nude, faced him, straddling his midsection. But the organs required for intercourse were lying in the sink. Tillie's vagina had been gouged from her body, and the big man's long dick and massive balls had been sliced away from his. Testicles still attached, the flaccid black penis had been inserted through the poor girl's canal, the bulbous head emerging from the incised section that no longer merged with a cervix.

Sheriff Stoner and Ranger Crow had arrived at the crack of dawn. The coroner and his assistant showed up shortly afterwards and had left with the remains a few minutes ago. Unlike Rosemary's red-faced admission that she'd peed on the floor, Nadia had felt no embarrassment explaining the vomit near the pool of urine hadn't come from either victim. She'd puked the moment she saw them.

It was approaching nine o'clock and Sheriff Stoner released the cowboys under the custody of a patrolman to perform their daily chores. The rest of them were told to remain in the dining room for the time being. Other than Dorian, only the cowhands had eaten anything for breakfast. No one else could summon an appetite.

Nadia had taken the chair beside Rosemary, who sat next to Nicole, seated at Montella's right, the madam occupying her usual spot at one end of the table. Dorian, who'd been told by Ranger Crow to shut up and sit back down after begging for permission to go outside for a smoke, begrudgingly dropped her butt beside Rico and the maid, sitting at mid-table on the other side. The lawmen stood just beyond Carlson's empty chair. She'd never seen him in that one but the prominent seats had always been reserved for him and Montella at mealtimes.

"Were the victims having a relationship, Miss Pace?" Ranger Crow inquired.

An angry sneer preceded Montella's answer. "If you mean *were they fucking*, the answer's no—at least not that I'm aware of. What's it going to take to get us out of here, Ranger?

Can't you see we're all sitting ducks?"

"Where exactly would you like to go?"

"Anywhere out of Tomahawk County."

"And why would you be safe out of the county?"

Shiny lips drawn taut, she raised her chin defiantly. "I'm not sure we would be, but it's certain we're not here."

The ranger scanned the notes he'd taken in the ballroom when he'd asked where everyone slept. "You were sleeping in the cot next to the female victim's, Miss Pace. When did you last see her alive?"

"Her name is Tillie, Ranger, not female victim. I last saw *Tillie* when we told each other goodnight from our respective torture devices we were given to sleep on. God I hate sleeping on a cot."

"And the butler?"

"Shortly before turning in. As we told you in the ballroom, he slept on the other side of the room next to Rico."

Ranger Crow looked at the cook. "When did you last see him alive?"

The broken-nose Italian folded two beefy arms across a flabby chest that had been firm and muscular in pictures Nadia had seen, taken during his boxing days. "When I went to bed. He was already snoring."

"And when did you last see the, um Tillie?"

"When she went to the ladies' side of the ballroom after we were released from the billiard room last night."

He glanced her way. "Have you ever seen the Ridgewall Ghost, Miss Mars?"

The ridiculous question surprised her and she couldn't help giggling. "Why would you ask me that?"

"Answer his question," the sheriff commanded.

"Of course not."

"I find it odd that Sheriff Stoner and I both saw it the very day you were brought out here."

Another laugh forced its way out. "And I'm to blame for

that?"

The Ranger started stroking his chin as a sardonic grin formed. "A few years ago some cowboys thought they were seeing a ghost on The Double Cross Ranch up in North Texas. I'm sure you've heard of it."

"Sure. Everybody knows about T. Wayford Cross, but this is the first I've heard about a ghost on his ranch."

"That ghost turned out to be a hologram rather than a spirit, and that's what I suspect Sheriff Stoner and I saw last night."

She gaped at him incredulously. "Well I didn't have anything to do with it. I don't know the first thing about how such things are done."

"Neither did the woman behind The Double Cross haunting. She hired a technician to do it for her, and that's what I suspect you've done." The Ranger looked around the room, apparently examining each face for any tell-tale signs of complicity. Eventually he settled his eyes back on her. "We'll connect the dots eventually, Miss Mars, so why don't you save us all a lot of time and inconvenience by telling us who you're protecting?"

"I'm not protecting anybody and have nothing to hide. I told the sheriff everything I know about Dody Massey and Carlson Loggins when I was staying in his jail. I'm sure he's filled you in, so there's nothing else I can tell you that you don't already know."

Nicole vaulted to her feet. "You told Sheriff Stoner about Carlson? How could you do that to him, Nadia?"

A dry laugh erupted from Montella. "In case you forgot, he fired her, Nikki. Nadia doesn't owe Carl anything. Besides, I'm sure Ranger Crow got plenty of information out of you, so don't come off so indignant."

Caramel features twisting from anger to shame, Nicole dropped back into her chair. "Montella's right, I'm being a hypocrite. Please forgive me, Nadia." She turned her attention to Ranger Crow and Sheriff Stoner. "You two have got to listen to me. The ghost has become a puppet of a voodoo priestess. That's who's killing everybody—none of us have a thing to do with it."

"I think Nicole's right," said Dorian while crossing her arms. The top of her bathrobe gapped open, exposing a goodly amount of cleavage. "How can Lambert and Tillie have been butchered so close to everybody without any of us hearing anything unless something supernatural's going on? Don't know that a voodoo priestess is behind it, but it's the ghost of Klell Ridgewall doing the slaughtering, you can bet yer fuckin' badges on that. And we're all gonna be dead if you don't get us away from here."

The lawmen's eyes were locked on Dorian's boobs as she spoke.

Ranger Crow finally shifted his gaze from the mammary flesh to Nicole. "Why are you so convinced the ghost is doing it, Miss Anderson?"

Nicole brightened, visibly excited at the chance to elaborate. "Angela saw the ghost inside the house the night Cynthia, Carolyn, and Babette were killed. That same night I dreamed that Angela and Sonya were horseback riding and Sonya's horse bucked her off and stomped her to death. Angela got killed at the restaurant the evening after the three girls were found in Babette's room that morning. And like Dorian said, none of us ever heard anything—neither in the mansion when Babette, Cynthia, and Carolyn were being hacked to death, nor at the restaurant while the ghost was mauling Angela. The very next day Sonya gets killed along with Carlson—confirming my premonition—and even though the bathroom where they were slain is near the billiard room where all of us were, none of us heard a sound. None of the cowboys heard anything when Munchie and Jeremy were killed either. The ghost appeared in the house again last night, and now Lambert and Tillie are dead."

A smile that appeared respectfully skeptical spread across the ranger's face. "The other ranch hands had already left the bunkhouse before the cook and ramrod were taken down, Miss Anderson, but I must confess it is mysterious that no one heard anything in the mansion, restaurant, or house at The Hog Farm when those murders took place. Just as mysterious as Nadia Mars being moved from one cell to another without remembering anything as she claims. But why do you insist that a voodoo priestess must be behind this?"

"Because people have been seeing Klell Ridgewall harmlessly appear and disappear for years," answered Nicole. "Someone has cast a spell on his spirit, giving him the power to act in the physical realm, making him think he's avenging the deaths of his wife and daughters. Only a highly skilled practitioner of black magic such as a voodoo priestess could perform such a feat."

Sheriff Stoner seemed to be giving her theory serious consideration, judging by the frown he wore, but Ranger Crow looked unimpressed.

Dorian stood up. "Dammit, fellers, I'm 'bout to have a nicotine fit. Can I please go outside for a smoke? I'll stand by a wender so you can see me."

Ranger Crow looked puzzled. "I said you couldn't leave the room, not that you couldn't smoke."

Montella scowled with indignance as Dorian hastily fished a pack of Camels and a butane lighter from the pocket of her robe and lit up. "Carl doesn't allow smoking in the house, Dorian, you know that."

Eyes glassy with relief, Dorian exhaled a cloud of smoke and grinned while dumping a handful of dinner mints on the table. "Don't reckon he has much say 'bout nothing now. Thanks, Ranger, you just made a friend for life. I'll use this here candy bowl as an ashtray."

Nadia almost sneezed when the rancid smell of secondhand smoke reached her nostrils, but managed to suppress it by holding a finger beneath them.

"Do you know a voodoo priestess, Miss Anderson?" queried Sheriff Stoner.

"No, not in America."

"Swamp country's full of 'em," declared Dorian, smoke streaming in diverse angles with her words. "Ain't nothin' meaner'n Cajun voodoo."

Nicole smiled at the sheriff. "You asked me that like you might think I'm on to something. Do you?"

"I met a man who makes a similar claim, but he didn't mention voodoo, just a dark power. I don't believe these murders are supernatural, but rather that someone's trying to make them look that way."

"But you saw the ghost yourself, Sheriff," Nicole protested. "You and Ranger Crow both."

"Yes, Ranger Crow and I did see something but neither of us are convinced it was the ghost of Klell Ridgewall."

From her peripheral vision Nadia noticed Montella was intently gazing at Sheriff Stoner, making her wonder if the blonde had a yen for him. It could have been her own increasing appreciation of Tomahawk County's Finest that had induced the thought but she didn't think so. Montella used to eyeball Carlson the same way. Her musing dissipated when Dorian spoke up again.

"Never mind who's doin' it—bum-fuck ghost or super-slick psycho. Are you fellers gonna haul our asses off this fuckin' ranch or leave us here to die?"

THIRTEEN

Gary moved two wetbacks brought in by the border patrol to the drunk tank, which couldn't be seen from main lockup. They'd be hauled back to Mexico in the morning. He'd done it to make room for seven new inmates. Four more would arrive before sundown.

The six women had been placed in two adjoining cells where female prisoners usually stayed. Like all the cells, each had two steel bunk beds and a toilet on the solid back wall, but they were the only ones equipped with stalls to prevent any male inmates across the way from seeing them use the commode. All the cell doors faced the dayroom—a secured area furnished with two exposed toilets, a lavatory, and a long steel table with benches attached. The ranch hands would spend the night on the opposite side after Lawrence Kerns brought them here when their chores were done. Rico Mircanti was already there, sitting on a bottom bunk, hands on knees, gazing blankly ahead.

"Okay, listen up everybody. I'll leave your cells unlocked but I'm keeping the visitor's door to the dayroom secured so no one can get in or out without a key. This pretty lady here is Ilian and she'll look in on you from time to time, and bring your supper in a couple of hours. Any questions before I go?"

Montella pouted. "Can't I just stay at your place again, Sheriff?"

* * * *

Jealousy rifled through Nadia over Montella's request. She smiled with relief when Sheriff Stoner denied it, and couldn't take her eyes off his khaki-covered butt as he walked away.

Ilian followed him through the dayroom door and turned to lock it. "Do any of you smoke?"

"Yeah, I do," said Dorian.

"Use that built in trash bin by the sink as an ashtray, not the floor. If I have to pick up a single cigarette butt that privilege will be revoked. This is my turf and I like to keep it tidy. I'm not just the dispatcher, I'm also a deputy." She patted the pistol at her side.

Nadia giggled. "Ilian, what's gotten into you? We're not under arrest."

"Oh yes you are, every one of you."

Ranger Crow stepped in from the waiting room as Dorian ejaculated, "Says who?!"

"Says him . . ." Ilian pointed at the ranger.

Nadia swallowed a gulp of shock. "Why?"

"Because you're all suspected accomplices," answered Ranger Crow. "You'll be allowed to use the dayroom until dinnertime, then your cell doors will be locked till morning. You have Sheriff Stoner to thank for that courtesy, not to mention being allowed to wear your own clothes and having most of the lights turned off at bedtime. Normally they all stay on in lockup twenty-four seven."

Rico scrambled up to the bars of the dayroom door. "Hey, you can't hold us without charging us with something!"

The ranger faced him and acquired a challenging grin that dared the portly Italian to say another word. "If we have to book you, we will, if that's how you want to play it. If so let's get that formality over with right now."

Waving him off, Rico walked over to the table and sat down.

"Anyone else want to get their mug shots taken?"

No one said anything, not even the sass queen Dorian.

Nadia couldn't believe Ilian's change in attitude. The sweet Mexican had turned into an apparent control freak. Ranger

Crow whispered something in her ear and left. Whatever he'd said caused a blushing smile to appear, indicating she'd just been commended for a job well done.

Dorian lit a cigarette and waltzed over to the lavatory as Montella, Nicole, Rosemary, and Selena sat down at the table with Rico. Nadia started to join them but a faint throb in her left temple announced an approaching headache, so she stretched out on a bottom bunk and closed her eyes.

* * * *

Dooly only picked at the meatloaf and mashed potatoes from Carla's Café because he couldn't keep his mind on the grub. Dorian sat across from him rubbing her bare foot on his crotch beneath the jailhouse table, burning a hole through him with a wanton stare that commenced after she'd vacuumed her plate a few minutes ago. She gave his hard a final push and her boobs shook as her toes found their way back into a slipper. A moment later she got up and headed for the toilets to smoke.

He hated they didn't have a closet to fuck in.

"What a weird ol' weary day," sighed Hank. He dropped a wadded up paper napkin on his empty plate and let out a tired groan.

"Whelp we learnt one thang fer sure this mornin', Hank—" Dorian trumpeted a loud burp, not bothering to cover her mouth "—the butler didn't do it."

The old cowboy grimaced as she cackled.

Dorian's sick jibe and the smell of her cigarette mingling with the dank air of the dayroom affected the taste of his chow. It also deflated his dick. Dooly put his fork down.

"Hey, I'll finish that fer ya if'n yer done."

"Have at it . . ." he pushed the half-eaten takeout meal to the center of the table.

Nadia Mars, a gorgeous newcomer to the ranch, did

likewise and glanced at Dorian, who could pass as her younger sister. At first sight the only notable difference between the two hot chicks appearance-wise was the color of their sexy eyes. "Eat the rest of mine too if you want—I never have liked meatloaf. I don't see why we couldn't order for ourselves."

"Because it's the cheapest dinner on the menu," said Ilian, sitting in a chair outside the bars. "Inmates always get the Blue Plate Special for supper. Maybe it'll be something different tomorrow night."

"You almost sound like you care."

"I do, Nadia."

"Then why have you been acting so rough? When I stayed here before, you treated me like a guest in your own home."

"You weren't being officially detained then. I must keep a professional distance from the inmates."

She grinned. "Does that mean we're still friends?"

Ilian nodded with a sealed smile.

Dooly had known the pretty Mexican and her boyfriend Alfredo since moving to Tomahawk County several years ago. Last summer the lovebirds had called it quits because of a lovers' spat and he'd toyed with the idea of asking her out, but they'd made up before he'd gotten the chance to do it.

Dorian came back to the table and started shoveling in the leftovers as if she hadn't eaten all day.

He got up and ambled to the outer wall to chat with Ilian. "Feels weird being locked up—never been in jail before. Where's Alfredo this evening?"

"Making his rounds. How've you been, Dooly?"

"Hangin' in the best I can with all this weird shit. How about yourself?"

"Same as you."

"Is Maton still kicking?"

"Mm hmm."

"That old dog'll probably outlive us all. Heard your sister

had her baby."

Her dark eyes flashed with joy. "Yeah, got a little niece."

"Congratulations. So what's your take on all these gory murders?"

A deep sigh escaped her. "All I know is I'll be so glad when the killers are brought to justice. I've been having weird dreams since this bloodbath started."

"So you don't think it could be just one whack-job acting alone, huh?"

"Oh gosh no. Gary set me straight on the fact it has to be at least two people doing it."

"Reckon it might be the ghost?" he joked with a wink.

Instead of the laugh he expected, fear swam over her face. "Honestly, Dooly? Deep down inside I am very frightened it might actually be Klell Ridgewall, because if it is, how do we stop him?"

* * * *

He discussed the matter with Heath during supper and finally decided to call in Dunmark Finley to hear what the man had to say. Gary phoned the metaphysical investigator from Carla's. Five minutes after they got to his office he showed up.

Gary rose from his desk and pointed to Heath, occupying the chair next to it. "This is Sergeant Heath Crow with the Texas Rangers, Mister Finley."

Finley shook Heath's extended hand. "You must be the man Sheriff Stoner thought I was when we met. It's a pleasure."

"Please have a seat," said Gary while crossing his arms, "and tell us what you think is happening on the Ridgewall Ranch."

Finley looked around.

"Use my chair, I'll stand."

"That's all right, Sheriff, I'll just stand too. Been on my ass in front of a computer all day in my motel room. All right then, to get to the point. I assume you're familiar with what happened to Klell Ridgewall's family way back when and the legend that stemmed from it."

"Mm hmm."

"How about you, Ranger Crow?"

"Yeah, the Sheriff filled me in."

Finley rubbed away an apparent itch under his nose and lowered his hand. "Contrary to what the two of you probably think, I don't believe in ghosts. There's no such thing."

Gary frowned. "You told me you saw Ridgewall seven times."

"Yeah, I know."

"Well did you, or didn't you?"

An insightful smirk rose on the metaphysical investigator's face, the kind of expression a teacher wears when about to surprise a student with an unexpected answer to a simple question. "Because of your reaction I used that term to keep from making you even more skeptical, but what I saw on those seven occasions was an apparition engineered by a demon. All genuine paranormal phenomena stem from one of two spiritual sources—the angelic or the demonic. No human spirit has ever returned to haunt anyone or anything after death, nor can it ever happen. When someone dies their spirit goes to one of two places and remains there, awaiting resurrection to heaven or hell. The ghost of Klell Ridgewall is a construction of mindless ectoplasm orchestrated by a fallen angel who obviously wasn't very high ranking when he chose to follow Lucifer in rebellion against The Almighty eons ago or his *light show*, if you will, would have more oomph.

"Recently some other demon possessing far greater power than that of our relatively harmless devil, has begun to wreck havoc in Tomahawk County for reasons presently unknown. And he'll continue this murderous rampage until he's spiritually bound from manifesting in the physical realm."

Heath exhaled a pungent sigh and rose to his feet. "I think we've heard enough."

Finley tightened his jaw. "I anticipated initial skepticism, but I'm the only one that can help you put an end to this. You're trained to deal with carnal evidence, not spiritual weaponry. Investigating this like you're looking for a human serial killer will leave you doing nothing but boxing at shadows. I'm not some eccentric crackpot who believes in spooks and UFOs, Ranger. I have two doctorates—one in theology, the other ancient history—which I earned at Oxford. I operate through an endowment from a scientific think tank that has over a billion dollars at its disposal, and the funding I've been allotted is large enough to afford me two full time assistants."

Gary squinted at him. "You don't talk like you're from England."

"I was born and raised in Raton, New Mexico. I got to Oxford via a Rhodes Scholarship."

"Very impressive credentials, Mister Finley," said Heath, stuffing his hands in his pockets, "but we don't think the devil's doing all this. However, we do think the killers want us to think the Ridgewall ghost is responsible. We know it's not just one person acting alone."

Finley heaved a sigh of resignation and turned to him. "All right, Sheriff, just don't say I didn't warn you. I didn't arrive at the conclusion I came to willy-nilly. I approached the first murders as if they'd been committed by human hands—even Angela Yang's—and only when I'd exhausted every other possibility did I come to see you. Everyone living on or near that ranch is in danger, and no one in Tomahawk County will be safe if this continues unhindered, not even the two of you. Demons don't play fair, gentlemen, and none of them ever display the tiniest drop of mercy. They're very limited as to what they can do in the physical realm except through a human agent, so someone on that ranch became inhabited by our killer, most likely becoming susceptible due to a grievously sinful way of life. When possessed by a demon, a man or woman can operate supernaturally."

Morbidly impressed, Gary couldn't help wondering if somebody in that ballroom might have slain Tillie and Lambert by superhuman means rather than merely sneaking the killers in and out through a large air conditioner vent, the only way anyone could have gotten in there since the doors were never left unguarded. All the silverware had been returned to the kitchen after supper and they'd have found any hidden weapons, having thoroughly searched the whole area. "Would you call running a whorehouse a grievously sinful way of life?"

Finley wrinkled his brow. "Was that what Carlson Loggins was doing?"

"Never mind that, answer my question."

"Well yeah, of course I would."

Gary cut his eyes to Heath. The expression on the ranger's face suggested their thoughts were jiving—Finley might be on to something. "Um, Mister Finley, if this is really what's happening, then exactly how does this process work—a demon possessing someone?"

"There are varying degrees to satanic manipulation," Finley informed with an erudite tone as if he was standing behind a lectern at a seminary assembly. "A demon first establishes a stronghold in a person's mind, the result of said person knowingly and deliberately persisting in sinful activity. That's why Satan and his minions tempt every member of the human race, to try to bring them under the devil's control. The tempting thoughts are what the Apostle Paul calls *darts* fired from the demon. When temptation is given into, that dart has hit the target, and many more will follow. Eventually, if the person doesn't repent, a spiritual stronghold is erected. Picture an arrow with a rope tied to it sticking in a man's head with a devil floating above holding the other end. This goes on all the time, but demons are clever, they make the man or woman think they're still committing the sin of their own free will. If the stronghold grows strong enough, the demon can enter that person.

"Though you didn't answer my question, I'm assuming Carlson Loggins was a pimp and the female victims were prostitutes. I asked around after the three hog farmers were killed and learned the sheriff before you operated a cathouse on that ranch, so the same hotbed of sin lies there as well. Using the legend of Klell Ridgewall seeking vengeance for the rape and decapitation of his wife and daughters, the demon has cut off the heads of every victim and left their bodies as if they died during some form of perverse sexual activity."

"Hold up a minute!" Shocked and angry, Gary took a step forward, glaring at the investigator. "How did you know about that? I only told the press the victims were decapitated, nothing more."

Apprehension flared in Finley's eyes. He looked as if he'd been left no recourse but to expose a friend's guilty secret. "Please don't blame him, Sheriff, but I got the information from the coroner. I've said nothing to anyone and have admonished my assistants to keep quiet as well."

A sense of betrayal wrenching his gut, Gary shook his head with disgust. Bob South knew he wanted to keep all that under wraps for the time being.

"I can see you're really upset so I need to give you the details, Sheriff. Because their heads were cut off like Ridgewall's women, I suspected the killer had also raped the female victims, being forced to do so by the demon. When the coroner told me none of them had been, I asked if the killer had left any form of sexual calling card. I knew by the look on his face when he told me no, that he was lying. So I bluffed and asked if Angela Yang appeared to be masturbating when she died. That caught him off guard and he asked who told me."

Heath shot Finley a harsh look of skepticism. "What prompted you to ask him that?"

"Because she was alone when she died. I couldn't see any other means for the killer to connect her death with illicit sexual activity."

Sucking in a heated breath, Gary brought a hand to his forehead, trying to reason everything out. His anger subsided but he still planned to give Bob a piece of his mind. Then again, Dunmark Finley might be lying about getting the medical examiner to blab. If so, one of the killers might be standing right in front of him. Determined to find out, he reached for the phone. "Excuse me, Mister Finley, I need to make a call."

A few minutes later he cradled the receiver. "Okay, your visit with the coroner checks out. You're obviously a very sharp individual, Mister Finley, but—"

"Sheriff, please don't patronize me. I'm on your side, believe me I am, and you need my help. And I'd appreciate it if you'd both quit calling me Mister Finley. My name is Dunmark."

Gary sniffed a gulp of air through his nose, irritated at being interrupted by the scholar. "Okay, Dunmark. As I was saying, you've obviously got a lot going for you upstairs, but what you're asking us to believe is really farfetched."

"I know it is, Sheriff Stoner."

"Gary."

Finley grinned. "I know it is, Gary."

"If this *is* the work of your demon, what do you suggest we do?"

"We need to find out who he's operating through and cast him out. If you'll look at Angela Yang's murder objectively, you'll see that what I'm saying isn't as farfetched as believing two or more homicidal maniacs followed her into the ladies room, managed to cut her head off, set up an intricate death scene, clean up the bloody mess, then themselves, and slip away unnoticed. Not to mention being able to perform the feat without being disturbed by any other female in that crowded restaurant needing to relieve herself."

* * * *

Gary stood beside Heath outside the open door, observing as Dunmark Finley made his way into the dayroom, preparing to speak. Ilian started clearing the table of disposable supper dishes furnished by Carla's. The only inmate not seated, Dorian leaned her shoulder against the toilet wall and ignited a cigarette.

Choosing a spot where everyone could see him, the investigator introduced himself. "Sheriff Stoner has given me permission to speak to you kind folks. I've invested the last ten years of my life investigating reported paranormal activity, and though ninety-five percent of the cases I've dealt with turned out to be either explainable by natural means or elaborate hoaxes, the Ridgewall Ranch phenomenon is the Real McCoy. However, the sword-waving confederate soldier so many residents of Tomahawk County have seen on the range disappearing at the stroke of midnight is not the spirit of Klell Ridgewall but the work of a demon . . . ."

FOURTEEN

Bolek Nowak highlighted a section of the message, copied it, then pressed *Alt* with his left thumb before toggling *Tab* with the pinkie of the same hand. The screen flashed to his word processor. He pasted the information, repeated the thumb-finger action to bring the email back, signed off, and returned to his electronic notes.

A lock of greasy blonde hair dropped over his right lens, smudging it. Swooping the offending strands back, Bolek removed his granny glasses, wiped away the smear, and repositioned the frame hooks behind his ears. "Ah, much better. So, my dear Dunmark, let us have a look at what you have learned, my friend."

Nadia Mars: Lived with the two females slain at a ranch called The Hog Farm. Squeamish when I asked if any of them had been having memory lapses or odd dreams of late. Wouldn't elaborate when I queried her, would only say she was born with a Gypsy curse of sometimes dreaming about bad things before they happen but is always powerless to prevent their occurrence. Sheriff told me she's a prostitute. Probable host for our demon but the jury's still out.

The two dead ranch hands are survived by four cowboys, none of whom strike me as suspicious. I think we can safely eliminate them.

Montella Pace: Served as madam for Carlson Loggins. She and the other women living on the Ridgewall Ranch, with the single exception of the maid, are all prostitutes, as were Loggins' six slain female employees. Highly unlikely any of them are possessed due to the fact they were sitting with the other diners when Angela Yang was killed at the restaurant.

However, two of them do stand out—a Jamaican named Nicole and a Cajun named Dorian. (Note: All these women are hot but Dorian is H.O.T. lol!)

Ilian Herrera: Stoner's deputized dispatcher. Told me she started having weird dreams around the time the murders started. She can't remember details, only that she keeps waking up to find she's still locked in a dream. Pure and sweet as apple pie, she's very sensitive and I believe the shock of the first murders rather than a demon is responsible for disturbing her sleep. It was the first homicide case Stoner and his entire staff have had to deal with.

All for now. Say hello to Lori for me, miss you guys!

Dunmark

Bolek scanned his notes written under the filename *Ridgewall* which preceded the section of Dunmark's email he'd pasted, hit *Save*, and rose from his desk. Lori had turned in for the night an hour ago. He walked over to the window and drew the blinds, hiding a breathtaking view of the Rocky Mountains bathed in moonlight. Dunmark had chosen to headquarter in Colorado Springs because his deceased grandmother had willed him her large split-level home, thus freeing up a large chunk of the money granted for constructing a building to house the research laboratory.

The phone rang.

"Yah?"

"Jest to, ze Bolek?"

"Ma, what are you doing up at this hour?"

"Vy you speaka de English to me, Bolek?"

Combing his hair back with his fingers, he made a sour face. It was almost dawn in Poland. "Przepraszam."

"*Apology accepted,"* she said in Polish. *"I called because I just woke up with an eerie premonition about Dunmark. Tell him* z dala od Ilian."

"Ilian?"

"Yes. I'm clueless why the name came to me, but Dunmark

will know. You will tell him, won't you, Bolek?"

"Obiecuje," he promised in his native tongue while crossing his fingers. He then told her goodbye and hung up the phone.

His mother was always having silly premonitions, and the so called wisdom supposed to accompany old age had only served to increase her superstitions. She'd never even met Dunmark Finley, why did she think he'd know what she meant?

Snickering at the woman's foolish panic attack, he headed for bed.

* * * *

Paralyzed with fear—the stark depths of which he'd never known could be experienced—dreadfully aware it wouldn't knowingly leave a living witness behind, Hank prayed the hideous entity wasn't aware its actions were being observed.

Trembling on the top bunk, he kept his eyes open only a crack, pretending to be asleep. He'd woken up needing to pee, and thank God he'd been sleeping on his side or he wouldn't have seen it the moment he opened his eyes. If he dared move a muscle the thing might notice and make him a part of the silent, ungodly commotion going down in the dayroom.

Silver flashed everywhere, a blade of light slicing off skin so fast it appeared to be vaporizing rather than actually cutting the flesh. One of eight hands, attached to snake-like arms extending from a blur of gray, held the knife. The other seven occupied themselves mopping up blood while arranging severed heads and mutilated bodies on the table after clasping the victims' mouths, preventing them from shrieking with pain and terror before death ended their agony. That area of the dayroom lay past the outer edge of dim light stemming from the ceiling. He couldn't tell who was being butchered, but from what little he could make out it appeared the horrifying creature had selected a man and two women.

The ghostly head never came into a discernable view during the whirlwind attack because the glowing weapon moved too rapidly to spotlight the silhouette. Hank's eyes flew all the way open involuntarily when the illumination ceased and something dropped to the floor next to the table where the decapitated bodies had been laid out. The momentum of the fall caused it to roll several feet towards him before coming to rest in an area better served by the low wattage light that kept total darkness at bay. A naked woman lay on her side with her back to him. He could see she had dark hair but the light was too dim to discern its texture or her complexion. She could have been black or white.

Suddenly the female began to vibrate on the concrete as if caught in the grip of an epileptic seizure. Heart pounding, he swallowed hard when the god awful being reappeared, engulfed the woman, and vanished, taking her with it.

Though terrified the thing might return, if he didn't get to the toilet immediately he'd have to spend the rest of the night on a wet mattress. Begging for the good Lord's protection, he climbed down the bunk and crossed the cell, keeping a wary eye on the dayroom as he relieved himself.

He glanced around. Dooley and Bobby Joe were accounted for, but he couldn't see well enough to tell whether Geraldo or Rico Mircanti remained in the next cell. Fearing one of them no longer did, he hurriedly climbed back in his bunk and pulled the blanket over his head with trembling fingers, praying that monster wouldn't come back for him—certain it would if even a whisper were to leave his lips.

* * * *

"Hell, send me to Huntsville and throw away the key if that's what you've gotta do but I'm not spending one more fucking night in your jail or anywhere else in Tomahawk County, Sheriff. I'm a law abiding man and I mean no disrespect, but you can't keep us here or we'll all wind up dead. It may not be Klell Ridgewall's ghost I saw, but whatever that goddamn killer is, it ain't human."

Gary rose from his chair, gritting his teeth—with hopelessness rather than anger—and wearily shook his head. "No need to apologize, Hank, I feel the same way."

Heath sat down at the desk and leaned towards the traumatized foreman, sitting a few feet away. "Funny how you could differentiate the victims' gender yet didn't recognize any of them."

Hank turned red with indignance. "I've got a lot of faults, Ranger Crow, but lying ain't one of them. I had no idea it was Rosemary, Selena, and Rico that fucking thing was slicing apart. It was all a blur and I couldn't see any colors but gray and silver. All I could tell was that two of them appeared to have tits and one didn't, and I wasn't even sure about that."

Gary feared he not only needed to evacuate the jail but the residents of Tomahawk County as well. Nadia's inability to recall being moved from her cell remained a mystery, but without question that silvery monster Hank saw last night had done it. Since it could not only pass through steel bars but somehow enabled its victims to as well, the thing appeared unstoppable. Dunmark Finley still called it a demon and felt the disappearing woman provided the human vessel the evil spirit needed to operate in the physical realm.

The only clue Hank could give about her identity was that she had dark hair. Three of the four females he currently held in custody fit that description: Nadia, Nicole, and Dorian. If none of them were the culprit, they were looking for a needle in a haystack because the majority of women residing in Tomahawk County were of Mexican descent.

He glanced at the metaphysical investigator, leaning against the wall with arms folded. "If that thing *is* a demon, how far away do I need to send the residents of this county to insure their safety?"

Dunmark cleared his throat. "If the inhabited woman gets evacuated too, even a trip to the moon will be futile."

"Yeah . . . that's what I figured." Gary started massaging his temples. "My gut says it's one of the women in this jail. What say you?"

"I'm inclined to agree with you."

Heath stood and turned towards Dunmark. "If you're right, don't we need a priest so he can perform an exorcism?"

The investigator lowered his arms and abandoned the wall. "It takes firm belief in Christ and a deep understanding of God's Word to cast out a demon—not reciting religious formalities, waving crosses, and sprinkling so called holy water. But it's too late for that anyway. A demon able to operate in the physical realm with this kind of power has its host under total lock and key. He hasn't wormed his way into her through a stronghold erected by the trickery of temptation. This bastard was invited in and she wants him to stay. We're dealing with a woman whose lust and self-centeredness puts Faust to shame."

Gary winced and dropped his hands. "Then what are we supposed to do, just shoot her?"

"Oh no, nothing like that. We have to convince her to renounce the demon by accepting Jesus Christ as her personal savior. When her dead spirit is quickened by the Holy Spirit, she'll want the devil to get out and we'll help her accomplish that."

He mulled that over and came to a conclusion. "The only safe bet is to move all three brunettes out of the county to some isolated place where there aren't any people before you try to convert whichever one of them it is."

Dunmark nodded. "May I suggest my research center in Colorado? I have specialized equipment that reads energy levels, sort of like a polygraph, that will most likely tell us who the host is. Once we determine that, we'll keep her sedated so the demon can't function through her as he's been doing. Then I'll try to get her to see the light."

"Is your place isolated?" asked Heath.

"Unfortunately no. It's located a few miles outside Colorado Springs in a country neighborhood. But the women need to be sedated while making the trip wherever you take them, so all we have to do is keep them that way until we locate our devil."

Gary picked up the phone. "I'll call the hospital and see about borrowing an ambulance. Hank, you and your boys are no longer suspects, you're free to go. I'll tell Tank to give your pistols back."

Character lines deepening with worry, the foreman eyed Dunmark. "You think it'll be safe for us to go back to work?"

"I think so. It's very unlikely the demon isn't residing inside one of the women in custody."

A sudden realization stabbed Gary like a knife and he hung up the phone before anyone at the hospital had time to answer. "That demon's not working through just one of them."

Dunmark furrowed his brow. "What makes you say that?"

"Hank said what he witnessed last night was over in a matter of seconds. That means Nicole Anderson could have killed Angela Yang instead of finding her already slain in the ladies room as she claims, the demon seeing to it she didn't get any blood on her so no one would suspect she did it. Montella was alone when she found Loggins and Sonya, so she could have done them in. Nadia can't remember being moved from her cell because the demon was operating through her to butcher Erma and Sally. Any of them could have taken down the butler and Tillie, and since they have black hair it was either Nadia or Nicole—possibly even Dorian the demon worked through last night."

Heath whistled through his teeth, a demoralized scowl clutching his face. "Oh hell, Gary, that makes sense."

"No it doesn't," said Dunmark. "Demons can't just hop from person to person and possess them at will."

"Apparently this one can. I'm convinced Gary's right because it not only explains why Nadia Mars can't remember being moved from her cell but also why she was spared."

Hank let out a sarcastic laugh and started scratching the back of his neck. "That thing looked like it can pretty much do anything it wants, I doubt it needs *anybody* to work through. It wouldn't surprise me none to find out it's an alien from outer space."

Dunmark donned a knowing look. "A lot of UFO sightings are the work of Satan, trying to deceive people into believing man is merely an evolutionary byproduct rather than God's creation. The devil can take on many forms."

"Well if he can look any scarier than what I saw last night, I hope to God I never see it."

Gary called the district attorney and waited with bated breath for Pete's secretary to connect them.

"Hope you've got something good for me this time, Gary."

"Pete, if you're not sitting down, you'd better. Bob South just hauled away three bodies from the jailhouse and . . . well there's no easy way to say this. The foreman of the Ridgewall Ranch saw them being slaughtered in the dayroom. It's not a team of serial killers like I thought. There's only one perpetrator and it's some type of supernatural creature . . . ."

* * * *

Lori Boon had been raised by ivy league parents in Rhode Island. The youngest of three girls, she'd always wanted a brother and now felt she had two—Dunmark and Bolek. She admired Dunmark's relentless dedication and ability to rough it for long periods of time, sometimes having to sleep in a tent and eat campfire food for days on end when trying to verify a sighting in a wilderness area. Unlike Bolek, who'd migrated from Poland to assist him ten months before she joined the team, she always felt guilty residing in the comfort of the research center during those periods.

Dunmark had lived on pennies while conducting his investigations solo until eight years ago when he'd finally received the financing he'd asked for. She'd met him and Bolek at a seminar in New York. Bored with her job, she'd jumped at the chance to become a Ghost Buster, as Dunmark had jokingly put it, even though he couldn't match the salary she made then. However, residing in this lovely home rent-free and not having to spend any money on groceries had actually worked out to a raise when considering income retained after necessities. Dunmark and Bolek completed their education at Oxford, where they'd become friends. She'd graduated from Brown with a master's degree in computer science, and during her college years had taken enough online medical courses to earn an associate's in applied science.

Wearing a helmet containing a hairnet of strategically placed sensors, she calibrated the readout levels of the customized electroencephalograph so they matched those on the computer monitor. Adjustments complete, she removed the headgear, set the equipment to standby, and went upstairs.

Seated at his desk in the living room, Bolek swirled around to face her—his thin pock-marked face looking studious as usual. "Dunmark says we can expect their arrival by ten o'clock."

"Central or mountain time?"

His lips formed a flat line. "Dammit, I forgot to ask."

A glance at her watch revealed the time to be eight fifty-two p.m. "Well they'll either be here in a few minutes or a little over an hour from now."

"It was fortuitous Dunmark was familiar with the Ridgewall ghost from years ago, yah? Otherwise he wouldn't have feared possible demonic activity when we saw that news piece on TV covering the first murders."

She nodded. "He told me he spent that whole summer

camped out on the Mexico side of the Rio Grande in that area, eating mostly pork and beans."

Bolek leaned back and fastened his hands to the back of his head. "Yah, he had to do that because the owner of the Ridgewall Ranch wouldn't give him permission to enter. He refused to leave until fully satisfied the manifestation was benign, so he each night he'd lay his bicycle in a raft and cross the water. With only the bicycle's headlight and a flashlight to see by, he'd peddle to a ridge where the sightings were most commonly reported."

"This is the most dangerous case we've ever been involved in, Bolek . . ." she lifted her glasses and soothed an itch on the bridge of her nose. "I'm trying not to let myself get scared."

"Me too, Lori."

* * * *

Gary helped Dunmark maneuver four gurneys into a big house the investigator called his research center. Each carried a sleeping beauty whose character could hardly be mistaken for that of Snow White's. Although he couldn't pinpoint a specific instance were Dorian had the opportunity to be used by the demon like Nicole, Montella, and Nadia, her black hair left the possibility she'd been the woman Hank saw.

Heath stayed behind to assist Tank and Alfredo in case the demon hadn't been transported out of Tomahawk County after all.

The cowpunchers had been taken back to the Ridgewall Ranch to resume their lives. Montella still didn't know she'd inherited Carlson Loggins' entire estate, but Hank Best did. Gary had informed him when he'd asked who he needed to talk to about keeping his job.

"I can't speak for Montella," he'd told the foreman, "but my guess is she'll keep you guys on the payroll until if and when she decides to sell the place."

Dunmark had phoned ahead to have his assistants move the furniture around in a downstairs den to make room for the gurneys. One of them appeared after the last prostitute had been carted in—a tall thin blonde man, whose brows rose high above his spectacles when he saw the girls.

"You did not exaggerate, Dunmark. These women *are* beautiful. You must be Sheriff Stoner."

Gary nodded.

"Pleased to make your acquaintance, Bolek Nowak at your service." He gestured with a slight bow as they shook hands.

An attractive woman strolled through the door. Well built on a slender scale, she had brown hair, pretty green eyes behind horn-rim glasses, and looked to be about his age, as did Bolek.

He introduced himself.

"Pleased to meet you, Gary. I'm Lori Boon."

"Which is which?" asked Bolek, eyeing the prostrate sleepers.

Dunmark started pointing. "The blonde is Montella, that's Nicole, the one over there is Nadia, and the one you keep cutting your eyes back to is Dorian."

Bolek covered his mouth to muffle a cough, then lowered his hand to reveal a grin of embarrassment. "It's hard to imagine any of them housing an evil spirit."

"They'll be coming to about four a.m., then you can give them the tranquilizer and we'll start the examinations," said Dunmark, who'd injected the women twice already—once in lockup, a second time at Santa Rosa, New Mexico.

Lori turned to her associate. "As always Dunmark arrived exactly when he said he would."

"And it was mountain time after all," said Bolek, still admiring Dorian. "I wonder what her rates are? Much more than I could afford, I'm sure. Um, not that I would ever make such an immoral proposition of course."

"Of course not," teased Dunmark.

Bolek heaved a sigh. "The name Dorian certainly fits her, does it not?"

"I can hear you," mumbled the Cajun hick. "Been pretending to be asleep for a good while."

Dunmark dropped his jaw. "That's impossible!"

Thick black lashes slowly parted as two deep-blue eyes struggled to focus. "The hell it is, dickhead. I'm awake ain't I?"

The surprise on Dunmark's face shifted to wariness as he looked his way. "She shouldn't have regained any degree of consciousness for at least six hours, Gary."

He motioned for the investigator to follow him. Once outside the room, he closed the door so Dorian couldn't hear. "Montella told me Dorian has a very unique metabolism. She eats and drinks enough for several people yet never gains weight, has been a heavy smoker since she was seven but never coughs, and hasn't aged at all in the ten years Montella's known her. Whatever enzyme or gene she has that keeps her body in perfect shape despite her abusing it, must have burned off the sedative."

Dunmark eyed him for a thoughtful moment. "So you don't suspect as I do, the demon is hiding inside her?"

"I'm not saying he isn't, just that her waking up so soon can be explained by her odd body chemistry, that's all."

"Let me explain something, Gary. When a person is demonized they can defy physical laws to a degree, such as walk on hot coals and not burn the soles of their feet, cut themselves without bleeding, levitate and such. She very likely owes her marvelous metabolism to a satanic agent. Though I've agreed to go along with your theory that the demon is working through different women, I still don't buy into it. I'm pretty satisfied Dorian is its host. The demon must have given the illusion she was still sitting with everyone else in that restaurant while in actuality she was hacking up Angela Yang, and did likewise in the billiard room while killing Carlson Loggins and Sonya Bain."

That struck a new chord of fear in him. "A demon can do that?"

"I hadn't considered that possibility until now, but it's certainly feasible. We'll start testing her immediately . . . ."

FIFTEEN

Hank bit into a baloney and cheese sandwich. The boys didn't much appreciate his efforts but since none of them knew how to cook much of anything more elaborate than bacon and eggs, which Geraldo had volunteered to make for tomorrow's breakfast, frying up a batch of baloney had been the best he could do. They were eating supper hours later than usual, due to spelling each other walking a bloated mare in circles so she wouldn't fall to the ground and twist her intestines into knots by kicking and rolling from the pain of sand colic. She'd finally farted it all out and her belly had deflated back to normal by ten-thirty. He could have delegated the chore to one hand but felt everybody, himself included, needed a little extra tiring out so they'd be able to fall asleep when hitting the hay instead of lying awake for hours worrying that Dunmark Finley might be mistaken and the ghastly creature hadn't been carted out of Tomahawk County after all.

"I don't want sandwiches for supper every night," bitched Bobby Joe, chewing a mouthful of potato chips. "Guess we'd better stock up on microwave dinners."

"Go right on ahead if you wanna pay for 'em out of your own pocket." Hank washed the bite down with coffee. "Until everything gets sorted out, Munchie's kitchen fund has got to be used sparingly. We may be working for free for all we know."

"How much is left in the cookie jar?"

"Not enough to eat steak every night, that's for sure."

"Aw come on, Hank, tell me."

"That's for me to know and you to find out."

Bobby Joe vacated his chair, went to the cabinet, and pulled the head off a ceramic naked lady Munchie had used to stash the grub money. "Hell it's empty."

"Mm hmm." Hank reduced his sandwich by another hefty chunk and chewed with the corners of his lips turned up.

"Why don't we butcher a steer, Hank?"

The grin vanished upon hearing his new ramrod's question. "We ain't thieves, Geraldo. That cattle belongs to Montella Pace, not us."

"Montella Pace?"

"Yeah. Sheriff Stoner told me this morning that Loggins left everything to her in his will, only she don't know it yet. He figures she'll keep us on after she finds out. Me, I figure she'll probably sell the place."

"Hell, Hank, I'll buy tomorrow's supper. Didn't know tonight's was on you."

He glanced at Dooly, who'd made the offer. A mass of thick brown bangs were plastered to his forehead as if still being pressed against it by the sweatband of his Stetson. "Busy day tomorrow, you won't have time to make a trip to town. Besides, it wasn't. I moved Munchie's stash."

"Why?"

"In case any of them patrolmen had sticky fingers. I wasn't worried about Lawrence Kerns, but I caught one of the others nosing around the bunkhouse like he was looking for something. Figured better safe than sorry."

Bobby Joe sat back down and grabbed his sandwich. "Where'd you move it to?"

"That's for me to know and you to find out."

"Not to change the subject," said Geraldo, "but what do you think that thing was you saw last night, Hank?"

The Mexican wore a questioning look that stemmed from curiosity or doubt, he couldn't tell which. "Dunmark Finley says it's a demon that hides inside one of the women that were locked up with us. If that ain't what it is, then I figure the thing came from outer space because it's damn sure not of this world."

"You sure you didn't dream it?"

That ticked him off and he shot Geraldo an angry scowl to show it. "You questioning my word, boy?"

"No, Hank, not at all. But since you slept on the bunk closest to the dayroom, I'm just wondering if maybe you heard the murders taking place in your sleep and your mind supplied such vivid images to match the sounds, you didn't know you were dreaming."

Seeing he wasn't being called a liar, Hank relaxed, shoved the last of his sandwich in his mouth, and set the record straight. "The sound of those murders couldn't have influenced my subconscious mind even if I *had* been asleep. That son-of-a-bitch managed to kill them without making any noise. I woke up because I needed to pee. If I hadn't been laying on my side and able to see it as soon as my eyes opened, there ain't a doubt in my mind I wouldn't be sitting here in the bunkhouse with you boys tonight. I'd be down in the morgue with those poor souls."

Bobby Joe sucked down some red soda pop and lowered the bottle, leaving a crimson circle centered on his fat lips. He looked like he'd just been kissed by a lipstick-coated mouth half the size of his own. "Man am I glad I didn't see it."

Dooly somberly nodded. "We're all four lucky to be alive."

"That we are, amigo." Melancholia swathed Geraldo's lean face the moment he said it. Tears sparkled in his eyes but none were falling. "I only wish my poor Sonya could say the same. We had such plans, she and I. She only pretended to be a whore like the others so she could bring Loggins to justice. I'll never find another like her. I'm doomed to a life without love."

Hank slathered mayonnaise on a slice of white bread and reached across the table to peel a circle of seared baloney from the stack. "You'll meet someone that'll make you feel different, hombre."

"No, Hank. I'll spend the rest of my life as a lonely cowboy like you."

"Yeah, married to his horse," snickered Bobby Joe.

Taking the jab with good humor, he grinned while topping the baloney with cheese and the other piece of bread. "Well she ain't won an argument with me yet, and never claims to have a headache when I wanna mount her."

The boys all laughed and he went to work on his second sandwich. Dooly and Geraldo turned in before he finished. Bobby Joe said goodnight while he was putting a third one together.

Hank watched him step into the hall, and turned back towards the table, mind awash with nagging doubts about what Montella would have planned for the ranch once she learned it was hers. Silence filled the house after he heard Bobby Joe's bedroom door close.

But only for a couple of minutes.

The hairs on the back of his neck stood on end as the angry screech of a bird of prey roared inside his head and a putrefied stench assaulted his nose. Fear rippled through his innards like a thousand squiggling centipedes, borne from an eerie comprehension that forced its way into the core of his being—mysteriously and ominously assuring him that he alone was meant to discern the reek of death and the evil wail.

Lunging to his feet, he turned to run but didn't manage a step.

Even if he hadn't been paralyzed by fright his numb legs couldn't carry him to safety. Mere inches away a glowing silver blade twirled in front of a hideous eagle-like face with searing yellow eyes and a sharp beak hungrily gaping to receive sustenance. Scaly claws manipulated the saber, and seven other deadly tentacles snaked out from a grotesque mass of gray shaped somewhat like a man-size bird. Hank's nostrils painfully collapsed between icy talons extending from a bony palm that gripped his mouth, forcing it to remain closed, locking a terrified scream within his lungs.

* * * *

Nadia couldn't believe Gary Stoner thought her capable of murder, and it hurt deeply that he did. He hadn't voiced it, but she couldn't fathom any other reason for her and the other three women being kept in confinement after the cowboys had been released. She assumed they'd been sedated so they wouldn't be able to tell where they'd been taken, but had no idea why they'd been moved from the jailhouse. The whole affair completely baffled her.

She glanced around and saw Montella rolling her head from side to side, starting to regain consciousness. Nicole was awake and groggily staring at the ceiling. Like her, they'd been strapped to a gurney. She couldn't locate Dorian.

A blonde man wearing a white lab coat walked in. "Ah, you are waking, that is good . . ." he pulled a hypodermic from a pocket of his lab coat and looked down at her through a pair of round glasses that glistened brightly beneath his oily forehead. "It's time to receive more medication. This will only relax you rather than put you to sleep."

"W-What are you doing?" Her voice sounded raspy. "Leave me alone."

"Not to worry, I'm Dunmark's assistant. Sheriff Stoner is here and we are assisting him. Please remain calm."

Hearing Gary was there helped to settle her nerves somewhat but did nothing to alleviate her confusion. "Where are we?"

"Colorado Springs."

"Why?"

"All in good time, mustn't worry about that now. I'll do you first, Nadia."

"How did you know my name?"

"Dunmark told me . . ." he slid the needle into her forearm

and seconds later she felt absolutely marvelous.

* * * *

Dooly slapped the top of his alarm clock and the nerve-jarring bell stopped ringing. Grateful to wake up in his own bed again, he yawned and stretched before gingerly climbing out of it. He ambled down the hall in his underwear, went into the big bathroom they all shared, and pulled his toothbrush from a holder mounted beneath a medicine cabinet with *Dew* inserted in the name slot.

"Is that you, Hank?" The voice belonged to Geraldo.

He turned to see a pair of bare feet resting on the floor of the only stall with the door closed. The Mexican ramrod was taking a morning dump. "No, it's me Dooly."

"Oh, good morning."

"Back atcha." He ran water over the bristles, squeezed toothpaste over them, and commenced brushing. The sound of a toilet flushing filled his ears by the time he began rinsing his mouth.

Geraldo, also in skivvies, began his morning ritual two mirrors away. A moment later Bobby Joe walked in naked, his long pecker swaying like a pendulum between his skinny legs.

It was the only thing about his homely friend Dooly envied.

Geraldo spat out a last mouthful of rinse water and daubed his lips with a towel. "Guess I'd better put on some clothes and get the bacon frying, eh, amigos."

"You'd better," said Dooly with a grin while heading for the door. He went back to his room, slipped into his duds, and made for the kitchen. When he got there he almost shit in his pants.

Hank's clothing had been neatly folded and stashed in one side of the double sink. His boots occupied the other basin. From inside a big cast iron skillet used to fry their baloney last night, the foreman's unseeing eyes were staring at the vent-hood above the stove. His body had been propped up against the cabinet in a sitting position with his naked butt on the floor. A mass of bloody goo, no longer flowing, streamed from a gory wound where once his gonads had been attached. The killer had wedged Hank's dick between his feet, making it appear he'd been using them to jack off.

SIXTEEN

They were an hour away from the Tomahawk County line. Gary had only managed a glorified nap between the conclusion of Dorian's testing and the start of the other women's, but the call he'd received at eight a.m.—nine Texas time—had driven away any trace of grogginess.

Hank Best had been decapitated and neutered.

Bolek and Lori would be driving to Tomahawk tomorrow, bringing some equipment with them to test the surviving ranch hands. Everyone needed a good night's rest before resuming the search for the murdering demon. It seemed unlikely Hank could have been mistaken about the dark-haired person being a woman, but he'd only seen the backside. The three remaining cowboys all wore their hair long—Geraldo's was black, Dooly's and Bobby Joe's dark brown—so they needed to be eliminated.

He drove the borrowed ambulance while Dunmark rode in back, keeping an eye on three slumbering hookers to alert him should any of them try to bail when they woke up. They weren't sedated, just exhausted, especially Dorian. Certain the demon resided within the Cajun hick, Dunmark had ran her through the battery of tests twice before finally acquiescing to the fact she was apparently possessed by an amazing metabolism rather than a devil. The other prostitutes had tested negative as well. Having gotten her nap out by the time he'd made a pit stop near the Texas-New Mexico border, Montella had begged to ride up front with him. Tired of having no one to talk to, he'd granted her request. She'd been trying to convince him not to charge any of them for blackmail and prostitution.

"Outside of your deputies and Ranger Crow, no other law enforcement agency knows. I've already notified all of Carl's clients we've gone out of business, and I'll inform all his victims they no longer have to fear exposure, I give you my word, Gary."

She'd never called him by his first name before and he guessed she mistakenly thought that would help her case. "Suppose I do that, and convince Heath not to say anything, what sort of legitimate occupation would you pursue?"

Still unaware she'd inherited Loggins' fortune, Montella turned her pretty head towards him and smiled. "You'll laugh when I tell you."

"Yeah? Well tell me and let's see."

"My goal is to become Mrs. Gary Stoner. Whether you send me to jail or not, I'm setting my cap for you, Sheriff."

Laugh he did. "Stop trying to hustle me, Montella."

"I'm not, I swear."

"What about being hooked on the thrill of the hunt and all that?"

Her breasts swelled with a deep breath. "I'm sick of living a secret life and disgusted at being a whore. I want my parents to be legitimately proud of me. I thought I'd found my dream man when I met Carl, but after you started to grow on me I realized he was nothing but a sweet-talking sex machine. You've shown me there's so much more to being a man than merely being great in the sack."

"Sure I have," he mocked, focusing on the road. "Sorry, you're out of luck."

"You can't overlook my past and give me a second chance, is that it?"

"Nope, everybody deserves a second chance."

"Why then?"

"I don't go for older women."

That prompted a dry laugh. "I'm only eight years older, Gary, and it's actually closer to seven since I only recently turned thirty-eight and you'll soon be thirty-one. It's not like I'm old enough to be your mother. I want to become a respectable lady and I know you can turn me into one."

"It's not gonna happen, Montella."

She shifted in the seat to face him. "Please tell me why. I know it's not really because of my age."

"You're too sophisticated for a guy like me."

"No I'm not."

"The hell you're not," he countered with a chuckle. "You and I wouldn't mix any better than oil and water."

"Dammit, Gary, I want to start a new life and I want to do it with you. Of course I'll probably have to spend some time in jail first since you're unwilling to help me avoid it."

Having no reason to keep it from her anymore, he decided to tell the madam a new life did await her, though it wouldn't include him. "I'll do everything I can to get you leniency like I told you. But even if you do have to do time, you can choose to live however and wherever you want when you're free again. Now that I know you're not connected to the murders I can tell you that I was only feeling you out about whether or not Loggins' left a will. You're his sole beneficiary. Congratulations."

That didn't seem to surprise her, the disappointment on her face lingered.

"Did you hear what I just said?"

"Mm hmm. I suspected you'd found a will by the way you kept quizzing me about it that night at your house, and knew if you had I'd been set up for life, otherwise Carl would have told me about it." Her brooding pout suddenly turned into an enthusiastic smile. "You could share it with me, Gary."

"Watch out, you're tempting now," he teased with a wink.

"I mean it. I took care of Carl's finances, none of his money in American banks can be garnished for back taxes because he never defrauded the IRS, except for what he listed as his occupation of course. All his tax shelters are legitimate enterprises and he has over fifty million in an account in the Cayman Islands that's untouchable."

He swerved to the other lane and passed a tanker truck. "You can talk till you're blue in the face but it won't change things. We're from two different worlds, and by that I don't mean what you did for Loggins. I'm a laidback country boy, satisfied with the simple pleasures in life, and you're a chic socialite."

Undaunted, she quickly said, "I'll give you the Ridgewall Ranch as a wedding present, mansion and all."

That stunned him. Montella made the offer like she knew he'd always wanted to be a cattleman, a dream he'd never told anyone in Tomahawk County.

He'd lived in the same house from birth until he got through seventh grade. Located in the country at the end of a row of identical houses provided for the employees of a small refinery that produced butane, it sat next to a small ranch owned by a middle-aged childless couple named Fred and Edith. They'd doted on him and his younger brother as if they were the kids they never had. Fred had patiently let them help with chores and they'd learned how to milk cows, make butter, castrate pigs, render lard, and skin goats before either could read. He'd later taught them how to ride a cutting horse to cull a cow from the herd, and the proper way to rope a calf. The joys of working with livestock had filled him and his younger brother with aspirations of becoming fulltime ranchers when they grew up.

A big oil company bought the refinery, offered his dad a better job, and they'd moved away from the plant. They never left Texas but his father's new position required them to relocate several times after that. Gary spent every summer on one ranch or another working for next to nothing in order to gain the knowledge and experience needed to one day manage his own. But harsh reality had set in by the time he finished high school. Lacking the means or credit to buy enough land and cattle to make a living, he gave up cow-punching, earned an associate degree in criminal justice at a junior college, and went into law enforcement.

But the dream had never died.

"Ah, you're thinking that over, I can tell." Montella's refined visage beamed with exhilaration. "What do you say, Sheriff? I'll make you a good wife and I'm still young enough to have kids if you want them. I promise I'll never cheat on you. I wouldn't have slept with anyone other than Carl if he hadn't made me do it for business reasons."

He eyed the road in silence, afraid to allow the conversation to continue for fear he'd give in to temptation. Besides the fact he'd love to own the Ridgewall Ranch, Montella was a beautiful woman, not some well-to-do wreck who had to hire a gigolo to satisfy her sexual needs.

The tempting blonde kept talking, sounding more confident by the moment.

* * * *

Bolek and Lori pulled up in a van around five p.m. Dunmark introduced his two assistants to Heath, Tank, and Ilian. Gary detected a distinct twinkle behind Lori's glasses when she shook hands with the ranger.

With the testing apparatus set up in the dayroom—Montella, Nadia, Nicole, and Dorian looking on from their cell—Dunmark asked for one of the cowpunchers to be brought in. Tank went to the drunk tank where the cowboys were being held, and returned with Geraldo. Lori beckoned him to take a seat, placed a helmet with electrical cables attached to it on his head, and strapped him to the specialized chair. Bolek administered a tranquilizer, and she began questioning the Mexican.

"Geraldo, I'm going to name a numerical sequence and ask you to continue it. Are you ready?"

He nodded.

"One, two, three, four, five, six. Which two numbers come next?"

"Seven, eight," said the relaxed ramrod slowly.

"Good. A, B, D, E, F, G as in God. Which letter of the alphabet did I leave out?"

"C."

Checking waveforms on a computer screen, she wrote on her clipboard and turned back to him. "Incorrect."

Geraldo frowned. "But you left off C, I'm certain."

"I did leave off the C as in Christ, but I also left off all the letters after G, didn't I?"

"Ah . . ." he grinned.

"But I have just lied, have I not, Geraldo?"

"Huh?"

"Your first answer was indeed correct because I asked which *letter* I left out—singular—not the plural *letters*. Does it trouble you that I lied?"

"Um no, not really."

She made another notation. "The entire New Testament is a compilation of letters, commonly referred to as epistles. Do you believe in God?"

"Oh yes, very much so."

"And Jesus?"

"Si, senorita," he proudly affirmed.

"Do you believe in the deity of Jesus Christ?"

"Absolutely."

"How about Satan, do you believe he exists?"

"Yes."

"Do you worship him?"

"Oh no, a thousand times no."

Lori set the clipboard on the dayroom table and crossed her arms, causing the lapels of her lab coat to part, revealing her breasts were straining against a green t-shirt and he'd underestimated their size. "Another sequence, if you please.

Ten, nine, eight. Which number comes next, Geraldo?"

"Seven."

"Does that number trouble you?"

The helmet moved back and forth.

"Answer verbally, please."

"No."

"How about the number six? Do you have any special feelings about it?"

"Um, no."

"How about six-six-six?"

He frowned again. "That's the mark of the beast."

"Very good. Are you aware that one, three, seven, ten, and twelve are Godly numbers?"

"No."

"Does it trouble you that they are?"

"No."

"Do you agree that justice calls for Satan to be cast into hell and bound forever—that he's a liar and the father thereof, a despicable, loathsome, ugly, vile creature, capable of nothing but evil . . .?"

Gary stood beside Ilian, listening as Lori continued quizzing Geraldo about the devil. The dispatcher seemed perturbed. He put his lips to her ear and whispered, "Is something wrong?"

She shook her head, but the troubled look in her eyes contradicted the negative answer.

"Everything okay at home?"

Instead of answering him she shouted, "Shut the fuck up, gringo bitch! It's God that should burn in hell forever!"

Startled, Lori turned towards Ilian while Dunmark and Bolek started running their direction, alarm tattooed on all three faces.

"Hurry, Bolek!" shouted the investigator.

Bolek hastily pulled a rubber-tipped bottle and a hypodermic from his lab coat as Dunmark yanked Ilian's wrists behind her back. "Help me, Gary, the demon's about to manifest!"

English curses and threats giving way to liquid Spanish, Ilian wriggled her right arm from the investigator's grasp. Though totally confused, Gary immediately grabbed it with both hands. She grew rapidly stronger so he hollered for Heath to help Dunmark, and Tank to take his place so he could wrap up her body.

The second Tank relieved him Gary leaned over and locked his arms around Ilian's waist, holding on for dear life, but she still would have broke free if Bolek hadn't stabbed her thigh and pressed the syringe plunger.

She collapsed over his left shoulder.

Holding the back of her knees, Gary straightened his posture slowly so she wouldn't slip off and crack her skull on the cement floor. "Open one of the cells, Tank!"

The baffled deputy hurried from the dayroom and returned with the keys. Heart pounding, mind reeling, Gary gently laid Ilian on a bottom bunk in the cell Rico Mircanti had occupied his last night on earth.

"My instincts failed me, Gary," said Dunmark, features ablaze with self-recrimination. "I just didn't think it could be her despite the fact she told me she's been having weird dreams since the murders started. When a demon operates through someone, that person's mind becomes overwhelmed in an effort to rationalize the manifestation. Usually the result is either a memory blackout or strange dreams. That foreman lost his life because of my incompetence."

"Oh, Dunmark, it is I who am the incompetent!" spouted Bolek, hammering the sides of his head with the pinkie side of closed fists, almost vibrating the wire frames off his pointy nose. "I had just read your email about that very thing when my mother called to tell me to warn you about someone named Ilian. 'Tell him to stay away from Ilian,' that's what she said. It should have rang a bell but I laughed off her premonition. I too have cost the life of that cowboy and shall never be able to forgive myself."

Still breathing hard, Gary shifted his gaze from the self-punishing assistant to Dunmark. "Ilian's the host, you're sure of it?"

He firmed his lips and nodded.

Hands now pressed against, rather than pounding it, Bolek bobbed his head up and down as well.

"How? She's a very moral, religious girl. I've never even heard her cuss before now."

Dunmark shrugged. "Who knows? She may have dabbled with the occult such as witchcraft, tarot cards, Ouija boards—consulted a fortune teller or psychic medium. Somehow she opened herself up to a devious spirit from hell."

"But she's nothing like the person you told me the host had to be—full of lust, extremely self-centered. She's none of those things."

Bolek exhaled a woeful sigh and finally lowered his hands. "On the surface perhaps, but you cannot know what goes on inside a person's mind, my friend."

Tank eyeballed the ceiling and groaned. "This is going to kill Alfredo."

"Mm hmm," Gary sadly agreed, glad the young Mexican was making his rounds. Seeing Ilian's insane outburst would have devastated him. "Let's hold off telling him as long as we can."

"We've got to move her anyway, Gary," said Heath. "We can buy some time if we do it before Alfredo gets back."

"Why do we have to move her?"

"The border patrol's bringing in a truckload of wetbacks. I took the call just before Dunmark's assistants arrived, and got sidetracked. Sorry I forgot to tell you."

"What about moving her to the Ridgewall mansion?" suggested Dunmark. "It could take days to liberate Ilian, maybe weeks. We might as well be comfortable."

Gary crossed the dayroom with Bolek at his heels, and approached the prostitutes' cell. The women had witnessed everything and all four were on edge. "Did you hear what Dunmark said, Montella?"

"Uh huh."

"It's your house now. Do you mind?"

A sexy smile blossomed. "It could easily be yours."

He winced. "Montella, please. Do you mind or not?"

"Take us with you?"

"Too dangerous."

Dorian grabbed the bars. "Lock us up in our bedrooms for all I care but please let us go home. Now that we know who the killer is, we can all finally get a good night's sleep."

Bolek put a hand on his shoulder. "We'll keep Ilian sedated. You can let them come with us. Besides, they can make themselves useful by cooking for us. Lori and I would welcome such a break from taking turns preparing meals."

"Excuse me . . .?" Dorian leered at him, the anger zooming from her blue orbs more intimidating than a charging wolf's. "Who died and made you boss, geek boy? You can't tell us what to do."

A heated blush flooded Bolek's pock-marked face. "Uh, I am not geek boy, my name is—"

"I know what the fuck yer name is, dickhead."

"That tears it!" snapped Gary, giving the Cajun bitch a threatening look of his own. "You're staying in jail, shit mouth."

She batted her eyes, exaggerating each flap of her long lashes. "Why Sheriff Stoner, you look so hunky when you're pissed. I'll behave, promise. I won't call Bolek no more names. Hell, I'll even cook fer ya. I make a mean-ass pot roast."

"Dorian goes with us or the mansion's off limits to everybody," stated Montella firmly, arms folded under her breasts, pulling the silky texture of her blouse beguilingly taut against the large mounds.

He tossed her a derisive smirk and turned to Bolek. "We'll take Ilian to my house. I'm sure these girls will love having a bunch of horny wetbacks whistling at them and making catcalls all night long."

Almost in perfect unison, four glamorous ladies of the night desperately pleaded with him to reconsider.

* * * *

Nadia had almost wept with relief when Gary finally relented after Dorian kept profusely apologizing as they all begged to be taken back to Montella's newly acquired mansion. The thought of spending a sleepless night in jail because of being harassed by a group of unknown men had been unbearable.

If she hadn't botched the blackmailing gig in Las Vegas Carlson might have mentioned her in his will since during her time with him she'd been second only to Montella as his favorite piece of ass. Now Montella had it all, so her fascination with The Francesco Brothers had not only caused her to lose the best job any hooker could hope for, but possibly a substantial portion of her former pimp's fortune as well.

Carlson had never mentioned any family so it hadn't come as too much of a surprise to hear he'd left everything to Montella, but she'd been thoroughly shocked to learn the murders had been committed by Ilian. She feared the Mexican sweetie must be the central character in her recurring dream. The nightmares had begun the same night Carlson's first three whores were slain. As they'd continued troubling her nights and more victims were being found in the daylight, she'd concluded the clairvoyant talent she despised had risen from a long period of dormancy to torment her once again.

The dream never deviated. A white dove gracefully coasted through a blue sky, occasionally flapping its wings to maintain altitude. Then an explosion of red startled her, and bloody feathers dithered earthward towards the mortified face of a little dark-haired girl gazing skyward, weeping as bits of mutilated bird rained upon her. When the remnants finally quit falling she looked down at the splatters, screaming in sorrow-filled rage, swearing she'd inflict the same fate on the ones who'd felled the dove.

A tall dark creature, somewhat resembling a locust, came up from behind the child and enfolded her within two blackish transparent wings, transforming her into a slimy gelatinous mass. Then a blinding flash of light engulfed the whole scene. When it dissipated, a naked woman the girl had grown up to be, stood atop a mound of bloody human body parts. Nadia could never make out the female's mature face before waking up terrified.

She glanced at Montella, sitting on a divan in the billiard room where they'd been told to stay. The new heiress had sounded serious about offering to share her mansion with Gary, but it could have been a bribe to persuade him not to press charges rather than true affection for the lawman. Wanting to know but afraid of the answer, she decided not to ask. Instead she turned her attention to Dorian and Nicole, playing pool. "Who's winning?"

"Nobody, we're just goofin' off tradin' break shots," said Dorian, an unlit Camel dangling from her lips. Montella wouldn't permit her to smoke it indoors.

"What do you think they're doing?"

"What, the sheriff and them? Casting out demons, I reckon." Dorian chalked the tip of her pool cue. "So who's manning the stove tonight?"

"Not me," declared Nicole, preparing to shoot.

Montella smiled. "I'll do it. I want to impress Gary with what great a cook I am. You know what they say, the way to a man's heart is through his stomach."

Dorian rolled her eyes. "The hell it is. Straight through his dick is more like it."

Nicole thrust her stick—the cue ball rammed the triangle and two solids sank in a corner while three stripes wound up in side pockets. "I'm going to have to agree with Dorian on that one, Montella."

Jealousy clawed at Nadia's insides, unnervingly hinting that a mere crush might not adequately describe her feelings for Gary Stoner any longer. Either way she couldn't restrain her mounting curiosity. "Were you serious when you told the sheriff you'd give him the mansion?"

The old familiar gleam of competitive resentment leapt into Montella's blue eyes. They narrowed as she gripped the front edge of the sofa and leaned forward. "You've got a thing for him too, haven't you."

Carlson once confided that Montella felt more threatened by her than any woman he'd ever slept with. Nadia had been flattered to hear him say it but the words hadn't been a revelation, she'd long been aware the statuesque blonde saw her as the only competition. Matching the lucky bitch's angry stare, she drew a quick breath and replied, "It would be futile if I did, wouldn't it. I could never compete with your newfound wealth, darling."

The capitulation caused Montella's shimmering lips to spread with a smile of satisfaction. She relaxed and languidly stretched her arms along the back of the couch. "And don't you forget it, *darling*."

Dorian's cigarette bobbled as a sarcastic chuckle flew out of her mouth. Taking a shot the moment Nicole lifted the rack, she ignored the scattering balls and eyed Montella. "Why are you interested in that square? Going after him makes about as much sense as trying to cure a case of the raw ass by wiping with sand paper."

Nadia laughed along with Nicole, but Montella reacted with a scowl. "Being honest doesn't make a man square, Dorian."

"Never said it did. Being boring does."

"How dare you call him boring, you don't know the first thing about the man."

"Neither do you, hot shot. But I can tell from being around him what little I have that he's the type that'll drive you out of your fucking mind. Early to bed, early to rise, watches sports on TV and little else, 'cepting cop shows and the like. He'll never take you out dancing and his idea of fun in the sack is strictly missionary. Probably won't even let you suck his dick on account of it'd remind him you're a whore."

"Was a whore . . .!" Montella launched from the sofa and slapped her hands on her hips. "I'm through with that way of life."

"Sure you are," Dorian retorted with a cynical grin. "Face up to it, Montella. You're too damn high-fallootin' for a man like him and you know it. You're used to champagne and caviar, not beer and peanuts—liver pate, not fried chicken gizzards—outwittin' the law, not abidin' by it—and there ain't no way his dick'll measure up to Carlson's magic wand."

"Humph!" Montella sat back down and crossed her legs, a supercilious leer embellishing her haughty bearing. "I can have champagne and caviar whenever I choose, and I want to obey the law from now on. As for his dick, I'll love it no matter what, simply because it belongs to him."

Nadia sympathized and actually felt tempted to root for her to win Gary over. After all, she had nothing to offer a man of integrity like that. Of course other than money, neither did Montella. But the issue was moot anyway because Dorian had correctly assessed the situation. Honest and forthright though he might be, the ex-madam would soon be bored silly if she succeeded in snagging the sheriff.

The door opened just wide enough for Deputy Green to stick his head through. "Everything all right?"

"Just hunkie-fuckin'-dorie," said Dorian, bent over the table, taking aim at the cue ball. "They gettin' them devils kicked out of Miss Prissy Pants?"

"Don't know. Gary's got me stationed in the hall so I can keep an eye on things. I'm here to escort you ladies to the kitchen so you can cook supper for everybody."

Dorian took her shot and a small wave of rolling thunder filled the room as fifteen kinetically energized globes bounded towards their destinations. "Care for a quick game of nine ball first?"

The deputy grinned, "You're on."

Nadia supposed he'd come to terms with Rosemary's death because she hadn't seen him look anything but depressed or dourly business-like since her murder until now. The hulking young lawman wore his heart on his sleeve. Anyone present when he and the pretty redhead were in the same vicinity could easily detect his infatuation with her, and the way she tried to conceal her irritation over it. Sadly, she could certainly relate, for every time she'd let her gaze linger on Gary's haunting gray eyes that so attracted her, an uncomfortable air had enveloped him very similar to Rosemary's reaction to Deputy Green's admiring glances.

SEVENTEEN

Geraldo had reached the top of the pecking order but at a horrible cost—the loss of dear Hank, a man he'd always respected and had come to love. When Lori Boon finally unstrapped him at the jailhouse, he'd still felt unnaturally relaxed due to the shot Bolek had given him. Knowing he might not feel so confident completely sober, he'd seized the opportunity to speak with Montella.

After much begging from the women, Sheriff Stoner had agreed to take them back to the ranch. As they'd crossed the dayroom he'd asked the sheriff if he could have a few words with the Ridgewall's new owner. The lawman had sensed what he wanted without being told.

"Montella," Sheriff Stoner had said, "I believe Geraldo, here, is wondering about his job. Does he need to file for unemployment or can he go back to work?"

She'd stood there tapping a long fingernail against her gleaming lips, mulling it over for several moments, during which time he'd begun to feel uneasy about the outcome. Then she'd vanquished his fear by saying, "Geraldo, I'm not familiar with ranching but I do know you've been shorthanded since loosing Munchie and Jeremy, and now your boss is gone as well. I've been informed that after Jeremy's death Hank promoted you to second in command. Do I have my facts straight?"

"Yes, ma'am," he'd replied, "and I know all the ins and outs of working cattle, so I respectfully ask that you let me take Hank's place as foreman."

"At your present wage?"

He'd cleared his throat and confidently stated, "It's only

proper that I receive a raise due to the increased responsibility."

Her deportment had immediately turned solemnly business-like, deflating his self-assurance. "I'm aware of what you make, Geraldo, because I take care of Carlson Loggins' payroll. Your current salary is quarter again the size of what the previous owner of the Ridgewall Ranch was paying you when Carl bought the place and gave all of you a raise."

"Um . . . yes, ma'am, that's true, but I wasn't ramrod then."

"I know, Jeremy Hicks was. I'm certainly not going to pay you what Carl was giving Hank because he had far greater experience than you. I will, however, raise your salary to what Jeremy was earning, which wasn't much lower than Hank's wage before Carl so generously inflated his pay. You can also hire a cook and two more hands, but they'll have to be satisfied with the rates Dooly and Bobby Joe are getting."

Her words had thrilled him. After Loggins bought the ranch Dooly and Bobby Joe had been making more than most ramrods did on other spreads, so he'd easily be able to recruit quality help.

He emptied two cans of pinto beans into a large skillet containing melted lard, minced onion and garlic, and started mashing them with a fork. He didn't know how to cook beans so had to rely on store-bought or those someone else had boiled.

Bobby Joe stepped into the kitchen alongside Dooly, sniffing the air like a hungry hound dog. "What you making for us, Geraldo?"

"Frijoles refritos."

"Huh?"

"Refried beans."

Dooly approached the stove and took a deep whiff. "Smells good. I see you whipped up a batch of tortilla's too."

Though flattered, he didn't want to raise any false hopes. "Unfortunately, vato, this is about as good as it gets with me.

I'll put an ad in the paper mañana for a new cook and a couple of more hands to help us out. Which one of you is man enough to fill my shoes as ramrod now that I'm the boss?"

"I ain't taking no orders from Dooly," Bobby Joe asserted, "and I know he don't want me bossing him around neither, so you'd best hire someone to be your second."

Dooly patted the fat-lipped cowboy on the back. "Now wait a minute, Bobby Joe, use your head. You'd much rather take orders from me than some stranger because you know I've got your back all the way. I've got more experience than you, so it's only right the job should go to me."

"Not on this ranch you don't."

"True, we came on the Ridgewall at the same time, but I wasn't a tenderfoot like you were when I arrived."

Geraldo nodded. "What he says is correct, Bobby Joe. The job is his."

Dooly jerked his hat off and let out a *yee-haw.* "How much of a raise will I get?"

"That'll be up to Montella."

Bobby Joe sat down at the table and yanked the brim of his Stetson over his eyes, sulking like an angry child.

"Aw, don't take it so hard, hoss . . ." Dooly seated himself across from the brooding cowboy. "We're still buds, nothing's changed."

"He's right, Bobby Joe. Just be thankful we won't be shorthanded much longer."

"Yeah," said Dooly, "and now that the sheriff has caught the killer, life can finally get back to normal. It's hard to believe that demon was hiding in Ilian, ain't it? Hope she comes out of this okay."

Bobby Joe eased his hat back and sighed. "Me too. I always liked that gal."

* * * *

Gary stowed his cell phone and went back inside Carlson Loggin's bedroom suite. He'd stepped into the hall to call Pete Lemmon and get him up to date. The last report the DA had received came from Heath, who'd informed him of Hank Best's death. Losing the foreman really exacerbated the nail-biting situation with the press because no one else had seen the demon. That had left Pete with no recourse but to make a public statement that the sheriff's department had several suspects in custody and no further details would be announced until the residents of Tomahawk County could be assured they no longer had a serial killer in their midst.

Ilian lay unconscious and spread eagle in the dead millionaire's bed. Dunmark had chosen it because the sturdy brass rails were ideal for securing the ends of leather restraints fastened around her wrists and ankles. Lori and Bolek had rigged up an intravenous drip device which not only kept her sleeping, but supplied glucose and electrolytes as well. Someone knocked on the door. Gary opened it to find Tank standing there.

"Supper's ready."

"Thanks, Tank. You eat with Dunmark and them, I'll stay here with Ilian. Have whoever gets done first come relieve me."

The big redhead rubbed his belly and grinned. "Just got through. Montella made me a plate before she set the table. You guys chow down, I'll watch over her."

Gary announced it was chowtime and headed downstairs, followed by Heath, Dunmark, Lori, and Bolek.

Montella had prepared chicken fried steak, mashed potatoes and gravy, an elaborate salad that looked like it had been put together to impress viewers of a cooking show, macaroni and cheese, and fluffy dinner rolls. She'd made enough to feed an army so Gary didn't hesitate to pile it on thick. He took a hefty bite of steak and discovered her promise that he'd never taste better hadn't been an empty boast.

Before he could tell her so Dunmark remarked, "Montella, this is the best chicken fried steak I've ever eaten."

"Thank you," she responded with a glittering smile, sitting at one end of the long dining table. "And what are your thoughts on it, Sheriff?"

Still chewing, he gave her a nod of approval from five chairs away—Heath, Lori, Bolek, and Dunmark sitting between them in that order. Across the table sat Nadia, an empty chair, Nicole, four empty chairs, and Dorian.

Gary scooped a forkful of mashed potatoes coated with cream gravy into his mouth. Both were delicious. Montella's excellent culinary skills surprised him. Having had her meals prepared by Rico Mircanti for so many years, he doubted she'd spent very much time slaving over a hot stove since teaming up with Loggins.

"So how long 'fore you get them devils outa Ilian?" said Dorian, sitting at Montella's left across from Dunmark, whom she'd queried while chewing.

"Hopefully soon, but realistically we're probably talking several days. And it's only one demon, not a multiple possession by the way."

"Ever run across one this mean before?"

Dunmark shook his head and took a sip of iced tea.

Dorian crammed her mouth full of macaroni and cheese. Yellow sauce oozed from the Cajun's lips but she left her napkin neatly folded on the table. "I'm intrigued by your work. Wouldn't mind bustin' devil ass fer a living. How much you make doin' this shit anyway?"

"We don't do this for money," answered Dunmark, smiling politely. "This is an occupation you more or less have to be called to, rather than choose. Few people are cut out for this job."

"Hmm, well maybe I'm one of 'em."

Montella giggled. "I highly doubt that, dear."

The mannerless beauty glowered at her, cheese trickling

from her mouth and an angry scowl making it appear she had rabies. "I might be for all you know!"

Ignoring her remark Montella looked his way. "So, Gary, did I exaggerate on my chicken fried steak?"

"No. I have to agree with Dunmark, this is the best I've ever had. Great mashed potatoes and gravy too, I might add."

Her eyes sparkled with prideful accomplishment. "I made the mac-and-cheese from scratch, it didn't come from a box."

"Guess I better try some then." He hadn't put any on his plate because there'd been no room for anything else after overloading it with only two of the available items on the table and smothering both with gravy.

"I see you're a meat and potatoes kind of guy. That's a very masculine trait which I admire. I'm sorry I couldn't find anything to make for dessert or I'd have whipped up something just for you."

Gary took a swig of iced tea and sighed while setting the glass down. "Would you please stop trying to hustle me?"

"She's not," said Nadia with a resentful tone as if defending her begrudgingly. "Montella likes that in a man. Carlson was a spud-loving carnivore."

"That may be, but I know she's only trying to convince me not to charge you girls."

"Why haven't you done so already?" asked Nicole.

Heath let out a small laugh. "Don't worry, we will when this is all over."

"How bad do you think it'll be, Ranger Crow?"

"Depends on the judge. If you were only guilty of solicitation you might have lucked out and got probation, but blackmail is a horse of a different color. You could all do serious time for it."

Nicole set her fork down, placed her elbows on the table, and leaned forward, resting her forehead on long interlocked fingers. "I just lost my appetite."

"You don't have to say nothin' to nobody, Sheriff," insisted

Dorian, eyeing him as if he'd made the statement instead of Heath. "We promise to be good little girls from now on, at least I do."

"It's not an option I'm free to take, neither is Ranger Crow. Your best bet—all of you—is to save your schmoozing for the district attorney. Nadia can probably get a deal if she's willing to testify against the corrupt sheriff I replaced, but the rest of you are out of luck since your boss is dead."

"We wouldn't testify against Carl anyway," said Montella. "At least not while he was alive."

"Hell, I would if it meant savin' my coon ass." Dorian spoke it with a mouth full of breaded beef.

Her confession pulled a hearty chortle from Bolek. "What do you mean by that?"

"A Cajun is a coonass. What nationality are you, anyway?"

"Polish."

"Ah, so you're a Polack, huh?"

"That is taken as a derogatory idiom by my people, so please do not refer to me as such. I'd sooner you call me geek boy. If you must use a term, Pole would be proper."

She gave him a taunting grin, slivers of steak clinging to her teeth. "What kind of pole do you have, geek boy?"

Bolek's pale face turned instantly crimson.

"Keep it up, Dorian, and I'll have Tank haul your ass back to jail."

Lips turning down, she flashed her blue eyes at him. "Sorry, Sheriff, I did promise not to call him that, didn't I. Won't happen again. I apologize, Bolek."

Lori rose from the table. "I'm going to look in on Ilian, be back in a few."

"I'll go with you," said Bolek, appearing relieved to have an excuse to get away from Dorian.

Montella waved for his attention as he watched them leave the room. "When can I speak with the district attorney, Gary?"

"I'll take you to see him tomorrow if you want."

"How about first thing in the morning?"

"Not a problem."

"Good. I'll be ready at eight sharp. Don't be late."

* * * *

Gary deposited Montella at Pete Lemmon's office and drove to the jailhouse. Alfredo walked in shortly after he got there.

"I couldn't get hold of Ilian last night and she's not here. Did she call in sick?"

Seeing no way around the inevitable, Gary broke the bad news.

As expected Alfredo took it hard. His face was a tortured portrait of shock, anguish, confusion, and anger. The poor boy just stood there gawking at him as he explained that Dunmark's assistants had come down from Colorado to test the ranch hands and Ilian's sudden outburst had shockingly revealed the demon was operating through her.

His gaping mouth finally closed and tears started flowing. "When did this happen?"

"Yesterday evening."

"Where is she now?"

"The Ridgewall Ranch. Dunmark has her sedated so the demon can't manifest."

Alfredo started wiping his eyes. The young Mexican's hands were shivering as if he'd just built a snowman without wearing gloves. "Does her mother know?"

"No. I told her we needed Ilian to accompany the border patrol on a special mission and she'd be gone several days. I'm hoping Dunmark can drive the demon out before I'm forced to come clean with Mrs. Herrera. I don't need a hysterical mother on my hands, or a panicked boyfriend, Alfredo. You can go see her, but don't let your emotions get the better of you or I'll have to bar you from the ranch. This is very serious business. Dunmark and his assistants can't afford to be distracted. We have to let them do their job so they can save her. Be back here in an hour. You'll have to be dispatcher in her absence."

The desk phone rang as Alfredo bounded out the door. He glanced at the Caller ID while reaching for the receiver. The DA certainly hadn't taken long to call him.

"Hey, Pete. Don't tell me you're through with Montella already."

"The woman has friends in high places. I just got off the phone with a U.S. Senator who called me at her request." A hearty laugh followed the statement.

"What's so funny about that?"

"You know the old saying 'Every dog has its day?' Well this ol' dog is finally going to have his. You think my ambition is limited to being a small town district attorney? Hell no, I've always hoped to advance my political career and he promised his support if I'd do him one small favor. Long story short, we're not pressing charges, she and the other women that worked for Loggins are free to go. I do, however, want you to bring Nadia Mars in, now that your metaphysical investigator is certain the demon wasn't working through her. I'm hoping she has enough on Dody that I can finally nail the sleazy bastard."

That put a smile on his face. "I'm pretty sure she does. You will go easy on her, I hope."

"Gary, not only will I give her total immunity, I'll make her the guest of honor at this year's Christmas party if she's got enough to bury that damn snake."

His lips stretched further. "That's what I was hoping you'd say."

* * * *

Gary steered his cruiser over the cattle guard and entered

the Ridgewall Ranch. Montella unfastened her seatbelt even though they had a quarter mile to go before reaching the mansion. He cut his eyes to her and grinned. "Must be nice to be so well connected. Or did that senator ask Pete to cut your slack because you've got something on him?"

"Wouldn't you like to know."

"Actually, no I wouldn't. So what are you going to do now that you've been cleared?"

She gave him knowing smile. "You really thought I was trying to hustle you, didn't you."

"Mm hmm."

"Well guess what, I wasn't. I still want to be your wife."

"You've got to be kidding me."

Her majestic mane bounced as she shook her head.

"Why would you want to spend your life with me when you've got the whole world at your fingertips?" he asked soberly, careful not to show how flattered he felt so she wouldn't be encouraged to keep trying.

"Why does any woman usually choose to spend her life with a particular man? Because she loves him."

"You can't love me, you barely know me. What's your real motive?"

"Dammit, there is no other motive."

"Oh, of course there's not," he derided with a smirk.

"You sure are a stubborn son-of-a-bitch, aren't you."

"I may be stubborn but I'm no S.O.B. My mama was a good girl."

"And that's what I long to be, Gary."

He gave her a warm smile. "And I hope you make it."

Montella's boobs shook as she brusquely crossed her arms while pouting at him. "Only not with you. Why?"

"It would never work." He stopped in front of the carport and killed the engine.

Walking behind Montella as she angrily hurried up the porch steps, he caught himself staring at her beautiful hips, swaying beneath the shiny black fabric of a tight-fitting dress. He quickly looked away. Allowing her beauty to fan the flames of temptation was a recipe for disaster, especially here on the Ridgewall Ranch. Half an hour later he descended the steps with Nadia Mars.

* * * *

Pulse tone dinging at regular intervals, Lori checked the meters and found everything par. Ilian slept peacefully, her pretty face looking like that of an angel rather than a drug-relaxed façade with a demon lurking behind it. She stepped out of the bedroom, closed the door, and made for the stairs, ready for some lunch. Dunmark had scheduled the first assault to take place immediately afterwards.

Her colleagues were already eating when she entered the dining room. One woman wasn't there—the amazingly beautiful Nadia Mars—but the rest were sitting at the table. Opposite the end Montella Pace occupied sat a stack of paper plates, napkins, and disposable cups. Loaves of three types of bread and an assortment of single-serving packages of chips rested beside a huge bowl of tuna salad and two pitchers of iced tea. Selecting two slices of rye, she fixed a sandwich, placed it on her plate, emptied a bag of potato chips beside it, and filled the cup.

Seeing an opportunity had come at last, she parked beside the handsome ranger. "Do you mind?"

He gave her a puzzled look that quickly faded. "Oh, you mean if you sit there. No, by all means."

His gaze turned straight forward the moment she sat down. Surely he'd take the hint since she'd chosen to sit beside him rather than opting for one of the other available chairs. She ate a bite and sipped some tea, hoping he would strike up a conversation. When it became evident he wasn't going to, she turned her head and smiled, feeling like an overly aggressive teenager with an incurable crush. "How long have you been with the Texas Rangers?"

"Since I left the marine corps eight years ago," he replied without facing her.

"So you were a marine, huh? Why'd you leave?"

"My hitch was up." He took a bite of sandwich.

Admiring the manliness of his smooth, muscular jaw as he chewed, she nibbled a chip and washed it down with tea, locating both from her peripheral vision. "Didn't want to be a lifer, huh?"

He shook his head, still looking forward.

You're either shy or you don't like me, she thought, studying the perfectly straight part of his dark-brown hair. "Do you ever miss being a marine?"

"Once a marine, always a marine."

"Okay . . . do you miss being in the corps?"

He turned and focused his pale-blue eyes on her, igniting a gush of excitement that eclipsed surprise over him visually acknowledging her presence again. She'd begun to think he never would.

"I grew up wanting to be a Texas Ranger but felt obligated to give fours years of my life to Uncle Sam first—do my part in the fight against terrorism—before spending the rest of it in service to the greatest state in the union."

Blood pressure escalating, she raised her tea in a toast. "Simper Fidelis, Ranger Crow."

The hunk tapped her cup with his own. "Simper Fi, ma'am."

"Please, call me Lori."

A bashful smile surfaced. "Only if you'll call me Heath."

So you were *only being standoffish because you're shy. Thank God!* "This is some strange case we have here, huh?"

"Oh yeah. I had no idea demon possession still happened in this day and time except in horror movies."

Recalling how that harsh reality had so radically changed her from a happy-go-lucky all American girl without a care in the world to a studious spiritual warrior, she exhaled a gloomy sigh. "Satan has kept it that way for the most part several centuries now, using the tactic that he doesn't really exist. But we're not terribly far from Armageddon, and the closer it comes, the more demonic activity will become visible. Are you a believer, Heath?"

"Yes, ma'am. I mean, Lori."

"I'll never forget the first manifestation I witnessed." She took a sip of tea and continued. "When I went to work for Dunmark I was just a computer geek with only a superficial understanding of the Bible and no experience in spiritual warfare. A missionary friend of Dunmark's called him from South America and asked for his help to deliver a six-year-old boy whose mother was a witch. We set up our gear in a hut outside the village the boy lived in. I got so scared when Bolek induced that evil spirit to make its presence known, Dunmark was forced to order me back to the village. Afterwards he explained that my allowing fear to override my faith could have cost every one of us our lives, including the little boy. I've kept my nose in the Bible since and haven't let a day go by without spending some quality devotional time with the Lord."

A glimmer of fear shone in Heath's heart-melting eyes. "I can see I wouldn't be any good at that. The little boy got delivered, I hope."

"Yeah, but no thanks to me." Searching for a tactful way to do it and finding none, she threw caution to the wind, hoping she wasn't moving too fast. "Um, forgive me for being rather forward, but I wonder if there's any possibility of us doing something together when this is over—you know, go out for a drink or have dinner."

He studied her for a moment and cleared his throat. "I don't date much, but if you think you can put up with my lack of social graces, sure."

A thrill raced through her, making it impossible to stop

grinning like a star-struck adolescent being asked out by the most popular boy in school. Her heart had gone pitter-pat upon meeting him and she now felt guiltily thankful for the demon. Their paths wouldn't have crossed otherwise. "I just hope you can put up with mine. I don't socialize much either."

Heath grinned back.

"Well if I ain't bein' hog-swallered, the ranger and Lori appear to be a-spoonin' and a-sparkin'."

She turned to see Dorian making a shame-on-you motion with her index fingers. The Cajun winked at her and lowered her hands. "Tell me what I need to learn to work with you and Dunmark now that I'm free to come and go as I please. I may not have much education but I catch on to things real quick."

Confused, she looked at Heath. "You're not charging her with anything?"

He shook his head. "Montella somehow got a senator to sweet-talk the district attorney into letting them all off the hook."

"Ah, that explains why Nadia Mars isn't here. She flew the coup already."

"No, Gary took her to the see the DA. She's not in the clear, at least for the moment."

* * * *

Bolek concentrated on his tuna sandwich, trying to keep from staring at the beautiful Dorian, wondering why she'd want to work with them. If the woman had any idea how monotonous it could be at times she'd never consider their research as a career. Sadly, The Great Tribulation could begin any day, and the nearer it drew, the more morbidly interesting his job would become as demonic activity increased. He firmly believed that some mortal man presently living, knowingly or unwittingly, waited to be personally indwelt by Satan and become the antichrist.

Lori hadn't gotten past the provoking-questions stage with Geraldo Toya before Ilian's manifestation made further probing ridiculously unnecessary. Dorian, on the other hand, had endured the full barrage not once but twice back in Colorado. The woman totally baffled him. Not only did she claim not to have any college education, but hadn't even earned a high school diploma. And yet on the intelligence quotient test—meant to determine if the subject somehow knew things beyond their apparent aptitude, a strong indicator of a supernatural presence—she'd registered at genius levels.

Like Dunmark and Lori, he'd initially found that to be proof she was demonized. Lori had administered that test first at Dunmark's request, certain he'd located the sullen spirit's host. When Lori hadn't been able to get a belligerent response from Dorian through the provoking theological quizzes, Dunmark had ordered another round of tests. But throughout the following interrogations, the second onslaught much more vigorous than the previous, no anger whatsoever towards God or Jesus had come forth. The three of them had finally concluded that Dorian was either a genius or the devil inhabiting her body inexplicably had genuine affection for The Almighty, the latter being extremely improbable. Now that they'd located the hellish being within Ilian, Bolek knew for certain the coonass indeed possessed a brain as astounding as her physical beauty.

And that drew him to her like a moth to the flame.

EIGHTEEN

Nadia agreed to testify against Dody Massey, and the district attorney's office had received assurance from the Mexican government they'd extradite the sleaze-ball back to Texas once they located him. True to his word, Pete granted her total immunity and placed her in his custody until the trial.

Gary unlocked the front door and beckoned her inside. A whiff of the dark-eyed Venus's beguiling perfume seduced his nostrils as she glanced around his modest living room. She hadn't dressed formal like Montella but looked fantastic in tight jeans and a purple turtleneck sweater.

"Do you rent this place or own it?"

Her tone made him chuckle. Nadia said it like she'd just stepped into an upscale residence instead of a working stiff's two-bedroom house. "It'll be all mine when the mortgage is paid off."

"It's cozy. Thanks for letting me stay here instead of keeping me in protective custody at the jailhouse."

Carrying the order from Carla's he'd phoned in before leaving Pete's office, he guided her into the kitchen for lunch—divvied up their burgers, fries, and drinks—sat down, and told her to do likewise.

She took a seat across from him and unwrapped her cheeseburger. "So this is where Montella stayed after Carlson got killed, huh? She told me about you hiding her out so everyone would think she was dead."

"Let's not talk about Montella."

"Okay, but I think you should know she's not the only one with a crush on you, Sheriff."

He frowned. "Someone told you Sonya had a crush on me?"

"Sonya? No, that's not who I was referring to. I never met the girl, but I was told she had a thing for Geraldo Toya."

"Oh. Tank thought she had a crush because she asked him a lot of questions about me. Who are you talking about?"

Nadia pulled the tab off a vat of takeout ketchup and dropped the disposable lid in the bag he'd emptied. "Never mind, I shouldn't have said anything."

That left only Dorian or Nicole. Nicole hadn't given any indication that he floated her boat, so he figured Dorian, being a troublemaker, must have teased Montella that she liked him too, trying to get a rise out of her. But even if she really had developed a crush it didn't matter—her crude ways had completely eroded the attraction he'd felt when they met. "Now you do understand that you can't leave Tomahawk County until after you testify, right?"

"Mm hmm." Her glamorous features turned wary. "I just hope I live long enough to do it."

"Pete was talking to the DPS about David Nevers when we left. The highway patrol will round him up and he'll be in my jail before nightfall."

She wrapped her pretty lips around a straw and drew some cola into her mouth. Innocent though the action was, it conjured such a strong erotic image in his mind he had to look away to keep an erection at bay. He couldn't help wishing that plastic tube was a part of his anatomy that had long been neglected.

"Is something wrong?"

"Mm mm."

"Are you worried David Nevers might give them the slip? Oh god, please tell me that's not what you're thinking."

He took a bite of his burger and eyed the large order of fries sitting before him. "I wasn't thinking that at all."

"Then what?" She set her drink on the table.

Making a mental note to shift his gaze each time her pouting lips and that stiff straw made contact, he faced her again. "What made you take such a wayward road?"

"What's a nice girl like me doing in a business like this is what you're asking, isn't it?" She wearily shook her head and sighed. "Do you have any idea how many times I've heard that?"

"Well you're hearing it again. What happened way back when that turned you into . . . ."

"A whore?"

Stabbing his own straw into his mouth, he vacuumed a swallow of root beer and nodded.

"I can sum it all up with two words. Carlson Loggins."

"You were straight before meeting him?"

She dipped a fry in her ketchup and bit off the red-coated end. "As an arrow."

"I wonder how many innocent girls that bastard has corrupted."

Responding with a shrug, she reached for her cola.

He tried to reroute his eyes but couldn't keep from watching her suck on the straw. His lengthening penis, aimed downward, got severely restricted by the crotch seam, and he had to use both hands to adjust his pants to alleviate the discomfort. It telescoped into the upper left leg of his trousers, pressing hotly against his inner thigh. He quickly retrieved the hamburger and held it near his face like a harmonica player waiting to embellish the chorus of a tune, relieved she didn't appear curious about the action. "How old were you when he . . . changed you?"

Nadia set the cup down and tossed him a sad smile. "He *changed me*, as you put it, seventeen years ago. Though I'd never turned tricks before, like most eighteen-year-olds in those days, I'd been around the block a few times. I had dreams of being a professional singer and was working as a backup vocalist with an otherwise all male cover band. We landed a gig playing the lounge of an exclusive country club in Houston and one night while we were performing Carlson and Montella came in. He never took his eyes off me and during a break he came over and introduced himself."

"Let me guess. He told you he could make you a star."

She laughed. "Hardly. He told me something someone should have long before—that I could barely carry a tune and was wasting my time trying to be a singer. He said, 'You must be sleeping with one of the members, otherwise I can't see why that band keeps you around. Honey, you have the face and body of a rock diva but not the vocal chords.'

"Well, though he was wrong about me sleeping with any of them, the leader had asked me to go with him and I'd turned him down. Carlson's bold statement made me realize the dude was only letting me stay with the group because he hoped to eventually win me over with his talent. I should have suspected it before then because the more important the gig, the less any of the songs I sang on made it to that evening's play list. I'd spend most of the show just shaking my booty and a tambourine. Anyway, Carlson then said, 'I work in the entertainment business too, honey—in the branch of it you were born for. You'll never make it as a rock star but if you come to work for me, I promise you'll be living like one right off the bat.'

"I was extremely enamored with him straight away, and when he asked if he could take me out to dinner the next night to discuss his proposal in more detail, I jumped at the chance. After he seduced me and promised sleeping with him would be a regular part of my life from then on, I agreed to whore out for him. The man was absolutely amazing in bed."

He finally tended to the burger and while chewing, reflected on Montella's statement about Loggins being a sex machine. "Montella said he was aces in the sack as well, and hearing you brag about him has gotten my curiosity up. What was so special about Carlson Loggins?"

She tilted her head forward with brows raised as her delectable lips formed a half grin. "You want to know if he was hung like a horse, is that it?"

He'd seen Loggins' penis when Bob South pulled it from Sonya's mouth, but that puny lump of flesh might have been much larger before shriveling in death. Plus he could have been one of those guys who more than quintuple in size when erect. "Was he?"

Nadia giggled and stabbed another fry in her ketchup. "Carlson was actually rather modestly endowed, but oh did he know what to do with it. And he could be so unbelievably charming—make a woman feel like she was the only girl on the face of this earth. After he sent me packing, I never missed the opulent lifestyle I'd been forced to leave behind nearly as much as I did those special nights I got to spend with him. He knew women inside out, and could push buttons most men don't even have a clue exist. I think it was a gift he was born with, one of those things you either have or you don't—impossible to learn." She popped the French fry between her grinning lips, closed them, and kept smiling as she chewed.

"Guess there's no use in asking for pointers then."

Nadia swallowed and cocked her head like a parrot trying to memorize a phrase from its master. "Are you considering taking Montella up on her offer?"

"No. What makes you say that?"

"Your statement about pointers."

He chomped another section of hamburger and sucked in a mouthful of root beer to wash it down. "I was hoping to get clued in to those buttons you spoke of, that's all."

"You don't strike me as the type of man that needs instructions on how to please a woman, Sheriff." She tossed him a playful smirk. "Am I mistaken in that assessment?"

"The few women I've been intimate with over the course of my life would have to answer that, but I think any guy hearing what you said about Loggins would be just as curious. I'm going to let you in on a little secret. I've been admiring you from afar as they say, long before we met."

Her eyes flew wide as a smile of surprise sprang to her sexy face. "You have?"

"Mm hmm, at Carla's Café."

She pinched the collar of her sweater and pulled it out a ways from her throat, long pink nails highlighted by the dark purple fabric. "Funny, I never caught you looking my way."

"Only because you weren't watching me." He reached for his fries, came away with a clump of three, and shoved them in his mouth.

"Oh I always watched you, and with caution. You were the enemy then." She released the elastic embroidery and it sprang back to her neck. "Were you aware of who I was? That I worked for Dody, I mean."

He shook his head. "I wanted to ask the waitresses about you, but didn't because I knew it would've started rumors. Being sheriff, I couldn't afford that. I quizzed Tank and Alfredo, but they didn't know anything about you either."

"Why didn't you just come over and introduce yourself?"

"I'd planned to if I could ever catch you alone, but you were always with the two gals I now know to be Sally and Erma."

She took a deep breath and exhaled it through a bewildered grin. "I had no idea you were attracted to me."

"Well I sure was."

The grin vanished with a falling countenance. "Was?"

"I don't think I have to spell it out."

"Oh . . ." her cheeks turned red. "You didn't know I was a whore."

He nodded.

She didn't touch her food afterwards, but he finished his.

"Remember when I said Montella wasn't the only one with a crush on you?"

"Yeah." He wadded up his burger wrapper and stuffed it in the white paper bag from Carla's.

"Well I'm the other culprit. The only reason I'm telling you is because I believe Montella is sincere about changing her life and wanting to spend it with you. I think being around you affected her the same way it did me. As you can imagine, we haven't been exposed to too many honest men. You're something special, Sheriff Stoner."

He pursed his lips and looked into space. Her statement sounded truthful and she certainly had nothing to gain by trying to hustle him. If only she wasn't a whore. His initial attraction to Dorian was mostly because the hick's hair, face, and body closely resembled hers, and he found it incredibly ironic they'd both turned out to be hookers. The image of another beautiful brunette—pregnant and falling to her death—sprang to the forefront of his mind, casting a pall of sadness over him.

"What's wrong?"

" Just missing my wife."

"Montella told me about the accident. I'm truly sorry."

Wishing he'd dodged her question, he heaved a sigh and rose from the table. Nadia would be fine without a bodyguard so long as she stayed put, and he needed to get away from her for awhile—let the exhilaration of knowing she had feelings for him mellow enough to become manageable. "Make yourself at home and keep the doors locked. I'm off to the Ridgewall Ranch to check on Ilian."

* * * *

Bolek pressed a cotton ball soaked with alcohol on Ilian's forearm and withdrew the hypo. The stimulant would take effect in a matter of seconds. He wiped the puncture point on the poor girl's vein and geared up for the task at hand.

Dunmark and Lori stood on either side of the big brass bed, the former holding a camcorder. Ranger Crow observed Ilian from a point near the closed door of the elaborately constructed master bedroom suite, the fingers of one hand hidden beneath a well defined bicep, the digits of the other exposed atop the opposing bulge.

"She's coming to," said Lori.

Lashes fluttering, lids slowly rising, the pretty Mexican's eyes darted rapidly back and forth, finally settling in the ranger's direction. "H-Heath . . . what happened to me? Am I dreaming again?"

Heath lowered his muscular arms. "No, Ilian, you're not dreaming. We brought you to the Ridgewall Ranch to cure you."

"C-Cure me?"

He took the liberty of intervening. "Remember me, Bolek Nowak? We met at the jailhouse, remember?"

Her dark orbs worriedly cut his way as she nodded. "What's wrong with me? What do I need to be cured of?"

Lori leaned over her. "Please tell me the last thing you remember before you fell asleep in the dayroom."

"You were talking to Geraldo Toya and suddenly I started dreaming. How can that be? I was awake."

"Yes, dear, you were awake when the dream started. Can you recall what you dreamed?"

Ilian wrinkled her brow, face reflecting failure to summon the memory. Tears forming, she rapidly shook her head, slapping the fluffy pillow with her cheeks.

"That's okay, don't worry about it. You do remember why Bolek and I came down here from Colorado, don't you?"

Nodding, she tried to rise. A panicked scowl seized her face upon seeing the restraints. "Y-You think the demon's in me?!"

"Yes, dear, and we'll need your help to make him leave."

Bolek grabbed her hand and gave it a reassuring squeeze. "Have you ever undergone hypnosis before, Ilian?"

"No," she muttered. Anxiety radiated from her stunned countenance that had turned sickly pale from confusion and fear.

"Before we can proceed, we need to hypnotize you so you can reveal to us what your subconscious mind has been hiding from you." He pulled a pocket watch from his lab coat. Clasping the end of a silver chain ten inches long, he dangled the shiny timepiece before her, slowly waving it back and forth. "Please keep your eyes fixed upon the watch and listen as Lori tells you a wonderful story . . . ."

* * * *

Nadia felt guilty but couldn't resist checking out Gary's bedroom, curious to see what the high sheriff wore when not in uniform. He preferred briefs rather than boxers, t-shirts rather than sleeveless undershirts, and tube socks. She left the chest of drawers and opened his closet. A dark suit, covered with clear plastic to keep dust at bay, separated a row of khaki uniforms from a slew of western shirts and blue jeans. The man liked cowboy boots and apparently didn't believe in throwing worn out ones away. They all had riding heels and the roughest of the lot had scuffed areas similar to the cowhands'. Opening a box with a white Stetson etched on the lid, she saw several sets of spurs and realized the marring came from them. Leather chaps crammed in a corner caught her eye. She picked them up and found another hat box beneath, containing pictures.

She carried it to the living room, settled on the sofa, and went through them one by one. *Ah, he used to work as a cowboy.* Those particular photographs had dates written on the back, and depicted an eager-looking youth progressing in age standing beside different drovers as he advanced in years. Montella had told her Gary was almost thirty-one, and since she couldn't find any cowboy pictures dated past the year he would have turned eighteen, he'd either given up cow-punching at that age, or hadn't posed for any more group shots after that.

"Wonder if Montella saw these while she was staying here," she mused aloud while returning the box and sitting the chaps back on top of it. With everything situated like she found it, she stretched out on Gary's bed, covered with an old fashioned country quilt. *I see you like a firm mattress, Mister Stoner.* A hint of his aftershave emanated from the pillows. It saddened her to think she'd never get to watch him lather up his face and scrape away a night's worth of stubble. She got up and went to his bathroom. Nestled between the two bedrooms, doorway centered in a short hall, it was the only one in the house.

Snooping in his medicine cabinet, she saw he used disposable razors and canned shaving cream, which mildly surprised her. She'd half expected to find a straight razor and a mug with a brush in it. She removed the lid from his aftershave and brought it to her nose, whiffing the pleasing fragrance with eyes closed. Then she did the same with his stick deodorant, relishing the manly smell. At length she covered the waxy dome, closed the mirror, and ambled to the living room . . . .

Relaxing in Gary's recliner, she pondered what the future would be like outside the world of prostitution. *What type of straight job could I get that's not boring and won't put me below the poverty line?* She chuckled at the notion of asking Montella for a job. *What the hell could I do for her, become her maid? I hate housework anyway and keeping that mansion spic and span would be a nightmare. She's given up the life so hooking for her is out of the question. Besides, I'm finished with the red light too.*

Hands behind her head, she closed her eyes and began toying with the idea of feeding the ranch hands. Cooking was something she enjoyed and could do quite well. If Montella let her stay in the mansion so she didn't have to fight off horny cowboys all night, and if the cowpunchers cleaned up after themselves, that wouldn't be such a bad gig. She wondered how much she should ask for if Montella agreed to it.

"Hello, Nadia."

She jerked her eyes open to see two menacing dark holes at the end of a double-barrel shotgun no more than a foot from her face. Dody Massey's bony wrinkled finger was twitching over the triggers, obviously about to pull them. The bastard had managed to sneak in without making a sound.

"Thought you wouldn't have to worry about laying eyes on me until they dragged my butt into the courtroom didn't you, slut. Well I snuck back into town after David Nevers told me about the first murders and have been laying low over at his place. Twenty minutes ago I heard some cars pull up so I peeked out the window and what did I see but two patrolmen with Pete Lemmon. I told Nevers not to let on I was there and hid in his coat closet so I could hear what was going on. They hauled his ass away after telling him you ratted us out to the fucking DA who placed you in Stoner's custody. Say your prayers, bitch."

NINETEEN

Gary entered Carlson Loggins' bedroom to find Bolek waving a watch in front of Ilian, Dunmark aiming a camcorder at her, and Heath raising a finger to his nose, signaling him to be quiet.

"She's under," said Lori softly from the other side of the bed.

Bolek placed the watch in his left hand, gently lowered the chain, and stashed it in his lab coat. "Ilian, you and I are going to take a journey together, floating backwards in time on the stream of your memory. Are you ready?"

Ilian nodded, eyes looking glassy and dreamlike.

"Good. I am navigating us to a specific time when your secret thoughts quit being your own and you had to share them with another. You can see the days fly by as we sail into your past. Tell me when it is time to anchor the ship."

Ilian's lips puckered and relaxed in rapid succession as if silently counting. She kept it up for several moments, then her eyes flared. "Stop!"

"Ah," said Bolek, "we have arrived?"

She nodded.

"Good, we have ceased moving. Now tell me where you are and what you see."

"I am in the country watching the doves fly overhead."

"How old are you?"

"Three."

"Very good. What is happening?"

"The beautiful birds are spreading their wings and I am wishing I could fly like them. But I can't because I'm just a little girl. I am jealous of their power of flight. One of them is on the ground watching me. He hops up on my shoulder and tells me he can make me fly."

Bolek frowned and glanced at Lori. "The bird is speaking to you?"

"Yes, he tells me he can make me fly."

"I see. Does he expect something in return?"

She nodded.

"What?"

"I must let him fly with me. He's a ghost bird. A hunter killed him and now he can't fly alone."

"Okay, continue on. Tell me what is happening now."

"I ask how he can make me fly, and he tells me he can only do it if I let him live inside me. I tell him 'Okay' and the next thing I know I am floating high in the sky—very high—and I grow frightened that I will fall. I tell him, 'Please leave me alone, I don't want to fly anymore. Please let me get safely back to the ground!' He leaves and I do fall. I wake up before hitting the ground and am shaking with relief that it was only a nightmare."

Bolek took her hand. "You were only three when you had this dream?"

"No. Though I'm three years old in the dream, I am really thirteen and have fallen asleep after committing a dreadful, wicked sin that I had never done before."

"And what was the sin?"

"Masturbation."

The heart monitor started beeping rapidly. Lori drug her right index finger across her throat.

Bolek nodded and released Ilian's hand. "We will speak more of this but first you must rest a moment."

Gary swallowed a lump of incredulity, dumbstruck over Ilian's tale. "Was that ghost bird the demon?"

"Shush!" commanded Dunmark and his assistants in unison, all three of them glaring at him with the same chastising frown.

"Sorry," he mouthed silently, feeling like an idiot.

When the beeps finally slowed to a steady pace, Bolek gave Lori an inquiring glance and she nodded.

"Okay, Ilian, we shall continue. Did guilt make you think you had committed a grievous sin or did someone tell you masturbating was such?"

"Someone told me."

"Who?"

"My priest."

"Why was the priest discussing masturbation with you?"

"He wasn't. He told me no one was supposed to touch my pee-pee but him."

Bolek's brows formed two steep rainbows high above his glasses, wrinkling his shiny forehead. "How old were you when he told you this?"

"Three."

"And did he ever touch your vagina?"

She nodded. "Many times."

"And you were only three?"

"Yes. He played with it until I reached puberty, then he never touched me again."

Exchanging a knowing look with Lori, Bolek folded his arms. "I see. What became of this priest?"

"He was sent to a parish in San Diego when I was fifteen and I never saw him again. He's dead now."

"When did he die?"

"Earlier this year."

"How did you learn of his death?"

"From one of my aunts who used to live here. My family and I, and all my relatives in Tomahawk County, have always attended the church he pastored. She moved to California a few years ago and lives near San Diego. She called my mother when she saw his obituary in the paper."

"What did he die of?"

"He committed suicide."

Bolek uncrossed his forearms, adjusted his spectacles, and sank his hands into the pockets of his lab coat. "Did you like it when he played with your pee-pee?"

"Not at first but I began to enjoy it as I got older."

"And did you feel guilty about enjoying it?"

"Yes, I felt dirty and ashamed."

"And you had never touched yourself erotically until the night you had that dream?"

"No. The guilt was unbearable. I swore I'd never do it again but couldn't resist the temptation. The more I did it, the guiltier I felt. My mother bought a vibrator to use on her arthritic neck and I started sneaking it to bed with me. Then when I was eighteen I bought some sex toys in a porn shop in San Antonio. One of them had special attachments for penetrating the anus and vagina while simultaneously stimulating the clitoris. I'd use it when I went to bed, and would often wake up in the middle of the night so horny I had to use it again to get back to sleep. I became hopelessly addicted to it."

Bolek took off his glasses and wiped a thin film of sweat from his brow. "We will now move to the place in time when you had the first dream where you woke up in another dream. Are you ready?"

"Yes."

"Good, we are sailing there now, tell me when to stop."

". . . Stop!"

"Now, Ilian—" he hooked the granny frames behind his ears "—I remind you that what you are about to experience is only a dream, a play taking place in your mind and nothing more. Understand?"

She nodded.

"Good, proceed. Tell me the first dream."

"I am putting golden chains around my neck, each has a talisman dangling from it and they feel cold against my breasts."

"So they are bare?"

"Yes, I'm totally nude, sitting in a soft chair with candles burning all around me. After I put on the last talisman I begin hanging fetishes on a wire rack. Somehow I know that some are meant to induce lust while others are for vengeance."

"What do the fetishes look like, Ilian?"

"They are about three inches long with bags at the bottom filled with some sort of beads, and each has a feather fanning out from a hook at the top. They are all a different color."

"Very well, proceed. What happens next?"

"I start chanting for Klell Ridgewall to rise from his grave and avenge his wife and daughters. I lie to him, saying the Indians have returned to torture and rape them once again. There is a boiling caldron and I watch the smoke rising until at last it takes on the form of a confederate colonel waving a long sword. But then something is wrong—the saber starts glowing as it shrinks to about half its size and the soldier melts into a gray blob.

"It frightens me and I wake up. I am very horny, unbelievably horny, and somehow know that my burning need can only be satisfied by three women. I then realize I must still be dreaming because I'm not bisexual. The next thing I know my alarm goes off and I wake up for real, recalling only that I woke up from a weird dream to discover I was still dreaming, unable to remember any details about either dream."

Bolek cut his eyes to Lori, then Dunmark, and lowered his gaze back to Ilian. "What do you do then?"

"I dress and go to work, and later that morning Carlson Loggins calls to report the first homicides—the three women that worked for him. Gary had gone to Carla's Café for breakfast so I call his cell and tell him. He instructs me to have Alfredo and Tank meet him at the office. When they leave I grow fatigued and fall asleep at my desk, something I had never done before. I again summon Klell Ridgewall and wake up in another dream, very horny again, knowing I need two men to satisfy me this time. I wake up at my desk very confused, again only able to recall that I woke up in a dream."

Once more Lori signaled him to stop.

"Thank you, Ilian. You must sleep now. We will continue at another time." Bolek reinserted the needle connected to the intravenous device by a tube.

Ilian closed her eyes a moment later.

Dunmark turned off the camcorder, placed it inside a case resting on Loggins' luxurious dresser, and started for the door.

Gary followed him into the hall.

"There's your first five murders, Gary. The demon killed the three women during the night. Then when it manifested in daylight and killed the cook and ramrod, Ilian's mind fathomed the action through a similar dream."

He harshly rubbed his face and dropped his hands, still grappling with the astonishing confessions of his sweet, demure dispatcher. "Was that ghost bird the demon?"

Dunmark nodded. "At least that's how her subconscious interprets it. He most likely had been trying to enter her since the molestations started, using the priest's unwillingness to resist pedophiliac lust to his advantage. Approaching puberty, she'd naturally find the episodes increasingly enjoyable as her hormones began making their presence known. The demon began establishing the stronghold through her deriving pleasure from the priest's actions even though she knew they were wrong. Then when she broke, what was in her mind, the fatal taboo by fondling herself, the demon was able to fully secure the stronghold. Knowing the fire had been lit, the bastard knew it wouldn't be long before she'd try to put it out on her own once the pedophile lost interest in her—an action that so defiled her conscience it enabled him to possess her, little by little through the years, until he finally gained full entrance. I was wrong, the demon wasn't invited in after all, but her lust eventually became so overpowering, he might as well have been.

"Now we have to convince Ilian that Jesus paid for her sins and can free her from bondage, not only to her sexual addiction, but will help her overcome the sin nature everyone's born with. Once she truly believes that and accepts Christ as her personal savior, the Holy Spirit will merge with her spirit, bringing it to life—the demon will no longer have a comfortable habitat and we'll be able to force it to flee."

He grimaced. "You mean that damn thing will be able to enter somebody else?"

Dunmark exhaled an edgy breath. "Hopefully not. We'll beseech God to send the fiend to hell and keep him there for eternity."

* * * *

He pulled the empty bottle from the calf's mouth, put it away, and mounted his horse. Bobby Joe would sure be pissed off if he knew. Taking advantage of Geraldo's absence, Dooly rode towards the mansion, hoping to catch Dorian having a smoke on the patio so he could talk her into a nooner at the bunkhouse. He wasn't about to go inside the mansion uninvited, figuring Montella would frown on it as much as Loggins and fire his ass. Geraldo had placed an ad in the newspaper by telephone and left for town. He'd be gone a good while, hitting all the feed stores to put up notices the Ridgewall Ranch was accepting applications for a cook and two experienced cowhands. He'd been instructed to help Bobby Joe after tending to the baby bull. It would take his homely pal a couple of hours to finish the chores Geraldo lined out, so he had plenty of time to cut off a piece.

The patio lay empty, but he knew it wouldn't be long before the chain-smoking nympho would head outside for a nicotine fix. He just hoped she'd be in as dire a need to smoke a dick as well. Pants swelling at the thought, he peered impatiently through the binoculars.

Not much time passed before the hot bitch came outside and lit up, but his stiffening pecker immediately started shrinking. That damn blonde dude had followed her.

"Shit!" Dropping the field glasses he pulled the reins hard right, spun his horse around, and galloped southward to help Bobby Joe.

* * * *

Watching thick smoke stream from her puckered lips and dainty nostrils, Bolek wondered why of all the addictive substances known to man, nicotine seemed to top the list. Dorian obviously relished the cursed tobacco weed. What imbecile had thought about inhaling smoke from it in the first place?

"That is very bad for you, you know."

She sneered at him. "Don't lecture me, Bolek. You said you wanted to talk to me in private, well here we are—get on with it."

"The way you speak, why does that change from time to time? Sometimes you talk properly, at others you sound—"

"Like a backwoods redneck? That's 'cause I am. Is that what you wanted to discuss with me? My vernacular."

"Um . . . no." He nervously folded his arms. "I am curious as to why you'd want to come to work for us."

Dorian sucked on her cigarette and exhaled smoke while speaking. "It seems like an interesting profession and I think I'd be good at it. I like fucking for the sake of fucking, because it feels good. Never once thought about getting paid for it until Carlson made me do it. I'm through with whoring. I wanna earn a worthwhile living, contribute something meaningful to society, make my life count for something."

Tapping his right index finger against his left bicep, he watched her take another deep drag. "I'm afraid you're simply not qualified for such work, and our budget wouldn't permit it even if you were."

Mocking laughter surged from her mouth with a bluish white cloud. "Forget the lack of dough for a minute and tell me what qualifications are required."

"To begin with, Dunmark is a doctor of both theology and ancient history, Lori and I have master's degrees, and you didn't even finish high school."

She snickered again. "Them demons won't listen unless you've got a college education, is that it?"

"No, of course that's not what I am saying."

"Listen, bub, ain't nothing I can't learn in a hurry when I've got a hankerin' fer it, and I got a bee in my bonnet to go into your line of work."

Her statement struck him humorous but he tried hard not to show it, fearing she'd think he was making fun of her. "You seem a very tenacious woman, I will give you that."

"And I'm the best piece of ass you'll ever have in your life. I'll let you fuck me if you'll help me convince Dunmark to bring me on the team."

Mind reeling, he took a step back and coughed. "That brings us to the second requirement—commitment to Christ, something you obviously know nothing about."

Free hand clasping her narrow waist, Dorian tossed the cigarette and raised her chin. "Okay, how do I make a commitment to Christ?"

"Are you serious?"

"Do you wonder what I look like naked? Of course I am."

Embarrassed by her remark, true though it was, he cleared his throat. "Well, first you must believe in Him."

"I do. Been acquainted with the Lord since I was no bigger'n a bug's ear. Know the Bible like the back of my hand. My spirit belongs totally to Him, but my body is mine all mine, and He takes care of it 'cause I asked Him to when I was little. Why you think I can eat my weight in groceries and yet every man that sees me grows fur on his tongue the moment he does? Why you think I can drink an alcoholic under the table and still walk a straight line? Why you think I look like I ain't turned twenty yet when I'm pushin' thirty? All because of my Lord and Savior Jesus Christ."

Utterly dumbfounded, stupefied with shock, he scratched his head, searching for the proper reply. None came.

"I'd like to take on that slimy spirit what's possessed that sweet little gal, and I believe I can do it—whup his ass all to hell 'cause greater is He that is in me than he that is in the world. Now I know I ain't no match for the devil but the devil ain't no match for The Almighty. Now ain't that right?"

"Uh . . . yah."

"Well then let's get it on. Let me at that son-of-a-bitch."

He'd never encountered anyone like her. Though vulgarly put, she spoke with a fire that seemed to stem from an unwavering faith in God's ability to protect and keep her. He decided to test the veracity of her statement about knowing the Bible. "You said you know God's word like the back of your hand. Please tell me what Jeremiah chapter forty-two, verse eleven says."

She grinned at him and ignited another cigarette. Wisps of smoke flittered around her lips as the white stick bobbled between them. "Which version you want it in? King James, New American Standard, what?"

"Uh, King James, please."

"Be not afraid of the king of Babylon, of whom ye are afraid—be not afraid of him, saith the Lord—for I am with you to save you, and to deliver you from his hand."

Incredible! he mentally gasped, for she'd quoted it verbatim. His mother had made him memorize it when he was a child, telling him to think of the king of Babylon as the bully who had it in for him in grade school.

Dorian puffed on the disgusting paper-wrapped weed, scissored it between two fingers, and finally removed it from her mouth.

He pulled out a miniature Bible he always kept on hand and requested quotes of verses from Ezekiel, Isaiah, Malachi, Proverbs, Psalms, Exodus, Judges, Matthew, Acts, First Corinthians, Galatians, Mark, Luke, John, Jude, and Revelation. Despite his best efforts to trip her up by searching for the most obscure verses he could find, she unerringly recited each one word for word as rapidly as he could silently read them. Gaping at her with awe, he closed the Bible and slid it back inside the inner pocket of his lab coat. "Totally, absolutely, stupendously amazing. Suppose I were to ask you to quote the book of Daniel in its entirety. Could you do it?"

As if she couldn't breathe without it, Dorian quickly filled her lungs with more tar and nicotine, lovely cheeks indenting from the suction. Grinning, she dropped the butt on the patio and languidly exhaled while grounding it out with the toe of her sneaker. "Listen, Bolek, I've got a photographic memory where the Bible's concerned. I've had a deep affinity with holy writ all my life. I can rattle off the whole thing from Genesis to Revelation if you want me to. 'In the beginning God created the heaven and the earth, and the earth was without form—"

"That won't be necessary," he said with a wave of his hand. "Dorian, I am *very* impressed—very impressed indeed."

"Enough to help me convince Dunmark to let me work with you guys?"

* * * *

"Well if it ain't Geraldo Toya come to call. How you been, cowboy?"

Geraldo grinned at the fat proprietor sitting on a stool behind the feed store counter, a safety pin holding up one of the straps of his overalls. "Hello, Ned."

"What can we do for you today?"

"Mind if I put this on your bulletin board?" He showed him

an index card worded the same as the ad would be when it appeared in the next edition of the local paper.

Ned scanned it and pointed towards a four-by-six section of corkboard, littered with various-size slips of paper advertising pigs for sale, stock trailers for rent, and the like. "Help yourself."

He retrieved a thumb tack from a tray beneath the advertisements and pinned the card to the board.

"I wouldn't hold my breath waiting for any responses. Folks now refer to the Ridgewall as The Death Ranch. I'm surprised you and the other hands are still willing to work there after what happened to Othello Vance, Jeremy Hicks, and Hank Best."

Geraldo wished he hadn't been ordered to keep his mouth shut. Sheriff Stoner didn't want the townsfolk knowing anything about the demon until Dunmark Finley confirmed Ilian had been delivered. It hadn't occurred to him until Ned mentioned it, but he probably wouldn't be able to get any help until the truth finally surfaced.

It looked like *The Death Ranch* would remain shorthanded a while longer.

Knowing morale would be low when he informed Dooly and Bobby Joe the three of them would have to shoulder a double load for a spell longer because of what people were thinking, he drove to the nearest grocery store, purchased a cookbook, and something tasty for supper. A good meal would brighten his vaqueros' spirits.

* * * *

Montella Pace glared at the sheriff from the end of the dining table. "What do you mean you're not having dinner with us? I made all this just for you, Gary?"

Lori suspected she was jealous of Nadia Mars, and didn't blame her—she would be too if that gorgeous vixen had been placed in Heath's custody.

The sheriff donned a grateful smile. "Good, then maybe you'll let me take some home with me so Nadia won't have to settle for takeout for supper."

"Oh hell . . ." Montella angrily rose from her chair and started for the kitchen. "There's a ton left on the stove, I'll fill you a big bowl."

From the corner of her eye Lori saw Heath trying to hold back a laugh. She poked him in the side and grinned. He winked and refocused on Montella's delicious beef stroganoff.

Bolek appeared preoccupied as he ate. Dorian slurped and burped, messily and loudly, rapidly emptying her plate. Left elbow on the table, Nicole was leaning on her hand, picking at her food.

Dunmark returned to the dining room, having excused himself to check on Ilian.

Lori looked up at him. "How's she doing?"

"Sleeping peacefully."

She pointed at Nicole, gazing absently at a cherry tomato impaled on a salad fork.

"What's wrong, Nicole?" Dunmark sensitively queried.

The contemplative Jamaican acknowledged him with a sad smile. "I really miss Rosemary. I just can't believe I've lost her too."

"I know it's hard to lose a friend, but her death wasn't in vain. Hank Best witnessing it expedited everything, and who knows how many lives were spared because of it?" He picked up his plate and advanced to the center of the table to fill it. "His would have been as well if I hadn't suffered a lapse in judgment."

Bolek groaned and tapped his chest. "I alone am to blame. If only I'd called you and relayed what Mama said, he'd still be alive."

"We both need to put it behind us, Bolek." Dunmark seated himself and unfolded a napkin. "There's nothing we can do to change what happened."

"A man that never makes mistakes is a man that never does anything," said Dorian, lips coated with white sauce from the stroganoff. "I know I can help you guys with this. Don't make another mistake by not letting me."

"What makes you say that?" Dunmark sliced open a dinner roll as he spoke.

"Because you guys haven't put all the pieces together, that's why."

"Oh? Well perhaps you'll enlighten me."

Lori could tell he'd tried not to appear condescending, but the way he was grinning undermined the effort.

Dorian forked a mass of dripping noodles into her mouth. "Let me be a part of your team from now on and I will."

"I'm afraid I can't do that."

Ravenously working her jaw as if she'd taken her first bite of food after a three day fast, she swallowed and said, "You guys are in over your head with this feller—he ain't your typical demon."

Bolek frowned at her. "How dare you make such a claim. What do you know about demons?"

"A hell of a lot more than you guys about this one."

TWENTY

Carrying two large storage bowls—one stuffed with beef stroganoff, the other salad—Gary pressed the doorbell with his elbow. When Nadia didn't answer, he stacked one on top of the other and tried the knob with his free hand, relieved to find it locked. *She must be on the pot,* he thought with a grin while fishing the key from his pocket.

His mirth turned to panic when he stepped inside.

A man lay sprawled out on his stomach, face embedded in the carpet a few feet from the couch, which had a gaping hole in the lower front. Someone had apparently blasted it with a shotgun at point blank range. Gary hastily set the bowls on his coffee table and turned the body over.

Dody Massey lay dead on his living room floor.

"Nadia! Nadia, are you here?!"

"Thank God you finally came home!" The door of his living room closet swung open to reveal Nadia crouched inside with a shotgun, tears streaming from her eyes. "I've been hiding in here for hours!"

He leaned in, took possession of the weapon, pulled Nadia to her feet, and turned towards the body. "What happened?"

She gazed fearfully at Dody's corpse. "Your whole life really does flash before your eyes when you think you're about to take your last breath. I was relaxing in the recliner with my eyes closed and never heard him come in. He spoke my name and I opened them to find he was bearing down on me with that shotgun. He told me he'd been hiding at David Nevers house and overheard the police tell Nevers I was going to testify against them. Then he told me to say my prayers. I scrunched my eyes shut and gritted my teeth, certain he was about to blow my head off. All of a sudden I heard a loud thump and the shotgun went off. I guess he must have had a heart attack. Knowing Dody never went anywhere without backup, when I saw one of the hammers still cocked and only one barrel had been fired, I grabbed the gun and hid in the closet. I just sat there trying to keep from screaming, aiming at the door, ready to shoot whoever opened it. My god, I've never been so fucking scared in my life."

Nadia buried her face in his shoulder, sobbing uncontrollably. Instinctively raising a hand to her back, he yanked the cell phone from his belt with the other and called Bob South, resisting a strong urge to pull her closer.

* * * *

"Next time you want to cheer us up, Geraldo, please don't do it with chow. I hate tuna casserole." Unable to stomach one more bite of the grub on his plate, Dooly buttered a slice of bread, forcing that to make do.

Geraldo looked hurt, as if he was a gourmet chef who'd just been told his cooking skills sucked. "Sorry, vato, I had no idea."

"I like it okay," said Bobby Joe cheerfully, chomping a mouthful of the stuff.

"Gracias. I followed the instructions in the cookbook to the letter. Maybe I'll try a meatloaf for tomorrow's supper. Does that suit you okay, Dooly?"

He offered an apologetic grin. "That'll be fine. Sorry to seem ungrateful, I'm sure you probably cooked it right. I just never have liked the taste of tuna-flavored macaroni."

Bobby Joe scooped another forkful over his fat bottom lip. "So Ned says we're working on The Death Ranch, huh?"

"Yeah, that's what everybody's calling it." Geraldo heaved a weary sigh. "And that means we probably won't be getting any help until the folks in Tomahawk County find out Klell

Ridgewall didn't do the killing."

* * * *

With Massey's sorry ass no longer contaminating his house, Gary microwaved the stroganoff, loaded two plates with it, filled two bowls with salad, set them on the table along with a couple of forks, and poured them each a glass of iced tea, insisting Nadia try to eat despite her protests that she had no appetite.

He supped heartily, marveling at how The Almighty had seen fit to spare Massey's intended victim by croaking the slime-ball with what Bob believed would prove to be a coronary thrombosis or stroke. "I don't know why you're still so strung out, Nadia. You should be celebrating the fact you obviously lead a charmed life."

She kept staring at the kitchen window like she'd been doing for the last five minutes. Dody had snuck into the house through it, quietly as the snake he'd been. If his corrupt predecessor had succeeded in silencing Nadia he'd have carried the guilt of not thinking to lock it for the rest of his life.

"Did anyone ever call about the hogs?" she muttered distantly, as if speaking to herself.

"The hogs?"

"Yeah, don't you remember . . .?" she finally abandoned the window and aimed her eyes at him. They were sad and misty. "I put an ad in the paper to sell all the livestock."

"Oh. Ilian never said anything about it so I assume no one has."

"My god, I hope they haven't starved to death. What's it been, nine days since Jared, Allen, and Carl were murdered? They haven't been fed since the day before."

"I'll call the county commissioner in the morning and tell him they've been abandoned. He'll take care of it. If they were in good health to begin with they'll survive, assuming they've had access to water all this time."

A weak smile appeared. "They do, thank God. Every pen is equipped with a self perpetuating tank. With all that's been going on I'd forgotten all about the poor critters."

Chewing a hefty bite of stroganoff, he picked up his tea and winked at her. "Maybe Dody fed them before he hid out at Nevers' place."

"That's not funny, Gary."

"Sorry." He liked the way his name sounded coming from her pretty mouth. "So what are you going to do after you testify against Nevers?"

She ran her fingers through her hair and shrugged. "I won't be going back to The Hog Farm, that's for sure. Except to get all my stuff of course."

"Wish you'd eat. It'll make you feel better."

"I suppose I should put a little something in my stomach." She sampled a tiny portion of sauce-coated noodles and raised her brows. "Oh, this is good."

"Montella made it."

Nadia imbibed a full bite of stroganoff and followed a nibble of salad with a sip of tea. "Speaking of Montella, I think I might ask her to hire me to cook for the cowboys."

"And live in the bunkhouse? You're not planning on anything illegal on the side, are you?"

She glared at him as if he had no right to suppose such a thing. "No, I'm not going to whore out to the cowboys. As a matter of fact I won't take the position unless she lets me sleep in the mansion. I enjoy living in the country, and now that Carlson's gone, I think Montella actually likes me."

"She didn't before?"

Blue and white highlights shimmered from her swirling black hair as she exaggeratedly shook her head. "She was *very* jealous of me."

"I can see why." It slipped out involuntarily and he wished

it hadn't, because the admission slapped a stimulated smile on her face.

"I'm flattered to hear you say that. She'd be jealous again if she knew I had feelings for you."

That stirred his insides, making him feel uncomfortably aroused. Why did Nadia Mars have to be a whore?

An awkward quiet hung heavy in the air when he didn't respond. Nadia uneasily scooted her chair a tad closer to the table and settled back onto it. "So . . . what's the latest on Ilian?"

He still hadn't gotten over the shock, and felt like a father having to deal with the pain of learning a trusted clergyman had turned his innocent daughter into a sex addict. "Bolek hypnotized her to find out when and how the demon possessed her."

"And did he find out?"

"Yeah, but I don't wanna talk about it."

"She and I became friends while I was staying at the jailhouse the first time. She comes off like such a sweet innocent thing. It blows my mind she committed the murders."

"Hold off on that garbage!" he snapped angrily. "That demon's the killer, not Ilian."

His reaction startled her, and yet she seemed excited by it, maybe even turned on. Her dark orbs simmered with a sultry radiance, and the slackness of her pretty mouth indicated arousal. "Heavens, I didn't mean it like that, Gary. What I meant was that I would never have imagined Ilian had such a dark side the devil could work through her."

The grotesque image of a perverted priest taking advantage of a three-year-old girl polluted his thoughts. It sickened him to the core and he hoped the bastard was rotting in hell. "Ilian never knew she was being used like that. According to Dunmark she'd go off into dreams that she couldn't recall after waking up when that demon manifested.

Bolek was able to make her remember them under hypnosis."

Nadia squinted with a thoughtful frown. "Those must be the dreams she told me she started having around the same time the murders began. She said she could only recall waking up in a dream within a dream."

"Yeah, those are the ones." He finished off the small remnant of stroganoff remaining on his plate, put the fork down, and wiped his mouth with a paper towel torn in half that served as a napkin since he didn't have any. The other section lay beside Nadia's barely touched food. "According to Dunmark, Ilian's mind rationalized the demon entering her as a dream about the ghost of a bird that got killed by a hunter. In the dream she's only three years old and the bird told her he could make her fly if she'd let him live inside her."

A sickly pale enveloped Nadia as if a stomach virus had just made its presence known by a gush of nausea. "My god, she *is* the girl in my recurring dream."

"What are you talking about?"

"I'm sure you won't believe this but I sometimes have clairvoyant dreams. A recurring one has been tormenting me lately—a flying dove being blown to smithereens with a little girl watching it from below . . . ."

When Nadia finished relaying her repeating nightmare, she pushed her plate away. "My stomach can't handle any more with these nerves. I suppose I'm still in protective custody?"

"Mm hmm, until you're through testifying against Nevers." As her mood had darkened he'd brightened his by reminding himself everything could only get better—the demon had been located and soon the residents of Tomahawk County would be rid of that devil as they'd already been liberated from a flesh and blood imp that used to be their sheriff. "It's a shame he's not an old man like Dody. Maybe then his ticker would give out too and spare the county the expense of a trial."

Nadia donned a worried pout. "Will I still have immunity now that Dody's dead?"

"Yeah, you don't have a thing to worry about. And now that we don't have to wait for Dody to be captured and hauled across the border before the judge can set a trial date, this should all be over with pretty quick."

She breathed a sigh of relief and reached for her tea. "Thank God. When can I get my car?"

He rose from the table. "We can drive out and get it right now if you want. And if you'll show me where their feed's located and hold a flashlight for me, I'll slop those hogs you're so worried about."

"You're not afraid I might just drive out of the county instead of following you home?"

"Nope. Because not only would I catch you, Pete would toss your immunity right out the window."

* * * *

After dinner Bolek followed his two colleagues up the elegant stairs ascending from the immense living room to the second floor.

Dunmark peeked at Ilian and closed the bedroom door, remaining in the hall. "Okay, guys, what are we to make of Dorian's statement?"

Lori folded her arms. "I don't put any stock in it. She's intrigued by what we do and is trying to bluff her way onto the team. Either that or she just likes being the center of attention."

"That may be, but she certainly knows her Bible."

"What makes you say that, Bolek?"

He turned to Dunmark, who'd spoken. "I was talking to her outside, and she told me she could quote the scriptures from cover to cover. Then she started doing it until I stopped her. This occurred after I had tested her by asking her to quote several verses which I was randomly selecting from all over the Bible. She unerringly quoted them all word for word."

Lori made a sour face. "Well that doesn't prove she's really knowledgeable about the demon we're dealing with."

"I agree, but I think we should hear her out. Dunmark, Dorian is a very remarkable woman, and if she's not just playing head games I think we should give her a fair listen."

Dunmark opened the door and motioned Lori inside. "Bolek and I will go talk to her and see what she has to say."

"Okay, but I think you're wasting your time."

They descended the stairs and found Dorian sitting in the living room with Montella and Nicole. Ranger Crow entered from the hall and asked where Lori was.

"She's watching Ilian," said Dunmark.

"Okay if I join her?"

"Of course."

As the ranger made his way to the second floor, Bolek approached Dorian, relaxing on a long divan. "Dunmark and I would like to have a word with you."

She jumped to her feet—causing her magnificent breasts to jostle beneath a black t-shirt—slipped on a blue jacket matching the color of her slacks, and grinned at him. "I knew you guys would come around. Let's go out on the patio so I can smoke while you give me the third degree."

They went down the hall and exited the mansion through a door in the kitchen. Dorian pulled a package of Camels from her jacket, freed a butane lighter tucked inside the cellophane, and lit up. The chilly night air accentuated the smoke streaming from her beautiful lips.

Dunmark took a step sideways to avoid the cloud. "All right, tell us what you think you know about the demon."

"When you introduced yourself at the jailhouse you said the ghost of Klell Ridgewall was really a demonic manifestation." She took another quick drag and exhaled. "I've never seen the ghost but everyone that has, says the same thing—he's holding a sword. Hank Best said the thing he saw was gray and had a long knife. Confederate gray, I'm wagering. Your demon and the ghost of Klell Ridgewall are one and the same. You can exorcise that devil from Ilian but it won't put an end to the killing. You'll have to deal with the person that's manipulating the colonel's ghost devil before this brutal shit will stop."

Bolek smiled at her. "We have the manipulator. It's the demon himself, making Ilian think she's responsible for summoning the ghost of Klell Ridgewall."

Dorian shook her head. "You're wrong."

"Then who is, pray tell?"

She shifted her focus to Dunmark. "Let me on your team and I'll tell ya."

"Come on, Bolek, we're wasting our time." Dunmark started for the house and he followed.

"The manipulator is Nadia Mars!" shouted Dorian.

He stopped and turned around, as did Dunmark. "What makes you think that?"

"I heard her talking in her sleep when we were in the pokey, the same night Hank saw the demon. Didn't think nothin' of it at the time so I rolled over on my side and dozed off. But hearing y'all discussing Ilian's dreams at the supper table made it click. Nadia was ordering somebody around in her sleep. Someone she called Gray Bird."

* * * *

Behind the wheel of her Shelby Cobra, Nadia kept a few car lengths back from Gary's taillights as they headed for town. He'd obviously worked with hogs before, knowing how much food they needed. Good thing too, since she hadn't a clue. All the pigs were much lighter than when she'd last seen them, but thankfully none had succumbed to starvation. Her ears still rang from their incredibly loud squeals of relief when he'd filled their troughs. He'd looked so masculine, heaving those heavy buckets into the air and dumping them over the fence, speaking to the swine as if they were his own, promising them they'd all be okay.

The goats had managed fine, having plenty of graze since the first freeze had yet to arrive. Gary had enticed them into the holding pen by sprinkling corn at the feet of a large buck with S-shaped horns the whole herd followed. After closing the gate he'd emptied the bucket, scattering the remaining yellow kernels on the ground for the baaing varmints.

Most of the chickens were still alive and roosting, apparently subsisting on insects and cannibalizing their eggs and dead comrades, according to Gary. But the poor rabbits hadn't survived the nine day fast, and she'd almost puked from the stench of death emanating from their hutches.

A strange thought sprang to her mind as she drove. Though the idea made her feel somewhat delusional, she couldn't help wondering if whatever killed Dody—heart attack or stroke—had happened strictly for her sake. Was it possible she possessed some unknown power much greater than clairvoyance?

TWENTY ONE

The day after Dody Massey attempted to blow her head off, Gary brought Nadia into the courtroom. He took a seat in back of the gallery as Pete Lemmon guided her down the aisle to the prosecution's table. Everyone stood when the judge entered, and a few minutes later Pete rattled off the charges against David Nevers.

Nadia didn't have to testify because the crooked patrolman threw himself on the mercy of the court. Though she never took the stand, her presence had been what prompted Nevers' confession, and Pete invited her to be his honored guest at the Christmas party held each December for all Tomahawk County employees. The whole proceeding took only forty minutes.

Gary escorted the tremendously relieved witness out of the courthouse and cut his eyes to her as they walked down a flight of concrete steps. "Still thinking about cooking for the cowpokes?"

She nodded. "I'll be on my way to see Montella as soon as we get back to your place."

He'd driven Nadia downtown in his cruiser, leaving her car at his house.

"Did you call the county commissioner about the livestock?"

"Not yet," he replied with a wink. "After I drop you off I'm heading out there to feed the hogs. I enjoyed slopping them so much last night, it got me to fooling around with the idea of trying to buy the place once all the red tape clears and the county clerk can tell me who owns it now."

Nadia moistened her lips and cast him a nervous smile. "I

have a confession to make. I was nosing around your closet yesterday and found a box of pictures. You were dressed as a cowhand in some of them. Watching you last night, I can tell you love ranch work."

"You went through my stuff?" He tried to sound pissed but the pleasure he felt over her being that curious about him defeated the purpose.

"Yeah, sorry." The smirk she wore testified she'd seen through his guise. "So am I to gather you're thinking of giving up law enforcement for hog farming?"

"No. Thinking about doing both—selling my house and moving out there if I can get my hands on the spread. It's big enough to raise a dozen head of cattle on, and small enough it won't eat up all my time."

She cringed as if he'd just stepped on her toes. "Doesn't it bother you that five people were killed in that house?"

"The house didn't kill them, the demon did."

"I can't believe you're not at least tempted to take Montella up on her offer."

He chuckled. "Oh I'm tempted but I'll never give in to it because I'd wind up becoming Mister Montella Pace if I did."

An admiring smile draped her face. "Most men would jump at the chance to marry a rich woman as beautiful as Montella even if it meant being henpecked."

"Maybe so, but not this cowboy."

* * * *

After slopping hogs, feeding chickens, and turning goats out to pasture, Gary headed for the jailhouse. When he stepped through the door Alfredo spun around in the dispatcher's chair, taking him in with anxious eyes. "Is Ilian okay?"

"Yeah, she's fine, Alfredo. I'm told she'll be good as new once she's free of that devil." He patted the young Mexican on the back and went to his office.

Tank walked in and pointed at the answering machine. "Dunmark left a message for you."

"Wonder why he didn't call my cell phone, he has the number."

The big redhead shrugged and hit the playback button.

"Gary," said Dunmark through the digital recording, *"it's probably nothing, but we'd like to reexamine Nadia Mars when it's convenient."*

He glanced at Tank and frowned. "Wonder what that's all about?"

* * * *

Something told her not to pass through the open gates of the Ridgewall Ranch—a peculiar, irresistible nudging from somewhere deep inside. Nadia instead made a u-turn and headed back for town. The strange sensation brought to mind what she'd started to tell Gary that morning but hadn't gotten the chance to. After showering she'd walked into the kitchen to see him sliding his cell phone into a holder on his belt. "That was Pete," he'd said. "We've got just enough time to grab a quick breakfast at Carla's before getting you to the courthouse. The judge expedited things and Nevers' trial is set to commence at nine o'clock. I'll have Tank haul him down there."

Nervousness over having to testify had totally distracted her, and when they'd left the courthouse she'd been so relieved it had completely slipped her mind until now. The recurring dream had haunted her again last night, but before the sight of the bloody body parts had startled her awake she'd recognized the girl's adult face.

The woman wasn't Ilian.

TWENTY TWO

Bolek stood with arms folded as Lori explained to Ilian that very few people, if any, get through life without masturbating at least once.

The sedated Mexican looked relieved. "Are you saying it's not a sin, Lori?"

"No, I'm not saying that, because usually the function is accompanied by fantasizing about having sex with someone the person isn't married to which makes it either adultery or fornication in the heart, both of which *are* sins. The act itself is never addressed Biblically so can't be technically labeled as such. However, anyone that deems it a sin is defiling their conscience when they do it, which makes them vulnerable to satanic manipulation."

Ilian's big brown eyes swelled with shame. "Like me?"

Lori nodded.

"I'm so embarrassed that you know my dirty secrets. I have no memory at all of telling them to you, or the dreams I still can't remember."

"You were under hypnosis, that's why you cannot recall," said Bolek.

"Would you tell them to me?"

"Sorry. It would not be wise to do so at this time." He looked at Lori. "Are you ready?"

"Yes, go ahead."

Reciting a rhyme he'd implanted in her mind yesterday before bringing her out of hypnosis, he watched Ilian's eyes glaze over, indicating she'd gone under again.

He waited until Dunmark switched on the camcorder and began. "Ilian, are you familiar with the name Gray Bird?"

* * * *

Hearing his office door open, Gary turned to see Nadia step in, looking troubled about something.

"How'd it go with Montella?" he asked warily, figuring she'd been turned down because of her expression.

"I didn't talk to her after all."

"How come?"

She took a deep breath and rubbed her temples as if trying to relieve a headache. "I drove out to the ranch but couldn't make myself pass through the gates."

"Why?"

"That's what I came to talk to you about."

* * * *

Dooly pulled his lunch from the saddle bag and sat down in the shade of the south stock tank. The nights had started cooling off but the early November days were still uncomfortably warm around noon. Unable to spare the time to rustle up a midday meal, Geraldo had told Bobby Joe and him they were on their own unless they wanted bacon and egg sandwiches. They'd both declined so Geraldo had only fried enough extra for his lunch while making breakfast. When Bobby Joe stuffed two hotdog buns with leftover tuna casserole, he'd called that gross, which had brought a snicker from Geraldo, who'd said, "That looks a lot more savory than that garbage you threw together, Dooly."

He'd squashed three pieces of baloney, two squares of pepper jack cheese, and a handful of corn chips between two slices of bread, one coated with peanut butter, the other barbecue sauce. Pulling it out of the baggie, he thought of poor Hank frying all that baloney for what turned out to be his last meal.

Geraldo and Bobby Joe were rounding up steers nearing

market weight. He'd been sent to replace the backflow valve on the windmill that'd been repaired the day Loggins and Sonya were killed. That chore had been completed before he'd dug out his chow, so he'd head to the corral after eating and join up with them when they brought the next few head in.

Expecting a raise now that he'd been named ramrod, he planned to call Montella as soon as he got to the bunkhouse after the workday ended and let her know he'd been promoted. While thinking on that he got an idea that made his pecker twitch. He'd ask if he could come up to the mansion to discuss his pay. That way he might have a shot at arranging a rendezvous with Dorian, which he could only do in person. Loggins had laid down the law that no cowhand could call the mansion except for pressing ranch business, and Montella hadn't dismissed that rule so he had to figure it still applied.

* * * *

"Why does Dunmark want to reexamine me?"

"Don't know. He left the message on the machine." Gary put a hand on Nadia's back and started for the door. "Come on, I'll treat you to lunch at Carla's on the way."

Her dark eyes turned apprehensive. "I'll have lunch with you but I won't go out there. If he wants to test me again he'll have to do it here or at your place."

The fear on her face didn't make any sense. "What's bugging you about being tested on the ranch? Ilian's sedated, she can't hurt you."

"It's not because of Ilian, Gary."

"Then what?"

"That's what I was trying to tell you before you interrupted me about Dunmark."

"All right, so what have you been trying to tell me?"

* * * *

"Sure looking forward to supper tonight, Geraldo," Bobby Joe spouted through a wide grin. "I *love* meatloaf."

"Sorry, vato, but we won't be having meatloaf after all. We'd be starving before it got done. When I made the offer last night I had no idea it was so complicated and that it takes ninety minutes to bake the damn thing after you get all the ingredients put together."

Bobby Joe's heavy lips drooped with disappointment. "Then what're you gonna make us?"

"Hamburger Helper, it's quick and easy." He swung his rope to dissuade one of six steers they were herding from turning around. "Ah, speaking of helper, Dooly's waiting for us I see."

The handsome young vaquero opened the gate when they neared the corral.

"Heeyah!" cried Bobby Joe, hurrying the six head through it before the other steers they'd rounded up to fatten could escape.

Dooly closed the gate and jumped on his mount from the rear like Roy Rogers.

Geraldo grinned at him. "Showoff! Is the windmill working okay?"

"Yep."

"Good. Let's round up another batch of steak on hooves."

They trotted along towards the Rio Grande. The herd had gathered on a hay-baited section of acreage half a mile from the corral, so they wouldn't be seeing the river today. He inhaled a deep breath of fresh air and emitted a blissful sigh. "Ah, there's nothing like working in the great outdoors. Aren't you glad you're not pushing a pencil in some stuffy old office, mi amigos?"

Dooly chuckled. "You sure are in a good mood. How come?"

"Because I got laid last night, my friend. Though it was only a wet dream I plan to turn it into reality. Hank said I would meet another and he was right."

"Who's the unlucky girl," sniggered Bobby Joe.

"A woman of my own breed. Ilian Herrera."

"You're shit outta luck, amigo," said Dooly, brows arched with surprise. "She's Alfredo Parra's woman. Better dream you up another chick."

"Not for long. When she's free of that demon I will show her the difference between a boy and a man. The deputy won't stand a chance once I do. And knowing him to be a gentleman like myself, he'll gracefully bow out."

Dooly took off his hat and ran a sleeve over his forehead. "I wouldn't count on that. Ilian once told me she and Alfredo have been thicker'n thieves since they were little kids, and they have wedding plans."

"Tisk tisk, they won't come to fruition."

"How can you be so sure?" inquired Bobby Joe.

"Because of the way she kept looking at me when she served us supper in jail. At the time I was still too hurt over losing Sonya to flirt back. But that dream I had last night was so real—so vividly, wonderfully real—I know it sounds crazy, but I woke up in love with her. I've thought of nothing all day but how beautiful she is."

* * * *

The hideous supernatural distortion of Ilian's features horrified Lori—skin bubbling as if stretched over boiling water, eyes popping in and out of their sockets in alternate succession, tongue stretching to impossible lengths, thrusting like a serpent's all over a grossly discolored face. Though Bolek's pale facade revealed him to be equally afraid, his voice didn't show it. He kept prodding the demon, forcing the godless entity to continue manifesting.

"You are bound by the chains of the righteousness of Christ who fills my spirit and those of my comrades. Why have you chosen this girl to defile?"

"Fuck you, *ty glupi Polaczec!*"

"You will speak to me in English and not Polish."

"Dlaczego? Czy wstydzisz sie swojej rasy?"

"No, I am not ashamed of my race and I am not a stupid Polack. I know you are trying to provoke me to anger but you cannot, for I am filled with the Holy Spirit who anoints me for the task of casting you out."

Lori started praying in tongues.

The demon glared at her through Ilian's eyes. "Stop that infernal nonsensical shit-speak, gringo bitch, or I'll rip your fucking lips off and eat them!"

She prayed louder.

Dunmark joined in, using his own prayer language while manning the camcorder.

Ilian's body began ratcheting on the bed, arms and legs straining to break free of the restraints nothing but the hand of God kept from being broken.

Bolek drew in a deep breath and pointed at the devil. "Very well, I no longer wish to know anything about you. Ilian has accepted Jesus as her personal savior and her newborn spirit seeks none but the Holy Ghost to reside within her so you must leave. Claiming my place through the blood of Christ as a son of The Living God, I command you—leave this woman and be bound where Yahweh sends you!"

A deafening ungodly squeal erupted from Ilian's foaming mouth as she arched her back with a violent thrust—spine forming a perfect arc, body hovering above the bed, hospital gown draping her like a table cloth. Then suddenly the appalling demonic face transformed into that of a lovely young woman, and she dropped to the mattress.

Joyful tears pouring from her eyes, Ilian raised her head and looked around the room. "He's gone, isn't he."

"Yah," said Bolek, wiping his sweaty brow with a trembling hand. "He is gone, never to bother you again. Let us give thanks."

As Ilian joined Bolek and Dunmark in praising the Lord for His mighty deliverance, Lori hurried for the hall to fetch Heath. Nobody outside the team could be in the room during the terminal function. The slightest doubt of the veracity of God's word would have empowered the demon to fully manifest and slaughter everyone present.

* * * *

Bolek slid the intravenous needle from Ilian's arm, unfastened the padded cuffs on her wrists and ankles, and helped her rise from the bed.

"Woo, I feel faint."

"The sedative will wear off soon. We finished just in time for dinner. Are you hungry?"

A bright smile sprang to her face. "Yes, ravenous."

He laughed and gave her a gentle hug. "You should be, after being fed through a vein for the last two days. I didn't give you a stimulant because you need solid food and it would likely suppress your appetite."

She gazed at him for several seconds, eyes filled with wonderment. "All my life I thought I was a true believer until today. Now I realize Jesus was little more to me than a make believe figure like Santa Claus. I wonder how many others are like I was."

"Far too many, I'm afraid," said Dunmark returning from the bathroom.

Bolek hurried past him. It had been hours since he'd last been able to relieve himself. Once he got his bladder blissfully emptied, he stepped to the lavatory, splashed water on his face, and combed his hair.

Lori and Heath were present when he returned to the

bedroom. Both were smiling at Ilian.

"Come on, dear," said Lori. "Let's get you cleaned up and dressed, then we'll go downstairs for dinner. If you gentlemen will excuse us . . . ."

* * * *

She'd talked Gary into letting her make dinner instead of dining at Carla's. Nadia had bought a fryer and fresh vegetables. He obviously enjoyed her fried chicken but hadn't bothered with the broccoli or carrots she'd steamed. Watching him finish off a second helping of mashed potatoes and gravy, she folded her hands together and rested them on a kitchen table she'd never planned to sit at again. He'd wanted to feed the animals and check out the house as a potential buyer, so she'd cooked their supper at The Hog Farm.

"You really are just a meat and potatoes guy, aren't you."

He blotted his lips with a cloth napkin whose red-and-white checks matched the tablecloth she'd dug out of a drawer for the occasion. "Suppose so. That was great, thanks."

His cell phone rang. Soon after he answered it his eyes lit up. "That's fantastic, Heath, thanks for calling! And she's a hundred percent okay? . . . Great, tell her I'll expect her to be at work in the morning . . . Of course I'm only kidding. Has Alfredo heard the news yet? . . . Okay, I'll call and tell him. Bye." He aimed his beaming smile her way while rising from the table. "Ilian's been liberated—they successfully cast that demon out a few minutes ago. Come on, let's go see her."

"I'm not going out there, Gary."

"Why?"

"I told you why. And I sure don't want to stay here alone, so please drop me off at your place so I can get my car."

"Where will you go?"

"I don't know. Probably get a motel room, I guess."

"Don't be silly. You can stay at my house for the time

being." He punched a button on his phone and brought it to his ear.

* * * *

Gary released Ilian from a rib-crunching hug and let her sit back down beside Alfredo to finish supper. He'd called the ecstatic deputy from The Hog Farm before driving Nadia to his house, so it hadn't surprised him to find the two lovebirds sitting together when he arrived. "Where's Heath?"

"He took Lori to town for dinner," said Dunmark with an odd grin. "I think they were planning on a date until Bolek said he wanted to tag along."

Montella smiled at him from the end of the dining table. "Are you sure you don't want to try some of Dorian's pot roast, Gary? It's delicious."

"Couldn't eat another bite . . ." he patted his stomach. "I'm full of Nadia's fried chicken."

Her lips thinned with agitation. She grabbed her napkin and started daubing them. "Where is she anyway?"

"Over at my place."

"Why didn't she come with you?"

"I need to talk to Dunmark about that very thing."

"She doesn't want to cooperate with us, huh? Well it's no longer necessary anyway."

"No, Dunmark, she just refuses to do it here."

Montella threw her napkin on the table. "Why that little bitch! Thinks she's too good for the likes of me now that she's no longer facing charges, is that it?"

He couldn't help laughing over her reaction. "That's not it at all. She's scared to come out here because of a premonition she had earlier today while she was driving out here to talk to you about the possibility of working for you as cook for the cowhands. She thinks it stemmed from a recurring dream she's been having and it scared her so bad she turned around and went back to town."

A shocked grin replaced Montella's scowl as she collapsed in her chair with a radical mood reversal. "Nadia wants to work for me? Well please tell her I'd love to accommodate her. Only she's certainly not going to live in the bunkhouse. She'll have her pick of rooms, except mine of course. I'm moving into Carl's now that Ilian's no longer occupying it."

"Shit!" yelled Dorian, flinging her arms across her stomach. The action caused her breasts to bobble dramatically, pulling his thoughts to Nadia's awesome bosom. "So you're kicking me and Nicole out?"

"Well *no!*" Montella laughingly bellowed. "You two can stay as long as you like."

"Then why are you offering up our rooms?"

"I meant she could have her pick of any room besides those occupied, you silly nitwit."

Nicole turned towards the blonde bombshell, face dripping with relief. "Can I work for you too? I'm not sure what you could use me for other than cleaning, but I certainly wouldn't expect you to pay me as much as Carlson did."

"Guess I need to apply for a job too," spouted Dorian resignedly, "since Dunmark won't take me aboard his ship. But don't count on Nadia cooking for the cowboys. Sooner or later mister hot shot investigator over there will figure out this demon shit ain't over with. Nadia's the one what's been a-yankin' that sucker's chain."

Gary frowned at her. "What are you talking about?"

"She overheard Nadia talking in her sleep to someone she called Gray Bird," said Dunmark, "but the name evoked nothing when Bolek had Ilian under hypnosis. Nadia was merely reacting to a dream."

Dorian cackled and leered at the investigator. "The hell she was. She was ordering that demon around, I tell ya."

A queasy sense of alarm rose in Gary's gut—the taunt-loving Cajun didn't seem to be bullshitting this time. "Um,

Dunmark, when you finish eating I need to speak with you privately."

* * * *

Nadia was thrilled Ilian had been delivered and would've loved seeing the sweet girl in her right mind again. But not on the Ridgewall Ranch. She'd thought about calling Montella but decided not to. Her feelings for Gary had grown too strong to be anywhere near him if they were destined to go unrequited. If he didn't want her, then she'd be seeking honest employment somewhere far away from Tomahawk County.

* * * *

Gary guided Dunmark down the hall and stopped near the library. "Why did you want to test Nadia again?"

"I didn't say test, I said reexamine. Dorian was so adamant Nadia was issuing commands to someone named Gray Bird I felt we should put her under hypnosis and try to find out what she was saying in her sleep. But after discovering the name had no affect on Ilian it became a moot point—especially now that the demon's been driven out and bound in whatever nether region God sent him to. After I show the district attorney the video and help you and Heath convince him he's not looking for a human killer, we'll be heading back to Colorado."

Dorian's certainty worried him despite Dunmark's lack of concern. "Pete Lemmon's already convinced, but the video will certainly help him out a lot. The poor guy's been racking his brains trying to figure out how to explain all these murders to the press without sounding like a madman. Nadia wants to talk to you about her dream, but she won't do it out here."

"Has she told it to you?"

"Yeah."

"Well fill me in."

Glancing down the hall to make sure no one had snuck out of the dining room to eavesdrop, he relayed the nightmare. "She was never able to tell who the woman was before waking up. After Ilian's outburst in the dayroom Nadia suspected it might be her and became convinced it was when I told her about Ilian's ghost bird. But last night she finally made out the face and it was Nicole's. After she had that premonition she's scared to go anywhere near the girl."

Dunmark narrowed his eyes. "Why did she suspect it was Ilian then? She's not black."

"I asked her the same thing. Nadia thinks the woman having Caucasian skin but Nicole's face means she was symbolizing both of them. The premonition convinced her of it, and she's always feared the recurring dream is about the murders. Now let me ask you something. Is Dorian sure it couldn't have been Nicole she overheard talking to this Gray Bird?"

TWENTY THREE

Dorian had gone outside to smoke when they returned to the dining room. Gary glanced at Nicole. Dunmark's assessment was bound to be correct—her Jamaican accent could hardly be mistaken as Nadia's, a native Texan. But he disagreed with the investigator's notion that the recurring dream most likely had no clairvoyant capacity at all. The little girl being so angry about the dove's death certainly could tie to Ilian's ghost bird, and a naked woman standing on a mass of human body parts so closely correlating with the actual slayings seemed too coincidental. On the other hand, he realized he might be putting too much stock in Nadia's nightmare because of a gut feeling they hadn't tied up all the loose ends.

"What did Dooly want when he dropped by earlier?" Nicole asked Montella.

"He wanted to discuss a pay raise with me. Geraldo promoted him to ramrod."

"Did you give him one?"

"No. I told him we'd have to wait and see how he handles the job when they get some new hands. Geraldo's looking for well seasoned men. That means they'll probably be much older than Dooly, and I'm not sure they'd respect such a young cowboy. Six months from now, if Geraldo thinks Dooly's handling things okay, I'll sweeten the pot a little."

Montella's reasoning impressed him, she sure seemed to have a head on her shoulders. Loggins must have picked up on that early since he'd self-servingly put her through college. It gave another indication he'd wind up pussy-whipped if he married her. He didn't care for bookkeeping and it would be so easy to let the little woman take charge of the finances while he focused on the livestock. Grinning inside, he couldn't help wondering if that would be such a bad thing.

"What would you do in that situation, Gary? With Dooly I mean."

The lighthearted muse evaporated. "It's your ranch."

"That doesn't answer my question. What would you do if it was your ranch? Would you have given him a raise?"

"It would depend on how good a hand he is. Since I don't know the facts on that, I couldn't say."

"Fair enough . . ." she raised her wine glass and took a sip. "All you have to do is say the word and it *will* be yours. Then you can see for yourself whether he deserves a raise or not."

He snickered and started for the hall. "Goodnight, Montella."

"Where are you going?" she cried after him.

"Home."

"To Nadia . . .?"

* * * *

Bolek felt like a mindless fool. *How could I have not sensed these two wanted to be alone?* They were sitting in a café called Carla's where they'd enjoyed a nice catfish dinner. He'd noticed the ranger giving Lori a romantic stare which she had blatantly reacted favorably to. It was at that moment he'd wanted to shoot himself for being such an idiot. He had to do something to salvage their plans. "Um, I feel under the weather suddenly, quite fatigued. I wonder, dear Heath, if I could impose upon you to drive me back to the ranch?"

The only thing that could have been brighter than the smile he felt inside at his request being granted was the delight Lori and the ranger tried to disguise. Though both expressed concern for his welfare, their countenances were practically glowing.

* * * *

Dooly had taken a double beating. Worried Montella might insist on discussing everything over the phone, he'd gone to the mansion without bothering to call. Not only had he been declined a raise, he hadn't been able to signal Dorian that he wanted to talk to her because Montella had stepped out on the front porch after Nicole answered the door and told him to wait there. He'd sulked all the way back to the bunkhouse and while wolfing down a plate of Geraldo's ground beef concoction had promised himself he'd fuck that bitch before turning in if he had to wait all night to catch her outside by herself.

Now within fifty feet of the patio and closing, he'd finally lucked out. Dorian was alone, sucking on a cigarette. His pants started tightening at the crotch the minute he saw her.

"Pssst!"

She turned his direction. "Dooly?"

"Yeah."

A lustful grin captured her gorgeous face. "Can you bring a blanket to the barn?"

His dick turned to stone. "Yeah."

"Meet you there in half an hour."

Biting his lip to keep from whooping for joy, he hurried back to the bunkhouse. Geraldo passed him as he neared the porch.

"Hey, hombre. Wondered where you took off to after chow."

"Yeah, I uh, just stepped out for some fresh air. Where you headed?"

"To the mansion. Montella called and told me to get over there pronto because she wants to discuss something with me. Oh, and she had some great news. Ilian's no longer possessed and is completely okay. Now the sheriff can tell everybody what happened and we can finally get some help around here."

"Hot dang, that is good news!"

"Simón. Well I'd best be on my way."

Dooly entered the bunkhouse to find Bobby Joe sprawled out on the couch watching TV.

"Where you been, Dew?"

He had to think of something fast because Bobby Joe wouldn't buy the fresh air bullshit and he didn't want to share Dorian. "Went to check on the calf."

"How is the little fella?"

"Fine, but it's kind of nippy out. Thought I'd dig out an old blanket to wrap around him."

Bobby Joe rose to a sitting position and reached for a boot. "They got that demon out of Ilian."

"Yeah, Geraldo just told me. Why are you putting your boots on?"

"Figured I'd go with you."

"Nah, chill out and watch your show, I don't need no help."

A cheesy grin spread across Bobby Joe's ugly mug. "Yes you do, you sly dog. Hell it's almost sixty degrees outside. Think I don't know you came back here to get a blanket because you're planning on fucking Dorian in the barn?"

Shit! "Okay, you caught me, but she didn't ask for you this time."

"She will after you pop your load, just like she did that night in the ballroom closet. One man ain't enough for that gal once her engine gets hot, and you know it."

Remembering how sore he'd been the morning after she'd worn them both out, he realized Bobby Joe was right. "Okay, let's grab a blanket and head that way."

* * * *

After a hot bath in Gary's tub Nadia went to the spare bedroom, did her chest exercises, applied makeup, and selected a change of clothes from her suitcase. Panties held towards the floor, she started to step into them but changed her mind when she heard the front door open. Tossing them on the bed, she slipped on a silky black robe, tied the sash, pulled it open at her breasts to expose the center of her chest, and made her way to the living room.

A hot rush flooded her body when Gary's eyes locked onto her cleavage. The come-on smile she'd faked countless times came of its own accord and had never been more sincere. "Just got out of the tub and was about to get dressed when I heard you come home. How's Ilian doing?"

Still gazing hungrily at the inner swells of her boobs, he nervously cleared his throat. "She's great . . . I um, told Dunmark your dream. He no longer needs to reexamine you."

Seeing the khaki was bulging below his belt buckle, she loosened the sash and dropped her robe to the floor. "I've fallen in love with you, Gary. Please give me a chance to make you love me . . . ."

* * * *

"Yes, you heard me right. Now what's your answer?"

Geraldo shook his head. "Sorry, Montella, it's not in me to shirk my responsibilities, and none of this makes any sense. Besides the fact you haven't told me why you're asking me to do this thing, Nadia Mars hasn't shown any indication she's attracted to me."

The regal blonde threw her head back and laughed. "Nadia's a whore. She's attracted to the high life. She'll jump at the chance believe me, and you can stash five grand in your piggy bank when you return."

Nicole entered the library. "Oh, so this is where you two went. There's nothing good on television tonight so I decided to find something to read."

Montella smiled at her. "By all means, dear, but be quick

about it and do your reading elsewhere. Geraldo and I are discussing business."

"Sorry, didn't mean to interrupt. I'll leave you two alone." She stepped into the hall and closed the door behind her.

His shapely employer rose and poured two brandies from a beautiful crystal decanter. Handing him one, she returned to the splendid antique chair she'd been sitting on when Nicole appeared. She took a sip and silently gazed at him over the rim of her glass.

Downing two nervous gulps in quick succession, he wiped his lips with the back of his hand. The liquor had gone down smooth and good—the highest quality he'd ever been served. Soothing warmth radiated from his stomach, relaxing him, making the sofa she'd bade him to occupy feel even more comfortable. Would he really be less of a man if he succeeded in talking Nadia Mars into accompanying him on a six week cruise? It wasn't like Montella had asked him to sleep with the woman, so he wouldn't be betraying his newfound love for Ilian. Again he pulled at the tumbler, feeling a deep sense of wellbeing—sitting in such an opulent setting, conversing with a very wealthy and beautiful woman, nerves becoming blissfully tranquilized by the brandy.

Ah but the ranch. They were sorely shorthanded as it was, and though Dooly could probably handle things for that amount of time with a full crew, having only Bobby Joe to help him would be far too great a burden to bear. Heaving a big sigh, he raised the glass to his lips, took another drink, and told her so.

The long painted nails and bejeweled rings of her free hand glistening as they passed through the air, she waved off his protest. "I'll get some help out here for Dooly and Bobby Joe while you're away, even if I have to charter a plane to fly in some cowboys who aren't afraid to work on this ranch. The nasty rumors about this place will have died down by the time you return and you can hire the hands you need if the temporary help doesn't want to stay on permanently."

He leaned forward. "You still haven't told me why you want me to take Nadia on a cruise."

Montella sipped her brandy and smiled. "I need her out of the way so I can win Sheriff Stoner over. If all goes as planned, you'll soon be answering to him instead of me because I'll be signing the ranch over to him."

"Ay yi yi! Why would you do such a thing?"

She laughed. "It's quite simple, Geraldo. I'll be giving it to him as a wedding present when I become his wife."

* * * *

Seeing Nadia naked had been more than Gary could bear and he'd been powerless to resist her. His voice had sounded foreign to him as he'd huskily muttered, "I'll need to make a run to the store first."

"Why?" she'd asked, the look on her sexy face indicating fear the fire she'd ignited might go out once his eyes were no longer glued to her hypnotizing body.

"For protection."

"Unless you're worried about infecting me with something, you don't need protection. And I'm on the pill."

Not wanting to waste a second more, he'd lowered his trousers and screwed her on the couch. Now he was naked too, and they were in his bed. Everything about the whore captivated and tormented him—her smell and taste, her deep kisses, large firm breasts, the way she moved and moaned, the tightness of her womanhood, the texture of her nipples and clitoris, the way both felt between his lips. It had been so long he'd forgotten what an orgasm felt like when not being produced by his own hand. Pumping back and forth inside her like a man possessed, when her pleasured moans turned orgasmic, he gritted his teeth as a second burst of hot semen gushed out, simultaneously sending him to heaven and hell.

Heaving for breath, he fell onto his back. Nadia rolled on top of him, flattening her beautiful tits against his hairy chest, resting her cheek against his, repeatedly declaring how much she loved him.

* * * *

Nicole answered the door when he rang the bell, and looked past him at the taillights rapidly moving towards the highway. "Where are Heath and Lori going?"

Bolek smiled while stepping inside. "I would imagine the two of them are discussing that very thing right now."

Frowning over his statement, she closed and locked the door. "I was about to have some ice cream. Care to join me?"

"Sounds good. What flavor?"

"We have every kind."

She led him to the hall entrance of the kitchen instead of going through the dining room, and retrieved a gallon bucket of vanilla from a large upright freezer. "What can I get you?"

"Vanilla will be fine."

A guilty smile crept across her face as she opened one of two refrigerators standing side by side. "It's fattening enough without it but I like chocolate on mine."

His mouth watered as she set a plastic bottle of chocolate syrup on a square table surrounded by four chairs. "Me too."

"Have a seat and I'll get us fixed up."

He did as she asked and watched her take two dessert bowls from an upper cabinet and place them on a gleaming white counter stretching the length of the wall, a window looming above a three-basin sink the only section without beautiful walnut storage units attached to it. Florescent lighting fastened above translucent panels covering the entire ceiling made the brass handles on the doors and drawers shine like gold. She retrieved a scoop, filled the bowls, dropped it in the sink, returned the ice cream tub to the freezer, stabbed a spoon in each mound of frozen sweetness, and carried them to the table.

"Is Ilian still here?"

"Mm mm, Alfredo took her home." She squirted a liberal pool of black syrup onto her ice cream. "All of us owe you, Dunmark, and Lori a huge debt of gratitude, Bolek. You guys most likely saved our lives."

"It is Dunmark you have to thank. He researched the Ridgewall legend some years ago and learned first hand the manifestations were real. If he hadn't, none of us would have suspected the murders could possibly have been supernatural when we heard about them on the news."

"I'm *so* glad this is finally all over with . . ." she handed him the bottle. "So that's why Dunmark came down here?"

Nodding, he coated his own dairy delight and imbibed a delicious spoonful. "We were watching the news and when a clip came on of Gary telling reporters that three women and two men had been beheaded on the Ridgewall Ranch, Dunmark left for Texas the next morning."

Nicole took a large bite and donned a faraway look while swallowing. "I feel foolish now, thinking a voodoo priestess was behind it all."

He cocked his right eyebrow. "You believe in voodoo?"

"Mm hmm. Does that offend you?"

"Indeed it does, for your sake. Jesus Christ is the way, the truth, and the life. No one comes to God except through Him."

"Oh I believe in Jesus too, Bolek." She took another bite.

"Nicole, I do not wish to start an argument but you cannot have it both ways with Jesus. You need to renounce that belief and asked Jesus to come into your heart."

* * * *

Geraldo got back to the bunkhouse a little after ten, not too surprised to find Dooly and Bobby Joe had already called it a night after being in the saddle all day rounding up steers. Whoever turned in last had left the TV on. Picking up the remote, he aimed it at the box to change channels, but hearing sports was up next on the local news, decided to relax on the couch, hoping to get a report on the Dallas Cowboys. Drowsy from fatigue and Montella's brandy, after he got comfortable his eyes refused to stay open. He turned off the television in the middle of a piece on Tony Romo and went to bed.

* * * *

"We must do things differently now, Gray Bird . . . Okay, fix it like you know I want it—the way I see it in my mind . . . Yes, yes, ahhhhhhhhhhh . . . So good—so very fucking good!"

TWENTY FOUR

Gary opened his eyes to see Nadia facing away from him, sleeping on her side. He crept out of bed so as not to wake her, turned off the alarm clock set to go off in twenty minutes, and headed for the bathroom.

Before he finished showering, Nadia slipped into the hot wet stream with him, her glorious nakedness completely overpowering his resistance as it had last night. Bodies melded together, they undulated with a sexual frenzy so intensely passionate that when she cried, "Oh my god, Gary, you've got me there already!" even though she couldn't possibly have really climaxed in such a short time, sperm erupted from his shaft as violently as scalding magma ripping the top off a virgin volcano.

A hooker's professional trick to get the john to pop prematurely so she could get on to the next one, he thought sadly. She'd wanted him bad last night but that had apparently cured her case of hot pants because this go-round had been nothing but a gratitude lay. Feeling awkward and gullible, he untangled himself from the lying tramp's arms and left her in the tub.

He quickly dressed and waited in the living room, diverting his eyes from the hall when she stepped out of the bathroom and went into the spare bedroom. The sound of a blow dryer could soon be heard behind the door. Half an hour later she reappeared—tantalizing breasts covered with a tight sweater, blue jeans hiding the exquisite razor-sculpted bush between her legs, lush raven hair immaculately in place, disturbingly beautiful face adorned with fresh makeup.

"Gary, I've never been so happy in my entire life. It was so wonderful waking up in your bed, smelling your aftershave on my pillow. I love you so much."

Trying not show how disgusted he felt, and not just over seeing through her charade, he cleared his throat and said, "I didn't bother making coffee because we're having breakfast at Carla's."

* * * *

Nadia gave him a troubled smile from across a booth in back, where he usually sat to distance himself from the noisy breakfast crowd that preferred the tables in front. "You've hardly spoken all morning, Gary. Is something wrong?"

Yeah, something's wrong. I've fallen in love with a whore. He shook his head.

"Then why are you being so quiet?"

Focusing on his coffee, he stirred it and took a sip. The waitress brought their orders and left to take care of more customers. Nadia kept gazing at him expectantly, awaiting an answer.

"Are you feeling guilty about what we did last night and this morning?"

Wincing, he looked away.

"You are, aren't you."

He nodded.

"Because of your wife?"

Instead of answering he seasoned his eggs and started eating.

"Gary, if you'd died young and your wife survived you, don't you think she would have eventually made love with someone else?"

The absurdity of her using that term nauseated him. He quit focusing on his food and glared at the manipulative slut. "We didn't make love, all we did was screw each other like two animals in heat."

Her features contorted with a jolt of pain and disbelief. "I can't believe you said that. I love you."

"No you don't. You took advantage of a lonely man because you were horny, that's all."

Nadia rolled her eyes and squinted at him like he was crazy. "God, Gary, that is so not true. I would never tell a man I loved him if I didn't mean it. Carlson Loggins is the only one besides you that's ever heard those words come out of my mouth. I meant it when I told him, and with all my heart I mean it when I say them to you. I'm not a whore anymore but a woman who's fallen madly in love, and I want to spend the rest of my life with you."

His cell phone rang. Matching her angry stare, he dug it out of his belt and yanked it to his ear. "Yeah?"

"Gary, it's Tank. We've got serious trouble. There's been another homicide on the Ridgewall Ranch . . . ."

* * * *

"I had no idea he was in the barn," said Geraldo with an emotional tremble in his voice. "I thought he'd gone to bed."

Gary wished he'd never heard of the Ridgewall Ranch or even Tomahawk County. He'd come to the bunkhouse to speak with the two hands after Bob South and his assistant carried away a decapitated and grossly emasculated Bobby Joe. Two things were radically different from the other murders. The incisions were jagged, indicating several whacks instead of one swift blow with a surgically sharp instrument, and blood was splattered everywhere.

Dooly, who'd discovered the body, sat at the kitchen table bawling so hard he couldn't speak coherently. The redness in the Mexican foreman's eyes signified he'd been weeping too. They were focused on him, squinting with pain and confusion. "I was told the demon had been cast out of Ilian, Sheriff—that's what I was told."

"Ilian had nothing to do with this, Geraldo," assured Dunmark, standing next to Heath. "We're either dealing with a human copycat killer or a different devil than the one cast out of her yesterday. And if it's the latter, then we have a complex web of evil that must be exposed quickly, because that means a malignant spirit purposely wanted us to think the demon of lust inhabiting Ilian committed the murders."

Jaw sagging, Gary leered at the investigator. "Are you saying Ilian's not responsible for any of the murders? That demon in her I mean."

Dunmark made a grim face and closed his eyes while roughly massaging the upper bridge of his nose. "If Bobby Joe wasn't killed by a human, that's exactly what I'm saying."

"Shit . . .!" Gary threw his notebook on the floor and kicked it across the kitchen.

Heath calmly walked over and picked it up. "I've been mulling over this Gray Bird Dorian said she heard Nadia speaking to in her sleep. Are you familiar with military slang, Dunmark?"

Slowly parting his eyelids, Dunmark lowered his hand and gave Heath a puzzled look. "Um, no not really."

"Well I find the name very interesting considering Klell Ridgewall was a confederate colonel."

"Why's that?"

"Because when a lieutenant colonel becomes a full colonel he's referred to as a full bird, and the confederacy wore gray as in Gray Bird."

Gary accepted the notebook from Heath and turned to see Dunmark wearing a cynical smile while saying, "If Dorian knows the term, then she most likely made up Gray Bird."

* * * *

Dooly wanted to kill himself. If he hadn't approached Dorian last night she wouldn't have told him to meet her in the barn—Bobby Joe wouldn't have wound up there, and he might still be alive.

They'd waited and waited but the bitch never showed. He'd finally thrown in the towel and gone to bed a quarter past midnight, but Bobby Joe just wouldn't give up, certain she'd come. Knowing he had to tell the lawmen about it, he looked up from the table and sobbed out, "I know why Bobby Joe was in the barn last night . . . ."

* * * *

After Dorian had been interrogated Dunmark said he needed to speak with Heath and him alone, so they went to the billiard room.

"Please sit down." The investigator eased onto a sofa as he spoke.

Heath settled into an armchair and Gary did likewise.

"What we could have here is a case of clever misdirection. If so, a master demon, if you will, is lurking in Nadia, Dorian, or Nicole. Bolek was visiting with Nicole last night until the wee hours of the morning so let's assume for a moment it isn't her. The master demon could have administered those dreams to Ilian, cleverly setting the stage for suspicion to eventually fall on Nicole through her belief that a voodoo priestess was manipulating Klell Ridgewall's spirit."

Gary cringed with confusion. "I don't follow."

"What I'm saying is the master demon could be responsible for making Ilian act like a voodoo priestess in her dreams, knowing Nicole had voiced her concerns about one controlling Ridgewall's ghost. It then could have satanically inspired Nadia to see the woman as Nicole in her dream. Since it would have to be powerful enough to override the devil that's been producing Klell Ridgewall's ghost all these years, and the spirit of lust that possessed Ilian, manipulating other people's dreams would be a cinch for such an entity.

Remember when I said we were dealing with a woman whose lust and self-centeredness would put Faust to shame?"

"Mm hmm."

"Which of the three do you perceive most fits that bill?"

"Dorian," he answered in synch with Heath.

Dunmark nodded. "Without doubt. However, the insidious creature may have set up an undetectable stronghold in Dorian before possessing one of the other two, continuing to pull her strings from within Nicole or Nadia. If, and I stress the word, it was in fact a demon rather than a copycat who killed Bobby Joe."

A sour pang pitted Gary's stomach over Nadia coming back under suspicion. The thought of her possibly being the depraved selfish person Dunmark had described in his office several days ago tore at his insides. The words he'd used sprang to his mind: *This bastard was invited in and she wants him to stay.*

Nadia hadn't shown any indications of having that type of personality but Dorian did in spades. He'd witnessed her insatiable lust for food, and Montella had told him she was a nymphomaniac which certainly fit the description of the person Dunmark had described as putting Faust to shame. He eyed the investigator. "If Bobby Joe wasn't butchered by a human copycat killer then I think you hit the nail on the head back in Colorado. Dorian's peculiar metabolism *is* demonic. She's the host."

Heath ran a hand over his face and stood up. "Gary, I've been thinking about what Dooly told us. Dorian initiated everything—named the place, the time, even told him to bring a blanket. Remember what she said when I asked her why she backed out?"

He nodded. "She said she hadn't been able to get away because Montella was talking to Geraldo, and having no idea when he'd be going back to the bunkhouse, was afraid he might catch her heading for the barn which might piss off

Montella because she'd know what Dorian was up to. What's your point?"

"I don't think it's much of a reach to say she could be sociopathic, and she's been trying to talk Dunmark into letting her join his team." Heath paused, apparently waiting for that to sink in. "Bobby Joe wasn't invited but went to the barn with Dooly anyway. What if she did go to the barn and saw Bobby Joe without being spotted by him or Dooly? Angry over him intruding, she sneaks close enough to eavesdrop on them, hears Dooly say he's been stood up and Bobby Joe swearing she'll come. She gets an idea and formulates a plan to convince Dunmark she was right about Nadia pulling the strings of the murdering demon.

"Counting on Bobby Joe holding out hope she'll eventually show, she goes to the slaughterhouse, gets a knife and ax, comes back to the barn and hides around a corner, waiting for Dooly to leave. When he does, she enters the barn, leaving the knife and ax outside, and lets Bobby Joe have his way with her—insisting he take off all his clothes first so he'll be completely nude like all the other victims. She sexually exhausts him and he falls asleep in her arms. She gets up, retrieves the knife and ax, slices his throat in his sleep, castrates him, and chops his head off. Naked during all this, she sneaks back to the slaughterhouse, washes the blood off herself and the implements, returns to the barn, puts her clothes on, and goes back to the mansion."

Appearing quite impressed by the speculation, Dunmark gave Heath a thumbs up and enthusiastically rose to his feet. "That could explain why there was so much blood left this time. I hate to say it for Dorian's sake, but hopefully she did do it, and there is no master demon at work here."

* * * *

Dorian didn't have an alibi and there were no locks on the

slaughterhouse doors, so she could have entered with ease and wiped her prints off the knob after cleaning the murder weapons. The DPS—who'd done a rush job at his request—had informed Gary no traces of blood were found on any of the many cutting instruments, and those obtained in the drains and traps of the industrial sinks were either bovine or caprine.

Geraldo had told him back at the ranch that they always used a lot of bleach when washing the butchering tools, a detail Dorian certainly could have been aware of. Being such a smart woman, she'd know better than to wash them in the sink. She could have filled a bucket with bleach water, cleaned the murder weapons in it, dumped the murky water outside, and put the knife and ax in their proper places. Then all she'd have to do is bleach the bucket several more times, discharging the water outdoors after each washing, and finally put it back where she found it, leaving it completely sanitized.

Bobby Joe's wounds were extremely sloppy compared to those of the other victims, so it appeared to be a copycat crime. Gary filed the faxed blood report and plopped down at his desk, hating he didn't have a shred of physical evidence. Unable to officially charge Dorian, he'd have to release her in forty-eight hours if something didn't turn up.

Heath and Dunmark felt positive she did it. He thought so too but wasn't sure a devil from hell inhabiting her body hadn't actually committed the crime rather than Dorian doing it to convince Dunmark he needed her help. If Bobby Joe had in fact been killed by a demon, then locking her up had been a useless move in trying to protect the residents of Tomahawk County. She wouldn't consent to being sedated and had threatened to sue the sheriff's department and Dunmark if anybody forced a needle into her.

"Hi, remember me?"

He turned to see Nadia standing in front of his office door. She'd managed to sneak in and close it without him hearing a sound. Strolling to the chair by his desk, she sat down and pierced him with her striking dark eyes. They reeked with vulnerability. "So where do we go from here, you and I?"

When Tank had called him about Bobby Joe eight hours ago, he'd dropped Nadia off at his house before driving to the ranch and hadn't spoken to her since. "Listen, I've got a lot on my mind and I don't have time for this."

The corners of her pouting lips turned up with a tiny smile. "I bet you haven't eaten since breakfast this morning, have you."

He shook his head.

"You must be starved. Why don't you let me fix you some dinner?"

"I don't have any appetite. Now I hate to be rude, but you're going to have to excuse me. If you want to cook supper at my place, that's fine, maybe I'll be hungry by the time I get home—but right now I don't need any distractions."

"Oh, is that what I am, a mere distraction?" She rose from the chair and gazed down at him, hurt clinging to her face.

Exhausted and irritated, he cinched his eyes closed and rubbed them furiously. Several bright spots danced before them when he raised his lids, disappearing a second later. "You know what I mean. Please wait for me at home. We'll discuss you and me later."

She donned a big smile which surprised him.

"What are you grinning about?"

"You said wait for me at home rather than your house. And that's what I want it to be, Gary—my home."

* * * *

"What do you mean you quit? You can't just bail on me, Geraldo!"

"I'm sorry, Montella, but this really is The Death Ranch, and I don't want to be the next casualty. I've had it. You owe me two weeks pay and I'd like to collect it now instead of waiting until the end of the month in case you wind up dead before then. Which you're liable to do if you don't leave too."

A sigh of exasperation gushed from her lustrous mouth. "Look, Dorian did it and now she's in jail. Dunmark Finley and Ranger Crow are convinced the stupid bitch went to those lengths to convince Dunmark he needs her on his team. Don't leave me high and dry like this, Geraldo. Please stay on."

"I'm sorry, Montella, I really am. But this place is haunted and that's all there is to it. Now may I please collect my pay?"

She stood with hands on hips, disbelief stamped on her angry face as if he was her husband requesting a divorce. "I can't believe this. First you turn down my offer to make an easy five thousand dollars, and now you quit on me altogether. Well don't you dare try to use me as a reference, you cowardly bastard. Come with me to my office and I'll cut you a check."

"Your office?" He wasn't aware she had one.

"Yeah," she ejaculated, eyes two burning spheres of blue fury. "My office."

He followed her upstairs and into a large bedroom that evidently also served as her workplace. She sat down at a very expensive femininely constructed desk and called up the ranch payroll on a computer. Scrolling down, she ran a manicured fingertip across a line, flashed over to a bookkeeping screen which had withholding information, somehow rapidly and effortlessly manipulated the keys despite her long nails, and soon a nearby printer sprang to life. A moment later she tore his check from a perforated line and handed it to him. "Get the fuck off my ranch, you ingrate."

Once again he tried to explain it wasn't ingratitude that compelled him to quit, but she gave him a look that chilled him to the bone as she pointed towards the door. He hurried through it, fearing she'd throw something at him.

"Hi, Geraldo," said Nicole with a wave as he entered the

hall.

"No time to chit-chat, must be leaving. It was good to know you . . . ."

* * * *

Dooly gave Geraldo a goodbye handshake on the front porch, went back inside the bunkhouse, and phoned Montella to tell her he'd be willing to take over as foreman if she'd pay him foreman's wages. Geraldo wasn't the only one scared shitless by Bobby Joe's death but he couldn't pass up what for him was the opportunity of a lifetime. Besides, he'd always believed that when your number's up, it's up, and he felt deep inside his wouldn't be drawn until he was a very old man.

"Hello?"

"Nicole?"

"Yes?"

"This is Dooly over at the bunkhouse. Could I speak to Montella please?"

"Sure, hold on . . . ."

* * * *

"Wow, there must be a million books in here." Dooly scanned the many volumes stuffed in numerous wood-framed shelves standing floor to high ceiling.

"Never mind the books," said Montella. "Do you really think you're capable of running this ranch?"

"Yep, all I need is some cowboys to line out and this place will run like clockwork."

She started doodling on a notepad sitting atop the reading table she occupied. "Aren't you afraid to continue working on *The Death Ranch?*"

The way she'd emphasized the morbid nickname made him grin. "Oh I'm scared, sure. Who wouldn't be? But I've always wanted to be in charge of a big ranch like this, and if you'll give me the chance to prove I can do it, I won't have to take orders until I'm forty like most punchers have to do before finally making foreman."

"Oh . . .?" she leaned back in her chair and locked eyes with him, a tricky smile on her face. "You don't like taking orders?"

"Didn't mean it like that. Of course I'd be taking orders from you. I'm talking about dudes like Jeremy Hicks who know damn well you can do their jobs as well if not better than they can, so they keep a feller bogged down with shit work so no one else can see they've got the capability of replacing them. That's what I meant."

Moving her lips as if chewing gum, she eyed him closely, evidently mulling everything over. He felt like he was back in school, waiting for a hot teacher to grant or refuse some special request. She kept it up for a good while, then suddenly brought her hands together and leaned forward. "If you can round up enough cowboys to take care of this ranch by sunset tomorrow, the job is yours. I'll pay them what you're making now and give you a thirty percent raise. If not, the deal's off, though you'll retain the option of staying on as a regular hand if you want to."

A big dose of adrenaline made him dizzy and he couldn't curb his enthusiasm. "Aw, thank you, Boss Lady, you won't regret it I promise!"

"Boss Lady," she giggled. "Corny but cute. Just call me Montella."

"Yes, ma'am."

"One last thing before you go, Dooly." Her beautiful gleaming mouth that looked capable of giving the best blowjob on the planet, stretched into a peculiar grin. "Don't worry about trying to find a cook, I'll take care of that."

TWENTY FIVE

Gary slid the Blue Plate Special from Carla's through the food slot, and the only inmate currently in lockup snatched it eagerly. Dorian sat down on a bunk and tore into the hamburger steak dinner.

"Damn, Sheriff, I thought suppertime was never gonna get here. Haven't had a bite to eat since you hauled my ass off the ranch earlier today." Gravy dribbled from her lips as she spoke. "Don't know why you guys think killing Bobby Joe was my doing. Figure I'm dead since that demon Gray Bird probably senses I'm on to him and will want to shut me up. It's down right despicable—an absolute travesty it's gonna take my death to make you idiots see I didn't make up the motherfucker."

She wolfed down several more mouthfuls, gulped a big swig of iced tea, and resumed her eating frenzy. "Would you at least bring Dooly in so I can get laid one last time before that thing slices me up? I'd let you do the honors but I know you're too high and mighty to dirty your dick on the likes of me."

Her animal savageness sickened him, but not nearly as much as the thought of her being innocent of Bobby Joe's murder frightened him. Dunmark had asserted that if Dorian wasn't guilty, the killer demon still held Tomahawk County in a death grip—a devil so powerful it had dominated both the unclean spirit that Ilian had been freed of and the imp producing the apparition of Klell Ridgewall atop his steed.

"No way, huh?" she said when he didn't answer. "Well thanks for at least letting me smoke in here, Sheriff."

He watched her light up and exhale. It hadn't taken the glutton hardly any time at all to scarf up every crumb on the disposable dinner plate.

"When Dunmark exorcises that demon out of Nadia—which he'll finally wise up and have to do after y'all find me without a head soon—I hope you'll give her a chance."

"A chance at what?"

"Winning you over, what else? She told me she's fallen in love with you."

He frowned at her. "When did she tell you that?"

"When you let her talk to me earlier."

Nadia must have asked Tank for permission to visit Dorian because she hadn't mentioned it to him.

"Listen, Sheriff, Nadia's totally innocent just like Ilian was—she ain't got no idea that demon's dwelling inside her. I know the gal inside and out, we've been friends for years. Says she's through with whoring and I believe her, just like I believed her when she told me she didn't know what true love was until you done went and stole her heart away. That made me so happy for her I got all warm and fuzzy inside and started crying, which got her water tap a-drippin' too.

"I asked if y'all had fucked yet. She wouldn't answer but the light in her eyes gave her away and I knew right then you had. I kept pestering her until she finally confessed that you'd pleasured her on your couch, your bed, and in your bathtub. Please give the woman a chance. True love is harder to find than the proverbial pot of gold at the end of a rainbow, and she truly loves you, lawman."

A rush of heated excitement had raced through him upon hearing Nadia's confided feelings, and for that brief moment he'd believed she really loved him. But her blabbing—and in ridiculous detail—about them having sex, splattered the emotion into a distorted hodgepodge as messy as a dozen eggs shattered on a kitchen floor. But another reaction remained unaffected by the quick emotional rollercoaster ride—confusion about Dorian. The hick sounded sincere, as if she truly cared about Nadia's welfare. That wasn't the heart of a killer sociopath. Could she be telling the truth after all?

"Dorian, would you mind telling me again what you were doing last night?"

She blew out another puff and shrugged. "Like I said, Dooly came up to the patio while I was outside smoking. I knew what the rascal wanted without having to ask, so I told him to sneak a blanket into the barn and meet me there in half an hour. A few minutes later Geraldo came walking up and said Montella wanted to talk to him about something. I took him inside to see her and asked Montella what was going on. She said they had some business to discuss. I asked how long it would take and she told me curtly it was none of my business. That got me to worrying. If Montella had decided to start fucking her cowboys—which I thought she might be planning on doing with Geraldo at the time—if she found out I was screwing Dooly she might kick me off the ranch, not wanting to share the stud.

"They went into the library and I thought about hurrying to the barn right then to wait on Dooly, but couldn't be certain when Geraldo would leave. If he saw me and told Montella about it, she'd have known damn well what I had planned. When he still hadn't left by the time I was supposed to be at the barn, I gave up and went to bed early, figuring Dooly would figure out soon enough I wasn't coming. I sure didn't think he'd wait for me so long, and I had no idea Bobby Joe would be coming too. I fell asleep watching TV and was in my room until breakfast this morning.

"I hate nobody can testify to that fact 'ceptin' me, but that's what happened, I never set foot in that barn last night. Ain't nobody hates violence worse'n me—I could never physically harm nobody much less kill 'em. Oh I like to taunt and tease and sometimes go over the edge verbally and all, but it's just harmless fun."

He sniffed a lungful of air through his nostrils. "Why are you refusing to be sedated?"

Dorian turned as somber as a frigid librarian. "Because I want to see what that damn Gray Bird looks like 'fore he guts me. I ain't like other folks, I've never wanted to die in my sleep. Life is to be lived to the fullest, and I don't want to experience my last moments through a hazy drug-induced fog."

She seemed to be telling the truth, and deep down inside he feared she was. "If you didn't make the whole thing up, are you absolutely positive it was Nadia you heard speaking to Gray Bird?"

Smoke funneled through her puckered lips. "Not a hundred percent, no. It was dark so I didn't see her mouth moving but it definitely came from her direction."

"Can you recall where everyone was sleeping that night?"

"Let's see . . . me, Nadia, and Selena were in one cell, and Montella, Nicole, and Rosemary were in the one next to it. Nadia and I were on bottom bunks, and I believe Nicole and Montella were too. Selena was in the bunk above me and I remember real clear that Rosemary was on a top bunk because she kept going on and on about how bad she missed Carlson and I finally told her to shut up so we could all get some sleep. I was about to doze off when I heard mumbling. It was hard to make out but I'm positive I heard the name Gray Bird and it was clear she was telling him to do something. I knew Nadia was talking in her sleep and didn't want to wake her so I just rolled over on my side, tuned her out, and drifted off."

He crossed his arms beneath his badge. "Who was closest to the next cell, you or Nadia?"

"Nadia."

"So it could have been one of the three women next door that was talking in her sleep, couldn't it?"

"Yeah, possibly, but I'm pretty dang sure it was Nadia."

Dunmark had logically stated Nicole's accent could never be mistaken for Nadia's, but since Dorian claimed to have heard mumbling it was equally logical she'd assumed the voice belonged to Nadia because they were in the same cell, and failed to detect a Jamaican nuance in the sleep talk.

* * * *

Bolek had tried his best to convert Nicole last night, speaking to her for several hours after they'd finished their ice cream. Alas, the silly woman refused to renounce her belief in voodoo because she firmly believed it to be real. Munching on a bite of cheese soufflé prepared by Montella, he gazed across the dining table at the lovely Jamaican, hoping his prayer would be answered.

At three that morning she'd let out a deep yawn and stretched her long arms saying, "I've really enjoyed talking with you all night, Bolek, but I'm afraid I'm going to have to bail on you and go to bed." After bidding her goodnight he'd gone upstairs to the bedroom Montella had graciously allotted him, knelt beside the bed, and besought the Lord to save Nicole.

His thoughts turned to the beautiful Dorian who'd been taken to jail. He rarely disagreed with Dunmark but didn't think she'd killed the unfortunate cowboy. True, the woman could be quite manipulative and for reasons that still eluded him seemed desperate to work with them, but he simply couldn't envision her going to such extremes to do it. It also troubled him that Dunmark had come to the conclusion Dorian had lied about hearing Nadia Mars speaking to someone named Gray Bird in her sleep. While that possibility was in no way incongruous with Dorian's behavior, what if she'd spoken the truth? Though Dunmark and Lori had both studied some psychology in college, he alone held a degree in the field, and every instinct he possessed insisted Bobby Joe's fate hadn't been decided by the Cajun genius.

* * * *

Heath treated her to dinner at a Mexican restaurant. Lori felt like a giddy teenager, sitting across from him at a cozy table for two. Last night they'd parked near the entry gates of the Ridgewall Ranch and necked until well past midnight after Bolek saved the day by lying about not feeling well. She didn't want to spend a moment away from Heath and dreaded leaving Tomahawk County. With him in El Paso and her in Colorado Springs they'd have to go weeks at a time without seeing each other.

Their waiter sat a burrito supreme before her and a platter of chili rellenos and tacos in front of Heath. "Will there be anything else?"

"That'll be all for now," he answered with a polite smile.

She silently gave thanks for their food while Heath filled two mugs from a frosty pitcher of beer. He handed her one, clicked his against it in salute, and she took a small sip.

He started dissecting a stuffed chili pepper. "I sure had a good time last night."

"So did I. Wasn't Bolek wonderful?"

"Mm hmm. There for awhile I thought he was never going to take the hint." He took a bite and winked. "Good chow."

"I should have told him we wanted to be alone—bless his heart, he had no idea." She dipped half a crispy triangle of corn tortilla into a bowl of guacamole and raised it to her mouth. Prepared with no additional ingredients other than the perfect amount of salt, the pulverized avocado tasted great. Sampling her salsa with the rest of the chip, she immediately had to cool her tongue with ice-cold beer. "This salsa's hot, be careful."

"Good, that's just how I like it . . ." he shoveled in a mouthful and engulfed the chip.

Grinning at him, she wondered how long he'd be able to hold out before quenching the raging inferno he'd just ignited in his oral cavity. She dropped her jaw when he repeated the process several more times, almost emptying the bowl before finally reaching for his beer.

"Wow, you really do like it hot, don't you."

He nodded and doused a taco with Tabasco sauce. Three quick bites later it was gone and he doctored another.

The way Heath relished Mexican food made her think of Dorian, who obviously lived to eat. Dunmark believed she killed Bobby Joe, Bolek didn't. Emotionally she leaned towards the Cajun's guilt because that would mean there were no more demons to be dealt with in Tomahawk County, but intellectually she had to agree with Bolek.

Heath's theory that she'd traversed the distance from the barn to the slaughterhouse in the nude after the murder seemed untenable to her. Though last night's temperature had been very moderate prior to midnight, it had dipped into the low forties afterwards. Since Dooly had left the barn around the time it started turning cold, Dorian would have been very chilly lying in wait outside while fully clothed, so it made no sense for such a brilliant woman to plot a murder which required walking naked a goodly distance to and from the slaughterhouse. To her way of thinking, had Dorian truly planned to murder Bobby Joe in order to get on the team, she'd have arranged for the murder to take place under much more comfortable circumstances.

Ironically, that very fact had only served to increase Dunmark's conviction when she'd spoken to him about it. "Don't you see?" he'd said. "She's counting on us all arriving at the same conclusion you did, Lori. That's why she was willing to suffer such discomfort. Don't underestimate her craftiness. She'd be what, an hour at most in the cold? Probably not even that long. An easy price to pay for what she perceived would get her off the hook should suspicion fall on her."

Hoping Dunmark's opinion would prove correct, she went to work on her burrito.

* * * *

Nadia had cooked dinner for the man she loved but it sat on Gary's stove untouched. An hour ago she'd stepped outside to see who was honking their horn and saw him waving for her to get in the cruiser. She'd ridden with him to The Hog Farm and he'd fed the livestock. Again sitting on the passenger side as they headed back to town, she eyed the fence posts whizzing by, supporting strands of barbwire stretching as far as the eye could see. Occasionally she'd glance to her left where the setting sun made the horizon look like multiple shades of red lipstick smears. He'd promised to eat when they got to his house but she could tell by his disposition he most likely still didn't have much of an appetite.

She knew Dorian couldn't have killed that cowhand and had told Gary as much. He'd refused to discuss the matter but she had a feeling he questioned her guilt too. Continuing to gaze through the window, she decided to break the silence despite the fact he wasn't in a talkative mood. "I made beans and cornbread in case you were wondering."

"Good." It sounded like an automatic response made to a stranger asking 'How are you?' in passing.

"And in case you were wondering about something else—" she turned to face him "—you're the best lover I've ever had, including Carlson Loggins."

An acerbic grimace assured he didn't believe her.

"I'm not patronizing you, Gary. I didn't know I wasn't really in love with him until I fell for you. You're wrong about us— we made love, we didn't merely have sex, and that's what makes you superior to Carlson. Sex was all we ever had. Not once did he ever make love to me, he just fucked me."

That only served to turn his expression even more sour. Smarting over his reaction, she turned back to the window. "Sorry, won't bring it up again."

* * * *

"No, vato, I'm not going back there." Geraldo reared his head back and emptied the shot glass, slamming it on the bar as tequila burned its way down his gullet. "Another please, patron."

Jerry the bartender replenished his vessel. "Well I don't blame you, Geraldo. I sure wouldn't work on that damn ranch."

"Death Ranch, you mean. And that's just what it is, my friend—the fucking Death Ranch. I hope Dooly wises up before it's too late. He's a good egg and one damn fine vaquero."

"Wonder why the ghost of Klell Ridgewall turned violent after all these years?"

The stupid question planted a frown on his face until he remembered the booze-serving gringo wasn't in the know. Well it was about time the whole town knew. "Listen, Jerry, I'm not supposed to say anything but it's not Klell Ridgewall doing it, it's a demon."

"That's not what I hear." A big, very handsome man he'd never seen before, bellied up to the bar and tilted a black Stetson back from his forehead, revealing a thick widow's peak of white hair. "The sheriff arrested a woman earlier today for killing that cowboy."

He squinted at the stranger, wondering how he knew Dorian had been taken into custody when Sheriff Stoner wanted it kept quiet for the time being. "Oh yeah? What's her name?"

"Don't know. I'll have a Coors Light, barkeep."

"Who told you this, vato?"

"That dude you were just talking about."

"Dooly?"

"Mm hmm. He's been spreading the word around town that the new owner of the Ridgewall Ranch is looking for hands."

Ay Chihuahua, he succeeded in talking Montella into making him foreman! His heart dropped. Blinded by ambition the poor kid had decided to play chicken with the grim reaper and had no chance of winning. "Do you know if he's found any takers?"

The man accepted a bottle from Jerry and downed a swallow. "Yeah, me for starters. I'm his new ramrod . . . ."

* * * *

Gary took a bite of beans mixed with crumbled cornbread. The flavorful chow whetted his appetite. Nadia sat with hands folded beneath her chin, watching him.

"How'd I do?"

"Mm-*mmm*," he replied while chewing, brows raised for emphasis.

Relaxing with a smile, she started in on her own helping.

The doorbell rang.

"Come on in, it's unlocked!" he hollered.

A moment later Heath and Lori stepped into the kitchen.

"Have a seat. Been to supper?"

Heath seated Lori and sat down across from her. "We just pigged out on Mexican food, Gary, but thanks. Wish I'd left some room, those beans sure look dandy."

"They are . . ." he scooped another spoonful into his mouth. "You make 'em?"

He shook his head and swallowed. "Never cooked a pot of beans in my life. This is Nadia's handiwork. What's up?"

Heath took off his hat and placed it on the table. "Lori doesn't think Dorian did it, and after hearing her reasons, I tend to agree. Thought I'd better let her run it by you."

"Dunmark has already informed me Lori doesn't think Dorian would brave the cold in the nude if that's what you dropped by to tell me. He also explained why that really convinces him she did it."

"Yeah well, while we were talking at the restaurant she said something I think you need to hear. Go ahead, Lori."

Lori took off her glasses, revealing her green eyes were even prettier without them. She massaged the upper bridge of her nose and put them back on. "You were present when we tested Dorian's IQ in Colorado, Gary. Remember how convinced Dunmark, Bolek, and I were that her abnormally high intelligence levels were evidence of a demon until she passed all the response tests with flying colors?"

"Mm hmm."

"Well if a woman that smart wanted to convince everyone the same demon that committed the other murders killed Bobby Joe, she'd have done it in a setting where she could more accurately mimic the other victims. She wouldn't have done it where she had no choice but to make crud incisions and leave too much blood behind. She would have procured a scalpel and bone-saw to behead him rather than doing it with a butcher knife and ax. According to Dooly she had Bobby Joe wrapped around her little finger and knew it, so she could have lured him anywhere at any time. Not only would she not want to walk naked through the cold outdoors, she'd know her efforts would make it look like the work of a copycat killer rather than a demon. In other words she'd have been acutely aware she was defeating her whole purpose. Does that sound like something a genius would do?"

Gary abandoned his spoon and locked his fingers together. "I've been wrestling with doubts about this all evening. Dammit, I don't think she did it either, and I don't think she made up Gray Bird. Why don't we get Dunmark and Bolek over here—have you guys hypnotize Nadia and see if it *was* her talking in her sleep to this Gray Bird? You don't mind do you, Nadia?"

She drew a deep breath and shook her head. "Do what you've gotta do . . . ."

* * * *

Taking every precaution, Bolek and Lori secured Nadia in the chair they'd brought with them from Colorado. They'd set it up in his living room.

Nadia shot him a worried look. "Gary, if they discover the worst, please believe me, I know nothing about it."

He gave her a reassuring smile. "I know."

"And one more thing. What I told you on the way back from The Hog Farm is the truth whether you believe it or not." She cut her eyes to Bolek and sighed. "Okay, let's get this over with."

* * * *

"I'll be back in half an hour to let you out," said Deputy Green, locking the visitor's door.

"Thanks for letting me see her."

"Not a problem."

Dooly watched him disappear into the front section of the jailhouse, then crossed the dayroom to Dorian's cell.

"Oh, you handsome cowboy, you ain't got no idea how glad I am to see you! You don't think I killed Bobby Joe, do you?"

"Of course not." He felt guilty about playing politics with everybody he'd talked to, but if he didn't pretend he believed the culprit had been nabbed, nobody would even consider working on the Ridgewall.

"Did the sheriff tell you I wanted you to come see me?"

"No, I was in town trying to round up some hands. Geraldo quit and Montella's gonna make me foreman if I can round up a crew by tomorrow evening. Figured you could use some company so I decided to drop by."

"It's like an act of God you did . . ." Dorian started tearing off her clothes. "Pull your dick out and stick it through the bars so I can suck it."

Her urgent demand and horny actions made him too stiff to get it through the zipper so he unfastened his jeans and slid them to his knees. Watching her pretty mouth hungrily close on his throbbing shaft, he grabbed the bars and heaved a pleasured sigh.

* * * *

Bolek pocketed the Swiss watch that had been in his family since the nineteenth century and began the session. "Nadia, please tell me the recurring dream that so concerns you."

He listened intently, occasionally glancing at Lori and Dunmark.

". . . and then I see a woman who I know is the little girl as an adult, and I wake up."

"And you had never been able to recognize her before the last time you dreamed it?"

"No."

"Nadia, we are going back to your dream now, to the very end. You can see the woman's face clearly, can you not?"

"Yes."

"Do you know her?"

"Yes."

"Who is she?"

"Montella Pace."

The name startled him. A quick look at Gary revealed he was beyond stunned. "Um, Nadia, are you certain the woman is Montella and not Nicole?"

"Yes . . . I'm certain."

"Do you remember telling Sheriff Stoner the woman was Nicole when you dreamed it last?"

"Yes."

"Does the woman still have dark hair?"

"Yes."

"But Montella is a blonde, is she not?"

"Yes . . . Montella's hair is blonde."

He turned to Dunmark and whispered, "Do you want me to pursue this or go on to Gray Bird?"

Dunmark eyed him over the camcorder. "Take her back to the first time she dreamed it and see if she can bring the face into focus."

"Nadia, we will now backtrack to the very first occurrence of the dream. Are you ready?"

She nodded.

"You are now at the end of it, at the point just before you wake up. The woman's face is coming into view, you can see it plainly. Do you know her?"

Nadia's eyes bolted wide. "Oh my god!"

"What's wrong?"

"The woman is me!"

"I see . . ." he yanked his glasses off and rubbed his eyes. "Nadia, please tell me some of your other dreams you felt were prophetic, the ones where bad things happened afterwards. Tell me the first one you ever had."

"My mother had a glass heart that was given to her by my father when they were dating. In my dream I was playing with it and dropped it. It shattered on the floor and I started crying."

He put his spectacles back on and folded his arms. "And what bad thing happened afterwards to make you think it was a glimpse into the future?"

"My father died of a heart attack two weeks later."

"How old were you when this occurred?"

"Seven."

"I see. Tell me the second clairvoyant dream you had."

Nadia frowned as her mind reached back into the past. "I dreamed I ate a chocolate bunny that I was told to leave alone until Easter Sunday. In real life when I woke up Easter morning I had itchy red splotches all over my face. My mother took me to the doctor and he discovered I was highly allergic to animal dander, so I had to give my pet rabbit away."

He asked her to tell him all of the so called prophetic dreams she'd had before the bird nightmare. When she relayed the last one he couldn't help grinning and noticed Lori doing the same. The only Gypsy curse Nadia Mars had was a tendency to have negative dreams. Her father's heart attack had convinced her she was clairvoyant, so she expected bad things to happen after every nightmare. Coincidences—most of which she'd have realized were quite extraneous if not for her father's death—had perpetuated the illusion.

"Nadia, do you know anyone named Gray Bird?"

She shook her head.

"Let us go back to the night you were in jail, the night the murders took place there. Can you see the cell?"

"Yes."

"Good. Now you have fallen asleep. Do you remember talking to Gray Bird?

"No."

"Dorian can hear you speaking. What are you saying in your sleep?"

"I'm not saying anything in my sleep. Dorian's mistaken."

"Can you hear anyone else talking while you are sleeping?"

"No."

"I am now speaking to Gray Bird. Answer me. Talk to me, Gray Bird, and tell me who you are."

Several moments passed without incident as he'd anticipated. He turned to Gary. "If Gray Bird is real, he has neither part nor lot with this woman. And her dream is merely a dream. No telling who the woman will look like if she dreams it again. She most likely had a horrifying experience as a small child seeing a bird shot by a hunter and it left a subconscious scar. In her childlike mind she felt the hunter should suffer the same fate as the bird, hence the human body parts are poetic justice—the hunter was blown to pieces just like the bird. Some event triggered that part of her mind and awakened it. Perhaps she witnessed a hog being slaughtered, or heard the unfortunate ranch hands discussing it. Then, getting reacquainted with Nicole and Montella, the woman's face became theirs because of guilt. They, like she once did, worked as prostitutes for Carlson Loggins."

Immense joy and relief shone in the sheriff's eyes. "So you're sure she's not demonized?"

"Absolutely positive."

Dunmark put the camcorder in its case. "I still think Dorian killed Bobby Joe, but to be thorough, I suppose we should call Nicole and tell her to come over so Bolek can probe her subconscious."

"I'll go get her," said Gary. "I don't trust her or Montella right now, because if Gray Bird's real, he's hiding inside one of them and I seriously doubt he'd allow his host to come here voluntarily to let us find out."

* * * *

Nadia rode with him as he drove towards the Ridgewall Ranch to pick up Nicole. Lori had injected her with a stimulant to counteract the sedative she'd been given. They'd been discussing her being under hypnosis.

"I can't remember telling Bolek any of that, Gary."

"Speaking of telling things, Dorian told me what you said."

"About what?"

He turned his head and grinned. "Me."

"What about you?"

"You know, what you told her in jail this afternoon."

"I didn't talk to Dorian this afternoon. I went to the jailhouse to see you and that's it."

Why did she want to spoil the mood with such a stupid lie when he'd been working up the nerve to tell her he loved her? "Look, I know you did. She couldn't have known what she told me otherwise. Beats the hell out of me why you refuse to admit it."

"I don't care what she told you, I haven't seen Dorian since you took me to the district attorney's office."

"You had to have or she couldn't have known about us having sex."

An angry scream pierced his ears. "I wouldn't discuss our love life with her or anyone else, goddammit! It's sacred to me because I'm in love with you. How dare that fucking bitch say I did."

"Hell, I'll settle this right now." He pulled out his cell and called Tank.

"What's up?"

"Did Nadia Mars ask to visit Dorian today?"

"Um, no. I said hi before she went into your office and she told me hello back. That's the only thing she said."

A bolt of fear rammed his gut. The tires screeched as he stomped on the brake and made a u-turn. He cut Tank off and called Dunmark.

TWENTY SIX

Dorian stared unblinkingly at Nadia, deep blue eyes burning with confusion. Nadia's dark orbs blazed with the same look of disbelief.

Gary kept glancing back and forth but couldn't spot a hint of pretense in either expression. There were only two possibilities: Nadia was lying and had somehow snuck into the dayroom without Tank knowing it, or Dorian knew they'd screwed—the number of times they'd done it, and the exact locations where they had—by supernatural means.

"Why are you doing this, Nadia? This afternoon you stood right where you are now, telling me all about your feelings for Sheriff Stoner." Dorian angrily shifted her gaze from Nadia and leered at him. "She's lying, Sheriff, and I'm totally hog-swallered as to why."

Nadia radically shook her head, boring a hole through him with her fuming glare. "Gary, this is the first time I've seen Dorian today, I swear to God."

Dorian plopped down on a bunk and slapped her knees, perplexity riveted to her face. "Hell, maybe I'm crazy. Maybe Dooly really didn't come see me either. Maybe I let some phantom play with my tits and finger me through the bars after sucking him dry. Shit fire in the dungeon, what the fuck is going on around here?"

Gary looked at Tank. "Dooly was here?"

"Yeah. I allowed him a thirty minute visit."

Dunmark stood with arms crossed, steadily appraising Dorian. Bolek and Lori were doing likewise.

Heath stepped closer to her cell. "Who let Nadia in to see you?"

A wave of renewed shock washed over the Cajun. She chewed on her lip for several moments, anxiety draining her complexion. "Fuck, I don't know. I was stretched out right here on this bunk with my eyes closed when she said hello. And that ain't right is it. I should have heard metal clanging when the dayroom door got locked behind her. After we'd visited for awhile I suddenly had to take a dump and she left while I was on the pot. I heard her say goodbye but didn't hear anyone let her out. Shit, shit, *shee-eye-it!*"

Rearing her head back, Dorian glared at the upper bunk, fearful confusion plastered to her face, teeth bared with a disbelieving scowl. She sat stiffly as if frozen in that pose for at least half a minute before finally leveling her chin. "I'm so sorry, Nadia, guess I'm losing my mind. I don't know how to explain any of this otherwise. It never occurred to me until Ranger Crow asked who let you in that I never saw you come in or leave, and that really fucks with my head. You really *weren't* here earlier were you."

"No," said Nadia in a soft empathetic tone, "I wasn't here."

Defeat embedded on her gorgeous visage, Dorian stood and raised her arms in surrender. "All right, I give. See-date away. Shoot me up and find out what the fuck's wrong with me...."

* * * *

The empty bunkhouse spooked him so he decided to turn in early. Dooly eased into his bed and turned off the lamp. He began to relax and smiled while recalling the kinky sex he'd had with Dorian a few hours ago. They'd agreed that when Sheriff Stoner finally saw the light and turned her loose, he'd ask Montella if she minded them courting. If she didn't they wouldn't have to hide their relationship. Otherwise they'd continue fucking on the sly.

There'd been a real down note though. She'd told him if the

sheriff and Dunmark didn't wise up and flush that demon Gray Bird out of Nadia real soon, the bastard would take her out before long because Dorian knew too much.

He'd hit pay dirt in town, latching on to a ramrod who'd promised to help him round up three hands tomorrow. Sonny Yoakum said he'd been punching cattle all his life and recently drifted to Tomahawk after a falling out with his dad, the only boss he'd ever had. The dude had been working for measly wages keeping the rodeo arena spruced up. Getting a blowjob from Dorian had been the perfect way to celebrate hiring his first hand.

Still smiling, he closed his eyes, looking forward to a good night's sleep.

"Hello, Dooly."

They flew open upon hearing the sultry feminine voice. He reached for the lamp on his nightstand and rolled the switch. "N-Nadia Mars?"

The gorgeous woman stood before him naked, her voluptuous body as beautiful as Dorian's.

"How'd you get in?" He was positive he'd locked the front and back doors.

"You should find a better place to hide the spare key than under the Welcome Mat. It's in the living room with my clothes." She tore the wrapper off a condom with her teeth and gave him a wicked smile. "I'm lonely. Mind if I spend a little time with you . . . ?"

* * * *

Dooly held the amazing woman in his arms, chuckling inside at how scared he'd been before. He'd thought for sure that demon Gray Bird was about to jump out of her and tear him to shreds. Thank God Dorian had been wrong about that. Instead of cutting his dick off, she'd worked it over good, leaving him totally relaxed and sated.

"How long have you had the hots for me?"

Nadia gazed at him with a lazy grin, a thick lock of black hair draped over one eye. "From the moment I first saw you."

"I never suspected a thing. Man, I'm so glad you're not shy or I'd have never known. What made you pick tonight to come on to me?"

"Oh, I don't know. I was just lonely, like I said."

"Does Montella know you're here? On the ranch I mean."

"Mm hmm. She called me while I was at Sheriff's Stoner's and hired me to cook for you. Isn't that wonderful?"

"Ah, so that's why she told me not worry about finding a cook." He ran a hand over her Dorian-like tits and sighed. "Damn this is great, we can do this every night."

"Well, not every night. I'll be living in the mansion . . ." she snuggled against him and closed her eyes.

So much for speaking to Montella about Dorian—he wasn't about to run the risk of losing Nadia by openly committing to the Cajun. Two of the hottest chicks he'd ever seen in his life were at his disposal and tomorrow he'd be promoted to foreman. How lucky could one man be?

* * * *

Frowning as if the fault lay with him, Bolek lowered his pocket watch. "It's no use. Dorian is one of those rare individuals who cannot be hypnotized."

"Then what the fuck am I supposed to do? How can I prove I'm innocent otherwise?" Dorian's beleaguered questions came out slurred due to her sedated state.

Lori put a supporting hand on Bolek's shoulder and gave it a comforting squeeze, trying not to show she felt equally disappointed. "You did what you could."

They'd decided to bring Dorian to Gary's house rather than haul the chair to the jail. When Dorian heard Nadia's psyche had already been probed for the presence of Gray Bird, she'd pled for them to test Nicole and Montella, swearing she'd really heard someone murmuring to the entity.

"If it wasn't Nadia then it had to have been Nicole or Montella," she'd said before receiving the injection. "It couldn't have been Rosemary or Selena because they both wouldn't have gotten croaked if the demon was hiding in one of them."

Heath checked his watch. "It's almost eleven. If you guys want to hypnotize Nicole and Montella tonight someone better head that way and get them."

"To save time let's just take the chair out there," said Dunmark. "I guess we should call and let them know we're coming since it's so late."

Dorian made a groggy face and mumbled, "Please take me too. I don't wanna die in jail."

* * * *

Montella let them in, staring daggers at Nadia as they made their way through the foyer to the living room. Dorian's persistent begging had gotten to him and he'd brought her along. She was now fully alert due to a stimulant Bolek had given her. Gary's nerves were pulsating with dread as much as keyed up with expectation.

Dunmark asked Montella where Nicole was.

"Right here . . ." the Jamaican stepped in from the hall.

Montella aimed a frown at her. "Where were you, I've been looking all over for you?"

"Just stepped outside for a breath of fresh air." Her caramel face knotted with a puzzled squint when she saw Nadia. "When did you come back to the mansion?"

"Just now. Why'd you ask me that?"

"Oh, you must have come in from the front or I'd have seen you—I was on the patio. Or did you change your mind about going to the bunkhouse to tell Dooly?"

Gary eyed Nicole, wondering what the hell she was talking about. "Yeah, she came in through the front door like the rest of us. What's going on?"

"That's what I'd like to know," said Montella, hands on her waist.

Nicole raised her brows. "She came out here with you, Sheriff?"

"Yeah, what's the big deal?"

Pointing a finger at Nadia, she fearfully started backing up—slowly as if trying not to alarm a coiled rattlesnake. "Either that's not really Nadia or the woman who told me Montella hired her to cook for the cowhands isn't Nadia."

"Are you stoned?" chortled Montella. "I haven't hired her yet."

"Nadia said you did . . ." she continued back-stepping.

Nadia dropped her jaw. "That's absurd! First Dorian and now you. I haven't been out here since I left to see the district attorney."

"So that's what's going on!" shouted Dorian, grinning with relief. "Don't you get it, guys? I'm not losing my mind after all. Gray Bird is impersonating Nadia."

An icy shudder reverberating through his gut, Gary cut his eyes to Dunmark as Nicole froze in her tracks. The panic on the investigator's face left no doubt he thought Dorian had solved the Nadia dilemma.

"Gary, we've got to get to the bunkhouse now, it may already be too late!"

* * * *

He'd driven Dunmark and Bolek to the bunkhouse, leaving Heath at the mansion to watch over the ladies. Sleepy-eyed, hair tousled, Dooly sat at the kitchen table with his hands wrapped around a steaming mug. Gary was relieved the young cowboy hadn't been harmed, yet very puzzled as to why. What purpose did the demon have for visiting Dorian, Nicole, and Dooly? Why had he left all three unscathed, and why was he pretending to be Nadia?

"Thanks for making me some coffee, this is good brew."

"My pleasure," said Bolek. "Now please continue, Dooly. You said Nadia surprised you in your bedroom shortly after you retired for the evening. What happened afterwards?"

Dooly took a sip of coffee and wiped his mouth. "Well I couldn't believe my eyes because she didn't have a stitch of clothes on. At first she scared the shit out of me because Dorian told me Gray Bird had killed Bobby Joe and was hiding in Nadia. So I just lay stiff as a board, not knowing what to do. Then she chewed the wrap off a rubber and it was obvious what she wanted from me was my dick rather than my life."

"So you had sex with her?"

He nodded.

Though he knew the woman Dooly screwed couldn't have been his Nadia, Gary felt sick to his stomach nonetheless. "And you were certain the woman was Nadia Mars?"

"Mm hmm."

"When did she leave?" asked Dunmark.

"Don't know. She was lying beside me when I fell asleep. What's this is all about anyway?"

Grimly pursing his lips, Gary sat down across from him, imagining how freaked out he'd be to receive such a mind boggling explanation. "Um, Dooly, the women who came to see you couldn't have been Nadia Mars because she was with me all evening. Understand?"

He seemed confused at first, then gave him a knowing grin. "Whatever you say, Sheriff. I won't tell anybody she was out here."

"No, that's not what I meant. Nadia really was with me all evening."

"Look, I don't know what's going on here but I'm dead positive the gal that came into my bedroom was Nadia Mars, there ain't a doubt in my mind."

"I understand why you think that but it wasn't her. Dorian thought she came to see her today too, but she didn't. We're pretty sure a demon is impersonating Nadia."

Dooly slowly turned his eyes to Bolek, then Dunmark, and finally back to him as the gravity of the situation finally hit home. "Oh shit, I think I'm gonna throw up . . . ."

* * * *

Lori sat beside Heath on a loveseat watching Nicole pace back and forth. Montella and Nadia were lounging in luxurious armchairs also observing her. Dorian lay on one of the couches, gazing at the ceiling. Gary had phoned Heath to notify him Dooly wasn't harmed, but had indeed been visited by a woman he'd thought to be Nadia.

"I just can't believe this. Who was it I talked to?"

Dorian hissed an exasperated sigh. "Gray Bird, Nicole, like I done told you half a dozen times. Same thing happened to me at the jailhouse."

"But why has he taken on Nadia's form?"

"Shit, he's a demon—who could know what goes on in his mind. I figure that motherfucker wanted me to think Nadia was talking to Gray Bird in her sleep at the jailhouse too. For some reason he wants us all to think he's possessed her."

Lori tended to agree with Dorian's assessment.

Heath leaned forward and clasped his hands together. "Nicole, take me through your conversation with the woman you thought was Nadia, starting with where you were when you first saw her."

She stopped pacing and turned towards him. "I had just got back from town after grocery shopping for Montella and picking up a slew of pie fillings and crusts for myself. I was in the kitchen when Nadia—at least who I thought was Nadia— came in and told me she had good news, she'd just been hired to cook for the cowboys. I congratulated her with a hug and she told me she was going to the bunkhouse to tell Dooly. She left and a moment later I saw her walk past the window over the kitchen sink, heading that direction."

"And what time was this?"

"About two hours ago and I'd been there since, baking pies for the pie eating contest at the county fair. I'll have to bake over a dozen more before I'm done. I'm doing it to honor Carlson's commitment he made when he volunteered Rico for it to ingratiate himself with the locals. It got stuffy in the kitchen so I went out on the patio for some fresh air. When I came back inside I heard you guys walking down the hall so I went to see what was going on, and when I saw Nadia I wondered why she'd walked all the way around the house to the front instead of coming in from the patio."

Montella eyed her suspiciously. "I checked the kitchen and patio when I was trying to find you after Gary called to make sure we hadn't gone to bed because he wanted to come out and talk to us. How is it I didn't see you, Nicole?"

She shrugged. "I must have been using the bathroom at the time. I was sipping green tea and as you well know it makes me have to pee a lot."

"Which bathroom did you use?" asked Heath.

"The half-bath in the kitchen."

"I didn't know it had one."

"The door's located in back of the pantry," explained Montella, apparently satisfied with Nicole's explanation.

The doorbell chimed and Nicole left to answer it. She returned with Dunmark, Bolek, Gary, and Dooly, who turned red-faced upon seeing Nadia.

Lori rose from the loveseat and headed towards the chair Heath had brought in after explaining to Montella and Nicole Gary hadn't wanted either of them to know beforehand they were to be hypnotized. "Who goes first, Dunmark . . .?"

* * * *

None of the women had undergone hypnosis when they'd tested them in Colorado. Unlike the completely unresponsive Dorian, Nicole succumbed easily. Bolek disposed of his watch and began.

"What is your name?"

"Nicole Anderson."

"And what is my name?"

"Bolek Nowak."

He glanced towards the entrance of the living room to ensure no one was eavesdropping from the hall. Certain they were about to encounter Gray Bird through Nicole or Montella, they couldn't chance anyone outside the team being present. Gary and Heath had escorted Montella, Nadia, Dorian, and Dooly from the room earlier. Satisfied they were alone, Bolek continued. "We will now speak of the woman you talked to earlier when you were in the kitchen. Do you recall telling Ranger Crow about it?"

"Yes."

"Who was this woman?"

"Nadia Mars."

Her answer spurred an uncomfortable stirring in his spirit. She should have said 'A woman I thought was Nadia Mars' or something similar. He inhaled a nervous breath and started singing. *"Jesus loves me this I know, for the Bible tells me so. Little ones to Him belong, they are weak but He is strong.* Are you familiar with that song, Nicole?"

She nodded.

"Good. Would you sing it with me?"

She nodded again.

"Very well, we shall begin. *Jesus loves me this I know* . . . ."

He watched her carefully as she sang along, her beautiful soprano as superior to his tinny alto as a Stradivarius to a Jew's harp. After repeating the song several times he subtly substituted Jesus with Satan when they again reached the chorus.

"*Yes, Satan loves me,*" she sang, "*yes, Satan loves me. Yes, Satan loves me, for the Bible tells me so.*"

His heart sank as she continued singing along, completely unperturbed by the change. They unquestionably had the master demon's host. "You have a beautiful voice, Nicole. As beautiful as a . . . *bird's.*"

The whites of her eyes began to yellow and the pupils dilated into long vertical slits of glowing red as thick black saliva oozed from the corners of lips rapidly turning gray and scaly.

He swallowed a lump of fear but forced himself to forge on. "In fact, I dare say your voice is as lovely as a *gray* bird's."

A violent sneer tore across Nicole's face, the corners of the hideous mouth stretching almost back to her ears, gaping as wide as a serpent's when about to engulf its prey. "You don't know who you're fucking with, Polack! You think I hadn't planned this all along, you pitiful fool? You're all dead before dawn, but first I'll force each of you to watch me eat your entrails while you writhe in exquisite excruciation. Ahhhhhhhh, I can almost taste them now . . . so good . . . sooooooooo very fucking good!"

The voice was guttural, deep, masculine, and vulgar. Demonic laughter bounced off the walls, raising fright goose bumps all over his skin. Trembling, he whispered to Lori, "Please tell Sheriff Stoner to take everyone to his house or the jail before we proceed further. I have a feeling we are dealing with a fallen angel that was not far below the rank of archangel before rebelling against God. And I'm sure I speak for Dunmark when I say we hold no ill will towards you if you wish to go with them."

Though her eyes had ballooned into two glistening green swells of fright, she firmed her jaw and whispered, "Fat chance, I'm here till the bitter end. Wait for me to get back before you say another word to that bastard . . . ."

* * * *

Gary could hardly grip the steering wheel his hands were shaking so badly. The sounds echoing down the hall as they'd hurried for the front door had been the most ungodly noises he'd ever heard in his life. Nadia sat on the passenger's side bawling hysterically. Montella was doing likewise, sitting in back with Dorian and Dooly, both of whom were mute with stark fear.

Heath's headlights reflected in the rearview mirror. The ranger had refused to leave unless Lori went with him, but once she convinced him that it would take the faith of all three members of the team to cast out that fearsome devil, and hers would be weakened if she had to worry about his safety, he'd reluctantly given in to her plea.

* * * *

Drying her eyes, Lori entered the living room. Heath's courage had brought on the tears—the helpless look on his face when she'd finally gotten it through his stubborn handsome head that he'd only be hurting rather than helping her if he didn't leave immediately.

The creature strapped to the chair could hardly be mistaken for Nicole. It looked as if a bird of prey and an octopus had suffered the same fate as the scientist and housefly in the movie *The Fly*—molecules scrambled together into a monstrous, repulsive glob.

Though he had to be as frightened as her, Dunmark somehow held the camcorder steady. The recording would be a blurry mess if she held the device in her shivering hands.

Face void of color, Bolek tried to give her a reassuring smile that failed miserably. He turned to the demon. "How long have you inhabited this woman?"

A grotesque beak, jutting from the lower part of what vaguely resembled an eagle's head with hideous yellow eyes, started moving. "Since the night of the first murders."

"On the Ridgewall Ranch?"

"Yeah, you ignorant piece of slimy Polack shit. You're wasting your time, pock-face. You can't drive me out of my home."

"Oh . . .?" he ran a quivering finger beneath his nose. "And why is that?"

"Nicole practices black magic. She begged for me to appear before her."

"How did she know about you?"

Laughter so loud it almost split Lori's eardrums erupted from the gray mass. "She didn't, you fool. She was trying to conjure Klell Ridgewall's ghost."

"And did she see it?"

"Hell no, she got me instead! Oh I've been having such delicious fun with you stupid pieces of shit. The limp-dick you cast out of Ilian Herrera was under my control but the weakling never killed anybody. I alone have enjoyed the thrill of the slaughter. And in case you're interested, you misdiagnosed Nadia Mars' recurring nightmare. Oh yes, those she'd had all her life were mere dreams brought on by the slut's meandering subconscious mind, but I injected the one about the little girl being enraged by the bird's death. The stupid bitch's fucked up psyche produced the adult identities of the girl as Montella and herself while you had her hypnotized. I only intended for the whore to see her as Nicole.

"It was Nicole that went to see Dorian in jail, and it was Nicole that fucked Dooly. It was a simple matter, making them both think they were seeing and hearing Nadia. Nicole thoroughly enjoyed fucking him by the way. Afterwards I planted an illusion—in the pure side of her persona that knows nothing of my existence—that she'd been at the mansion the whole time and had spoken with Nadia, who'd told her she was going to the bunkhouse. After I finish with you all, Nicole and I will travel to many other locations, leaving a plethora of mysterious murders for the fucked up authorities to uselessly ponder."

The walls reverberated with the sounds of sadistic hilarity.

Lori cupped her hands over her lower face to keep from hyperventilating.

"Why did you spare Nadia when you killed Erma and Sally?" Bolek's voice sounded amazingly strong considering the fear emanating from his features.

"None of your fucking business, you cock-sucking Polack!"

A flash of anger in Bolek's eyes revealed the insult had gotten to him. But only momentarily. He drew a breath and said, "How is it you eluded detection when we tested Nicole in Colorado?"

"Idiot, I can come and go from Nicole as I please, she relishes the power I bring her. I merely left her body before your bungling leader stuck that fucking needle in her arm and put her in the ambulance. I forced my way into the Mexican bitch for most of the slayings until you dealt with her and eliminated my entryway by casting out my inferior. I carved up the cowboy in the barn through Nicole. We did it when she excused herself to use the bathroom while you were trying to convert her."

She could tell by the way he grimaced, that revelation smote Bolek like a whip, but he managed to continue. "Did Nicole kill Angela?"

"The Chinese bitch? No, I used Ilian."

"And you used Ilian for Erma and Sally as well?"

"Not that it's any of your fucking business but yeah, I did. While her parents were dozing in the hospital I spirited her away to the jailhouse. I grabbed the two sluts and zapped us all to The Hog Farm, allowing Nicole to see the fun through my eyes as I skinned their faces and heads. Oh what sensual pleasure she derived, taking it all in from the comfort of her bed. I got Ilian back to the hospital before anyone noticed her absence."

"Why have you only selected certain people to attack rather than killing everyone on the ranch?"

Again the walls shook with horrific laughter. "Nicole's bedroom door was open when I first appeared to her. Babette saw me from the hall on her way to the bathroom. She ran back to her room and told the other two cunts who were playing Monopoly with her, so the three of them had to be silenced. I zapped the game back in a drawer and took care of business. Nicole so enjoyed the shedding of their blood, she demanded more. She wanted to feel the experience of making a man die in exquisite agony so she selected the ramrod and cook, being they were her least favorite of the cowboys. Nicole lay in her bed masturbating while I again linked her psyche to mine through Ilian so she could witness the splendid carnage. Afterwards she sat down to a hearty breakfast. Mmm, she so enjoyed her biscuits and gravy that morning.

"Carlson Loggins choosing Sonya rather than Nicole to accompany him for a sexual liaison was his fatal mistake. She'd known by the look on his face he was horny, so she signaled him with a shake of her butt while leaning over a pool table that she was feeling quite randy as well. When he left with Sonya she'd felt so slighted it inspired her dark half to summon me within her mind. I entered Ilian, transported her to the mansion, and my-my did Nicole's secret personality have a hard time not manifesting due to the immense pleasure derived from witnessing me torture the two swine.

"Unfortunately for her dear friend Rosemary, she saw me emerge from Nicole in the jailhouse so she had to go. Nicole had only intended to taste the blood of Rico and Selena that night. I purposely allowed Hank Best to witness their slaughter so he could tell you ameba-brained idiots about me. It was all part of the plan. He was the logical choice to lure you fools back from Colorado."

Bolek had a prolonged coughing fit. When he finally quit hacking he pulled a handkerchief from the inside pocket of his lab coat and blew his nose. "Again I ask—why did you spare Nadia?"

"To cast suspicion on her, you imbecilic dribble of Polack piss. I butchered Angela Yang to make it look like Nadia wanted revenge because the slut replaced her, then killed the three hog farmers to get the sheriff acquainted with her. I sliced up Lambert and Tillie without Nicole's direction as well because it was Nadia's first night in the mansion. She's going to take the fall for all the murders. Nicole doesn't want any harm to come to Montella or Dorian. Whichever one of them discovers your pitiful bodies when they return to the mansion will also find a written confession in a suicide note from Nadia, whose body will be lying alongside yours.

"Nicole didn't leave Dooly's bedroom empty handed earlier tonight. She stole his pistol, the one I will force Nadia to use when she fires a single shot through the roof of her mouth after I whisk her out here. When the sheriff wakes up to an empty bed in the morning and finds the bitch's body in this very room, even he will have to conclude Nadia was demonized and had tried to make Nicole—who'll be found restrained in this chair—the scapegoat."

Bolek hacked again and cleared his throat. "What is your name?"

A shrill spray of wicked laughs emerged from the demon. "Gray Bird, of course."

"No, I mean your given name. The one bestowed upon you by The Most High before you rebelled against Him?"

"Enough of this drivel, you're beginning to bore me, pock-face. It's party time—prepare to die . . .!"

* * * *

"Hurry, Gray Bird, slit his fucking throat—do it now—hurry, hurry, hurry . . .! Yesssssssss mmmmmmmmmm, look at that delicious blood. Now the other—bash his head in with that fucking camcorder, then take the bitch apart and show me her spleen!"

Something pierced her neck, dispelling the erotic pleasure flooding her dark soul . . . .

* * * *

Gary had almost reached the city limits when Heath called. He immediately phoned the hospital, made a u-turn, and speed-dialed the panicked ranger to assure him an ambulance was on the way. With the cruiser floor-boarded he soon overtook Heath's personal vehicle which didn't have a suped-up engine, and arrived at the Ridgewall Ranch in half the time it would have taken driving the speed limit.

Montella gave him her house keys and he told everyone not to get out of the car until Heath arrived. Gary let himself in through the front door, ran through the foyer, down the hall, and into the living room.

Lori was leaning over Bolek, pressing her hands against his bleeding neck, begging him to hang on. Splayed out on the floor like Bolek, Dunmark lay unconscious, the broken pieces of his camcorder littering the floor near his head. The restraints of the specially constructed chair were hanging in shards but Nicole was still sitting on it, head leaning towards her left shoulder. Her gaping eyes would never again close on their own. A syringe protruded from the side of the dead Jamaican's neck.

He knelt beside Lori, who'd called Heath and said she didn't have time to explain but needed him to get an emergency medical crew out to the ranch immediately. Not knowing the hospital's number, Heath had passed the mission on to him. "Is there anything I can do to help?"

She looked at him with tear-soaked eyes, sadly shook her head, and refocused on her bleeding coworker.

"Did the demon escape?"

"No . . . he's gone for good."

"Did you stick that hypodermic in Nicole's neck?"

Her eyes slammed shut as she gritted her teeth and slowly nodded.

Seeing she was in no mood to answer questions, he decided to wait until the emergency team took over before getting all the details. He rose to his feet and examined Dunmark. Two patches of blood in his sandy hair were drying. The bleeding had stopped but at the moment only God knew what damage may have been done to his brain. He wondered why the demon had chose to pound Dunmark's head with the camcorder rather than use its knife, and why the beast had only wounded Bolek on the side of the neck instead of lethally cutting his throat.

He let his eyes wander to the stairs, recalling the first time he'd climbed them and the shocking scene that had followed. Lawrence Kerns' statement at The Hog Farm rose in his thoughts—*Talk about being baptized by fire.* The patrolman had used the proper term all right. That's exactly what had happened to him and his staff.

None of them would ever be the same.

It amazed him that so many people nowadays claimed to be agnostic or altogether atheistic. How could anyone doubt the existence of God? The evil rapidly growing all around the planet proved the devil was real and doing his damndest to corrupt the entire human race. What possible motivation could the prince of darkness have other than trying to win a war against his creator?

His stomach knotted as it dawned on him he wouldn't be thinking that way if the reality of spiritual warfare hadn't been horrendously revealed to him. Intellectually acknowledging the existence of something and really believing it were two radically different things.

Heath ran into the room calling Lori's name and hurried to her side. "What happened?"

She broke down and through a torrent of tears cried, "The bastard cut his carotid artery. Bolek's lost so much blood he's not going to last much longer—the paramedics had better get here soon. If he hadn't turned to run when Gray Bird attacked, the knife would have severed his trachea, esophagus, all the blood vessels in front of his spine, and he'd have died almost instantly. After delivering that one blow the beast went after Dunmark."

"How did the demon break free? I thought they couldn't do that with their host tranquilized."

A painful grimace latched onto her face. "Nicole was psychotic—a complete split personality—she had a hidden dark side that was so evil it was manipulating the demon instead of the other way around. Our faith was powerless to stop Gray Bird because that part of Nicole wanted him to act. One moment he was strapped in the chair, fully manifesting, and the next a long glowing knife suddenly appeared in one of his many hands and he broke free. I heard Nicole ordering him to cut Bolek's throat and was shocked to see her sitting in the chair, completely separated from the devil that had sprang from it. While she was watching him smash the camcorder on Dunmark's head at her command, I came up from behind and injected air into her jugular vein. I was forced to do it—she'd have killed us all otherwise. Gray Bird dematerialized when she expired, and I begged the Lord to bind him in the deepest regions of hell."

Heath took off his hat and raked a hand through his hair. "Is this the end of it?"

"Yes . . . the killing spree is finally over. Bolek managed to get all the details about the murders before Nicole ordered the attack. This whole nightmare started because of a tragic coincidence." Sniffing heavily between sentences, Lori relayed the information her unconscious colleague had extracted from the demon.

Heath pulled out a handkerchief, gently wiped her eyes, placed it around her nose, and commanded her to blow. The weeping investigator complied and thanked him. With her hands the only thing keeping Bolek from bleeding to death, she hadn't dared do it herself.

"Why didn't Gray Bird just work directly through Nicole from the beginning instead of using Ilian?"

He'd started to ask that very thing before Heath beat him to it.

"We'll never know for certain, but I can only assume Nicole's dark half wasn't willing, so Gray Bird chose the nearest available human he could enter to keep his existence a secret. Apparently that personality's taste for violent death grew so strong that when Gray Bird couldn't satisfy her depraved cravings through Ilian anymore, she had no choice but to be the human vessel the demon required to operate through."

TWENTY SEVEN

Heath and Lori had followed the ambulance, leaving him alone with Nicole until the coroner arrived. As Bob South and his assistant carted off her remains, Gary thought about the pretty Jamaican pleading for Heath and him to believe her allegation about a voodoo priestess manipulating Klell Ridgewall's ghost, clueless that all the murders stemmed from a malicious personality lurking within her. If only Babette hadn't happened by when Gray Bird first appeared, the Mister Hyde aspect of her psyche might never have developed a taste for shedding human blood.

For several minutes he stood gazing at the chair she'd been taken from, two emotions whirling in his head—tremendous relief that the butchering demon had finally been eliminated, bitter sorrow that the monster's host couldn't be spared. His first homicide case had turned out to be a startling revelation. An invisible war ceaselessly raged in the spirit realm and there wouldn't be peace on earth, good will towards man until Jesus Christ reigned over the human race.

He left the living room and headed for the foyer. Nadia, Montella, Dorian, and Dooly were gathered near the entrance. The women's eyes were puffy from crying and the color still hadn't returned to Dooly's young cheeks.

Nadia locked her arms around his neck. "Poor Nicole."

"Yeah . . ." he squeezed her tight.

"The coroner wouldn't tell us anything," said Dorian, voice devoid of its customary sassy edge. "We'd like to know what happened."

Tears were streaming down the Cajun's cheeks by the time he finished, revealing she also had a hidden side. Beneath that uncouth gluttonous rebel rouser lay a sweet, caring woman. "So many dead because Babette had to potty. What a fucked up case of being in the wrong place at the wrong time."

Montella inhaled a deep breath and discharged a heavy sigh. "Come on, everybody. Let's settle our nerves with alcohol in the ballroom . . . ."

* * * *

Seated at the bar beside Nadia, who was nursing a bourbon and water, Gary allowed himself one bottle of Budweiser. Dorian and Dooly sat on the other side of her chasing tequila shots with tap beer while Montella, perched on a stool to the young cowboy's left, had opted for brandy.

Dorian leaned forward and looked his way. "Do you think it's really over at last, Sheriff?"

"Lori assured me it is." *Let's just hope she's right,* he thought, wondering if he could resist the temptation to resign if it turned out she wasn't.

"Damn shame I'm not gonna get to work with those guys, I know I could be a real asset to their team. I got a good look at Dunmark when they wheeled him past us. Looks like he'll make it out of this okay but I'm not so sure about Bolek, those bandages on his neck were awfully bloody. Hope he pulls through."

"Me too," agreed Nadia. "So what *are* you planning to do now?"

"Guess I'll kiss Montella's ass so she'll give me something to do around here."

Dooly grinned and patted Dorian on the back, spirits clearly brightened by booze. "Ever thought about trying your hand at cow punching?"

Montella giggled. "Now there's a thought that should have occurred to me. Honey, you'd look right at home wielding a branding iron."

An appalled scowl rolled over Dorian's face as if she'd just spotted a dead roach in her soup after slurping a spoonful. "I could never burn a poor cow like that, but I could cook for Dooly and whatever new hands come aboard, since Nadia doesn't want to anymore."

Nadia tossed her a teasing smile. "How do you know?"

"Hell, everybody knows it's only a matter of time before you and the high sheriff get hitched. Cupid done smacked your bow-hinds together forever."

Montella loudly cleared her throat and spun her stool ninety degrees. "Dooly, I've been thinking things over . . . ."

* * * *

Lori stood beside the hospital bed clutching Heath's hand. Dunmark still hadn't regained consciousness but his mouth had fallen open and he'd started stretching his jaw, indicating he would any second. Bolek was undergoing emergency surgery to repair his lacerated carotid artery. If not for the blood transfusion he'd received in route to the hospital her valiant coworker would have died before getting there.

The top of Dunmark's head resembled the back of a double-humped camel, but miraculously the lumps on his scalp had only bled from being scraped rather than gashed open by the camcorder. Though the video camera had been destroyed, its flashcard lay within a pocket of her lab coat, unharmed.

Dunmark's eyelids began to flutter and soon parted. She freed her hand from Heath's and leaned over to check his pupils. "Thank God, it looks like you're going to be all right."

"The d-demon . . . what happened to the—"

"He's gone. It's all over." She caressed his face and smiled.

"Is Nicole all right?"

She'd dammed up her despondency but Dunmark's query broke her resolve and she couldn't hold back the tears any longer. There'd been no other option, but that didn't lessen the horrid guilt of taking a life. "She didn't make it."

Heath put a hand on her shoulder and gave it a reassuring squeeze. On the way to the hospital he'd reminded her that Nicole's death had saved not only two lives but most likely countless others. He'd borne the same dark emotions the first time his duty demanded lethal action, and promised the guilt would pass.

Dunmark tried to sit up but she flattened her palms on his chest to prevent it. "You just lie there until the doctor looks you over."

Moisture welled in his eyes. "Bolek didn't make it either, did he."

"Bolek's going to be fine." She soothed his brow with a gentle stroke of her hand. "He's in surgery. The paramedics arrived just in the nick of time, thank God."

* * * *

Despite knowing it had been Nicole rather than her in his bed, Dooly still couldn't look at Nadia Mars without blushing. It totally blew his mind that such a thing could happen. Turning his thoughts back to the good news he'd just received, he let the unbelievable experience with the Jamaican flitter away and took another shot of tequila. Montella had rescinded her condition and officially named him the foreman of the Ridgewall Ranch, along with raising his pay thirty percent as promised.

Dorian dropped her left hand on his crotch, pressed hard against it, and pulled away before anyone could get wise to the action. He grinned at the Cajun beauty, wishing he could grab her tits.

Montella went behind the bar and came back to her stool with a can of mixed nuts which she placed on the counter.

He helped himself to a handful as did Dorian.

"Thanks for the beer, Montella," said Sheriff Stoner. "I'll be shoving off now."

Nadia shot him an anxious look and jumped to her feet. "You *are* planning on taking me with you I hope."

Tomahawk County's Finest slid an arm around her waist and walked her towards the front ballroom exit.

Montella seemed mighty displeased about it. She took a long pull of brandy and kept her glaring eyes on the couple until they disappeared into the hall, then she let out a "Dammit!" while slamming the tumbler on the bar so hard he couldn't believe it hadn't shattered.

Dorian giggled and said, "Chill out, honey, it's for the best."

"Oh yeah?" Montella heatedly replied. "Well for your information, my dear, it cost you a ritzy vacation. I'd planned to hire Nadia to cook for the hands on the condition she'd accompany you on a six week cruise. I was going to send you along to make sure she stayed on that damn boat. I'd planned to have Nicole take care of the cowboys in the meantime and try my best to seduce Gary—make him fall in love and marry me before y'all got back. Nadia wouldn't have been able to stand being around him under those circumstances and would've left Tomahawk County for good. I came up with that plan after Geraldo turned down the offer. I knew Nadia would never get anywhere with Gary after I informed him she'd accompanied Geraldo on a forty-two day love fest. Now it's time I faced the fucking truth—I've lost him to her."

"Don't take it so hard, Montella . . ." Dorian shoved a handful of nuts in her mouth. "Like I done told you before, you'd wind up bored out of your mind if you got stuck with Sheriff Stoner. You're just infatuated with him 'cause he's got integrity and a nice butt. That'd wear off in no time. Nadia, on the other hand, is slap-dab mad dog in love with him. You might as well let true love take its course 'cause he feels the same about her, as any fool can see. Now you gonna let me cook for Dooly and your new cowboys or what?"

Montella slapped the bar with a jewelry-laden hand. "I hate you, you know that?"

"Why?"

"Because you're right. Not only about Gary and Nadia, but my infatuation with him wearing off and leaving me bored with the situation if I'd won him over. The job is yours, smartass."

A sly grin sprang up. "So how much you gonna pay me?"

TWENTY EIGHT

When he got to his office Gary called the county clerk and learned Dody Massey still owned The Hog Farm but was in serious arrears with the taxes on all of his numerous properties. Except for the house and the acre it stood on, The Hog Farm wasn't subject to property tax, being agriculturally exempt, but he owed a small fortune in back taxes on the residence. None of Dody's relatives were willing to pay the amount due plus interest accrued through penalties, so city hall had agreed to let him purchase the ranch for a paltry fifteen thousand dollars.

While he pondered what to name his new spread, Ilian waltzed in, her pretty smile brightening an already wonderful morning. "What are you doing in uniform? I told you to take a week off."

"I need to get back to work. I'm going stir crazy sitting around the house."

He laughed. "Well in that case, why are you showing up two hours late?"

Alfredo stuck his head through the door before she could answer. Ilian quickly looked away as a dejected scowl latched onto the deputy's face. "I'm off to make my morning rounds, Gary."

The hostile look on Alfredo's mug and Ilian's refusal to make eye contact worried him. "What's wrong?"

"Ask her . . ." he stormed off without bothering to close the door.

"Did you two have a fight?"

Ilian drew a quick breath and shook her head. "I broke up with him. I hadn't intended for this to be my first day back at work because I didn't want to face him. But I started going crazy with dread, knowing I had to sooner or later, so I decided to get it over with. I feel awful about hurting him but had no choice. Geraldo Toya called me last night, drunk as a skunk, telling me he'd fallen in love with me and wanted to marry me. I told him to propose when he was sober and then I'd believe it wasn't just the booze talking. Well it wasn't—he called me first thing this morning. I phoned Alfredo right after we hung up.

"All these years I thought I was in love with Alfredo, but that changed when the patrolman brought the Ridgewall ranch hands to the jailhouse. The moment I saw Geraldo my eyes were opened to the truth—I hadn't known what true love was until that very moment. I'd seen him around town but not up close, and we'd never spoken. I can't explain what happened but I knew he was really the one for me. Unfortunately I couldn't seem to catch his eye, so I planned to go ahead and marry Alfredo, hoping that over time I'd develop the same special feelings for him that have been overwhelming me since falling for Geraldo. Until that drunken vaquero called me last night I didn't think he even knew I was alive. Thank God he did. Now Alfredo's free to find his one true love the way I have mine."

Her shocking news hit him hard for Alfredo's sake, but he couldn't argue against the inability to resist true love because he certainly hadn't been able to. It *would* be only a matter of time before Nadia and he got hitched, just as Dorian had said last night. "What's Geraldo planning on doing, now that he's no longer foreman of the Ridgewall Ranch?"

She shrugged. "Don't know. If nothing else he can always work at my father's hardware store. One thing for sure, he's not going to live on a ranch if he continues being a cowhand. That hombre's gonna sleep with me every night."

Dunmark walked in with Heath and Lori, who was carrying a box of DVDs.

Gary rose from his desk. "I'm surprised to see you on your feet so soon, Dunmark."

The investigator gingerly touched a patch of hair rising in front of a valley formed by another protuberance an inch behind it. "Thankfully the only swelling was above my hard head or I could have been in trouble. They released me when I cleared the concussion protocols."

"How's Bolek doing after his surgery?"

"He's going to be okay," answered Lori with a serene smile. "He'll have to stay in the hospital a few more days to recuperate though."

"I guess you guys will be heading back to Colorado after he gets out, huh?"

"Lori will . . ." Dunmark stuck out his hand. "I'm on my way back now, just came in to say goodbye."

He crossed palms with the rescuer of Tomahawk County and patted him on the back. "You're my hero, Dunmark— along with Lori and Bolek of course. I don't *even* want to think about what would have happened if you hadn't shown up. Whatever amount that think tank is funding you, it isn't nearly enough, my friend. Hope you'll pay us a visit every now and then."

"Count on it. And our door is always open to you as well."

"How about you, Heath? Are you bailing on me today too?"

Heath draped his arm across Lori's shoulders and grinned. "My captain gave me permission to loiter around your county until my girl takes Bolek home."

The irony of it all tugged at his gut. If that killer demon hadn't manifested, Heath and Lori would never have met, and he'd have never gotten to know Nadia. Under any other circumstance, once he learned she'd been one of Dody's whores he'd have dismissed any possibility of romancing her. "You guys can stay at The Hog Farm if you want. I'm proud to say I'm its new owner. I'll be moving out there as soon as it's deeded to me."

"Thanks," said Heath, "I'll take you up on that if Montella doesn't want to extend her hospitality a while longer."

"Here you go, Gary . . ." Lori handed him the box.

"What's this?"

"Copies of all the videos for the district attorney."

"Oh, Pete will need these." He set the real-life horror movies on his desk and sighed. "I wonder who'll open the first souvenir shop once word of this gets out. Tomahawk is bound to get invaded by curious tourists."

"Along with a slew of occultists I'm sure," Lori added sympathetically.

"Now you guys are positive Gray Bird can't come back, right?"

Dunmark nodded. "The odds against another set of freaky circumstances coming together to allow that demon such access to the physical realm are astronomical even if the fiend hasn't been bound in hell like Lori prayed for. When Nicole tried to conjure Klell Ridgewall's ghost she unwittingly opened a gateway that allowed that beast to appear, and her dark half welcomed him to dwell inside her. The benign imp behind the Klell Ridgewall sightings might still be able to manifest but the spirit of lust that possessed Ilian has been permanently imprisoned by the Lord—Lori, Bolek, and I felt it in our spirits at the moment of deliverance."

* * * *

Dooly introduced Sonny Yoakum to Montella on the front porch of the mansion. She folded her arms beneath her big tits and gave him a hard going-over as he recited the ranching skills and experience he'd acquired while working for his father. When he finished, Sonny nervously took off his hat.

"My, what a rich head of hair," she purred. "Do you color it?"

"Um no, ma'am, why?"

"Just wondering. Tell me, Sonny, are you an honest man?"

"Yes, ma'am. Except when it comes to poker."

An odd smile came to her. She seemed to be undressing him with her eyes. "How old are you?"

"Thirty-six."

Montella's glossy lips spread further. "I assume you've heard about what happened on this ranch recently."

"Yes, ma'am."

"The murders I mean. The reason we got nicknamed The Death Ranch."

"Yes, ma'am."

"And yet you're not afraid to work here. Why?"

"Dooly told me the sheriff caught the killer."

Sonny didn't know anything about what happened last night with Nicole, and he hoped Montella wouldn't scare him off by mentioning it. Unfortunately she laid it all out and he groaned inside, certain the big cowboy would turn tail and run.

"I'm sure what I've just told you is far more frightening than any rumors you may have heard, but I want you and everyone else who works here to know what really happened so I can't be accused of misleading you. Now that you know the facts are you still interested in the job?"

Dooly had geared up to beg him to reconsider—grovel like a dog if need be—but it hadn't been necessary. Though he'd flinched and grimaced while hearing the gruesome details, Sonny nodded.

"I assume you've been informed of the base pay rate?"

"Yes, ma'am, and it's almost triple what I was making at the rodeo arena so I'm glad to get it, especially with room and board thrown in."

Montella raised her chin as if she'd been insulted. "That wage is for regular hands. As Dooly's second in command you'll be earning fifteen percent more."

"Well that makes it plum juicy, ma'am, much obliged."

He'd told Sonny his pay would most likely be above a regular hand's but couldn't guarantee it. The way Montella kept lustfully ogling the big fella, it surprised him she hadn't hiked it more.

"You're a good deal older than Dooly and have far more ranching experience. Are you sure you won't mind taking orders from such a young buck?"

Sonny put his hat back on and shot her a confident smile while crossing his Herculean arms over his equally impressive chest. "We talked enough ranching yesterday to let me know he's got the basic know-how to run this spread. I can teach him how to deal with whatever comes up he's not familiar with and I'll have his back all the way if any of the punchers get uppity with him. They'll all learn soon enough nobody wants to get on my bad side. I'm the type of ol' boy who leaves the job behind at the end of the day—planning for the next one like cattle bosses have to do just ain't up my alley, so there won't be any conflict with me trying to become lead dog. We'll make a fine team and your ranch couldn't be in better hands, ma'am."

His response brought a hot blush to Montella's cheeks.

"I understand you're single. Have you ever been married, Sonny?"

"Came close once but it didn't work out."

"Oh? What happened?"

"She wanted me to give up ranching and take up a more lucrative occupation. When I wouldn't do it, she gave me an ultimatum. Seeing she loved money more than me, I called it quits and never looked back."

Her sultry gaze heated up several degrees. "Okay, you're hired. Your first chore as Dooly's ramrod will be to help him round up some more hands and a cook. When you get back from town, come up to the mansion so I can record your social security number and other pertinent facts about you."

"Thought Dorian was gonna cook for us."

"Change of plans, Dooly," she said while still hotly eyeballing Sonny. "It'll be news to her too. I'm sending her to Houston to find three women Carl fired three years ago and bring them here to take care of the mansion. I'll place an ad for a chef in the Houston Chronicle, have her interview the applicants, and choose the one she feels most comfortable with. Dorian has an uncanny ability to size people up. When she comes back she'll be working as my personal assistant so you'll have to find a cook after all. Well, as John Wayne would say, 'You're burning daylight,' so off with you two and good luck finding quality help."

He was glad Dorian wouldn't be around the other hands three times a day after all, but sure hoped she wouldn't be gone long. As they made their way to his pickup he grinned at Sonny. "Montella sure took a shine to you, dude. The way she was looking you over I half expected her to tell me to take a walk and leave you two alone for awhile."

Sonny let out a laugh. "I sure didn't see it that way."

"Don't you know how to read women?"

"Not real well, no. I get fooled about eight out of ten times I think I've got one pegged."

A twinge of sadness settled in his gut. Bobby Joe had the same problem. "Well trust me, you soaked her panties, and before long she'll be taking 'em off for you, hoss."

The big cowboy's brows shot up. "You've had a piece of *that* classy lady?"

"Nah, Montella thinks of me as a kid. She looks at you and sees a man."

* * * *

Geraldo sat on the motel bed, rubbing his temples. Aspirin had taken away most of the pain but his head continued to throb from a hangover. He'd rented the place for a week and left the phone number at the bar, the rodeo arena, and all the feed stores in town, hoping some rancher would call, needing a spare hand. In spite of his misery he couldn't quit smiling. Ilian had accepted his proposal and promised to break it off with Alfredo immediately. He felt sorry for the deputy but had to be true to his heart.

Dooly had called a short while ago, having gotten his number at one of the feed stores. It pleased him no end to know the young cowboy was still alive but he couldn't help wondering for how long. He'd said Nicole wound up being the butchering demon's host and the killings had for sure ceased this time, but the same claim had been made after Ilian's deliverance. Hopefully the Ridgewall Ranch *was* really safe at last. Either way he'd never set foot on it again. Montella would have him arrested for trespassing.

* * * *

Bolek tried to shake Nicole from his thoughts but couldn't. How had she gone through life without such a severe neurological abnormality being detected? He couldn't imagine her parents, siblings, or some close friend hadn't at least suspected she had a problem, for surely someone must have witnessed her other personality. The venom in her voice when she'd commanded Gray Bird to slit his throat, and her almost orgasmic reaction to the blood squirting from his nicked carotid artery, still made him shiver inside—the way it had before consciousness slipped away. Nonetheless he felt so despondent over her death a part of him almost wished Lori had failed to save his life.

Dorian might be a genius but she was a fool for wanting to work with them. If she were to taste but a modicum of the emotional torment pressing upon him at the moment she'd shed that ridiculous notion in a heartbeat.

"Knock, knock," said a feminine voice as the door to his hospital room opened a crack. "May we come in?"

It took him a moment to recognize the voice as Montella's. "Yes, please do."

She entered and behind her came the woman he'd just been thinking about. Montella held a vase stuffed with mixed flowers and Dorian was carrying a cluster of yellow roses.

The beautiful coonass set them beside a large bouquet Lori had brought him that morning, then leaned over and kissed him on the cheek. "That there bandage looks a heap better than them bloody rags you's wearing when them paramedics wheeled you out of the mansion last night, Bolek."

Somehow a smile found its way out. "Yah . . . I would imagine so."

"How are you feeling?" asked Montella while placing her gift with the others.

"No physical pain, just some mild discomfort from the stitches, but inside I hurt deeply and weep for Nicole."

"So do we, you dear, sweet, brave man. Thank you so much. You, Lori, and Dunmark all deserve a medal. Dorian and I probably wouldn't have been alive much longer if you hadn't done what you did."

"Not so, the demon told me Nicole did not want either of you to be harmed."

Montella frowned. "I wonder why?"

"I'll tell you why," snickered Dorian. "With you dead, she'd have been forced to leave the mansion, and she wanted me around because we both cook better than her. She doesn't like having to eat her own vittles."

Didn't like, he almost corrected aloud, trying not to let her cavalier remark anger him.

"Speaking of vittles, Montella's gonna whoop up a feast fer supper tonight. Dooly done rounded up a new crew and she invited them to the mansion to celebrate your victory over Gray Bird. I'll ask one of the nurses if I can bring you a plate."

* * * *

Lori yearned for Heath to make love to her but dared not tell him so, lest he think her promiscuous. They were parked near a ridge on the Ridgewall Ranch, looking at the stars through the windshield of his pickup.

"Wasn't it nice of Montella to let us continue staying at her place until Bolek gets out of the hospital?"

It was the first thing he'd said since turning the engine off ten minutes ago. The time had come for them to discuss the future of their relationship and he apparently felt as awkward about it as she did. "And very generous of her to feed us as well. That was quite a sumptuous feast she prepared for everyone to celebrate the ranch being demon free. Did you see the way she was making eyes at that new hand Sonny Yoakum?"

"Yeah . . ." he turned towards her. "So what are we going to do about us, Lori?"

She scooted beside him and leaned her head on his shoulder. "Our careers make everything so damn difficult. I can't leave Dunmark and Bolek, they depend on me too much, and I know you can't give up being a Texas Ranger so I wouldn't dream of asking you to."

He cleared his throat. "You're right about that but I can't give you up either because I love you."

She'd sensed his feelings had grown as strong as hers but neither of them had verbalized it. Hearing the words so overwhelmed her she couldn't hold back any longer. "I love you too, Heath. Forgive me if I sound like a tramp but I want you so badly I can't help it. Let's spend the rest of our time in Tomahawk County in a motel room, starting right now."

A flash of light made them both look towards the ridge to see a confederate officer galloping towards them on a white horse, holding a long sword high in the air. He pulled the reins back to make the phantom steed rear up on its hind legs, and before the apparition disappeared Lori could have sworn she saw a smile of gratitude on the colonel's face.

Heath gaped at his watch with an awestruck frown, so she glanced down at hers.

It was straight up midnight.

About the Author

Arley Owens, Jr. is a musician, composer, poet, artist, author, producer, and rancher who resides in his native Texas with his lovely wife Cristi.
He's a member of the musical group TORN PAGE.

Website:
http://www.tornpageband.com

Other books by Arley Owens, Jr.
A Tale of the Mojave
The Cyrus Syndrome
A Texas Ghost Story
Incident in Baltimore

READ ARLEY OWENS, JR. ON YOUR KINDLE:
http://www.amazon.com/author/arleyowens

SHORTY MAE PRODUCTIONS
P.O. BOX 81102
MIDLAND, TEXAS 79708